The Displaced

FALL OF A FORTRESS

By Frieda Watt

Dedicated to Stuart

Visit the Author at www.friedawatt.com

Get notified about the next book in the series by subscribing at www.friedawatt.com/contact

ISBN (ebook): 978-1-7752722-0-5

ISBN (Paperback-Large Print): 978-1-7752722-3-6

ISBN (Paperback-Small Print): 978-1-7752722-4-3

ISBN (Paperback): 978-1-7752722-1-2

ISBN (Hardcover): 978-1-7752722-2-9

Acknowledgments

First, I would like to thank my Mom and Dad for bravely packing three kids in the back of a station wagon and driving us across the country to see what makes Canada so great. That trip to Cape Breton Island really impacted me. Thank you to my longsuffering editor Kathryn Dean, your advice has made me a better writer and this book so much more interesting. Thank you to Nancy Grove for reading the very first rough draft and for the research books. Thank you to my children, Grace, Laura and Emma for being patient when inspiration struck, during the many trips to the library and for eating pancakes for dinner. Finally, thank you to Stuart for all your love and support. I could not have done it without you.

Table of Contents

To The Reader

If you enjoy reading this novel, please take the time to write a short review on *Amazon.com* at www.goo.gl/c6XkKo

Thank you,

Frieda Watt

PART ONE: LOUISBOURG 1744

Chapter 1

THE SOUND OF SHEEP'S HOOVES THUNDERING against the sun-hardened road was the first sign that something was not right. The island fortress that housed the city of Louisbourg saw many interesting characters enter its port, but panicked sheep surging through the wide main street on a June afternoon was unheard of. The fortress of Louisbourg sat on the eastern edge of Île-Royale, the last vestige of the French Empire on the east coast of the continent. The guardian of the mighty Gulf of the Saint-Laurent, the massive structure was an intimidating reminder to anyone who travelled the North Atlantic to Quebec, the centre of France's power in North America.

Though cut off from the rest of the French Empire by the ocean and by British lands, the fortress's stone walls rose proudly above the stormy Atlantic. A bustling city second only to the capital, Louisbourg provided all the modern comforts for its citizens and garrison, and as an international port, it played host to ships from all over the globe. Unfortunately, at the moment, it was being terrorized by sheep.

Pierre was the sixteen-year-old son of Augustus Thibault, a very successful, widowed merchant in the city. Pierre's father had a hand in everything from wheat and livestock to shoes and pots. One of his largest ships, the *Jonas*, had sailed from the capital with this cargo of sheep, which were meant to supplement the failing flocks of the farmers around the fortress.

Pierre had been placed in charge of transporting the summer flock to the farms surrounding the city, but the animals, after so many days cramped aboard the rocking vessel, found the promise of dry land too appealing and rushed to freedom the moment the little delivery boats reached the wharf.

Louisbourg boasted a market, where cattle, fruit, vegetables, and fresh fish were sold. Located in the heart of the city, it was an unofficial gathering place for many of the townspeople. The vendors heard the commotion and shouts of warning, but it was too late. The flood of sheep rounded the corner. Terrified by the other livestock and the mass of people in the marketplace, what had hitherto been a chase turned into a stampede. The flock splintered, overturning tables of vegetables and leaving terrified poultry in their wake. Oblivious to the traffic, they raced between the legs of horses and surged along the busy thoroughfares, knocking children and pedestrians down as they went.

Pierre ran helplessly behind the pack. Being the son of a merchant, he had very little shepherding experience. Though just sixteen, he stood head and shoulders above most people. His broad shoulders promised strength to come, but his large bones held very little meat—and he had absolutely no idea how he was supposed to contain the thirty charging balls of wool currently streaking through the dirt streets.

Marie-Christine Lévesque had the misfortune of stepping out of the apothecary's shop near the hospital just as one group of ewes came charging by. Unaware of the over-anxious sheep until it was too late, she tried her best to jump out of the way but lost her balance on the stone step and went tumbling to the ground, the headache cure she'd recently purchased for her aunt stomped to bits by the hooves of the rampaging beasts.

Pierre came running up behind them, cursing under his breath. He paused, bending to help Marie up. Even in his distressed state, he noticed how slim she was and how easy it was to pull her up.

"I'm sorry," he said. "You're not hurt, are you?"

Marie shook her chestnut hair, looking around for the glass vial which, until a moment ago, had contained lavender oil. "Are those your sheep?" she asked, annoyed but trying to straighten her hat and keep some sense of decorum about her.

"Yes." Pierre's blue eyes gazed after the animals, wincing as more shouts filled the air. "Well, they're supposed to be, but they've escaped."

"Did you let them out?" she asked, trying her best to brush the dirt off her many cotton skirts. Pierre had a record for letting animals out of their pens at market.

"Of course not!" he snapped. The panic in his chest was making it difficult to breathe.

Marie sighed, resigned, as the sounds of more destruction echoed off the surrounding buildings. "Do you need help?"

"Would you?" The relief on his freckled face was clear.

"Are they branded?"

"Do you brand sheep?" he asked anxiously.

"I don't know."

"Right. Well, just get any sheep that's running wild, and I'll sort it out after we've captured all of them."

***

Four hours later, Pierre and Marie, along with Marie's twin, Nicolas, and her best friend, Elise Sarrazin, found themselves in the cramped, wood-panelled office of Father Allard. All four were exhausted, mud splattered, and bruised from their tangle with the flock. Marie's hat was missing; Elise's usually pristine, freckled face was covered in dirt; and Pierre's left hand was swollen after being stomped on repeatedly by a particularly vicious ram. Only Nic had survived unscathed.

The flock had put up a magnificent fight, and their antics were finally put to an end only with the assistance of several irate farmers and soldiers. The sheep had been herded into a green pasture not far from the city gates. The animals would be delivered the next day after some much-needed rest.

Father Allard was the priest in charge of discipline at the Lycée Notre-Dame, the formal school run by the nuns. It was a job he'd done since he'd arrived at the fortress as a young priest, freshly graduated from seminary in Normandy. His long-running relationship with both Nicolas and Pierre had begun when Nic arrived at the fortress six years previously—a relationship that had almost made the priest quit the cloth.

All four of the teens sat in silence, waiting as Father Allard massaged his temples behind his plain, maple desk. Pierre, Nic, Marie, and Elise had finished their formal schooling the previous spring, and at that time, the priest had hoped he would never again have to deal with what he called the "devil's duo." Yet here they sat, having been delivered to him by the city's major himself, Jean-François Eurry de la Pérelle. Major Pérelle had the unenviable task of overseeing the entire fortress's military administration. He was not pleased to become involved with the perpetrator of the sheep fiasco.

Nic and Pierre had been friends since the moment they'd met. Pierre was a year older than the other three. Nic and his twin sister, Marie, had arrived at the fortress at the age of nine, and the two boys had met at school. Both were intelligent but bored by the classroom, and they quickly bonded as the chief troublemakers of the school.

As a twin, Marie did everything with Nic until she was old enough to put her foot down and not be swept into his various schemes. Nic teased her but never allowed Pierre or anyone else to *really* upset her. All the same, Marie often found herself dealing with the aftermath of her brother's behaviour. Elise was generally a good sport about the troubles the boys caused. She was willing to put up with occasional antics from Nic and Pierre if it meant she had a friend in Marie, and she was also disinclined to object because she was quiet and reserved.

"I am very much hoping there is a better explanation for this than you were bored and looking for something to do," the middle-aged priest sighed, the firelight gleaming off his bald pate.

Both Nic and Pierre shifted uncomfortably. Five years ago, they'd been caught freeing pigs in the city market. That incident had initiated their close relationship with the priest before them, and it was impossible to deny the similarity between the two events.

Pierre spoke up first. His always unruly blond hair was standing on end after the afternoon's events. He was hunched over on his stool in an effort not to look as large as he really was.

"Yes, sir. See, the sheep came from Quebec. They're to help boost the flocks that we have here. My father sent me to deliver them to the farmers. It's just that sheep don't really like being kept on boats and this was a long trip because they had to go around the British." He paused to confirm that the priest understood the current political situation. "The sheep kind of stampeded when the boats reached the wharf," he finished lamely, a slight blush to his high cheek bones.

Father Allard rested his head in his hands for a moment, trying not to blame the situation on Augustus—but without success. "And why would your father put you up to such a task?"

Pierre shifted his large frame on the hard stool. "He's trying to give me some more responsibilities. He's hoping I'll take over the business one day."

The priest's mouth fell open in horror. He quickly closed it and crossed himself. "And how does Monsieur Thibault feel about how this situation played out?"

"It could have been worse?" Pierre asked hopefully. He had already seen his father briefly and knew that his father's fury was beyond words, but the priest didn't need to know that.

Nic chuckled beside him. It took much more than Father Allard to ruin his amicable mood. Nic was short and compact, his black hair tied neatly at the back of his head. Since he was usually the instigator of whatever troublesome scheme he and Pierre became involved in, it felt good to have Pierre take all the blame this time.

Father Allard stood up. He was almost as tall as Pierre, but he was as slim as Pierre was broad. "Those sheep ... knocked over almost the entire market, causing hundreds of *livres* in damages, knocking several citizens to the ground, including Major de la Pérelle. They ate Lady Isabelle's prized roses and would have escaped capture if the soldiers at the city gates hadn't been thinking quickly and shut the doors. Which I will remind you happens only during the day for the grimmest of circumstances." He gave both boys a look of deepest loathing. A vein was pulsing unpleasantly near his temple.

"Technically, we are at war," Nic piped up, his swarthy features alight with amusement. "And we've been in that position since we declared war on the British in March. Too bad we didn't find out about it until May 3rd." The European nations that ruled the continent were once again at war, trying to expand their immense Empires. Louisbourg was completely dependent on the shipping channels from France and Quebec for any kind of news of what was going on in the rest of the world. As a result, the fortress had been at war for two months and not even known.

Father Allard was silent for a moment as if praying for strength. He changed direction.

"Mesdemoiselles, I was not aware that chasing after sheep was a worthwhile pastime for ladies such as yourselves."

Marie glanced over at Elise, who blushed deeply. Elise was the youngest in her family, with three older brothers, all in the French military, like their father, and her parents cared deeply about her standing within the social fabric of the fortress. It was their hope that she would marry well and lift them from the financially tight life of a military family.

"I don't think sheep care what your station in life is when you're pursuing them," Marie said coldly. She never liked it when someone blamed her for being a woman. "The sheep were wreaking havoc, and we tried to stop them. Would you have preferred us to stand by and let them escape? or let them continue ruining Lady Isabelle's garden?"

Elise gave Marie a slight smile. Father Allard glared at Marie but ignored her remarks and turned back to the boys. This was exactly why he didn't like the Lévesque twins: not enough discipline at home. "While I may not be your schoolmaster anymore and no longer have the ability to punish you, I will be informing the people who do have that happy privilege," he smiled unpleasantly, showing a row of deep yellow teeth.

Pierre nervously ran his hand through his tangled hair. His father was already waiting outside, and the consequences were not going to be pleasant. Nic stared sullenly at the priest.

"If I have to deal with either of you again, I will personally make sure that you both spend several days in the iron collar." He pointed a bony hand to the door, and the four of them retreated as quickly as possible into the dark corridor.

Augustus Thibault was just outside Father Allard's office, leaning against the corridor wall and waiting impatiently for the conclusion of the meeting. He was a large man with thick muscles padding his tall frame, acquired during the labours of his youth on the family farm. He was the son of a *habitant*, the youngest of fourteen. Since the family farm in Trois-Rivières was not large enough to support all the posterity, he and three of his brothers left when they were old enough to find jobs of their own. Through hard work, bribery, and sheer luck, he had built a successful merchant business for himself.

Right now, though, Augustus did not look pleased. His blue eyes flashed dangerously behind the wire frames of his glasses. He hadn't worked his entire life for his son to ruin it all with his carelessness.

His son looked a great deal like him. They were both tall and blue-eyed. Augustus's hair had once been golden but was now streaked liberally with grey. His son had his straight nose, high cheek bones, and square jaw, but as the two of them met in the hallway, their differences became more prominent than their similarities. It was clear who was in charge. Pierre walked silently beside his father, looking dejected.

The other three headed home. Louisbourg might be a large place, but news of what happened and their involvement would eventually reach Marie's guardians and Elise's parents. No one would be happy to hear that they had been involved.

***

Marie left her brother and friend after only a block. She needed to replace the lavender oil the sheep had destroyed, and it didn't take much convincing for Nic to see Elise home. Elise was gorgeous, with copper hair, green eyes, and a flawless complexion. She hadn't come to appreciate her own beauty yet, but that didn't stop Nic from being attracted to her.

Marie stomped through the streets, fuming. Groups of soldiers in their blue coats and white shirts and trousers punctuated daily life. The previous month, the French army had attacked the fishing grounds of Grassy Island, part of the Canso Islands, which lay to the southeast of Louisbourg, completely obliterating the community there. That was a military victory, but the citizens of Louisbourg weren't too impressed. It did not inspire much confidence that the army was capable of burning a village to the ground. If the French could do that, what would the British do?

The apothecary gave her a very disapproving look as he handed her the second vial of lavender oil. Marie knew she looked as if she'd fallen into a ditch. Her best grey skirt was ripped, and her blue jacket and fichu were so muddy, she wouldn't be wearing them for some time. Worse, the whole disaster had been caused by Nic and Pierre—again. Although Nic wasn't malicious, he was always causing problems, and he struggled to understand the consequences of his actions. He wanted to make people laugh. As for Pierre, Marie didn't completely understand why he always went along with Nic's schemes. However, she suspected that Pierre caused trouble to get his father's attention. It was a stupid way of going about it, but it was effective—too effective. Since Pierre lacked Nic's charisma, he usually ended up worse off than his partner.

Marie found Nic waiting for her near their home. Apparently, he didn't want to face their guardians alone. The twins had been orphaned at nine and sent to live with their mother's sister, Annette, in the great fortress. Annette had married Claude-Jean des Babineaux, a nobleman from the French countryside, with an estate in France and official standing at Versailles. He was Master of the Quay, the leader of the Admiralty Court, a title given to him by the Duke of Penthièvre, the Admiral of France. He was wealthy and became wealthier by accepting the bribes his excisemen collected from the smugglers and pirates who frequented the harbour. Claude was responsible for all marine matters. Nothing went in or out of the harbour without his knowledge.

When Claude arrived in Louisbourg, he had the engineers build him a large, two-storey, whitewashed stone manor house on the quay overlooking the harbour, with several shuttered windows and a large, well-tended garden in the back. It was one of the most impressive homes in the city. The house was intended to show the power of the spirit of New France to anyone who visited the fortress. It was also designed to stroke Claude's considerable ego.

"They won't make a big deal of this," Nic reassured her as he pushed open the heavy oak front door. "We were only trying to help."

Unfortunately, Annette was waiting for them. She was a small, nervous woman, her nervosity made worse by her husband's temper and her frequent headaches. It was always possible to judge her mental state by the way she was dressed. Annette never left the house in less than perfect condition. Her dark hair was always dramatically pinned on top of her head, her eyes and lips painted on, and her clothes immaculately pressed. Today, however, her hair hung loose behind her back, and her eye makeup was smudged. She had clearly worked herself into a hysterical frenzy.

"Where have you been?" Annette demanded. While petite, she had the ability to radiate a great deal of energy. Marie had left her in bed this morning, too ill to move. Evidently, her indignation at the gossip spreading around town had propelled her out of bed. "Is it true that you had something to do with the sheep running wild this afternoon?"

Marie tried her best to explain, but her aunt seemed to have made up her mind on the subject. She was cross at Marie for involving herself but was convinced that Nic was somehow responsible for the whole fiasco. Unfortunately, he had enough of a history that her suspicions weren't entirely unrealistic.

"I've tried my best. I really have. But every time I think things are going well, you go and pull a stunt like this!" She was pacing up and down the carpeted entryway, wringing her hands.

Annette was not one to sit quietly when upset. She cried and blamed herself and carried on until the person she was talking to eventually apologized. She had just begun her performance when Claude emerged from his study. He wasn't a large man—not much taller than his nephew—but with a barrel chest and thick limbs. His white hair and round spectacles aged him, adding some fragility to his appearance, but he was as strong and robust as any young man in their twenties. From the ugly look on his face, it was obvious that he, like everyone else, knew about the sheep and wasn't satisfied that it was an accident.

"What happened?" He stood in front of Nic, his dark eyes only slits. Claude seemed to live in a constant state of disapproval. Already well into his forties, he had very little patience for his wife's charges. He clearly didn't believe they'd been doing anyone a service. Whenever Claude spent time with

Nic, he was condescending at best and cruel at worst, but years before, Nic had decided he wouldn't be bullied by his uncle.

Nic spoke without making eye contact, his black eyes focused on the floor, trying his best to keep his own anger in check.

"How many times do I have to tell you not to waste your time with that farmer's son?" Claude spit, stepping closer to Nic's face. Marie could smell the whisky on his breath from where she stood.

Nic rolled his eyes. "He's not a farmer." The Thibaults' agricultural roots were Claude's most common complaint about them.

"Of course, he is. His success is nothing more than the result of bribing the right people," Claude said, just above a whisper. Then he crossed the threshold from disapproval to fury. Annette retreated into another room, and Marie could feel the danger rising. She silently prayed that Nic would keep his mouth shut, something he wasn't usually capable of.

"Like you?" Nic mocked. He was too angry to be cautious. Claude's face drained of colour. "You think you're so much better than the rest of us? Augustus is as rich as you. That's why you hate him—"

The rest of Nic's words were cut off. Claude hit him as hard as he could in the jaw, knocking his nephew to the floor. Marie clapped her hands over her mouth to stifle a scream. Nic didn't get up immediately; it was a moment before Marie heard his moans as he came back to consciousness. Claude stomped away.

Marie bent down to help Nic up, but he brushed her off. "I'm fine," he panted, rising to his feet. He didn't look at her but went up the stairs and locked himself in his room.

***

It was no secret that Claude was never enthusiastic about taking the twins. He was not one to keep his opinions to himself. After Nic and Marie's parents died in Quebec, the twins were taken in by Annette, their mother's sister. However, the twins' mother's brother, Joseph-Jean Dumas, expressed a desire to take the children in. He was a General and a rising star in the French military in Canada, who lived in his parents' former house just around the corner from Nic and Marie's family.

However, travel for his military service and the lack of a spouse worked against Joseph-Jean. Annette, as the children's aunt, argued that the children needed a woman's love and a permanent home. Annette had won out, completely ignoring her husband's objections. Claude had no children of his own, and he had no desire to become a surrogate father.

Marie often wondered whether Annette had permanently damaged her marriage by becoming guardian to her and Nic. Annette had married Claude simply because he was available and wealthy. A broken engagement had left her feeling vulnerable when she first met Claude. He had taken Annette because she was beautiful, reminding him of the refined women of Versailles. He was desperately lonely in the remote island fortress, and Annette, as the daughter of a General, seemed to be the best choice he had in the colony. They got along well enough for a while, but cracks soon appeared in their union. Annette was not the submissive woman Claude had hoped she would be. He usually ignored her outbursts and hysterics, having no patience for such weakness. Annette hoped the children would bring a positive change to the house. Sadly, the opposite came true. The children were wild and untamed just like the rest of the colony, further adding to the problem. Marie could remember nothing but fighting between them.

Nic appeared the next morning after Claude left for the day, a dark, purpling mark at the edge of his chin. He hadn't shaved, in hopes that the black stubble would draw attention away from it. Marie said nothing as the two of them went toward the kitchen in search of breakfast.

The Babineaux house was one of the largest in the city. Despite the grandeur of their home and the luxurious furnishings shipped from Europe, the twins preferred to eat at the scrubbed wooden table in the kitchen in the presence of Madame Badeau, the housekeeper.

Madame Badeau was shorter than both the twins and carried her considerable weight around her hips. Her iron-grey curls poked out of the white linen cap she always wore, and she was never seen without an apron stuffed full of the odds and ends that she felt might come in handy. While Claude liked to consider himself the master of his domain, it was Madame Badeau who really ran the house. She was the only one to whom Claude showed any respect, most likely because he had never learned to cook for himself.

The estate employed two maids as well as Madame Badeau, and then there was Claude's personal servant, who was not an employee but a slave from the West Indies named Ferdinand. In his mid-twenties, Ferdinand had already passed the life expectancy for most slaves. The twins rarely saw him. He was devoted to his master and spent most of his day attached to Claude.

Nic sat down without looking at anyone. He knew she wouldn't let him off without a scolding. After she served them their brown bread with lard and a boiled egg each, she pushed his black hair away from his face with her massive hand.

"Let me see how bad it is." She turned Nic's jaw toward the light. Though his eyes and hair were dark, his skin was pale enough that any mark showed clearly. "You need to learn to keep your mouth shut," she said, then let him get to his breakfast.

"How is this my fault?" Nic challenged. He was tired of being chastised for his uncle's temper.

Madame Badeau sighed. "You never poke a sleeping dragon in the eye and then complain when he burns the village down." Nic rolled his eyes. "I saw that. Now drink your milk." She slammed a mug down in front of him.

"We were just helping," he grumbled, picking up the mug.

Madame Badeau harrumphed but gave him a narrow smile. "That Thibault boy will be the death of you. But at least you stick together."

Marie watched Nic and Madame Badeau as she downed her bread and lard. It was cozy here in the kitchen—in contrast to the rest of the house. She always thought that the great manor felt empty. Though it was filled to capacity with some of the finest things that money could buy, it was far too big for the four residents who lived in it. They could go days without seeing other members of the family, though that was a relief when it came to her uncle. The kitchen was also the warmest place in the house. Except for the few hottest days of the summer months, the heat from the ovens was a welcome relief. The cramped kitchen felt more like home than the rest of the massive house ever could.

Marie finished up her breakfast and then pulled her linen apron from its peg and pinned it on. She almost made it to the back door before Madame Badeau handed her a hat with the warning that it was sunny. Grudgingly, Marie accepted it and tucked her waist-length chestnut braid under the fabric, pulling the brown ribbon tight under her chin.

She wouldn't have been at risk for a sunburn even without her hat. Nic sunburned easily, but she wasn't as pale as he was. People usually assumed they couldn't be twins because they looked so different. Nic was taller with a stocky build, while Marie was slender. Her hazel eyes were wide, framed with long, dark lashes, and placed perfectly on either side of a petite, straight nose. Nic was the spitting image of their father, while Marie wasn't really sure where she'd come from. Her mother had been tall and willowy. Marie was simply small.

The garden behind the Babineaux home provided a large portion of the produce the family ate, as well as kitchen herbs and spices. Annette had planted it at the beginning of her marriage, hoping to develop a green thumb. She wasn't successful, and Marie soon took over the weeding, planting, and grooming. Sometimes Nic would help her, but he preferred to spend as much time as possible away from the property.

Two rows of apples and plums lined the far end of the garden. Rows of onions, turnips, and cabbage were already sprouting in the black dirt in their raised beds. Strawberries and gooseberries grew on the side opposite to the fruit trees near a stone bench erected in memory of her mother. A large pen with chickens, goats, and pigs filled the far corner near the vegetables. Claude's two horses were kept separate from the rest of the livestock in their own stone stable. Marie never took care of those horses. That was a job Claude entrusted only to Ferdinand.

Marie settled herself between the rows of onions, sitting cross-legged on the warm earth. A tribe of grubs had moved in during the spring months, gorging themselves on the tender new leaves, and Marie was waging a losing battle against them. This was starting to be a huge problem, since the garden was especially important this year.

The fortress was completely dependent on supplies coming from Europe, the Valley of the Saint-Laurent, Île Saint-Jean, and the West Indies for such basic items as wheat and sugar, and those supplies were now being cut off by the British navy. Many ships leaving from France to bring supplies to Louisbourg were also being captured just off the coast of Europe, and the shipping season had only just begun. No one was outright starving, but tight rationing was in place to try to stretch the available supplies. At least there would be mutton, Marie thought ruefully.

The sun beat down as she pinched the offending grubs from the stalks of the growing plants. She dropped each squirming white body into a clay jar of water she kept beside her. She felt a bit like an executioner as she dropped the bugs into a watery death. With every drop, she imagined tiny death screams. She purposely kept her face turned away from the mouth of the jar.

A shadow crossed the neatly kept squares of budding life. Looking up, Marie saw Pierre's tall frame silhouetted against the sun. She was surprised to see him. He didn't usually visit, preferring to meet Nic somewhere in the city. Three years ago, he had been unceremoniously removed from the house when Claude missed a bribe from one of Augustus's captains. It wasn't Augustus's fault. All his captains knew to line Claude's pockets, but it was easier for Claude to blame the merchant than a sea captain who was no longer in town. Pierre had been careful about his visits ever since.

"How goes the annihilation?" he teased, his wide grin lighting up his face. Marie was surprised to notice that he was starting to look a bit physically attractive. Too bad he was still such an idiot most of the time, horsing around with her equally brain-dead brother. If he ever grew out of that behaviour, Marie observed, some girl might actually fall for him some day.

Marie struggled to her feet, her joints stiff after being in one position for so long. She wiped her hands on the corner of her apron. "I'll get every last one of them if it's the last thing I do. What brings you here?"

Pierre looked rather embarrassed. "I came to apologize for yesterday."

Marie's mouth fell open. She wasn't aware that Pierre knew what an apology was. For a moment, she was too surprised to say anything.

"Well, apology accepted." Marie tried to cover her shock by brushing off her skirt. "It was an accident. But if I were you, I'd stay away from livestock for a while."

"You don't need to worry about that! I've been reassigned to a clerk job for the foreseeable future," he said, looking more than disappointed. "Maybe for the rest of my life."

"At least he didn't fire you," Marie joked, feeling a little badly for him.

Pierre shrugged. His father tried his best, but he found raising his son alone to be a challenge. Neither of them knew how to relate to the other. "Wouldn't put it past him. He didn't get where he is today by giving people fourth and fifth chances." He paused, lost in thought, then seemed to remember where he was.

Pierre looked down awkwardly, scratching the back of his neck. "When I saw Nic's shiner, I thought it might be best to apologize to everyone else involved." He gazed across at the stable, where Ferdinand's glossy black face was visible, watching them carefully. Claude's slave was not naturally inclined to gossip, but he knew all about the enmity between his master and Pierre's father, and he knew Claude would not be happy to know Pierre was frequenting the premises. "I'd better go before Claude finds out I'm here."

He took a step forward, knocking Marie's clay jar over. Water quickly spread along the raised row, darkening the soil as it went. The collection of bugs so carefully dropped into the jar splashed against the stocks of the new plants.

Marie jumped out of the way, trying to stay clear of the incoming wave of pests.

"I'm sorry," Pierre exclaimed in horror, completely mortified. He tried to step out of the way but lost his balance, smashing the row of cabbages as his body landed.

Exasperated, Marie shouted, "What is wrong with you?"

Pierre's pale, freckled face was beet red. "I-I didn't mean to," he stammered, pulling himself to his feet. He withered under the look Marie gave him. "Let me help." He quickly scooped up the jar.

Marie snatched it from him. "You've done enough," she snapped. Some of the slugs weren't dead and were slowly climbing up the fresh shoots.

Pierre admitted defeat. He hadn't come to apologize on his own. It was his father who had sent him. Afraid of what his father would do if he refused, Pierre had obeyed him, but whatever Augustus was expecting to be gained from this encounter, Pierre had ruined it. He quickly retreated from the garden, careful not to crush anymore vegetables.

***

The hot July sun warmed Marie's face and chest as she and Elise sat on the grass, gazing out at the turbulent North Atlantic. A stiff breeze blew the tall, golden grass, tickling Marie's bare forearms. She stared out at the ocean, watching the waves crash into the rocky shore. The ocean seemed to have a life of its own, changing its mood and purpose whenever it fancied. Today, it was a royal blue with powerful white caps that slammed into the rocky coast, soaking anyone who came too close in freezing spray. To Marie, gazing at the ocean was one of the best things about living in Louisbourg.

Elise sat beside Marie, her hair tied neatly under her broad-brimmed hat. Marie's hair blew wild behind her. Marie didn't know that redheads reacted badly to the sun until she met her friend. Elise could burn doing the simplest of outdoor chores. Even hanging out the laundry could reduce her to the colour of a nightshade berry. No matter the heat, Elise always wore a hat, because as she said, she had enough freckles as it was.

"You're so proper," Marie muttered, lying down in the grass so that all she could see was the blue sky. Annette would berate her later for allowing the sun to darken her skin, but she didn't care. Louisbourg was a long way away from the centres of arts, culture, and fashion, where a young woman's looks were scrutinized and judged harshly. Complexions were meant to be pale, but here in the colonies, staying out of the sun was unrealistic.

Annette had the best of intentions when she'd brought the twins from the capital. However, she wasn't prepared for two high-spirited nine-year-olds who refused to sit still. At first, she'd tried to tame Nic from following his wild ways, and she'd attempted to educate Marie in the refined, lady-like behaviour expected of her. But eventually, Annette gave up, hoping only to keep the twins alive and out of prison.

Elise made a face. "What do you expect? Some of us have a reputation to uphold." Elise was the youngest in her family, but originally there'd been ten older siblings, not three. The other seven had died in the smallpox outbreak of 1732, which had decimated the fortress. The four youngest Sarrazin children had managed to survive, becoming the miracles of the epidemic. As a result, Elise's parents were fiercely protective of her and her reputation.

Marie laughed. Nic had caused so much trouble as a child that his behaviour had affected her reputation as well—to the point that people were often impressed that she could hold an intelligent conversation when they discovered the two were twins. Marie and Elise had first met at school. They sat next to each other in the classroom, and neither really fit in with the rest of the girls. Marie was a stranger and Elise was too afraid to talk. Eventually, Marie had coaxed Elise into telling her something about herself, and from there, the friendship grew. There were only so many times you could have your braids tied to the back of your chair or your school bag hidden in a tree by Nic and Pierre before you became best friends.

Elise and Marie gazed out at the bay in front of them, which housed the Louisbourg harbour and lighthouse. The harbour was filled with all sorts of ships—from the French navy's massive warships (providing some peace of mind) to the smallest fishing boats. But the vessels the girls could see represented only a fraction of the ones usually present during the summer months. The British navy was obviously doing a good job of blocking French ships from reaching the fortress.

Cod was the fundamental reason why Louisbourg existed. Thousands of barrels of salted cod and cod liver oil were shipped all over the world from the city's harbour. So every summer, Louisbourg's population swelled well beyond its walls with fishermen from Europe who came to cast their nets for a season before returning home. The buildings lining the city's wide streets had been purposely built low, so the wind could dry the cod stretched across the many wooden racks that lined Rochefort Point and the surrounding plains. This meant that all of Louisbourg and the surrounding area stank of fish during the summer months. The smell filled every corner and even coated the mosquitoes in the oily film of curing cod. The low buildings would also be less vulnerable to the cannonballs and mortar shells of the British if the enemy ever arrived. This building code was a stipulation that many people chose to ignore.

Elise picked at a few pieces of grass and began braiding them between her fingers. "It's too hot." She threw the braid into the wind and picked up her skirts to let the breeze touch her legs. Marie turned and gazed at the fishermen in the distance, bent over their drying racks. Her waist-length hair danced around her face. It was too hot to stay indoors knitting. She couldn't imagine salting fish in this heat. Looking toward the fortress, she watched the soldiers walking along the tops of the ramparts. This was her favourite view of the city—seen from among the tall grasses near the edge of the water with the mighty city to her right.

The short walls that lined the quay framed her view, and the city's patchwork of buildings were a welcoming sight behind the rocking masts of the harbour. Grand stone houses mixed with modest wood cottages, and inns intermingled with taverns and the homes of artisans and merchants. Louisbourg was the largest port stationed at the mouth of the Gulf of the Saint-Laurent. The warm summer months saw Louisbourg swell almost to the size of the capital, Quebec.

During the winter, the city hibernated. Only the permanent residents stayed and braved the icy winds blowing off the open ocean, so during that cold season, the garrison outnumbered the civilians. Since May, only a few more soldiers had been added to the ranks. The British blockade was making it impossible for the help sent from France to get through.

"It's so hot today," Elise laughed, "that my mother refused to do any baking."

"But there's so little bread to make," Marie replied. There were always food shortages in Louisbourg. Wheat was usually the first thing to run low, the closest supplier of the grain beyond Île-Royale being Île Saint-Jean, some three hundred miles away. Ocean travel wasn't the most reliable method of getting food to the people of the city, so there were often periods of rationing. Most people were surprised when Marie announced she had never heard of rations until moving here. But this time was different. Because they were now at war, no one knew when this period of deprivation would end.

Elise plucked one of the golden blades that danced around them and nibbled on the end, making a face. "Doesn't taste the best."

Marie laughed. "It's July. There is actual food around." She waved a slender hand at the fields and forests surrounding them—filled with vegetation and berries.

A shout came flying across the air. Elise shielded her eyes against the bright sun. "It looks like Pierre," she said, mortified, pushing her skirts back around her ankles.

Marie shrugged. "Hopefully, he doesn't want us to help him with something," Elise groaned. They were both thinking of the sheep.

"I don't see Nic," Elise said with concern. Usually, the two boys were inseparable.

Pierre's loping gait carried him easily to where the girls were sitting. "Hello, ladies." His cheeks were pink and his blond curls damp from the heat. Elise looked him over suspiciously. He noticed. "I haven't done anything this time," he said, holding up his hands in supplication, feigning hurt that she looked skeptical.

"Then why are you here?" Elise folded her arms across her chest. It wasn't that she didn't like Pierre, but she wasn't about to get sucked into another plot. The memories of the last encounter were too fresh.

Pierre shrugged, his linen shirt billowing away from his thin chest in the breeze. "Couldn't stand the smell of drying fish anymore. Thought I'd come say hello."

Elise exchanged a meaningful look with Marie which puzzled her. "Well, I think I must be going," Elise continued. "My mother's doing the laundry today. I really should go and help her." As she retreated, she gave Marie a look that clearly stated she expected to be informed about the rest of the afternoon's events.

Marie sighed inwardly as she scrambled to her feet. She knew perfectly well that Elise had nothing to do at home, and Marie was going to have to spend the next day explaining away the ridiculous ideas Elise had obviously got into her head. The glare of the sun was making it almost impossible for Marie to see, but she grabbed as much of her hair as she could and awkwardly held it by her side. She looked at Pierre expectantly.

"Have I offended her?" he asked, looking after the retreating figure.

"She's still not over the sheep thing."

"I see. I guess she doesn't forgive easily," he said, though he didn't seem particularly concerned.

"No, she just doesn't want any trouble today. It's too hot."

"It sure is. A letter came from my Uncle Tomas in Quebec. Apparently, the entire city shut down a few weeks ago because of the heat. People were getting ill, so everyone just closed up shop and stayed home or found a cool place to go. It's not that bad here, but can we find some shade?"

Marie laughed and waved toward the surrounding forest.

"Well, let's go over there," Pierre said with enthusiasm, and the two of them headed toward the shade of the large trees. When they came to the edge of the woods, they found a crude path that had been worn among the ferns and decomposing leaves.

"What brings you here today?" Marie asked as they tramped along.

"I can't just come and visit?" Pierre said as he pushed a birch branch out of his way and held it back for Marie.

"You can. I'm just not sure why you would." Pierre was Nic's friend first, and most of Marie's interactions with him were through Nic. Until a year ago, Marie had never really been welcomed by the duo.

Pierre smiled and pulled a handkerchief from his pocket. Unwrapping it, he produced four dark brown squares of something that seemed to have melted slightly around the edges.

"What is that?" Marie asked.

"It's chocolate—from the West Indies. I brought it because I thought you and Elise might like some."

Marie picked up one of the squares. It melted quickly, sticking to her fingers. She knew it was a delicacy, but it was one she'd never tried. "Don't people usually drink this?" she asked.

"Yes, usually, it's like coffee, so it's supposed to be hot, but I didn't think a hot drink would go over well today."

Marie licked the chocolate experimentally. It tasted bitter but not unpleasant. "Where did you get this?" A woodpecker cackled overhead.

"The *Persephone* came in today. Unfortunately, no one can control what ships make it and which ones don't, so we don't have enough wheat, but we do have chocolate."

Marie laughed and popped the square into her mouth. She began to chew on it until Pierre told her to just let it melt. She did that but felt rather silly walking through the forest with her mouth stuffed with the exotic food.

"Does your father know you took this?" Marie asked suspiciously once the treat had dissolved.

"Of course. Don't look so surprised. We do actually talk to each other from time to time." Pierre often joked about the lack of a typical father-son relationship between him and Augustus, but Marie wasn't sure if this state of affairs really bothered him or not.

"How is your father?" she hedged.

Pierre shrugged. "Same as always. Busy with work."

Deeper within the forest, the trees were so tall and thick that the light streaming down through their branches looked green. It was peaceful there, the noise of the city left behind.

Pierre broke the silence. "There's a creek not far from here," he said. Most farmers and fishermen had wells or at least a neighbour who would share their water. But some of them made the trip to the creek, as it offered a welcome break from the daily routine—especially on a day as hot as this.

Pierre took over the lead, trying to find a spot that wasn't crowded with children also looking for a break from the midday heat. Their mothers and older sisters reclined on the mossy banks, watching them lazily. After a short while, Pierre found a bend in the creek's path that no one had claimed yet. He sat down on a mossy log by the edge of it and began to strip off his shoes and socks.

Marie didn't follow suit because she had another problem to contend with. That chocolate was good, but now her mouth was covered in a thick film. She bent down at the edge of the creek to take a sip. The rushing water was cold and clear against her fingers.

"Where's Nic today?" It felt strange to have only Pierre for company.

"I don't know," Pierre shrugged. "I told him where I was headed, but he didn't want to come."

"I'm not very exciting when you've spent most of your life with me," Marie admitted.

Pierre laughed. It was a low, husky sound that seemed to come from his stomach. He grabbed some raspberries from a nearby bush and tossed some to Marie. "Now what would make this more exciting?"

"I could constantly remind you of all the things you should be doing instead of bugging me," Marie teased, sitting down beside him, taking extra care that her skirts didn't drag in the mud.

"Is that what siblings do to each other all day?" Pierre asked, curious.

"Basically." Marie pulled her own stockings off and dangled her feet in the water. Minnows swam around her ankles, trying to determine whether or not they were a threat.

"My father had so many siblings I think he wanted to spare me the tragedy." Pierre walked right into the creek, sighing with relief as the clear water reached his thin calves.

"I can't believe your grandmother gave birth fourteen times."

"Only six," Pierre corrected her. "My grandfather was married twice. His first wife died giving birth to number ten, and two of her kids didn't survive."

Marie shuddered. Childbirth was not something she was looking forward to—especially here in the colony, where having as many children as possible was encouraged. "Your father probably realized what you were like and figured it wasn't worth the risk to have another."

Pierre threw his head back and laughed again, the sound booming off the jack pines. "Probably," he said, wading toward her. "You should come in."

She shook her head. "If I come home even a little wet, Madame Badeau will kill me."

Pierre looked confused.

"Do you have any idea how long it takes this many layers to dry?"

Pierre shrugged. He didn't spend any time worrying about women's fashions. But if someone were to ask him, he'd say that as far as he was concerned, women wore too many layers. "I won't let you get wet," Pierre said. There was a gleam in his eye that Marie didn't trust.

"I don't think so."

Pierre reached out his hand. "Come on, you'll be fine."

Marie stared at the water racing over the smooth stones. It did look inviting. Cautiously, she took a step in and grabbed Pierre's hand to keep her balance on the slippery rocks. Without warning, he pulled her forward and she lost her balance and tumbled into the water.

Coughing and spluttering, she sat up, pushing her curtain of hair away from her face. Completely soaked, she was silently cursing herself for being so stupid. Pierre was doubled over laughing.

"I'm sorry," he gasped between breaths. "I couldn't help myself."

Marie sat for a moment, watching the water speed over her many skirts, trying to figure out what to do next. Then she sprang forward. Pierre yelped and jumped out of the way. There was no way Marie could push him into the water. He was simply too large. But that didn't stop her from splashing him as much as she could for a good five minutes.

"Truce!" he shouted over and over, trying to escape the torrents of water. The two of them stood staring at each other, water dripping from their hair and faces. Marie stayed crouched, ready to defend herself if necessary.

"You're a feisty one." Pierre said, pushing back the hair that was plastered to the side of his face.

"You don't grow up with Nic and not learn how to defend yourself."

Pierre stood up, his hands raised in surrender. They hadn't realized how loud they were being until a group of bare-chested children came around the bend, their faces curious as they watched the standoff between the two teenagers.

"I promise I won't do anything else," Pierre pleaded, a wide grin playing on his lips.

"Ah-huh." Marie continued to watch him like a hawk. "Then you get out first."

He shook his head, dropping water from his blond hair into his eyes. "Ladies first."

Marie paused for a moment, thinking. As fast as she could, she climbed back on shore, her soaked petticoats weighing her down. She slipped her shoes back on, picked up her stockings, and then grabbed Pierre's shoes.

"Hey!" he yelled, still in the middle of the creek. "I need those."

Marie gave him a wicked smile and took off back to the city.

***

Madame Badeau wasn't pleased about the state Marie was in or the amount of water that was dripping onto her clean floors. The layers of petticoats were hanging in the garden, weighing the line down heavily. Marie was given the task of scrubbing the kitchen floor to make up for her watery indiscretion. Nic lolled in the doorway, watching her. He was envious of how Pierre had chosen to spend his afternoon and hadn't been shy about sharing his opinion ever since Marie arrived home, trailing puddles behind her. He didn't say anything as he watched her intently scrubbing the wood floors, sweat rolling down her forehead. Marie had the impression that he felt this was a worthy punishment for stealing his best friend for the afternoon.

It was close to dinnertime when Pierre appeared on the doorstep. Marie had the misfortune of being the one to answer the door. To her surprise, Pierre didn't seem angry at all. He had dried off, but his hair was as unruly as ever despite the fact that he'd tried to wrestle it into a braid.

"I thought I would trade you these for my shoes." He handed her half a dozen taper candles. "They're from the mainland." He seemed a little sheepish.

Marie bit her lip to keep from laughing. "I steal your shoes and you bring me candles?" Marie knew that it took at least a week to make candles. It involved standing close to a pot of melted wax for a long time. So Pierre was saving her a lot of work. Marie stepped inside and then returned with the stolen footwear.

"My father naturally wanted to know where my shoes were. After I finally told him, he suggested I go and apologize." His high cheekbones were slightly pink.

"Really?"

Pierre rolled his eyes. "I didn't want to, given how the last apology went, so I thought candles might be better."

Marie laughed aloud. "Yes, I think I prefer candles."

Pierre nodded and slipped his soft leather shoes onto his bare feet. "Next time there won't be any 'Ladies First' nonsense," he said darkly, wiggling his toes to bring some warmth back to them.

"That was your first mistake, assuming that I'm a lady."

"Ah-huh," Pierre said, then waved goodbye, walked out into the street, and mixed in with the evening traffic of sailors coming off the ships in search of dinner.

The harbour was almost empty, but the men who occupied the boats knew they would be called upon if the British launched an attack that summer. With the exception of those on the warships, none were in the military and none had much training. The garrison and a few sailors, that was all that stood between the citizens of Louisbourg and the largest navy in the world.

Marie closed the door to find Nic waiting for her in the shadows of the sitting room. He looked distinctly grumpy.

"You know he's never given anyone gifts before," he grumbled.

Chapter 2

THE HARVEST WAS WELL UNDERWAY, and the race was on to gather as much of the crop as possible before the deadly frost came and coated everything in a thin layer of ice. The farmers around Louisbourg were bringing their crops to the government warehouses. With the British barricading the waters, these storehouses were more important than ever.

Annette was the organizer of many charitable events in the fortress. While anxious and prone to hysteria, she really did have the best of intentions. Her endeavours also usually took her out of the house, absences that helped her marriage survive. At the beginning of September, she decided to help the government package and organize the autumn bounty. She insisted that a certain amount must be set aside for the poor, who would otherwise starve, being unable to buy from the government's stash.

Marie hadn't been keen on the idea of packing crates when there was a garrison of soldiers looking for things to do when not training or standing watch. So, unwilling to suffer alone, she'd dragged Elise along with her. When they arrived at the dusty warehouse it was vacant, except for long tables set in the middle and empty crates and barrels. The compact dirt floors and rough stone walls were lit by torches on the walls. It was a dreary place to spend an afternoon. The smell of the floor varnish (created from cow dung and blood) made Elise gag.

Marie was surprised to see Sophie de la Rocque and Charlotte Duchambon standing by one of the tables. Sophie was the daughter of the King's Engineer. She lived for gossip, held grudges, and thought she was better than the rest of them. Marie couldn't stand her. As for Charlotte, Marie wasn't well acquainted with her, but she did know she was the daughter of the Governor, Louis Du Pont Duchambon, and so had some status in the colony. Charlotte had difficulty connecting with people, though, as she suffered from a debilitating stutter. When Marie had interacted with her, Charlotte had barely spoken.

Marie's thoughts were interrupted by the arrival of Annette, along with a long line of wagons of produce. As soon as each wagon drew up to the main door, it was quickly unloaded by soldiers looking for extra wages. There were a few members of the Swiss guard, but most were cadets from northern France. Then the task of sorting cabbages from onions, rotten from fresh, soon began.

"I can't wait until your aunt goes back to getting people to make quilts," Elise muttered, tossing a grub-filled cabbage into the bad pile. All around them, the room bustled. The soldiers continued to unload empty crates for the women to fill with good produce and then took the full ones away. Annette had succeeded in convincing a large number of upper-class ladies to come and lend a hand, and their presence only added to the liveliness of the crowd. "This isn't as bad as the time Annette decided to have us host the fundraiser for supplies for the school," Marie pointed out, trying not to breathe through her nose. Charlotte glanced at Marie and rolled her brown eyes.

A grimace crossed Elise's beautiful features. The gambling night had raised a lot of funds for the school, though one engineer went without food for a month, having gambled away his month's wages. However, Annette forgot to secure help for the cleanup afterwards, and Marie and Elise were among those forced to scrub chewing tobacco off the floor of the Engineer's property.

"With a track record like that, it's a wonder she gets anyone to help," Elise muttered. Help might have been a strong word. Most of the women were happily gossiping at their tables, hardly touching the produce. Realizing that the work wasn't getting done, the soldiers started sorting through the cabbages.

About then, Sophie came bouncing over, dark curls swinging. She never worked at these events, using them purely as social gatherings instead.

"So tell me, Marie," Sophie began, oblivious to her peers' efforts to fill the crates. "What's this about you and Pierre Thibault swimming together in the creek in the forest? What's your excuse this time?"

Marie threw Elise a look. Elise busied herself with the cabbage, suddenly finding the pile of heads quite fascinating.

"What about him?" she responded coolly.

"Well," Sophie said, leaning on the table. "Someone told me about your jaunt in the woods." Her green eyes twinkled.

Elise's cheeks were red. She forgot about the smell around her and inhaled deeply, doubling over at the stench of the warehouse.

"He's my brother's best friend. Obviously, I see a lot of him." Marie tried to keep her voice steady.

Sophie pouted in disappointment. "But he's more interested in you than he's been before," she wheedled. It was well known Sophie lusted after anyone with good bone structure, of which Pierre was included.

Marie sighed, forcefully pushing the last of the onions into a crate. "He's a friend, Sophie. Let it go."

"More than a friend?"

Marie slammed the crate on the tabletop. "It's none of your business who I spend my time with. You're not my mother and you're wrong."

"Does Annette know?"

"Does your mother know you've been sneaking into dark corners with my brother?" Marie snapped.

Sophie looked as if she'd been slapped. Both Elise and Charlotte did little to cover their laughter. Humiliated, Sophie turned on her heel and stomped off, pushing her way past a group of soldiers.

"I'm sorry, Marie. I didn't tell her much. She just asked where you were last Thursday." Elise's green eyes were wide with concern. "I shouldn't have told her."

Marie brushed the comment off. "Don't worry about it. She's not the only one."

"That b-b-b-busy b-body can spin y-y-y-yarns out of a g-g-g-grain of s-s-s-salt," Charlotte blurted.

Marie and Elise both stared, open mouthed, at Charlotte. It was the first time they'd heard her speak in months.

***

The end of September brought shorter days, and the evening air bore the promise of colder days to come. Any fishermen who'd made the treacherous voyage from France had left for home, and most of the harvest was gathered in, the storehouses packed to the rafters in preparation for the long, frozen months of winter. The citizens of Louisbourg knew that, all too soon, they would be waking up to the sight of frost covering the ground. The winter would last for a long, long time, so it was no wonder that the residents of the fortress weren't ready to say goodbye to the summer months yet.

Dusk was falling, but the city was just beginning to stir as people got ready to go out to the Harvest Festival just outside the city walls. Marie was pinning up the last of her hair when a knock came at the front door. Marie headed down the stairs and opened the door to the sight of Elise, her pale cheeks red from the bite of the chilled air, and her younger cousin, Diane, who was standing beside her, practically bursting with excitement. Both had pulled their overcoats out of storage and were wearing them for the first time that season.

Marie had no idea where Annette was, an occurrence that had been happening more and more in recent weeks. Her charitable activities kept her busy during the day, but where she was in the evening was anyone's guess. Unconcerned, Marie put on her grey, woollen cloak, waved to Madame Badeau, and followed Elise and Diane into the evening.

Like Elise's family, Diane's was in the military, but unlike her cousin, she was the oldest of seven girls. Her father was one of the officers responsible for trying to train the city's militia. It was a thankless job with little pay. Diane was also as dark as Elise was fair. This was her first experience out on her own, and she practically glowed with anticipation as the trio walked along.

The usually dark streets were lit by paper lanterns as citizens filled the city streets that led beyond the walls. There was a festive feeling in the air. Small children ran beyond the reach of their parents, darting in and out of the shadows created by the fading sun.

Soldiers lined the streets, keeping a close eye on the proceedings. The white and blue of the French uniform contrasted with the red and white of the Swiss Kerr regiment—both solemn reminders of what would likely be coming next summer. Now that the fishermen had left, there were more military men than civilians in the fortress. The ever-present guards stood beside the gates. Unconcerned with security during such a festival, their muskets leaned, neglected, against the thick stone walls. The weather was becoming too cold for these soldiers' thin uniforms, so wool blankets were draped over their shoulders to provide a little comfort from the biting air. They laughed and joked with those leaving, appearing to be completely unconcerned that a war was raging around them. Marie wondered if any of these men had been at the Grassy Islands or Annapolis Royal.

Just beyond the walls, a massive bonfire raged, casting light and heat for hundreds of yards. A fiddler stood a stone's throw from the blaze, scratching out a jig for all to hear. More musicians were coming to join him, unpacking their instruments and livening up the festivities even more. It seemed that most of the residents of the city had left their homes for the night to be part of the country dance, and with the harvest over, there was much to celebrate.

Claude, however, felt that attendance at such gatherings was beneath any member of his family. But with Claude in Quebec on orders from Governor Duchambon, there was little that he could do to stop Marie from being out there with the crowd. Marie didn't care about class structures. In fact, New France as a whole was famous for lacking the proper divide between the classes, and nowhere was that more apparent than in Louisbourg. Only a handful of families with aristocratic blood lived within its walls. Most wealthy people were like Augustus, part of the burgeoning bourgeoisie, something Claude abhorred.

Back at the bonfire, fruit and vegetables that hadn't been claimed by the government were gathered and spread out on flannel sheets on the ground. It appeared that a steer had even been slaughtered for the occasion. Marie was surprised. She thought that all spare cattle were the property of the garrison, used to supplement rations, but here, in front of her eyes, most of the soldiers were already into the bouillon, the cheapest alcohol, trying to forget that they were trapped on the island for the winter. If the soldiers were eating, some official must have given permission for the feast to happen.

Elise scoured the crowd for people that she and her companions might know. Sophie de la Rocque wouldn't be there and neither would Charlotte, this type of gathering being considered inappropriate to their station in life. There were a few young women that Marie knew by sight from school, but she wasn't in the mood to try to make new friends. Elise led Diane over to the blankets, with Marie following behind, when a voice whispered in her ear, "Hello, beautiful."

Startled, Marie turned to find herself face to face with Pierre, who was looking warm in a new thick, black wool jacket. His face was alive with the excitement of the festival. She laughed to cover her surprise. "You scared me!" she accused, flustered. She had to shout to be heard over the crowd.

Pierre chuckled. "Sorry. Just trying to get your attention."

Marie looked around and spotted Nic a few steps away, looking unenthusiastic in a grey, woollen cap. He'd spent the better part of his time recently trying to convince Marie that Pierre wasn't worth her time.

"You know he's had his hands on a few girls," Nic had pointed out angrily one afternoon when he'd been forced once again to share his free time with his sister. (The garden had needed weeding and Madame Badeau had made him help.)

"So have you. What's your point?"

Nic's pale face went through several colour transformations before settling on beet red. "I have not!"

Marie laughed at him. "Sophie de la Rocque, Anne de la Forêt ... and, oh, how about Pasqueline Bellamy? I'm sure Claude would like to hear you've been running around with a fishmonger's daughter."

Nic hadn't said any more on the subject after that, but he wasn't happy that Pierre seemed to be showing interest in Marie and was spending less time with him. When Marie was in his presence, he often resorted to angry looks, stony silences, and muttered annoyance. Right now, Nic was so angry that he stepped away from Marie and Pierre and stared furiously at the bonfire. Elise and Diane had sat down on one of the blankets and were accepting pieces of beef from one of the soldiers tending the fire.

As Pierre and Marie were standing there in the middle of the crowd, it occurred to Marie that Nic should start looking for a serious relationship, and she said as much to Pierre.

Pierre looked around. Being several inches taller than most people, he had a better view of the gathering than Marie did. "Any ideas?" He stood on his toes, scanning the people milling around. "You know he's had plenty of interactions with girls."

"I mean more than flighty flirtations and dark, sordid affairs."

Pierre nodded and continued looking around.

As Marie looked in the opposite direction, she realized that she knew most of the people here only by sight. Technically, it was Nic's job to protect her from any unsavoury exchanges that could ruin her reputation, but just now, she felt more protected by the hulking figure of Pierre than the slouching, sullen character Nic was becoming.

"Well, there's always Elise's cousin, Diane," Marie said. "She's only fourteen, but that's just one year younger than Nic."

Pierre walked over to where Nic was standing, apparently trying to make sense of the flames in front of him. The aroma of cooking beef filled the air as hunks of animal were mounted on stakes near the flames. "Come on, Nic," Pierre said. "We're here to have fun, so why don't you join the rest of us?" After a great deal of coercion, Nic finally followed Pierre to where Marie was, and Marie led them over to Elise and Diane. She made the introductions.

Elise didn't seem very interested in conversing with Nic. She'd spent enough time dealing with him in school. Besides, there was a large group of soldiers standing a few yards away that had caught her eye. But Diane was eager for any attention. She might have been younger than the rest, but her raven hair, full red lips, and hazel eyes were starting to turn men's heads. Pierre wrapped his hand around Marie's elbow and motioned for her to follow him.

"Do you think it's safe leaving Nic with the two of them?" Marie asked.

He gave her a quizzical look.

"He won't corrupt them, I mean."

Pierre glanced back. "How much damage can he do? Unlike me, Elise is smart enough not to fall for his crazy schemes. And, yes, I do know what I'm implying about my own intelligence."

Marie coughed to cover her laughter. "But what about Diane?" she said.

"Too naïve. He'd see her as a little sister more than anything else."

They walked around the fire to the other side, where the fiddler and his companions had attracted a large crowd of spectators. A few of the fishermen's wives could be seen in the light of the fire, dancing a jig.

"Want to join them?" Pierre asked, one eyebrow cocked.

Marie snorted in disbelief. "You think I can do that? I can barely make my way through a simple set at a ball. I'd end up on my back with a twisted ankle."

Pierre grinned. "You sure?" He bent his legs and began a very poor impression of the dancing women. Marie doubled over, laughing.

She was happy to watch as the gathering grew into a dance. There was an unrestrained air among the inhabitants as they celebrated the end of the summer season. Farmers and fishermen gathered in groups to catch up after so many weeks of continuous labour. They'd shed their usual grubby work clothes for their Sunday best, so most were almost unrecognizable. Soldiers relaxed with jugs of bouillon, celebrating the summer that had passed without a British invasion. Even young children were present, trying their best to stay awake in their mothers' arms.

"Come here," Pierre said, looking back at Marie over his shoulder. "I want to show you something."

Marie glanced over at Nic, who wasn't paying them any attention. If anyone caught her and Pierre sneaking off into the darkness, there would be hell to pay, especially if Nic was the one making the discovery. He held her to a higher standard than he held himself.

"Nothing will happen. I promise." For once, there was no mischievous glint in his eye. She decided to trust him.

***

Pierre led Marie away from the bonfire and the celebration, but they stayed within view of the walls. Away from the warmth of the fire, the air was cold, and Marie pulled her grey cloak closer around her. She'd left her hat at home and now regretted choosing vanity over practicality. Pierre saw her discomfort and passed her his toque.

"It'll ruin your hair, but I'll pretend to not notice." Marie's bare ears were too cold for her to complain.

There was no moon, and the world seemed dark after the light of the festival. It was also difficult to navigate the uneven terrain. Stumbling over a rabbit hole, Marie grabbed Pierre's hand and let him lead. He seemed to have a particular spot in mind, but she was surprised when he sat down on a seemingly random patch of grass, resting his elbows on his long, folded legs.

"Why here?"

He motioned for her to sit. She kept a few feet between them, settling on the dying grass. Pierre didn't seem to mind. "What are we looking at?" she whispered. The thirty-foot-high walls and embankments might be an astounding feat of engineering, but she saw them every day.

Pierre pointed to the sky. Marie looked up, not sure what she was supposed to be seeing, but Pierre seemed intent on spotting something in particular. Suddenly, a pin prick of light went shooting across the inky blackness. A moment later, two more fell behind the hospital's spire.

Marie gasped. She heard Pierre chuckle in the darkness. "Shooting stars. There's been a shower of them the last few nights. I've been coming out to watch."

Marie never suspected him of being a stargazer. The faint light showed the dim profile of his face, his chiselled features recognizable even in the dark. He looked a little nervous. "Never saw this coming, did you?"

"No," Marie admitted, impressed. "I always thought you were more concerned with things a little closer to home."

Pierre smiled, the faint light flashing against his teeth. "I own a telescope."

"What?"

"Not a very big one, but it helps."

Marie leaned back, her elbows carrying her weight in the dry grass. She wondered how many more secrets Pierre held from the world. "Who would have thought you'd be spending time watching the stars? What other secrets are you hiding?"

He scratched his chin, thinking. "None really ... Well, remember that time you found frogs in your bed?"

"It's kind of hard to forget a dozen frogs hopping around under your covers," Marie pointed out. "I knew that was you."

"It wasn't!" Pierre insisted. "I got the frogs down at the marsh, and I wasn't sure what I was going to do with them. But I didn't put those frogs in your bed. Nic did that all by himself. I just took some of the blame."

Marie snickered. "Right. You think I'm stupid."

"I do not!" Pierre said indignantly. "I'm the one who cut six inches off your braid at school. I'm the one who started the snowball fight that ended up with Nic getting a cut on his forehead. I'll even admit that I'm the one who broke Annette's vase from Versailles, but I didn't put the frogs in your bed."

Marie began to swell with exasperation. "You broke that vase? I had to scrub the floors for a month because Annette thought I was lying to protect Nic."

Pierre blushed in the darkness. "Sorry about that," he said meekly.

"She still brings that up to this day, and it was almost five years ago!" Marie couldn't believe she'd been punished for Pierre's clumsiness. "All that time and Nic never said a word, and I never heard him complain when he was punished for actually breaking the vase. Ferdinand made him clean out the stables."

"Sorry," Pierre repeated in a small voice. "Nic figured I would probably get beaten for that stunt."

"You're lucky Claude didn't hit *Nic* for that," Marie huffed.

"Do you believe me about the frogs at least?"

For a moment Pierre thought she might explode, but instead, Marie began to laugh.

"Yes, I believe you," she hiccupped, finally calming down. "But if I ever find out I was punished for something else you did, I'll hurt you."

Pierre chuckled, the moonlight shining off his grin. "That's the worst of it. I promise."

Marie wasn't completely convinced. They continued to sit, staring up as more faint rays of light tumbled from the sky. Pierre eventually asked, "Do you like it here?"

Marie was surprised by the question. "Of course."

"I just mean you were born in Quebec, and you've seen the world outside the island. I just wondered how Louisbourg compared."

Marie looked up at the heavens. "It's the same stars over Quebec as here." Then she paused. "People are wealthier in Quebec or more civilized as they would put it. The pirates and smugglers hide there because they're afraid of the law, whereas here, they move around unmolested. There's more nobility in Quebec, more people from Europe visiting." Pierre nodded. He'd heard as much. "There's more food too. They can sustain themselves on what they grow. I don't remember being hungry because of low food supplies until I came here."

"We definitely never have enough of anything here," Pierre remarked.

"But I love the ocean and the sky, how you can't tell where one ends and the other begins. I love the wilderness, the forests that haven't been tamed yet." She stopped, embarrassed. "I sound ridiculous, don't I?"

Pierre shook his head. "No. You sound happy."

She smiled. "I mean I miss my parents, but I don't want to leave here."

"What happened to them?" Pierre always wanted to ask but had never had the courage to inquire before now. "You don't have to talk about it if you don't want to." He already half-hoped she wouldn't want to say anything.

Marie pulled her cloak closer around her. "There was a fire that ripped through three homes before it was contained. Ours was the second house. The maid got Nic and me out. My parents were upstairs with our brother."

"You had a brother?" Pierre was startled. This was new information.

Marie nodded sadly. "François. He was two at the time. Don't mention him to Nic. He doesn't like to talk about it."

"I didn't know that."

"Few do, but apparently you've been keeping a few things to yourself over the years as well." Marie touched the end of her nose, which was starting to sting from the chill.

"You look cold," Pierre said, watching her rub her face. "I think that's enough stargazing for one night."

"Can we do this again?" Marie asked eagerly. She'd never spent time looking up at the minuscule pinpoints of light like this before. Now that she thought about it, it seemed a little ridiculous to ignore that amazing sight.

"Yes, of course we can do this again ... if Claude ever lets you leave the house with me, that is. I doubt he would be very pleased about that. And it's not very often that there's a festival we can go to and then sneak away from." Pierre helped Marie get up. "At least you wore gloves."

"I'm not completely hopeless," Marie said, flexing her wool-covered fingers.

Back at the celebrations, the warmth of the firelight was welcome after the gloom of the night. Marie stood close to the flames, letting the heat thaw her extremely cold toes and fingers. Pierre came back to where she was sitting, carrying a cotton cloth filled with some of the roasted beef. In the firelight, she could see that Pierre's ears and cheeks were red from the elements. Marie stripped off her wool gloves and gladly accepted some of the steaming meat.

As they stood silently munching, Nic rounded the corner, eyes blazing. He had clearly noticed their absence. Marching up to them, he stopped just a hair from Marie's nose. "Where have you been?" he demanded, his chest puffed out in indignation. Marie had a very strong impression of Madame Badeau as he stood with his arms folded across his chest. She fought the impulse to laugh. This wasn't a good time to mention the resemblance.

"What are you talking about? We've been here the whole time, haven't we?" Marie looked up at Pierre, who nodded enthusiastically.

"You have not! I've spent the last half hour looking for you!" Nic said heatedly.

Marie wiped her greasy fingers on the cloth. "I thought you were with Diane and Elise."

Nic huffed. "It didn't end well."

Marie bit her lip to keep from laughing. "What happened?"

He just shook his head. "Let's just say there are some levels of madness even I am not willing to deal with." Marie purposely avoided Pierre's eye and tried to look concerned.

"So I'll ask you again," Nic said. "Where were you?" He directed his comments toward his friend. Pierre might be taller, but he seemed to shrink under Nic's stern gaze.

"There's a group of soldiers over there," Marie said, pointing abstractly across the blaze, "who challenged Pierre to a bit of cards." It seemed like a plausible idea that Nic wouldn't be able to verify.

"Yes, I thought it would be fun," Pierre said, catching on. "Went and played, but I lost miserably. My father won't be very pleased." He rubbed the back of his neck. "Marie here was quite sensible, though. She tried to talk me out of it."

Nic didn't look even slightly convinced. He was about to say more when the image of Diane emerged from the crowd. He quickly ducked behind Pierre's towering silhouette. Pierre and Marie exchanged a look. Diane glanced around for a moment and then walked away, frustrated.

"She's gone." Marie worked to keep her voice steady.

Nic peeked around Pierre's black jacket cautiously, his grey cap lopsided. "Okay, Marie," he whispered from his less than dignified position. Clearly, he'd led Diane to believe something about his intentions that were not true. "If we go home now, I won't ask you anything else about where you've been."

Marie stifled a laugh and was sorely tempted to alert Diane as to her brother's whereabouts, but after some hesitation, she decided to let him off the hook. She bade Pierre a hasty goodbye and slowly headed back into the city and to the safety of being inside the walls.

***

September 30th dawned bright and clear. The first frost glittered on the ground and encased the trees' colourful leaves in shimmering ice. Marie awoke to a cold house, her breath clearly visible. She dressed quickly, trying to expose as little skin as possible. When she walked into the kitchen, she was informed that Nic had already left for the day, but where he'd gone Madame Badeau didn't know. She had a suspicion that his plans for his birthday would not be approved by Annette, so that was probably why he'd left before he could be interrogated.

The roaring fires in the ovens were a welcome relief. The maids lit fires in all the fireplaces in the house, but there was still always a chill in the morning— except in the kitchen. Madame Badeau placed a cup of coffee in front of Marie once she settled onto the wooden bench.

"What's the occasion?" Marie teased, gladly accepting the steaming cup and wrapping her fingers around the warm porcelain.

"It's not every day someone turns sixteen." Madame Badeau gave Marie an affectionate pat on the cheek before bustling off into the cold cellar below the kitchen.

Marie stood by the window, sipping the hot delicacy. She looked around at the things in the kitchen. She always found it amusing that while Claude did his best to fill his home with all the luxuries of France, he still had the same dishes as everyone else on the continent. Despite his opulent taste, the same, plain, blue and white china that almost everyone else owned filled his cupboards.

Marie traced the blue flowers that encircled the rim of her mug. She liked the intricate patterns, and it amazed her that something so fragile could have survived the turbulent Atlantic crossing.

After finishing her coffee, she settled herself near the warmth of the fire, picking up a quilt she was working on. Annette's latest charitable cause was to provide the marginalized with whatever they needed. The nuns at the Hôpital du Roi were attempting to get their patients who were well enough to knit outerwear, but the enterprise was not going well. Most of the men felt knitting was a woman's job and weren't eager to learn, and many of the female patients were slow, since they were still convalescing. So large numbers of women from the city were enlisted to knit or quilt blankets. With the winter months coming, those blankets would be greatly appreciated. For her part, Marie preferred quilting to sorting vegetables and was eager to keep Annette going with these types of projects. As she was threading her needle, she heard Annette moving throughout the upper level of the house. It was still relatively early in the morning for her aunt to be starting her day, but Marie paid little attention to the sounds.

After only a few stitches, Marie's thoughts turned to Pierre. She felt silly thinking about him as often as she did. She wasn't sure what to make of the time they were spending together. Of course, Nic still wasn't happy to be sharing his best friend with her. He continued to warn her that she wasn't the first person to receive Pierre's attention, but that didn't bother Marie. He hadn't asked her to go into any deserted alcoves yet, and she doubted that was his intention. What she found surprising was how much she enjoyed his company. She had known him for years as a school troublemaker, but he was surprising her ... there was a sensitive soul beneath the bravado.

The front door blew open, bringing with it a blast of chilled air that found its way right to the kitchen. Marie heard Nic yelling a greeting, and she went to meet him, laying her sewing on the table.

Marie stopped in the doorway. Nic wasn't wearing his regular clothes. Instead, he was wearing the blue military jacket of the fortress's garrison. His dark eyes shone with excitement, but his hunched shoulders showed his nerves.

Annette appeared at the top of the stairs. Marie saw her own shock mirrored in her aunt's face.

"I've ah ... ," Nic cleared his throat. "I've enlisted."

Annette let out a cry of despair. Marie tried her best not to roll her eyes but just said, "Why would you do that?" Annette came running down the stairs, a robe over her night clothes, stopping just a few inches from her nephew. "What on earth possessed you to do this?"

Nic's cheeks flushed. This wasn't the reaction he'd been expecting. "What do you mean? I'm sixteen. I'm old enough to start my military career."

"Why, though?" Annette's voice was becoming higher and higher. Soon only dogs would be able to hear it. "There was no need for you to do that!"

Marie saw Madame Badeau peering out from the kitchen. She made a quick assessment of the situation and then retreated. Marie thought of joining her.

"No need?" Nic exploded. "We're at war. We won at the Canso Islands and brought British prisoners here. A dramatic defeat for the Brits! You think the British will endure an attack on their fishing fleets and just let it go? Though it's not really a victory because the British prisoners are eating our already scarce food supplies."

"None of that concerns you." Tears were forming in the corners of Annette's eyes.

"Of course, it concerns me. I'm one of the men living here. It's my duty to protect my country!" Nic's temper was rising to meet his aunt's. "I either join the militia or I join the military. I picked the military."

Annette pushed out her chest indignantly. "But this is just irresponsible."

Marie had heard enough. Their shouts followed her as she entered the kitchen. Madame Badeau gave her a knowing nod. Wrapping her cloak around her and putting a hat on her head, Marie exited through the back entrance, ignoring Ferdinand, who was watching her intently.

Despite the cold, the streets were teeming with activity. Marie passed the butcher, who was busy slaughtering a pig in the entranceway. Several residents were waiting patiently for the fresh meat. She sidestepped the pool of steaming blood that was blossoming out onto the dirt road as the pig let out a final squeal.

Marie didn't know where she was heading until she arrived: the large stone warehouse with a sign jutting out from the wall, saying "A. Thibault, Merchant and Trader."

The Thibault warehouse was located right near Augustus's residence, at the corner of Orléans Street and Champlain Street. His business was once situated on Rochefort Point, but an extension of the fortress wall and the addition of the Maurepas Bastion meant that he'd had to relocate. Marie climbed the hill to the sturdy, two-storey home. The bottom of the house was made of rubblestone but the second floor and the warehouse were constructed of wood. The warehouse sat right beside the home, with a garden and stables for pigs and chickens behind. The street was filled with labourers loading the last of the summer's merchandise from the few ships that hadn't yet left. Frost meant snow was soon to follow, and once the snow flew, no more trade would be carried out until the spring thaw. Hundreds of pounds of salted cod needed to be shipped before the ice came. Hopefully, the ships heading east to France would be free from encounters with the British navy.

Augustus Thibault's office occupied the entire main floor of his house. He often entertained the captains and representatives of the Master of the Quay, the excisemen looking for taxes, who came through his door. Augustus employed two clerks and a dozen labourers during the summer when business was flourishing.

That morning, the office was busy with end-of-year affairs. Two captains sat near Augustus, impatiently waiting as he finished preparing the documents they would need for travel. No one noticed Marie as she stepped in quietly.

She spotted Pierre on the far side of the room, bent over his father's desk, receiving instruction. Despite the sheep fiasco, he was showing an aptitude for running the business side of things. As long as he stayed away from livestock, and if his father finally forgave him, he might be successful. Marie waited near the entrance for him to finish before making her way across the room. His spot in the office was at least warm—since it was nearest to the stone fireplace. Pierre looked up, surprised. "What are you doing here?"

Marie now felt badly that she had come. Obviously, they were very busy. She should have waited until office hours were over instead of disturbing him now. "Do you have a moment?" Clearly, he didn't.

Augustus looked up from his papers briefly as his son conferred with him. The two ships' captains glared at Marie for delaying their departure. "You have time," Augustus said, nodding at Marie. "You can't be too long, though," he added as if concerned that his goodwill would be taken advantage of.

Pierre grabbed his jacket from the back of his chair and led Marie outside into the streets.

Many of the men there were soldiers, who were working for various merchants and traders to supplement their meagre military incomes. As Pierre buttoned his jacket, Marie watched them for a moment, trying to imagine Nic among them.

"Are you all right?" Pierre took her arm and led her away from the labourers toward the quieter interior of the city. "Something must be wrong if you came all the way here in the middle of business hours."

"Did you know that Nic was thinking of joining the army?" There was no point in wasting time on pleasantries when he needed to return to the office. She could see the muscles in Pierre's jaw begin to work.

"He mentioned it," Pierre said, slowly watching a horse and wagon pass in front of them, laden with barrels. "Why?"

Marie felt hot tears spring to her eyes. She blinked quickly to prevent them from spilling over. "He enlisted this morning."

"And he didn't tell you first?" Pierre guessed.

"No! And why didn't you tell me?" She knew it wasn't Pierre's fault, but she had to blame someone. She was scared and hurt that Nic hadn't told her his plans. He must have been considering this for some time. It couldn't have been an impulse decision.

Pierre stopped walking and turned to face her. "I thought you knew." He pulled her out of the way as another horse and cart went by, headed for the harbour.

"Well, I didn't," she said thickly, staring at the dirt.

Pierre pulled her close, in a one-arm hug. "I'm sorry," he said after a while.

She buried her face against the scratchy wool of his dark jacket. She felt stupid for being upset. If Nic wanted to join the military, that was his right. As the nephew of Claude-Jean des Babineaux and General Joseph-Jean Dumas, it would be possible for him to have a successful career. Claude's noble stock and Joseph's high-placed command could only help Nic. Marie sniffed and straightened up. Pierre smiled down at her. For the first time, she realized there were flecks of yellow mixed in with the blue of his eyes. "Sometimes he just makes me so angry," she mumbled.

Pierre laughed. "It's a man thing. Sometimes we act before thinking."

Marie continued to talk, spilling all her fears and worries. The problem wasn't just losing Nic to the military, with him living in the barracks, she would be stuck in the mansion on her own. Pierre listened carefully, never interrupting. From time to time, he would agree but that was it. Marie was consoled in part because she knew she wasn't being completely ridiculous if Pierre could understand. "I'm sorry to have dragged you away from work like this," she said after she finished her complaints.

"Not a problem." He seemed to mean it. "I think I'll have a talk with Nic about including you in his life goals. How did Annette take it?"

Marie sighed. "I left them screaming at each other."

"That's to be expected. The weapons are all locked up?"

Marie gave him a look. "Oh. Ha-ha."

Pierre elbowed her in the ribs. "It's better than not saying anything to each other at all."

They looped around the block and found themselves facing the harbour once more. Marie wasn't sure what had made her run to Pierre, but she was grateful he hadn't pushed her away.

"Hungry?" he asked when she seemed to have a handle on her emotions.

"What do you have?"

He led her into the dark warehouse, where barrels of wheat and bundles of food were stacked against the walls. It was surprisingly warm among the packets of food. At a first glance, it appeared that there were plenty of supplies to feed the city all winter, but usually the warehouses were packed to the rafters with barely enough room to walk between the rows. This was all the city had to eat until spring.

Pierre reached up and pulled down a small package wrapped in white linen and tied up with string. Cutting through the strings with his pocket knife, he pulled open the wrapping to reveal white cake flour. Marie grinned. She hadn't seen that since before the war started.

"It's for the Governor," Pierre smirked. "Thought you might like some white bread for your birthday."

"You remembered."

"I'm not a complete idiot." Some soldiers appeared at the door, carrying the last of one ship's cargo. Rum sloshed around inside the heavy barrels. Pierre hesitated. "I need to get back to work."

Marie nodded, cradling the flour carefully in her arms. "Thank you."

He shrugged but then grinned before he headed back toward the office. "Don't mention it. I'll give your brother hell next time I see him."

***

That night, Marie sat in bed listening to the shouts and screams reverberating through the house. Annette had told Claude about Nic's actions, and Claude supported Nic. That wasn't what Annette wanted to hear, and now the two of them were dealing with their problems the only way they knew how. Not for the first time, Marie wondered if life would have been better with Uncle Joseph Dumas back in Quebec.

The door opened a crack and Nic's head appeared. His hair was down, falling fuzzy all around his face. It made him look more childlike despite the black stubble on his face. "Can I come in?"

Marie nodded, and the noise from the argument downstairs decreased as he closed the door. He climbed onto her bed. The ropes that held the mattress up sagged under his weight.

"You're disappointed in me, aren't you?" Nic asked, looking down at her.

Marie made a noncommittal noise. "I just wish you'd told me."

"Pierre mentioned that. I think he might punch me if I ever make you cry again." Marie laughed weakly. "I didn't mean to upset you," Nic went on. "I wanted it to be a surprise. I knew Annette wouldn't agree, and I was trying to avoid the argument until the last minute. Are you worried?"

Marie shook her head. "No. Yes. There's a war going on. What if the British arrive? If you go to fight, you may not come back." She could remember her mother having the same conversation with her father many years before. "Why, though? You don't have to do this to support yourself."

Nic leaned against the wall, the candlelight throwing his dark features in sharp relief. "Do you like Claude?"

Marie snorted. "Who does?"

"Not his wife, that's for sure." Nic scratched the back of his head. "I don't want to owe Claude anything. I know Annette has these ideas of me taking over his position as if I were his son, but I'm not doing that. I don't want to be his son. I want to get out of this house and not depend on either of them anymore."

Marie had to agree that the idea had merit.

The shouts below them were subsiding. As usual, the twins heard the slam of the front door. Claude had left. He would return hours later, having spent the night with the seedy underside of the fortress, consuming enough liquor to forget his anger.

"But the military?" Marie went on. "You're educated. You could do so many things. You could go to France and study there." She was grasping at straws. She knew Nic loved the wilderness of New France too much to leave it.

"Father was an Officer, Uncle Joseph is a General, Grandpère was a General. I'd rather follow in their footsteps."

Marie could hear the soft sound of Annette sobbing and the calming voice of Madame Badeau trying to reassure her. The servants employed in this house never lacked for entertainment.

"If you get killed, I'm never going to forgive you," Marie said crossly.

He laughed. "I'll try my best."

"Will you go and live with the garrison in the King's Bastion now?" The King's Bastion was the largest building on the island. It housed the whole garrison, as well as the Governor's apartments. It was a monument to the French military, visible for miles from both land and sea.

Nic noticed her concern. "Yes. You'll be here all alone." That wasn't entirely true. Nic was still trying to come to terms with his sister's friendship with Pierre. He might be losing his best friend, but it could be worse. In fact, it might be a good thing to have Pierre check in on Marie from time to time. At base, though, Nic thought Pierre was being a bit stupid. While he was envious of his friend and sister, Nic couldn't imagine spending time with only one girl.

The thought of being alone with Annette and Claude in the house terrified Marie. For a moment, she wanted to explode at Nic, but she held her tongue. There was nothing he could do about his situation now. "You're abandoning me?"

"You could always get married," Nic suggested, unable to keep from laughing.

Marie hit him with her pillow. "That'll solve all my problems. I can spend my time taking care of some cranky old man."

"He doesn't have to be old."

"Who would you suggest?"

Nic didn't have an answer. Marie felt slightly vindicated. It might be acceptable to marry at sixteen when your father was a fisherman, but things had changed among the upper classes in the eighteenth century.

"When do you leave?" Marie said with a resigned sigh.

"Tomorrow, but I'll still be in Louisbourg. I'll come and visit as often as I can. And if either Claude or Annette gives you a hard time, I'll come sort it out."

Marie didn't find that promise as reassuring as it was meant to be.

***

Three days after Nic's enlistment in the military, Madame Badeau announced that Claude would be having a formal dinner that night. Marie was sitting at the scrubbed table in the kitchen when the news was divulged. If Annette hadn't been in the room, Marie really would have made her feelings clear, but instead, she settled on a simple "Why?"

"Your uncle wants to have the leaders of the military over for dinner to formally introduce Nic to them," Annette sniffed. It was clear that she was still injured by Claude's attitude toward the whole thing.

Marie kept her opinions to herself until Annette had left. Claude hated parties, but every now and then he could be called on to host a gathering over dinner. It was his chance to network with the other powerful and important people in the city. Introductions could be made, business dealings were brought forward, and relationships strengthened. But the gatherings were incredibly boring and served no one in the house except Claude.

"Do I have to go to that dinner?" Marie asked the housekeeper when Annette had finally left.

Madame Badeau looked deeply annoyed. Every person in the house knew Claude wasn't doing this for Nic. Claude was thrilled that Nic was now out of the house, no longer dependent on his uncle for anything. This dinner was an excuse for Claude to play the role of doting uncle. He could introduce Nic to some powerful people, strengthen his own personal ties with the military, and convince himself that despite his terrible treatment of his nephew, he really was helping the boy out.

"Of course you do," Madame Badeau snapped. "It'll be two hours ... three tops. You'll survive." Marie wasn't so sure. Claude expected his family to show all the refinement and poise one might find in any family in the countryside around Paris. But Marie couldn't stand such behaviour. She found it false and burdensome.

Late that afternoon, Marie sat in her room, having her long hair wrestled into a fashionable but impractical updo by one of the maids. "This is all your fault," she glared at Nic, who was sitting on the other side of the room.

Nic smiled pleasantly. This was the first time he'd been home since their birthday. "I don't know what you're complaining about. We're having duck. You love duck." He was wearing his new uniform, which didn't make Marie feel any better.

The twins presented themselves at the appointed hour to greet the guests. François Bigot, the Finance Commissary; Governor Louis Du Pont Duchambon; and Commander Joseph Marin de la Malgue, the military leader, were among the handful of people invited. None of them had brought their wives.

"This is my nephew, Nicolas," Claude said, clapping a hand on Nic's shoulder as he introduced him to de la Malgue. There was almost a note of pride in Claude's voice. "His father was Lieutenant Caleb Lévesque; his grandfather, General Garan Dumas."

De la Malgue shook Nic's hand enthusiastically. "I knew your father!" he boomed. "I always liked him. I'm glad you're following in his footsteps." Nic couldn't help but look pleased.

Marie sat down opposite Nic. None of the guests ever spoke to her at these events. None of them were even mildly interested in her. Apparently, it didn't matter that she was also the descendant of these military officials. Marie glared at Nic as the first course of split pea soup was laid before them. Nic smirked back at her.

"I have one of the finest Pauillac wines here," Claude announced from the head of the table. Ferdinand produced several green-glass bottles and set them around the table.

François Bigot smacked his lips. "You always know how to spoil me, Claude," the Commissary said.

Claude smiled. "If it isn't from Bordeaux, it isn't worth having. You, of all people, should know that." Bigot roared with laughter. He was from Bordeaux himself.

Marie was amazed at how easily the conversation flowed. Claude kept his guests laughing with his stories of mad ship captains and the ingenious lengths to which smugglers would go to hide their illegal cargo.

"I wish these men would realize that I know who makes their living with illegal dealings," Claude lamented. "If you give me a cut, I'll let you on your way. The other night, I had one ship with sugar on it." He paused for dramatic effect. "The poor captain, barely old enough to shave, thought it best to pack the cargo hold with wheat over the sugar."

Governor Duchambon started laughing. "You can't be serious."

Claude's dark eyes sparkled. "I don't know what the man was thinking. But when we boarded the cargo hold, it was filled with rats. I never thought that many rats could live in one place."

All the men in the room roared with laughter.

"They were fat as well." Claude shook his head. "Eating all that sugar. I'm glad I didn't have to clean up after that one."

Nic was involved in the conversation, though the men around the table knew little about the newest officer in the fortress. Claude was able to expertly steer the conversation around any sins Nic might want forgotten.

Marie watched it all, detached. No one wanted her opinion. When Claude was like this, charming and funny, playing the room like a violin, it was easy to see why Annette would have fallen for him. The darkness that consumed him was so well hidden that no one would ever suspect it was there.

As the last of the sugar pie was scraped from the plates, Claude stood, raising his wine glass. "Now before we retire for the night, gentlemen, I would like to propose a toast." Nic's pale face turned beet red. "To Nicolas. May you bring your family honour as you serve your King and country with your many abilities. You will do well."

Nic purposely avoided his sister's eye. Marie couldn't wait to bring this up in front of Pierre. Nic would die of embarrassment.

Later that night, after everyone had left, Marie sat in her room trying to untangle the ridiculous hairstyle that was pinned to her head.

Nic was there too, collapsed into an armchair a few feet from Marie. He was in no hurry to get back to the King's Bastion. "How are things here?" he asked.

"Well, after that performance, I think it's safe to say you're Claude's favourite child."

Nic rolled his eyes. "It's nice to know he can still act like a human being when the situation calls for it," he grumbled. "You know what I mean?" Marie knew, and she also knew they were never going to bring up this topic again.

Marie sighed, trying without success to extract a hair pin. "It's been three days since you enlisted. Claude hasn't said a word about it until tonight. He doesn't talk to anyone—except for giving instructions to Madame Badeau."

Nic nodded. "If he gives you any trouble—I mean any at all—you tell me."

"I don't know," Marie mused, finally seizing hold of the hair pin and pulling it out with several hairs still attached. "You might be too busy. What was it again? 'Serving your King and country with your many abilities'?"

Nic glared at her. "If you ever bring that up again ... ," but he couldn't think of a threat bad enough. He departed shortly afterward, leaving Marie feeling very lonely.

***

December 27th, the anniversary of her parents' death, always found Marie at the Governor's Chapel. It was the only chapel in the city, built for military use, but civilians came there to worship and pray as well, since no parish church had ever been built. Land had been set aside for a community church near the hospital, but construction had never begun. Therefore, the opulent Chapel was used by everyone, civilian or military, who called the fortress home. And that is why, on that cold December day, Marie was sitting inside the Governor's Chapel, which was attached to the Governor's residence and barracks at the King's Bastion.

The white walls and gold-leaf trim were calming, but Marie felt uncomfortable under the severe gaze coming from an oil painting of Louis IX at the front of the church. He might be the patron saint of the military, but Marie felt he was looking down on all the worshippers, silently casting judgement on them. She realized that she might be feeling nettled only because anything to do with the military bothered her, now that Nic had enlisted. Since the fateful day of Nic's entering the army, she hadn't seen much of him. He now lived in the Officers' apartments in the King's Bastion, visiting only sporadically. The pilgrimage to the Chapel was something they had always done together, but now his duties were keeping him away.

Marie didn't doubt that if her father had lived, Nic would be wearing a French uniform anyway. It probably wouldn't have mattered as much to her, however, if her parents had still been alive. As it was, she often felt that it was Nic and her against the world, so she depended on him greatly for emotional sustenance. They couldn't rely on Claude for support, and as much as Annette loved them, she wasn't much of a parent. It was always the two of them, but now Nic had the military and Marie couldn't be part of that.

So, Marie was alone on the Lévesque day of mourning. Elise couldn't accompany her because she was sick in bed with a cold. Marie had thought of asking Pierre, but he was busy working. At any rate, she didn't feel comfortable asking him, although she had no doubt he would have come if she'd spoken to him about it. Unable to stand being alone with her grief any longer, Marie left the church before the mass started and wandered aimlessly to the edge of Rochefort Point to watch the churning Atlantic. Annette would be cross that

Marie had skipped mass on such a personal day, but Marie didn't care, let Annette pray for the dead herself.

After a half hour or so by the water, Marie turned back down the quay, her mind still far away with her parents and Nic. Snow had fallen the night before, but a narrow path had been cleared by those brave enough to face the cold. As Marie re-entered the city by the Maurepas Gate, she was almost knocked down by a large figure wrapped in several layers of black fur. Scrambling to keep her balance, Marie grabbed the person's outer layer of fur. If she had been outside the city walls, she might have mistaken the figure for a bear.

"Whoa, there," said the bear-like person. Marie was shocked to realize she was hearing the deep voice of Augustus Thibault. He grabbed Marie's arm to prevent her from falling into the snowbank beside her. Then he pushed back his large, shaggy hat, revealing the bright eyes that were so very much like his son's. The muscles around his mouth were constricted with worry.

"What are you doing out here, Marie? You need to get indoors right away." He seemed annoyed to find her walking alone in the streets—something he was well aware she did on a regular basis. Without waiting for an answer, he seized her upper right arm and steered her forcefully toward her destination.

The city was quiet except for the distant beat of military drums. The harbour was silent, the ocean turbulent, and they were under no threat from invaders. "What's going on?" Marie asked. The urgency of the man's actions was frightening her.

"Is Claude home?" Augustus inquired, scanning the streets.

"Probably not. He was meeting with Governor Duchambon when I left." She tried to shake her arm free, but Augustus kept a firm hold with his leather-gloved hand.

"Annette?" He seemed oblivious to Marie's struggles to free herself.

"I assume she's still there."

Augustus cursed under his breath. Marie saw nothing out of the ordinary. The streets were deserted, but that was to be expected on a day as cold as this. But then she noticed that Augustus's other leather-covered hand, the one not forcing her toward home, was wrapped tightly around the butt of a pistol.

She wasn't sorry to be rid of him once she reached the front door of Claude's manor because she was disturbed by his odd behaviour—including the fact that he'd followed her in without invitation.

Annette came to meet them at the entrance to the sitting room. "What's going on?" She was rightly shocked to see the merchant standing in the middle of her foyer.

Marie shrugged. Augustus continued to look agitated, pulling the heavy dead bolt across the front door.

"Is Claude home?" he demanded.

Annette shook her head, perplexed. "I don't expect him home until tonight."

Augustus swore under his breath.

"What is the matter?"

"The garrison has mutinied." Augustus looked out one of the front windows beside the front door in a state of distraction.

"What do you mean 'mutinied'?" Marie asked.

"They're contesting their lack of food and wages. They were promised spoils from the raid on the Canso Islands, but those were never delivered to them. It was a fair incentive for a full-on attack against the British, which was a particularly dangerous undertaking. Apparently, they've had enough."

Marie glanced at Annette. Neither of them had heard these complaints from Nic. When Annette pointed this out, Augustus didn't even respond at first. He just kept standing guard in front of the window as if he expected a group of renegade soldiers to come barrelling down the street at any moment. "Nic's an officer. It's the cadets who've mutinied. Apparently, they aren't being paid. The officers are, but they aren't passing the money down."

Madame Badeau emerged from the back of the house, wiping her hands on her apron. The news was as unsettling to her as it was to the rest of them. One of the maids began to cry, but the housekeeper shooed her away, annoyed.

"Don't you supply the rations?" Marie asked. Annette looked at her furiously. It might be an impertinent question, but Marie didn't care.

Augustus sighed and ran his hand through his greying hair. "I've given the military everything they've asked for. There shouldn't be a problem. The garrison of Louisbourg are the best outfitted soldiers on the continent. I don't know what they're complaining about." He broke off, mumbling to himself like a madman.

The sound of distant musket fire ruptured the air. Annette clutched Marie's arm. "What do we do?" Annette asked in no more than a whisper. The panic in her voice was clear. The garrison outnumbered them all, and there weren't enough guns in private hands to counteract the military. If they took over the city, there was little anyone could do about it.

"I don't know. I just received word myself and thought it prudent to come check on you." The Thibaults' home was much closer to the King's Bastion than theirs, so Augustus would easily have heard the commotion as it was starting. Marie wondered why she and Annette and Claude were first on his list of neighbours, but she wasn't complaining.

"I'll stay until Claude comes home," said Augustus. "It's not safe for women to be alone."

Marie wanted to point out that Ferdinand could protect them but then remembered he was at Governor Duchambon's with Claude. Annette looked as if she too wanted to challenge Augustus's idea, but more musket fire soon ripped through the air and that stopped her from raising any objections.

Annette and Augustus moved into the sitting room, which gave them a clear view of the street. Augustus kept his pistol within arm's reach on the painted table between them.

Marie went to the kitchen and sat with Madame Badeau. The housekeeper settled her considerable weight onto a chair at the table, opposite Marie, a kettle of tea sitting between them. Madame Badeau left only once to check on the other servants. She reappeared a quarter of an hour later, looking annoyed with the rest of the staff, who were too busy fretting about the current situation to do their work.

Annette and Augustus were worried about the fate of the fortress, but Marie was more concerned about Nic. He was new to the military, a very junior officer but an officer nonetheless. What did this mutiny consist of? Were the mutineers being violent toward the officers? Had all the cadets revolted or just a few? Neither Marie nor Madame Badeau said anything. They just sat waiting for some form of news, the unanswered questions weighing heavily on their souls. The sporadic gunfire continued throughout the afternoon, grating on the nerves of those waiting inside.

Claude arrived as the sun was setting, and for the first time in Marie's memory, Annette rushed to the front door to greet him. He seemed to have aged in the last few hours. His hair seemed whiter and his walk more stooped than when he had left that morning. "The soldiers have taken over," was all he said.

Augustus slipped out the kitchen door when it was announced that the master was home. Claude may have been overwhelmed by the day's events, but that wouldn't have stopped him from going ballistic if he found the son of a *habitant* in his home.

Claude collapsed into the stuffed armchair by the fire in the sitting room, completely drained. Annette handed him a glass of rum and knelt at his feet, begging for news. He emptied his cup in one gulp and set the glass on the painted table, recently vacated by Augustus's pistol.

"The army has three demands," he sighed, his cheeks wobbling as air escaped from his mouth. "They're tired of stale vegetables and rotten bread. They complain that the British prisoners from Canso are being fed better than they are, that their wages are going toward keeping the enemy alive, and that the good flour is being sold to the civilians here instead of being given to them."

"But of course it is," Annette objected. "Are we expected to eat rotten flour on top of starving?"

Marie wanted to point out that things didn't get much worse than what the army was being forced to eat—moldy bread made from flour mixed with sawdust—but she kept her peace.

Claude ignored his wife's comments and rubbed his hands together. "They also want their wages for the manual labour they've been performing for the King and other citizens. And they're demanding the booty they were promised from the expedition to Canso." Claude sighed again, the firelight reflecting off his round spectacles, momentarily obscuring his eyes. "They've taken over the Bastion and the rest of the fort. They refuse to do anything until their demands are met. They've completely taken over the government offices and are patrolling the streets as we speak. Governor Duchambon is still meeting with the leaders, trying to sort things out. But I fear they will sell us to the British when spring comes."

"What about Nic?" Marie had left the kitchen to listen from the doorway to the sitting room and couldn't refrain any longer.

Claude and Annette both looked at her as if surprised to be reminded they had a nephew in the middle of the crisis.

"Is he all right?"

"I don't see why he wouldn't be," Claude said coldly. "But if he's in cahoots with the rest of these scoundrels, I hope they shoot him for it."

Annette let the comment pass. Enraged at them both, Marie fled to the sanctuary of her room. It wasn't Nic's fault that this was happening. He'd been a member of the garrison for only three months. Would he be punished along with the rest of the officers? She had a mad desire to run out of the house in search of him, but she knew it would be dangerous and futile with disgruntled soldiers roaming the streets.

She thought back to the night of the bonfire. The soldiers huddled at the gate had been wrapped in multiple layers of wool blankets, unable to get close enough to the heat of the flames. She hadn't thought much of it at the time, but now she realized they hadn't been given proper outerwear. If they were being fed with similar neglect and if they had really not been given the spoils of war that they'd been promised, it was no wonder they were in a state of mutiny.

Marie curled up under her covers, pulling the quilt tight under her chin. Thoughts of Nic, Elise's brothers and father, and the cadets of the garrison swirled in her head as she tossed and turned on the feather mattress. Was

Claude right? Would the soldiers sell the fortress to the British if given the chance?

Chapter 3

SHE DIDN'T REALIZE SHE'D DRIFTED OFF until she was awakened by sunlight streaming in through the window. The fire had gone out and the air was like ice. She crawled out of bed, her quilt still wrapped tightly around her, grabbed her clothes, and headed down to the kitchen, where it was sure to be warm enough to change without getting frozen. Madame Badeau wouldn't mind.

The house was silent, and the streets were deserted of all regular life. The shouts of soldiers parading through the streets sent a chill down her spine. She saw a few silhouettes move past the windows in the sitting room and went to check that they were locked.

Marie found Madame Badeau in her usual place, operating the stove. Ferdinand was near the door, keeping watch. The fire gave welcome relief to her frozen body, even if it did nothing to calm her nerves.

"Where is everyone?" Marie sat on the floor near the hearth, trying to thaw her frozen muscles.

"They drank themselves to sleep last night." Madame Badeau's thin lips were pursed in displeasure as she slammed a pot of water on the stove. "Of all the concerns they had, they never once mentioned Nic."

She was in such a foul mood, Marie felt it best not to mention Claude's comment of the night before. "Do you know anything more yet?"

Madame Badeau shook her head as she stoked the fire. Marie could hear the voices of the other servants, but they refused to emerge from their quarters. "Antoine, the cooper's apprentice from down the street, stopped by this morning. I think he was hoping your uncle had classified information he might share. He told me he ran into a pack of soldiers, drunk and looking for a fight. He escaped by convincing them his brother was in the garrison."

"Does Antoine have a brother?"

Madame Badeau laughed darkly. "Poor soul's an orphan. Most of the garrison's in a similar position—with no family on this continent except for the ones they make themselves."

"I'm still so worried about Nic ... Why wouldn't he send word?" Marie fretted.

"Oh, Nic will be fine," Ferdinand said in a deep voice that echoed around the kitchen. "He's talked his way out of plenty of bad situations."

Marie didn't look convinced.

"When he was thirteen, he took one of my horses without permission. Almost killed the poor beast, he rode her so hard. I was going to tan his hide, but somehow he got the better of me." Ferdinand smiled and Marie felt a bit better.

It was a tense day. Claude left as soon as he stopped throwing up. Annette wandered around the house, wringing her hands. The servants were still fearful of leaving their bedrooms. Marie tried her best to avoid them all.

The sound of drums, which usually signalled the call for all soldiers to make their way back to the barracks, continued to beat, sending unknown messages to those stationed throughout the city. There was a different sound to these beats. They were calls for the townspeople to submit to the mutineers.

***

Four days after the mutiny began, Marie still hadn't left the house. Claude came home every night with the daily news, but Marie refused to even look at him.

She did listen in on his conversations with Annette, though, and from those, she gleaned the information that the Swiss Regiment, the mercenaries from Switzerland, had started the mutiny, pressuring the French to join them. The Swiss had assembled in the courtyard outside the barracks, announcing their intentions and refusing to take orders. Then they went searching for the French troops, who promised to stand in solidarity with them. By the end of that first day, the entire garrison was part of the mutiny, except for the officers.

Governor Duchambon gave the men everything they'd asked for, but the soldiers continued to defy orders. From what Marie could understand, the soldiers were running about town, causing whatever disorder they wished, threatening merchants who would not sell at the low prices they demanded, and treating the officers as their slaves. They knew the townspeople were powerless to stop their new regime and abused the power they gave themselves.

A curfew was set in place, and people quickly abided by those orders. Women and children didn't leave the safety of their homes, and men tried to keep the city running as normally as possible, but the soldiers were bent on creating chaos.

On the fifth day of the mutiny, as 1745 started, Pierre arrived at the kitchen door. He was wearing a blue soldier's jacket over his thick overcoat and so had made it through the city relatively easily. Madame Badeau shrieked at his appearance, convinced the rebellious soldiers had come to plunder the house. It took some time, but he was eventually able to convince her that he had better intentions than robbing and plundering.

Marie ran to the kitchen at the sound of the commotion, a candlestick in her hands. She felt almost sick with relief to see Pierre.

"Did you join the mutiny?" Once the happiness of seeing him evaporated, the presence of the jacket concerned her.

"No!" He was upset that she would even think such a thing. "A gang of them came to the warehouse two days ago, and one of them left their jacket. I've been using it ever since. It makes travel easier." He shook his hair out of his face.

Madame Badeau hustled the servants away. They'd all finally left their apartments, but now they needed to be sent off to give Pierre and Marie some privacy.

"Can I leave with you?" Marie whispered. "I haven't left the house since this all started, and I'm going mad worrying about Nic."

"No," Pierre answered, his usually jovial face serious. "It's not safe out there. They'll only harass you if you're lucky. Rape you if you're not."

Marie felt weak at the knees. Madame Badeau was obviously listening in the other room and swore loudly.

"I saw Nic," he said, watching her carefully.

"Is he part of the gangs?"

"No. He's at the mercy of the gangs ... but he seems fine," he added hastily. "They haven't hurt him at least." Pierre didn't think it wise to tell Marie that the rebel soldiers were treating Nic as a slave and starving him and depriving him of sleep, just for their own entertainment.

"Do you think they will?"

"I don't know." Pierre looked completely defeated. "A group of them threatened my father with a sword if he didn't charge them what they wanted to pay for blankets. My father's a big man and could probably have taken one or two of them on, but not a group like that." Pierre paused and looked out the window. "They now have everything they want, but they won't stop. François Bigot, the Finance Commissary, has been doing his best to smooth things over. He's trying to send a letter to France or Quebec, but he's being watched day and night."

"What is Quebec going to do?" Marie began to feel trapped. The citizens and officers and administrators were all alone on the island in the middle of winter because no assistance would be coming from the direction of the frozen Saint-Laurent River. And no army could cross the freezing landscapes of New France and the British territories to save them.

"Beats me what Quebec can do." Pierre began to chew the inside of his cheek. "The Saint-Laurent is nothing but a block of ice." The hopelessness in his voice was clear.

"I'm glad you have no military aspirations," Marie said quietly. "I don't know what I'd do if everyone I knew was involved in this."

Pierre ran his hands through his hair, making it look even wilder than usual. "The thing is, as terrible as the conditions are for the garrison, it's worse everywhere else in the French Empire. None of the soldiers have enough food or clothing. Nowhere else do they even have a barracks. Most are made to live with civilians. I don't understand why our soldiers are still rebelling. Everyone is eating rationed food, even the Governor. Do they want the rest of us to starve so they have enough?" Pierre paced the length of the room. Each trajectory didn't last for many minutes, though, as his long legs could cover the room in three steps.

"Are you all right?" Marie asked gently. She had never seen him so worked up, and his fear frightened her.

"Of course, I am," he laughed darkly. "No one is looking to hurt me. I might be the son of a merchant, but as long as my father has things to sell, we'll be fine." He leaned his head against the wooden frame of the door between the kitchen and the rest of the house. "You're the one I'm worried about. Claude's gone all day, and there's so much stuff to steal here. I'm surprised they haven't ransacked the place yet."

"Thanks for that cheery thought." Marie threw Pierre a dirty look. "While you're at it, why don't you tell me that they'll sell us all to the British in a few months."

Pierre sighed and lifted his head. "I'm sorry. I didn't mean to frighten you. I just don't trust Claude to take care of you." He glanced about quickly as if concerned that the master of the house might be listening.

"That makes two of us, but I think he'd like to shoot every last one of them," Marie admitted. She told him what Claude had said a few nights previously.

"How can you be happy living here with him?" Pierre wasn't trying to be nasty; he really meant it.

"It's a big house," Marie explained. "I just stay out of his way as much as possible."

Pierre shook his head in exasperation. "You can come live with my father and me if it gets to be too much. You shouldn't have to deal with this." Marie knew he was joking, but she detected a small grain of truth underneath the humour.

"Last year, my Uncle Joseph wrote to offer his place to either Nic or me if we ever want to visit Quebec. He does that every few years, as if he knows this isn't the happiest place. He's not at his home very often, as he's usually the first person to be sent somewhere for a thankless military errand because he has no family. Sometimes I wish I'd taken him up on the offer."

Pierre was quiet for a moment. "Has Claude ever hit you?"

Marie shook her head, her long braid swinging down her back. "No, only Nic. And usually Nic would have said something beforehand to get him going."

"Well, I'm glad you stayed. But if you ever need me to clock Claude in the head, I'll be more than happy to oblige."

Pierre stayed for a few hours. His father was aware of where he was and was willing to part with him for that time. Madame Badeau put him to work chopping firewood and fixing one of the kitchen shelves. He didn't seem to mind helping out, and he was rewarded with a steaming bowl of thin onion soup for supper.

Anxious as always, Annette stayed by the window of the sitting room, keeping a watchful eye out for her husband, even though he wasn't due back until nightfall. She didn't relax until Pierre had finally left.

***

Epiphany came, but no one dared enter the Governor's Chapel to celebrate the occasion. People met elsewhere, cowering together in sitting rooms. Annette refused to leave the house, and she forbade Marie from leaving as well. To make up for her lack of external piety, Annette fasted for two days. Marie went along with it only to stop her aunt from complaining. Annette's nervosity and headaches were never helped by fasts.

As the winter progressed, the disorder in Louisbourg was replaced by an uneasy truce. The mutineers still continued to control the fortress, but François Bigot's tact seemed to be defusing the aggression. That and the officers' refusal to give any orders. Very slowly, life began to return to normal.

As February approached, Marie was still waiting for Nic to come home, even for a short visit. He'd sent a few notes saying he was fine regardless of the unrest, and Annette treated the hastily scribbled notes as if they were manna from heaven. But they did little to calm Marie's nerves. Marie was also terrified for Elise and her mother. Being so closely related to so many officers made them prime targets for the garrison's anger.

Marie refused to speak to Claude, mostly because of what he'd said about hoping Nic would be shot if he was part of the revolt, but Claude didn't even notice. While the disturbance to civilians was decreasing, the government was still struggling to end the mutiny. Behind the scenes, the ground was also being laid to eventually bring the leaders of the mutiny to justice.

Marie left home only a handful of times, always accompanied by Ferdinand, and never after dark.

The ecclesiastical leaders did what they could to denounce the actions of the garrison, but with the garrison outnumbering the inhabitants, they went only so far for fear of bringing violence upon themselves.

Then one blustery day in February, Pierre arrived at the front door. When Marie let him in, he announced that he was taking her to see Nic, something he had heretofore refused to do.

"Why now?" Marie asked as she put on her grey cloak. She had begged him to take her to see Nic every time Pierre saw him. She was beginning to get angry at both of them.

"Things have finally calmed down enough." He held her hand to keep from slipping on the hard snow of the road. The truth was that the cadets were calming down and no longer abusing the officers. However, Nic didn't want Marie travelling the city unless he could count on her returning home whole. The women who had been unlucky enough to be caught outside at the beginning of the mutiny had suffered more than anyone else. Nic finally felt safe having Marie leave home for a short while. However, Pierre wasn't going to let Marie know that. As always in the middle of winter, the city seemed to be encased under several layers of ice. In the middle of the streets, the snow was tightly compacted from the traffic of so many months, with dirt showing through in the busiest areas. Fires were lit at street corners, offering some comfort to those who had to be out. Horses draped in wool blankets pulled sleds, transporting people or provisions. Except for a few soldiers standing menacingly in the background, life seemed to have returned to something like normal, even if the tension was still palpable.

Pierre and Marie moved quickly, the frozen ground crunching under their boots. The muscular young man kept a protective arm around his charge, his right hand resting on the dagger in his belt. His hypervigilance made Marie more nervous, but she couldn't imagine anyone giving Pierre trouble—not with his bulk and the soldier's blue coat he was still wearing as a disguise.

Nic met them just outside the Dauphin's Gate under the dark shadow of the ramparts.

There was a tavern not far from the walls, frequented by the armed forces. It was a rough place even in the best of times. That's why Nic was standing outside that building. He didn't trust that they'd be safe if they went in.

It was a tearful reunion. Nic was remarkably thinner than Marie had ever seen him, with dark bags under his eyes, but he seemed whole otherwise. As a junior officer, there was little he could do in the present situation except try to keep his head down. He could understand why the soldiers were furious, although he didn't think that justified their committing treason against their King. He told Marie that his superiors were the ones getting harassed by the mutineers the most but that he was being ordered around like the rest of the officers. He said nothing about being starved and sleep deprived. There was no point in making Marie more upset. Nic did say he was worried about what the British would do in the spring, though he was more optimistic now that the daily routine of life was beginning again.

Marie didn't want to leave Nic, but after a few minutes, he insisted on getting back to the King's Bastion before anyone noticed he was missing. He didn't want to give anyone an excuse to molest her. He promised to send word as often as he could, but the infrequency of his earlier messages didn't reassure Marie very much.

Pierre hustled Marie home quickly after Nic and Marie had said their goodbyes. He said nothing until they reached the house.

"It'll work out," he promised gently as he dropped her off in the snow-filled back garden. "The river won't stay frozen forever. Help will come when the ice breaks up."

"That's still months away," Marie pointed out. Ships wouldn't come until April.

Pierre nodded. The British were coming, and the garrison was furious and refusing to fight. Even if help came from Quebec or Montreal, what would that accomplish? The situation was bleak.

Louisbourg had never before felt so far away from civilization. There was no help for them while the winter reigned, and for the first time, Marie realized just how dependent they were on the rest of the world.

***

The spring of 1745 came slowly, with rain and fog engulfing the island. Some days, the fog was so thick the beam of the lighthouse was no more than a bright smudge against the gloom. Fortunately, whatever feelings motivated the soldiers to begin the mutiny had begun to dwindle. The military hierarchy still lay in ruins, but the fear that had gripped the city was melting with the snow.

Though the Saint-Laurent River was thawing and the ferocious ocean storms of winter had subsided, no ships were entering the harbour yet. The threat of the British navy's blockade was still enough to keep even the bravest captains from making the voyage. Even the fishing grounds were heavily patrolled after the attack at Canso in the previous spring. Marie had heard no news from Quebec. The government there knew of Louisbourg's precarious position, but whatever the capital might be doing about the situation, they weren't sending reinforcements.

Then, at the beginning of May, a group of Mi'kmaq travelling from the south of the island reported that British ships had been seen heading for Île-Royale. Governor Duchambon had kept that information as private as possible, but now that the news had trickled out, it quickly became part of the word on the street.

Claude blamed the mutineers for trying to incite a panic, but privately Marie felt they were just as afraid of a British attack as everyone else. With no assistance coming from either Quebec or France, the fortress would be completely on its own. The raid on the Canso Islands may have seemed like a good idea at the time, but now, with a British fleet bent on revenge staring them in the face, it seemed foolhardy at best.

On the morning of May 8th, Marie sat in the garden trying unsuccessfully to win the war against the weeds that were snaking their way through the vegetable beds. The grubs seemed to have got the message that this garden was not a friendly one and had not returned, but the weeds had appeared again, just as they always did. Elise sat next to Marie, planting potatoes. Elise wasn't very good at keeping anything alive, so Marie often helped her with the

Sarrazins' garden. In return, Elise did routine gardening jobs for Marie that were difficult to mess up.

Marie hadn't seen much of Elise during the height of the mutiny. She and her mother had kept a low profile, staying indoors as much as possible. Even the bakery business had been closed so as not to draw attention to the family. Luckily, while the soldiers took issue with her father the Lieutenant, Elise and her mother had not been harassed. This was partly because they'd spent most of the time at Elise's cousin Diane's house. Though it was safer there than in their own home, Diane had numerous siblings, and the role of chief childminder had fallen to Elise. With so many little people running around, she often wondered if it would have been better to take her chances at her own house.

As Marie sat focused on her labours, listening to Elise complain about the inability of toddlers to cooperate, a cry rang out somewhere along the harbour wall. It was answered by another and then another. Fearing another mutiny, the girls sprang up and ran to the fence to see what was happening. Unlike the last mutiny, a great deal of activity was going on in and around the fort: people were riding horses, gardening, drying laundry. But all were now in the same position as Marie and Elise, looking toward the sounds.

The shout came again—except this time, Marie and Elise could hear exactly what was being said: "The British!" The words seemed to ripple through the air as people heard and then understood. Surely, it couldn't be. It couldn't be.

Throwing open the garden gate, Marie ran down the street, skirts held above her knees, dodging puddles and pedestrians alike. She could hear Elise behind her, struggling to keep up.

A crowd was gathering along the docks, pushing and straining to see for themselves. Only six months had passed since the mutiny had started, and now the enemy was at the gates. After several minutes of elbowing, Marie and Elise made it to the front of the pack.

Marie had never seen such a sight in her life. She had seen a handful of warships from time to time, since a few were still stationed in the harbour. But now, ninety British warships were floating silently outside the harbour entrance. On each ship, three levels of cannons rose above the water, three masts stood taller than any tree, and at the end of each mast, there was the blue and red flag of Britain—not the white flag of the French colonies.

Even if the garrison fell into line and tried to protect them, it was obvious that they were doomed. French soldiers were scampering around the thirty mounted cannons that made up the Island Battery. The Royal Battery and lighthouse were the only other protection the harbour had, but everyone knew that the ammunition for every cannon was in low supply.

Elise grabbed Marie's hand and squeezed it. "What are we going to do?"

Marie shook her head, her mouth open in horrified amazement. Louisbourg was prepared for a sea battle, but as she looked at the British floating army, she suddenly realized how small and vulnerable the French navy really was. The rebellious garrison was the only defence they had. Marie turned and looked at the wide expanse of wilderness around them. It was perfect for a raid; no military outposts had ever been established around the fortress.

A murmur of fear was spreading through the crowd. Marie felt as if her blood had turned to ice.

"Surely, they'll defend us," Elise whispered, staring up toward the barracks.

Members of the garrison came running to the docks, their white and blue uniforms mixing with the greys and browns of the townspeople. They looked stunned at the sight that greeted them. The citizens were silent, looking to the soldiers who stood in their midst. Most of those soldiers couldn't have been more than seventeen. They looked terrified as they watched the invading warships and scattered back to the barracks. Marie exchanged a glance with Elise and knew her friend wasn't any more reassured than she was. There was nothing they could do but watch, and wait.

***

The garrison did rise to the call to arms. The leaders of the mutiny were executed in public for all to see. So their reign of mischief was over, but the battle for Louisbourg was just beginning.

The British wasted no time in assembling their forces. By May 11th, they had stormed the beaches and established their armies on land. Meanwhile, the French military were taking an inventory of their ammunition, and the results confirmed that the fortress didn't have enough cannonballs or gunpowder to engage the British now. So it was decided that the soldiers would wait to fully engage once the real battles began.

Within a few days, the invaders had mobilized, quickly overtaking the Island Battery and the lighthouse. From those locations, as well as the bluffs above the city, they unloaded their massive artillery and aimed it at the fortress.

At first, it seemed as if the British were content to wait outside the gates while the inhabitants of Louisbourg slowly starved to death. This tactic was effective enough, since what had merely been food rationing had now turned into the likelihood of outright starvation. The farmers and other inhabitants who lived beyond the city walls were now crowded into the relative safety of the fortress, and that made for more mouths to feed. After three weeks, though, the enemy decided that this method wasn't going to work, and they began direct attacks.

Marie was right when she first thought that the wilderness would give the British an advantage. Under cover of the surrounding forest, the British had slowly rolled their cannons and mortars within range of the walls. The French militia braved the elements to harass the British infantry but without success. The British claimed the open fields, opening fire on the town, ripping holes through roofs and shattering the stone ramparts.

The siege wasn't being fought just by the army on land. The British warships exchanged cannon fire daily with the ships in the harbour. The French ships were so outnumbered, though, that they could do little more than answer the offending British volleys.

Six weeks after the British ships had first appeared, the siege was still going on. The noise of gunfire was deafening, even inside the Babineaux home, and the entire fortress was gripped with fear. It was becoming increasingly clear that the French were not going to win the battle. They were outnumbered and starved. The clergy encouraged fasting and prayer to save the city, but Marie thought it wasn't really fasting when there was nothing but dwindling stores of salted cod to eat. Some priests were preaching that Armageddon had arrived and that people needed to prepare themselves for Judgement Day.

The army was running dangerously low on ammunition, to the point where British cannonballs were being picked up and shot back at them. The sick and injured were increasing at an alarming rate, and no one was sure what would happen when the conquering army marched through the gate.

Marie sat with her back against the sitting room wall, the farthest point in the house from the projectiles coming in off the water. Her legs were stretched out in front of her on the wooden floor. As was the case for everyone else in the fortress, the wait was driving Marie mad. All the citizens of the city were staying indoors as much as possible, praying that their homes and other buildings would keep them safe from the flying mortars.

Marie was helping at the hospital most days, although with the limited amount of knowledge she possessed, she was sometimes more hindrance than help. Annette had suggested that Marie do this service, and Marie had been happy to comply, partly because it was a way of escaping from the house. It also kept her mind busy and made her feel that she was contributing to the cause. On this particular day, she had been sent home around noon after spending most of the previous day tending to the wounded. She did need a rest, but now that she was back at the manor, there was nothing to do but listen to her empty stomach rumble and pray that the next projectile wasn't coming for her. She tried to keep her mind off Nic.

Elise was sitting beside Marie—also leaning against the wall. With all of her brothers and father involved in the siege, she had nothing to do but worry and keep her mother company. That didn't take up all her time, though, since her mother had abandoned the bakery, as there were no ingredients left to bake with. So Elise spent a lot of her time with Marie when Marie wasn't at the hospital. She'd tried to help there but quickly realized she didn't have the stomach for all the blood and bile at the facility.

"Have you heard anything?" Marie asked tentatively. Nic was still terrible at sending updates home. Marie resigned herself to the fact that someone would either tell her of his death or she would see him at the end of the attacks.

Elise's auburn hair fell untended down her back. She was chewing on a piece of straw. She claimed that chewing helped the hunger pains, but Marie found it made her even more aware of the movements of her empty stomach.

"My brother Charles did send a note back yesterday," Elise said as she pulled a partially knitted pair of gloves out of her bag and started untangling the needles from the wool. She had trouble sitting still, and knitting helped calm her down. "But all he said was that everyone is still alive."

"At least that's something." Marie started rolling some grey wool into a ball while Elise's bone needles clicked away beside her.

Elise shrugged. "Even if someone was dead or injured, I doubt he would say so. 'We must keep our spirits high,'" she said in an uncanny imitation of her oldest brother.

There was a knock at the door. Marie struggled to her feet, her leg having fallen asleep from being so long in one position. It was Pierre. He stood as tall and gangling as ever, with a loaf of bread clutched triumphantly in his large hands.

Marie let out a squeal of joy. Bread was so tightly rationed that only the military and militia had any to eat. Marie thought back to the fall, when Pierre had shown her the inside of Augustus's warehouse. It had seemed like so much food then, but now almost all of it was gone.

Pierre grinned, his wide smile showing most of his teeth. "I found some bread," he said casually. "Mind if I come in?"

Marie hurried him into the house. He had joined the militia, as had every able-bodied man in Louisbourg, but he visited whenever he wasn't needed. Marie had a strong suspicion that Nic had asked him to keep an eye on her.

"How did you get this?" Marie asked. Pierre held the loaf delicately, as if it were made of gold.

Pierre flopped himself down onto the floor beside Elise. Her face lit up when she saw the bread close up.

"It's Louisbourg. You can get anything for a price." He tore the loaf into three pieces and passed two of them to Elise and Marie. "You should know better than anyone else."

Marie scowled as Elise laughed. Claude was a favourite among pirates and smugglers for looking the other way for a price. Marie looked around the richly decorated room, financed by all the times he'd feigned ignorance.

"I don't take bribes," Marie said, nettled.

Elise elbowed her in the ribs. "Claude's not the only one." Then she bit into the crusty loaf with a sigh of contentment.

Pierre and Marie followed suit. There was sawdust mixed with the flour, but none of them cared.

"The soldiers are selling parts of their rations," Pierre said after his first mouthful.

"Why?" Marie asked.

Pierre shrugged, unconcerned. "Damned if I know. Probably looking for extra money for drink. Goodness knows we have enough of that to get us through."

Marie leaned her head against the wall, picking crumbs off her bodice. It felt wonderful to eat something that wasn't fish. She glanced over Elise's copper crown at Pierre, who was still devouring his meal. She was beginning to depend on his regular visits.

He looked over and gave her a significant look. Marie looked at him stupidly. He bent his head toward Elise's. "I don't mean to be rude, Elise, but can I talk to Marie alone for a moment?"

Marie's heart skipped a beat. Elise grinned. Apparently, Marie had confided too much in her over the last few days. She watched Elise skip happily into the front foyer as another round of explosions ripped through the air.

"What's going on?" Marie asked. She was worried that there was news of Nic. Bad news.

Pierre stood up and stretched his long frame. He looked thin. Maybe if he could have regular meals not interrupted by international conflict, he could get some meat on his bones.

"I'm leaving tomorrow," Pierre said glumly, not looking at Marie.

"What are you talking about?" She felt her palms growing sweaty. He couldn't leave, not now. "No one's leaving. We're completely surrounded by the British."

Pierre sighed and leaned one shoulder against the wall beside her. "I know that. But some people are still sneaking out."

That was true. People were deserting, and others were abandoning the fortress in a desperate attempt to reach Île Saint-Jean or Quebec.

"Those people are dead." Marie said bluntly. "The British are on the entire island, making sure we'll all be conquered."

Pierre shrugged as if that was inconsequential. "I know that, but my father feels otherwise."

Marie had a sinking feeling. Ever since his mother's death, Pierre and Augustus were strangers living in the same house. Pierre often joked that they didn't know how to relate to each other, but she knew now that, deep down, it bothered him. They never fought, but they never bonded either. "Your father wants you to try to leave the fortress right now?"

Pierre nodded.

Marie couldn't believe it. "But why? It's suicide!"

Pierre rubbed the back of his neck. "He believes that everyone will be shipped off to France when the British come through the gates."

"Well, he's more optimistic than Father Allard anyway." She was thinking of the previous Sunday when the priest told a very packed Chapel to prepare to meet their maker. He had been so hysterical that she was surprised he hadn't suggested desertion.

"My father did a lot of business with New England before the war started. He doesn't believe the enemy's as bloodthirsty as some people do."

Marie nodded. A great deal of trade was done with New England during peace time. "But why not come to France with us?"

His lips twisted at the sound of "us." "My father was planning this before the siege, back when the blockades started. He believes there will be more opportunity on the mainland. Besides, I have family in Quebec."

"You have family everywhere."

He smiled. "True, but the Procurator General in Quebec, Dominique Renault, is looking for an assistant-apprentice. He is in charge of all the legal proceedings, appointments, and laws that are drafted. He doesn't have any sons and is looking for someone to help him. My father's brother—Uncle Tomas—is a friend of his and recommended me. I can read and write, and goodness knows I like to argue. My father knows I'm not happy living with him, and he thought a change of scenery would do me some good."

"I thought you were eventually going to take over from your father."

"I thought so too," Pierre said heavily. "But I think I messed up one too many times."

"You don't have to go!" Marie exploded. "Aren't you too old to be an apprentice? And getting off the island is impossible, never mind trying to get to Quebec."

"I know that," Pierre said quietly. He picked up a knick-knack, a very ugly miniature canoe, from the mantle over the fireplace and began fiddling with it. "But what can I do? Will my father be able to build a business in France? Everyone who goes will be a ward of the state. You'll be fine because you'll have Claude's connections, but what about everyone else? There's opportunity in Quebec." He recited the last part formally as if from memory.

"Do you want to go?" It wasn't the question she wanted to ask, but this one was easier. Her vision blurred as she looked at the floor. He was doing this to please his father, a desperate attempt to win his approval.

Pierre stepped toward her and gently wrapped his arms around her. She had never been this close to him and realized that she might never be this close again. "I'll go," he said quietly. "My father's right about one thing. He and I aren't happy together."

But what about me? Marie thought. She wanted to cry. She'd been hoping for something more between them and suspected their feelings for each other had been growing for some time, but she knew it wouldn't happen now with the Atlantic likely separating them.

Pierre placed his hand under Marie's chin and tilted her face upward. Gently, he kissed her. She threw her arms around him, not wanting ever to let go. He pulled her closer. Then, after a moment, they broke apart.

"If I make it to Quebec, I'll send you word," he promised.

If.

Marie blinked rapidly and watched Pierre go out the door. Her protector deserting her just when she needed him most.

PART TWO: QUEBEC 1745

Chapter 4

PIERRE HAD LEFT THE ISLAND ONLY ONCE BEFORE—when he was twelve. His grandmother had died, and his father had insisted on travelling home with his wife and son to the family farm near Trois-Rivières. His grandmother had come to New France as a *fille du roi* and had no family to speak of except her descendants in the colony. For a boy of his age, the trip went from one exciting event to the next as he met cousins, aunts, and uncles he had heard of but had never met. It was exciting, that is, until his mother contracted pneumonia. The family returned to Louisbourg shortly afterwards, but she succumbed a month later in the fortress.

Pierre couldn't think about that now. His journey off the island was harrowing enough without thinking of past grief. He and the men he was travelling with had left the fortress on May 26th, but that was no journey to freedom, as British troops were patrolling the forests, determined to rid the island of any inferior French who might be hiding in the bush. The leader of their band, Samuel, had been a *coureur de bois* in his youth and was expert at guiding them through the wilderness and around the invaders. He knew all the paths the streams took, where the stony outcrops were for hiding, and the fastest route to the ocean. To avoid detection, they travelled at night, far away from the light of the British fires. Once, they climbed the trees in a stand of tamaracks to evade some drunken Redcoats. It had been a tense moment, but they survived, although covered in tree sap and needles.

One day, they came across a group of Mi'kmaq hunters who were also being terrorized by the British invasion. The hunters helped their little group steer clear of the roaming invaders, and the last of the trip was uneventful thanks to their help.

The fugitives' destination was Baie des Espagnols, some forty-five miles from Louisbourg, and it took four days to reach it. Luckily, the British hadn't made it there yet. In fact, there were very few boats of any kind in the harbour. However, the men did manage to find a humble merchant vessel bobbing in the harbour. They'd heard a rumour that a captain from Acadia was shuttling French refugees off the island, and when they went up to the boat, they discovered that the rumour was true. The captain had been born a French citizen, but after the Treaty of Utrecht in 1713, which gave Acadia to the British, its inhabitants were in no position to lift arms against their conquerors. So the area north and west of Halifax was now firmly in British hands. All the same, this captain, like most people in Acadia, refused to pledge allegiance to the King of England and was doing all he could to help his countrymen escape from the bombardment of Louisbourg.

The captain didn't leave for Quebec right away. He waited a whole two weeks after Pierre and his companions had arrived at the harbour. The journey to Quebec took six weeks, and he wanted to take as many refugees to the capital as possible. But on June 13th, after four days of no more escapees emerging from the forest, the vessel left.

Pierre didn't enjoy boats. He'd learned that much as a child, and nothing was different on this day as his ship was rolling away from the west coast of Île-Royale. The Gulf of the Saint-Laurent might be part of the Saint-Laurent

River, but it didn't act like a river. Its currents were as fast and powerful as the ocean's. The boat was tossed around in the forceful waves, rolling frighteningly from side to side.

Pierre leaned his large body against the damp wooden rail of the ship's deck. Feeling the wind on his face helped reduce his anxiety. Surprisingly, the sailors had only good things to say about the weather as they manoeuvred the small boat through the rushing waters. But Pierre soon became oblivious to the elements around him as seasickness overcame him. For the first few days, he was violently ill, hanging his head over the side of the rail with increasing frequency. He finally got his sea legs on the fourth day, so he offered to help the crew, but his proposals to give assistance were rebuffed. It was just as well. He knew as much about sailing as he did about blacksmithing. After he admitted to not knowing which side was port, his instructions were to sit down and enjoy the voyage. Once aboard the ship, no one breathed easily until they'd passed the British colony of Acadia—the entire mainland just west of Île-Royale, but fortunately, wherever the British navy was, it wasn't concerned with the small vessel heading toward Quebec. Once the ship passed Acadia, Pierre knew they would make it to the capital.

Pierre sincerely hoped his father had no idea how dangerous the journey would be. If he had any idea, Pierre would say that his father had sent him away knowing there was a good chance he'd die en route. Fortunately, Samuel the *coureur de bois* was among them. Without him and his knowledge of the island's interior, Pierre didn't doubt that they'd all be sitting back at a British camp now. Or shot, but he wanted to think as positively as he could.

By the beginning of August, the ship was passing the peaceful, rolling hills of the Saint-Laurent Valley. It seemed impossible that such tranquillity could exist when the mighty fortress of Louisbourg lay in ruins behind him. He tried not to be angry with his father for sending him away. Augustus's logic was sound, since getting a job as assistant to the Procurator General was a tremendous opportunity for him, but Pierre couldn't help feeling that his abrupt departure had less to do with his own future and more to do with his father's.

Pierre tried to keep thoughts of the fortress out of his mind. No matter what he'd told Marie, he wasn't sure what the conquering British would do. It was nice to think that the inhabitants would be peacefully removed and shipped back to France, but that was only one of many possibilities. And even being banished to France, stripped of all land and worldly possessions, would be difficult. France had its own problems without dealing with displaced citizens of New France.

A shout came from one of the masts. Land was in sight. Pierre chuckled. Land had been in sight for most of the voyage. It was the capital that was now coming into view. He struggled to his feet and made his way to the bow. He'd learned that term at least. It was the 4th of August, and the air was hot and sticky. The water was teeming with boats of every kind. Fishing boats, massive cargo carriers, merchant vessels, and even the birchbark canoes of Native people jockeyed for space in the harbour where the Saint-Charles River met the Saint-Laurent.

The city jutted out of the water, built on a sheer, black, rocky cliff that dropped into the river. The Lower Town sat at the level of the two rivers, with protective batteries and the harbour surrounding it. The Upper Town soared above the rivers, with buildings taller than Pierre had ever seen silhouetted against the blue sky. There were no height restrictions on Quebec's buildings because the city's defences were completely natural. No army could possibly scale the massive cliffs where it was situated. The Algonquins named the place

Kebek, meaning "where the river narrows." It was a desirable place for the French empire to establish a stronghold, as its natural fortifications provided safety for a growing and vulnerable city. The south shore of Quebec was built on the large cliff, which provided advantageous higher ground against any invading enemy. To the north and east lay the Saint-Charles River. Although not as effective as the high cliffs to the south, it nevertheless provided a place of vulnerability for any attackers who would first have to cross its narrow waters. The land to the west was also protected, not by natural fortifications, but because it was accessible only by passing through the narrow section of the Saint-Laurent River that the French defended. The river was less than a mile wide at this point, well within range of the French cannons. Any enemy troops that passed through the area would be met with complete annihilation.

Enthralled, Pierre exited the ship, not at all sorry to be leaving the rocking, stinking bucket behind. The docks were packed with men unloading freight, while massive work horses stomped the hard ground, their carts laden with goods coming into the city from along the Valley of the Saint-Laurent. Travellers met their loved ones. People were haggling over prices right on the docks, and everywhere there was something to see. With a pang of sadness, Pierre remembered that Louisbourg had been like this once, before the war started.

He exited the fray, craning his neck up to get a better look at the buildings around him. The air was fresh—unlike the salty sea air that had always filled his nostrils in Louisbourg. And there was no smell of salted cod like the one that perpetually hung around the fortress on Île-Royale.

Pierre squinted in the bright sunlight. Rows of neat stone buildings lined the dirt streets of the Lower Town. Roads crisscrossed the hillside so people could travel relatively easily between the upper and lower parts of the city.

Gardens filled with wildflowers and vegetables filled the squares in front of the houses, and bird song could be heard in the tranquil air. As Pierre walked along, he entered a crowded square. At its side, there stood a small, stone church, with round windows and a tall spire—a reminder of reverence in the midst of the bustle of the day. A well stood in front of the church, and women and children were gathering water there and talking about the day's events. Stone houses, all attached to each other, stood around the rest of the square. The sight of them reminded Pierre of Marie's parents. No wonder they hadn't had time to escape the fire that killed them.

Here, it was as if no war was going on at all. Quebec's citizens carried on as if nothing out of the ordinary was happening in the colony. Stalls lined with fresh fruits and vegetables were stationed every few yards in the streets leading up from the harbour. Clearly, no one was starving. Pierre felt a rush of anger about the normalcy of life here when his own entire world lay shattered on the Atlantic coast.

In his frustration, he crushed a piece of paper he was carrying in his pocket and then remembered how important that little slip of paper was. His uncle's address was written on it. He'd been told that the house was near Notre-Dame-des-Victoires, which he hoped was the large stone church he had just passed.

All the same, after his harrowing journey, he was in no hurry to show up at his uncle's door. It was a relief to be alone for a while, doing nothing more than taking in the sights and mingling with the crowd. He wandered aimlessly through the streets, his rucksack of possessions slung over his shoulder until he was ready to look up his uncle's address again and ask for directions to the place.

Like his brother, Tomas Thibault had become a merchant and had shown a flair for business as well. Corruption wasn't as prevalent here as it was in Louisbourg, but Louisbourg was in a category of its own, being a trading centre where nobody did anything unless his pockets were lined.

After a few twists and turns, Pierre found Uncle Tomas's home at the end of a cul-de-sac. It was a three-storey townhouse that was attached to its neighbour on one side. The two houses were divided by a thick firewall, which stuck up about three feet above each roof. Pierre wondered absently if Marie's home had had that feature. All the houses he had seen so far were protected in that way.

The house was only a short stroll from Notre-Dame-des-Victoires, but it also backed onto the harbour, making for easy access to the vaulted cellars in the basement that housed the most potentially profitable merchandise of all: alcohol.

Pierre had met his Uncle Tomas once when he was a child. Tomas's two sons were a few years older than he was, so both would be in their early twenties now, but he had no idea what to expect as he knocked sharply on the front door. He just hoped they would give him a slightly more welcoming greeting than the one he typically received from his father.

Tomas answered the door. He was as tall as his brother and nephew but painfully thin, his pale skin stretched tightly over his sharp cheekbones. Pierre immediately thought of a cadaver. Had it not been for Tomas's reddish beard and dancing blue eyes, he might have been mistaken for one.

Tomas greeted his nephew with a bone-cracking bear hug and ushered him into the house. For someone so thin, his strength was surprising. Pierre wasn't used to being greeted with such warmth. He looked around the house amazed. He had been led to believe that his father was the more successful of the two brothers, but this didn't seem to be the case. While nothing compared to the expensive taste of a nobleman like Claude, fine wooden furniture and paintings of landscapes filled the rooms, and a gilded mirror hung opposite the front door. He thought that maybe his father's home would have looked like this if his mother hadn't been gone for so many years, but then he remembered that Tomas's wife had died in childbirth twenty years before.

He caught a glimpse of himself in one of the mirrors and realized that he looked every part of the exhausted, starving refugee.

Tomas watched him kindly. "You look as if you could sleep for days."

Pierre just nodded. His uncle no doubt wanted information that only he could give about what was really happening on the island, but he couldn't launch into that now. He was afraid that a simple statement would start a flood of information that he couldn't control. He wasn't ready to give so much horrible news right now. He was too bone weary and didn't want to start things off on such a negative note.

Tomas seemed to be content with silence for the time being. He showed Pierre the room where he'd be spending the night, then left him in peace there and ordered one of his servants to take a bowl of thick beef stew to his nephew. Pierre's rucksack fell to the floor with a heavy thunk, and when the food arrived, he devoured it as if he was a wild animal. He hadn't had any meat or fish since his departure from the fortress, and before that, everyone had been surviving on the stores of salted cod from the summer before. He moaned as he bit into a crusty loaf of fresh brown bread. With his stomach full and the presence of a soft feather bed that wasn't swaying with wave action, he collapsed into bed without undressing.

He awoke several hours later, the pink rays of the setting sun streaking across his quilt. He stretched deliciously, debating whether he should undress and keep sleeping or go downstairs to see his family and find more food. His stomach rumbled loudly. He chose food.

He found his uncle and two cousins in the dining room clearly halfway through their evening meal. Not wanting to interrupt, he turned away, but one of the boys spotted him and called for him to come and take a seat at the table.

Pierre would never have recognized his cousins as being part of his family if he'd met them on the street. The grown men they'd become didn't match up with the boys he remembered chasing around the countryside when he was last in Quebec. Neither of them were as tall as he was, though they would never be considered short. Daniel, the oldest, had mousy brown hair and brown eyes. He had a clean, round, shaven face and a quick smile. His brother, Jean, surprised Pierre. He looked more like Nic than the rest of his family, with black hair, dark eyes, and a bushy beard that obscured most of his face.

"I don't want to interrupt," Pierre said hastily.

"Nonsense," Tomas boomed. "I'm not about to let my nephew starve under my roof." Pierre was about to say he wasn't starving when his stomach announced the opposite. Tomas laughed and called for another plate.

Pierre spent the rest of the evening with his uncle and cousins and couldn't believe how easily they all related to each other. Dinnertimes with his father were usually silent affairs, but here, the atmosphere was jovial, with each man apparently trying to outdo the others with the sound of his voice.

Daniel worked in the family business, hoping to take over in a few years when Tomas finally decided to retire. The war with Britain had not spared the colony along the rushing river as Pierre had originally supposed. The ship traffic had thinned considerably, and supplies were dwindling. However, unlike the case in Louisbourg, the colony had a good quantity of its own food supplies and livestock. Tomas's business was suffering, but it wasn't in danger of folding.

Jean seemed to be the odd one out. He apparently had no desire to work in the warehouse or offices. He'd worked as a trapper for most of his youth, never officially finishing school, and had spent the last season as a *voyageur*.

"Went all the way to Les Saults de Sainte-Marie to trade with the Ojibway," he boasted proudly. "Took the better part of the season to get there and back, but I made enough on that one voyage to live off for a year."

Pierre's eyes went wide with amazement. He had heard of the mighty rapids of the Sainte-Marie River, but he had never met anyone who'd travelled there. On any map he had ever seen, it looked unimaginably far away.

Jean laughed when Pierre expressed his amazement. "It wasn't easy—portaging those canoes and all that cargo, but with twelve men per canoe, it makes the job easier."

"That's astounding."

Jean shrugged as if it were not a big deal. "Didn't you have *voyageurs* in Louisbourg?"

Voyageurs did pass through Louisbourg from time to time, but those men were strangers to Pierre. They appeared inside the fortress walls only sporadically, with fantastical tales of the interior. Pierre never thought of them as living, breathing men before.

"Will you go again next year?" Pierre asked, still enthralled by his cousin's courage.

Daniel chuckled, pushing his peas around on his plate. "He only did the one year. Couldn't stand the smell of the bear and skunk oil they put on to keep the bugs away. Made him sick."

Jean seemed unembarrassed. "I'd rather be eaten alive by mosquitoes than wear that stuff again. I thought I was going to suffocate from the smell the first night I put it on."

Pierre wasn't sure whether Jean was joking or not, but he laughed along with the rest of them. Jean then started rambling on about how he now worked as a clerk in one of the government-run warehouses. Pierre thought that must be a boring occupation for someone who had once paddled deep into the continent, but Jean didn't reveal what he thought about his current job.

"I can take you to see Dominique Renault tomorrow," Tomas offered, draining his glass of wine. "He's an old friend of mine; he'll treat you well."

"He also has four daughters," Daniel piped up happily. "Beautiful girls, them."

Tomas rolled his eyes. "Leave him alone. Pierre's here to work."

For some reason, the comment bothered Pierre deeply. His mind raced back to Louisbourg, to the large manor house by the water. Was Marie still there?

"Has there been any news about Louisbourg?" Pierre asked. The atmosphere around the table changed dramatically. Daniel and Jean busied themselves with their almost empty plates.

Tomas leaned back in his chair, staring at the ceiling. "Not yet," he said finally. "A few people from Louisbourg arrived before you, but they would, of course, know less than you."

Pierre nodded.

"What was it like there?" Daniel asked, staring at him from across the table. A quick glance at Jean told Pierre that he was listening even though his bushy head was bent over his plate.

Pierre shrugged. He didn't want to talk about it, but the silence continued to stretch. "Augustus was still alive when I left. Very few people have died if you don't include the soldiers." He stared at a grease mark on the linen tablecloth, not wanting to make eye contact. "The British had begun bombing before I left. The army is running out of artillery, so whatever the British send over is being collected and sent back. There isn't any food. The walls are starting to crumble despite their great thickness. There's ... ," his voice failed him. He tried to clear the lump in his throat, but it wouldn't budge.

"That's enough," Tomas said, standing up. "I'm sure word will come eventually. In the meantime, let's not dwell on what we can't control." He gave his sons a sharp look.

Pierre felt thoroughly embarrassed, but Jean broke the tension.

"Vivienne, Renault's wife, is an excellent cook. We'll be rolling you onto the boat by the time you leave."

Everyone laughed. Even Pierre managed a chuckle.

"But don't get too fat. Remember his daughters."

"Daniel!"

***

With a full stomach for the first time in months, Pierre slept like the dead until the sound of cannon fire jolted him from sleep. Heart hammering out of his chest, he sat up drenched in sweat, his hand automatically reaching for the dagger he'd put on his nightstand. It took him a moment to remember that he wasn't in his room in Louisbourg. The bear skin rug on the floor was his first clue. Panting, he slowly crept to the window to see what the problem was.

The sun was barely above the horizon. With the ever-present mist of the fortress absent, he could see clearly down to the street below. A Clydesdale was standing not far from Pierre's window, looking far too big for its city surroundings, attached to a cart full of barrels. One of the barrels had slipped off the back, cracking open and spilling its contents of grain all over the dirt road.

Annoyed at himself, Pierre sat back on the bed and threw the pillow over his head to block out the light. He was in terrible shape if a cracked barrel of wheat could cause him this much anxiety. He tried to go back to sleep, but he couldn't. Eventually, he gave up and dressed in the clean clothes he had carried with him all the way from Île-Royale. He tried his best to wash the grime off his face and hands. But by the time he felt clean again, the water in the wash basin in his room looked like mud. He also shaved off the bushy beard that had grown with alarming speed during his journey.

Pierre looked in the glass hanging over the wash basin. His cheeks were sunken from lack of proper food, and there were dark bags under his eyes. There was also a haunted look in his eye that he didn't recognize, but this was as good as he was going to get.

As quietly as he could, he crept down the stairs and out of the house. He left a note to his uncle on the hall table, thanking him for the hospitality and for the job recommendation and saying that he looked forward to more visits despite the intensity of learning his new responsibilities. Tomas would happily have accompanied him to Dominique Renault's office, but Pierre felt more comfortable going there alone. He'd enjoyed spending time with his uncle and cousins the night before, but he'd felt like an outsider, an interloper who didn't really belong. He wondered if he would ever feel normal again among these people who hadn't experienced the horrors of war. The last attack on Quebec had been in 1690. His father hadn't even been born yet.

The city was waking up. The smell of fresh-baked bread hung in the air, the docks were filling with sailors and labourers, and vendors were setting up their stalls in the markets. He suddenly realized that most people didn't even know the fate of Louisbourg, so how could they mourn it?

As Procurator General for the area of the Saint-Laurent Valley and the Great Lakes interior, Dominique Renault was in charge of all investigation and prosecution of crime. There were very few actual lawyers in New France, since one could be considered a lawyer only if he had graduated from law school. Since the closest one was in Paris, most judges and criminal advocates had studied under someone in Quebec and attended lectures of the few lawyers who did give classes in the colony. They'd also done their best to personally study the law. Obviously, it was far from a perfect system. Often, those enforcing justice had as little knowledge as those they were prosecuting.

As Procurator, Renault sat on the Superior Council, the governing body of New France. He answered only to the Intendant, the official in charge of all things civil and financial. The Intendant was second only to the Governor, the viceroy of the King. The Governor was in charge of the entire French colony, spanning all of Canada and south to the Gulf of Mexico. The Governor oversaw every aspect of colonial life from the civil to the military. As for Renault, he had a say in all the laws and regulations of Canada. Little went on in his area of jurisdiction that he didn't know about and even less that he couldn't control.

Renault lived in the Upper Town with the rest of the members of the governing body. His home near Sainte-Anne Street looked over the cliffs to the Saint-Charles River. As Pierre approached the place, he found the sounds of the water comforting, since they reminded him of the ocean's waves at home during peace time.

Renault's offices were located on the first floor of his home, the family dwelling being on the second and third floors. Renault employed two clerks, both of whom had been hired when in their late twenties. Judges, police officers, and criminal advocates all sought meetings with him on a regular basis. He also travelled around the colony, trying to govern and restore order to the small settlements that dotted the countryside. He was a busy and powerful man but a man without a son.

After graduating from law school, Renault borrowed the money he needed to secure his position from his father and travelled to New France. As a young man, Renault sought adventure and the colonies were sufficiently wild to fill that need. He became wealthy and well respected, but as his body aged and his joints started to ache with arthritis, he found he wasn't able to keep up with his workload. With no son or other close relative to help him, he found himself in a problematical position. His clerks were competent, but they were nearing middle age themselves. With the vast majority of the population illiterate, it seemed he would have to send for someone from France, who would know nothing of the world he was stepping into.

Renault had talked over the problem with his good friend, Tomas Thibault, and that is how Tomas ended up recommending Pierre as an assistant-apprentice. Pierre was intelligent and well educated and familiar with the ways of New France, even though he was from the far-flung region of Île-Royale. His father was willing to send him, hoping to give the boy a second chance where no one knew of his youthful indiscretions. Renault decided to hire him.

Pierre stood at the carved oak door, trying to work up the nerve to open it. Then he noticed a little brass bell suspended above the doorframe by a thin wire. His father had one just like it above his own door. Another comforting sight from home. The bell tinkled just as it did in front of his father's office, bringing a smile to his lips. He pushed the door open and walked in.

Pierre had been expecting something like his father's operation, a utilitarian work space that put function and practicality above all else. Instead, he was greeted by a handsome room with a large stone fireplace and lit by sunlight coming through several large windows. Most of the room was occupied by what Pierre imagined was Renault's personal space, including a large oak desk and padded chairs. That must be where he held most of his meetings and did most of his paperwork. Around the corner, in a separate room, were two plain wooden tables with spindle stools.

The office was empty, although some documents were spread out on the desk, suggesting that someone had been there not long ago. Dust mots swirled through the air, and a general smell of paper and ink filled the office. Pierre walked slowly around the room. He had to duck slightly to pass under the exposed rafters that spanned its length. Footsteps on the stairs leading down from Renault's living quarters announced his arrival.

Dominique Renault was in his early fifties. Having lived the last thirty years in Quebec, he considered himself a Canadian through and through. His black hair hadn't gone grey yet, apart from the white at his temples, but his goatee was streaked liberally with white hairs.

"Are you Pierre?" His low, gravelly voice sounded loud in the quiet room.

"Yes." Pierre stuck out his hand.

Renault had a strong handshake. "Excellent. Otherwise, I would have asked you what you were doing in my office." He looked Pierre over; his yellow eyes reminded Pierre of a hawk's. "Is your uncle here?"

"No, I came on my own."

Renault was a muscular man despite his age, well dressed to demonstrate his station in life, and he held himself with an air of authority.

The Procurator General continued to gaze at Pierre with his piercing yellow eyes. "You survived the trip. I am of the understanding that it was a dangerous one." Something about the way he said it made Pierre realize that Renault understood the magnitude of what Pierre had endured.

Standing in this refined space, Pierre felt slightly healed. The plight of Louisbourg wasn't completely forgotten then. "It went as well as it could have."

Renault nodded sadly. "Do you think they will prevail?"

Pierre shook his head. "I'm surprised they've lasted as long as they have."

There was a pause, each lost in his own thoughts of Louisbourg. Renault was the first to break the silence.

"Best show you around." He clapped a hand on Pierre's shoulder—with some difficulty, since he had to stretch to reach it. "This is my office. The clerks Fortin and Gagné work over there, in their own room." He pointed to the small room off the main area. "You don't need to worry about them. Hocquart, the Intendant, and I use them for drafting laws. Nice gents, but they keep to themselves."

The full office was larger than Pierre had supposed. Behind the main room was a modest study filled floor to ceiling with books of all types. This was Renault's private space, where he went to work and think without interruption. Most of the books had apparently come with Renault from the motherland, and Pierre had never seen so many books in his life. Renault chuckled as the young man stared openly.

"It's quite the collection, yes," he mused. "I often lend them out to those interested. It is possibly the largest collection in the colony." He allowed Pierre a few minutes to properly appreciate the collection before pulling him away to other things.

Pierre wasn't to work with the clerks. He was given a small desk in the corner of Renault's large office so he could listen to all that went on. Pierre had his own bedroom, tucked behind the clerk's room and across from the study, which was far more than he had expected. He knew most apprentices slept on the floors of their work spaces. He felt slightly more at ease knowing he had his own place to sleep just beyond the office. Renault gave Pierre some time to clean up more before introducing him to the two clerks. Both men weren't very interested in him, but they were cordial.

The Procurator General brought him back over to the large oak desk in the front room of the office. "Being an assistant is not the most exciting job," he conceded, "but the more you learn, the more you'll be able to do. In half an hour, I have a meeting with Hocquart, and you will accompany me there. I wish only for you to observe and take notes."

A short time later, laden with paper, quills, and ink, Pierre stepped up into Renault's carriage for the trip to the Intendant's office.

The Upper Town sat on top of the cliff overlooking the Plains of Abraham and the Saint-Laurent, separated from the docks and warehouses by the soaring cliffs. Renault told Pierre that Quebec didn't feel much like a city to him; it was more like one of the small country towns that dotted the European continent. Pierre had to take Renault's word for it, since he'd never been to France.

The government offices were near the military offices that had been built up along the fortifications of the city. Upon entering the imposing stone building, Pierre was once again struck by the opulence around him. Perhaps life was more comfortable here in the capital because it was surrounded and therefore protected by the rest of the colony. While the offices of Louisbourg were decorated, they were filled only with the essentials, but here, great attention was paid to decorative detail. Pierre had never seen so many vases filled with cut flowers in his life.

Pierre was introduced to the Intendant, the most powerful man in New France. Gilles Hocquart was of average height and chubby, with one of those powdered wigs that Pierre thought were ridiculous. He betrayed none of his thoughts, of course, and settled himself in a corner, hastily scribbling away as the two men discussed business. Pierre felt rather awkward when they discussed him and the unknown fate of Louisbourg as if he wasn't present, but their conversation wasn't one he was invited to join.

Afterwards, when they had returned to Renault's office, the Procurator General sat down with Pierre and asked about his experiences during the siege of the fortress. Renault was sympathetic to how difficult it was for Pierre to articulate his experiences during the ordeal, and he listened carefully as his assistant explained the mutiny as well as the food and artillery shortages.

Renault wanted to know every detail, always prodding further and further below the surface. It was the first time Pierre had spoken of the people he had left behind. He became exhausted as he brought them back to the forefront of his mind. He explained how Nic had been treated as a slave and how he had been deprived of food and sleep just to entertain the soldiers. He remembered how the bombs had fallen and how the military had begged the population to collect any ammunition found in the walls and in craters in the ground so they could be shot back at the enemy.

Pierre was about to speak of Marie but found he didn't have the voice for it—partly because he felt guilty. As soon as he'd escaped the island and found himself in the relative safety of the boat heading for Quebec, he regretted not having saved her from British hands.

"Did the whole garrison fight?" Renault asked, bringing Pierre back to the mutiny. Renault had been a part of the decision to not send reinforcements to Louisbourg. It was one that he admitted to wrestling with for some time, and he was not completely comfortable with the final decision.

"They all did—as did the militia."

That seemed to satisfy Renault, but he was still furious about the behaviour of the soldiers. "Those kinds of actions are the greatest threat to the colony," he huffed. "I hope the leaders were dealt with appropriately."

Pierre nodded. He had watched the executions along with everyone else.

"As soon as I hear anything about the fate of the fortress, I will let you know," Renault promised. "But now to dinner. I shan't deprive my dear wife of the opportunity to fatten you up."

Jean had not exaggerated about Vivienne Renault's cooking ability. Renault could easily have afforded a cook, but his wife wouldn't hear of it. Cooking was one of Vivienne's great loves. She spent most of her time puttering around the kitchen, preparing the elaborate dishes she served to her guests. Anyone who had sat at her table was always amazed by what they were treated to. No sooner had Pierre taken his place around the dinner table than a heaping plate of chicken and vegetables was placed in front of him by one of the Renaults' servants. As soon as he was finished, Vivienne insisted he take seconds, though no one else was finished.

"Did they not feed you in Louisbourg?" she asked, aghast, as she watched him continue to eat. Although she possessed all the grace and poise of a well-born woman, Vivienne was passionate and sometimes prone to outbursts like this.

Feeling rather sheepish, Pierre put down his knife and fork. "Ah, no, Ma'am, there wasn't very much food once the war started. The British navy prevented most of the supply ships from reaching us."

Vivienne's red lips opened in horror. "Did you know about this?" she hissed at her husband.

Renault nodded warily. "Of course, dear. But there is little anyone can do. As the boy said, a complete British blockade is in effect."

Vivienne didn't look as if she accepted that answer, but she held her tongue. All the same, Pierre had a suspicion that Renault had not heard the last of her thoughts on the subject. The Renaults' four daughters said little as they watched their guest eat, but, Pierre thought, Daniel had been right when he'd said they were beautiful. They all had dark hair and pale skin like their father, but they'd inherited fine features from their mother and had learned to imitate her poise.

Alone in his room that night, after cleaning the office space and setting everything up for the next day, Pierre opened one of the books Renault kept in his library. He hadn't understood most of the details that Hocquart and Renault had discussed at the government offices, but he was determined to learn.

His room wasn't large. In fact, it was hardly big enough for the bed and desk that occupied it, and the bed ended up being Pierre's chair. His reading method was to put his book on the desk and sit on the edge of the bed with his knees tucked under the table. The single candle burned several inches before he finally retired for the night.

***

After a week, pierre found he had settled into a simple routine. He was the first one to wake up every morning to open the curtains to let in the sunlight and to organize the notes and files that everyone needed for the day before any of them arrived. Once Renault did present himself, Pierre took notes for the various meetings he had and accompanied him on his travels.

The prison in Quebec was one of their frequent destinations. Renault didn't usually deal with the everyday cases, but someone, be it a judge or an official dealing with a crime, would sometimes ask for advice that involved his interviewing a prisoner. Every so often, a well-connected convict insisted on a conference, but when Renault complied with those requests, he complained bitterly all the way there and back.

The prison was a large stone building with thick walls and barred windows attached to the military buildings. There were no separate accommodations for military and civilians. Pierre wasn't sure if he had ever seen a place as depressing as this and was always grateful when they left. Each dark cell, bare except for a thin layer of hay, must be a terrible place to be even if the person accused deserved their dreadful quarters. No one stayed in that place very long, as justice was handed down as swiftly as possible. Most people preferred corporal punishment to being imprisoned, and the judges were happy to comply.

The courthouse was another of their frequent stops. Renault often complained about the well-known fact that the judges sometimes knew less about the law than the accused. So if Renault's only job had been to make sure that justice was actually being served around the colony, he would have been busy enough. However, he also sat on the Superior Council. Pierre was surprised when he was invited to attend one of their meetings only four days after his arrival. Sixteen men served on the Council, including the Governor, the Intendant, the Bishop, and the leader of the militia. Again, Pierre sat in a corner furiously scribbling notes. The men were more than interested in hearing about Louisbourg, but Pierre was spared from recounting his stories again by Renault, who passed along the information Pierre had already given him.

On the first Sunday in September, a blustering and rainy day, Pierre accompanied the Renaults to Notre-Dame de Québec in the centre of the Upper Town. The church was larger than any that Pierre had ever seen, and it had large windows and an intricate, majestic altar.

Pierre sat at the front with the Renaults and the rest of the important figures and their families, well aware that his large frame was being discussed by those behind him. The refugee from Louisbourg was an interesting new topic for gossip.

Before the morose priest began the mass, he cleared his throat to make an announcement. Pierre wasn't paying much attention, being focused, instead, on the building's elaborate windows, when he heard the word "Louisbourg." His heart stopped. Louisbourg had capitulated, the inhabitants deported to France, and the garrison to prisons in Boston and the rest of New England.

Murmurs rippled throughout the congregation, but Pierre didn't hear them. His ears were ringing. He felt his hands begin to tremble, so he gripped the top of the pew in front of him, but that didn't help. Overcome, he stood up, ran down the aisle, and burst out the front doors into the early autumn rain. He collapsed on the steps, taking deep gulps of fresh air. Louisbourg had fallen almost two months before, but the news had reached Quebec only now. News travelled painfully slowly between the two cities, and that was one of the colony's greatest vulnerabilities. So Louisbourg was gone, quite likely along with everyone he knew in it.

He heard the heavy church door swing open and sensed Renault settling down beside him.

"Sorry," Pierre mumbled, trying to wipe his eyes surreptitiously.

Renault shook his head. "My dear boy, what on earth for?"

"Making a scene."

Renault scoffed. "That would be distressing news for anyone."

Augustus would have been admonishing him, but now that was all irrelevant, as his father was on his way to France.

Renault and Pierre sat in silence, watching the rain fall, the heavy droplets slowly soaking through their outer layers of clothing. Of course, Pierre had known this was coming. Louisbourg could not have survived indefinitely against the British. But the shock felt unbearable. And then there was Marie. Where was she right now, at this moment? In material terms, Claude would be able to provide her with a good life in France, unlike some of the poor who were now completely destitute, but Pierre's heart hurt, knowing she was so far away.

"Do you know where the survivors will go?"

"France is a big country," Renault sighed. "I have no idea, but your father will send word eventually; it's only a matter of time."

"The river will be frozen by the time they reach France. I won't hear anything until spring."

A reassuring hand was placed on his shoulder. "I know. But spring will be here soon enough."

Chapter 5

THE DAYS CONTINUED MUCH THE SAME, with little break in routine. Pierre was forbidden to work on holy days as was the rest of the colony, but other than that, he worked every day except Sunday. He divided his evenings and Sundays between Renault's home and his Uncle Tomas's, though after he'd been in the capital for two months, he was surprised to have Renault invite him to join the family for dinner every night. Pierre had heard the stories of the abuse and neglect that apprentices suffered during their training, but life with Renault was far different. Pierre felt as if he was the prodigal son being welcomed back after a long absence.

During some of his off hours, Pierre continued to work his way through Renault's library, memorizing all the rules and regulations that he could. He hadn't told Renault he was doing this, but after a few months, Renault started asking him his opinion about certain points of law. When Pierre was able to answer with more than wild guesses, Renault made a point of asking him more often, usually when he was least expecting it. This kept him on his toes, but he rarely answered incorrectly, and the pile of books in his room kept steadily growing.

Renault's four daughters were in various stages of adolescence. The eldest, Martine, was sixteen, only a year younger than Pierre. It took him about a month to realize that none of them would be against him showing interest in any of them. More alarming was his master's apparent approval of the situation.

He confided in his cousins about this strange turn of events, but Jean laughed and Daniel teased him for being worried.

"I would love it if even one of them showed me some attention," Daniel smiled.

Pierre let the subject go.

While things were going well during the day, he slept badly at night. Usually, he poured over his books as long as possible, putting off the hour of sleep. That didn't help, though. Every night, the bombs fell on Louisbourg, the fortress crumbled around him, and Marie was always there calling his name, begging for help. He'd always wake up in a cold sweat, grateful that he slept alone in the office, where no one could hear his cries. He had dark circles under his eyes from lack of sleep, but his work kept him so busy during the day that Louisbourg only haunted him in the quiet hours of the night. Renault had recommended a glass of brandy before bed, but that didn't help either.

Winter came, and it was colder and more brutal than any he had ever experienced. The Saint-Laurent froze over, the ice thick enough that a man could skate on it. People flocked to the frozen surface with their bone skates strapped to their boots. Skating on the river was the preferred place for such activity. Many younger people took to skating through the icy streets of the city. But this was frowned upon because people were sometimes cut off or knocked over by those going at breakneck speed.

Despite the cold and the several feet of snow that covered the countryside, life went on. Most inhabitants of the colony were stuck wherever they had been when the first of the winter storms blew. The King's Highway between the capital and Montreal was passable, but few were brave enough to undertake that journey. Fishermen built temporary huts along the edge of the frozen river, fishing through small holes cut in the ice. Hunters and trappers still ventured beyond the walls of the city, in attempts to get high prices for fresh meat, their feet shod with large snowshoes of the type that Native people wore. At least some must have been successful because Vivienne continued to serve fresh rabbit throughout the winter months.

As April of 1746 approached, the river began to groan and creak. More than once, the sounds made Pierre wake up in the middle of night, certain that the city was under attack. When the ice finally shattered completely and great boulders of ice flowed down the river, the city began waiting anxiously for the first ships from France.

Pierre wondered if any would actually come. With Louisbourg now in the hands of the British, would it be possible for French ships to make the long trip west into the Valley of the Saint-Laurent. He was fearful and on edge most of the time. Renault noticed but didn't say a word. There was nothing he could do, though he was worried about what would happen if no news came for Pierre. He'd heard enough from his protégé to know that the relationship between him and his father wasn't the strongest. However, he couldn't imagine any father dropping all communication and abandoning his son to an unknown fate.

Snow still covered the ground in most places except the streets. The warmer temperatures and rain had turned those into rivers of mud and winter muck—debris that had been hidden all winter by snow. Pieces of leather lost from bridles and reins, bits of broken snowshoes, single gloves without their mates, and human waste ran through the streets. Quebec was definitely not at its best, and the dirt-blackened snow that lined the streets didn't add to the city's charm either.

Late one afternoon in April, Pierre was sidestepping the puddles and rivers in the streets, heading back to the office. He'd spent the whole day at the courthouse without Renault. He'd been promoted to dealing with Judge Caron on his own. This could have been interesting, but the Judge was far too old to be still dispensing justice. He could barely remember what he'd eaten for breakfast let alone the laws of New France. Fortunately, some notary was usually around to make sure things didn't get too out of control. Renault was trying to have the man peacefully retired, but so far, Caron had been resistant. Once a week, Pierre went to try to talk some sense into him, but today's meeting had gone as well as they usually had. Caron had thrown a shoe at him and accused him of being a British spy.

Pierre was exhausted. Dealing with Caron was always a daunting task. He wished Renault or Hocquart would just strip the judge of his responsibilities, but Renault felt that would be unkind given the number of years Caron had served before losing his mind.

The bell above the door announced Pierre's arrival. He wasn't looking forward to entering the main room despite the warm fire crackling in the fireplace, as he was feeling distinctly nettled and not very charitable toward his master. As he was mulling over ways to free himself from the Caron job, he was surprised to see his Uncle Tomas sitting in the chair he usually occupied beside Renault.

"How did the great, honourable Caron behave today?" Renault asked, trying not to sound too pleased that he'd dumped the errand on Pierre.

Pierre stripped off his black wool coat and hung it on one of the pegs at the entrance. "Well, he accused me of treason only twice before he threw me out, so I guess that's an improvement."

Tomas laughed. "Can't you get rid of that old geezer?"

Renault leaned back, lacing his fingers behind his head. "I continue to try to sell him on the south of France at this time of year, but he insists on doing his civic duty. Once Hocquart gets back from Montreal, I'll ask him to have a heart-to-heart with the man, hopefully before he accuses some poor twelve-year-old pickpocket of betraying the King."

Pierre rolled his eyes, there was a council meeting tonight that was sure to go late, those men loved to hear themselves speak. They were trying to decide how to proceed with normal life since the war had entered its second year and didn't show any signs of stopping. There was a shortage of men since the army continued needing reinforcements and the farms were suffering as a result. Since Louisbourg had been lost, Quebec needed to be prepared in case an invasion occurred. Everyone had an opinion and none of them agreed.

Pierre sat down opposite his uncle and his employer. "What brings you here today, Uncle Tomas?"

Tomas leaned forward and handed Pierre a weathered envelope. "Arrived today. Thought you might want it." His blue eyes danced as he watched his nephew hastily tear open the envelope. "Who's it from?"

Pierre scanned the letter quickly. "Augustus."

Renault sighed with relief. Maybe with news from home, Pierre would finally relax or at least sleep more. He could see the paper shaking in Pierre's hands. The young man was beside himself with anxiety. "You can go and read it alone," Renault said.

Pierre hastily retreated to his room, closed the door quietly, and sat on his bed. It was a short note, written in his father's untidy scrawl. Two ships had taken the majority of the civilians back to France. It was a stormy voyage, but almost everyone had survived. Augustus had listed the dead just in case, but the names meant nothing to Pierre.

His father was renting a cottage in the countryside between Paris and Versailles, though how he was making an income he didn't say. But Pierre knew his father had enough investments and savings in gold to live on those for a long time. Generally, merchants didn't conduct business miles away from port. As far as his father knew, Nic was imprisoned in Boston with the rest of the garrison, awaiting the end of the war before being released. The British weren't complete barbarians, so he would be kept alive, but his life there would be an ordeal nonetheless.

Pierre's heart skipped a beat as he reached the end of the letter. His father's cottage was less than a mile from where Marie and Annette were staying at the Babineaux estate. Claude had taken up his spot in Court once again and was campaigning for those displaced by the war. Annette refused to join her husband at the palace and lived in the countryside away from the drama of the Court. Elise was living somewhere nearby with her mother. Claude had arranged for them to live comfortably.

Now that it was April, it would take roughly two months for a letter to reach France by ship. If he sent a reply right away, there was a good chance he could get an answer back before the river froze again.

He cleared his desk of the various tomes that were balanced precariously there, sorted through the papers strewn around, found a few that were blank, and began to write. Before he knew it, he had filled three pages front and back. He was about to race off to the harbour when he thought of his father and scribbled a hasty reply, informing him that he was fine and learning much.

Tomas and Renault were still sitting in the front office, not discussing anything of great importance judging by the half-empty brandy bottle between them.

Renault glanced at the overstuffed envelope in his assistant's hand and laughed. "Telling him your life story, are you?"

Tomas leaned forward and read the name printed across the front. He gave his nephew a shrewd look. "I would suggest at least sending your father a paragraph."

Pierre said nothing but flashed him the second envelope bearing his father's name.

"Who's the other letter for?" Renault asked, his interest piqued, but Pierre ignored him.

"I'll be back, I'm just heading down to the harbour." He rushed out without waiting for a reply.

The summer that followed was cool, and during that whole season, the winds of war continued to blow over the colony. No attacks were launched against the French towns and villages along the Saint-Laurent Valley, but the power of the British navy continued to make its presence felt. The men on the vessels that arrived from France and the West Indies told harrowing stories of barely escaping from the massive British warships they'd encountered en route to Quebec. Pierre often wondered if his letter would even reach Marie, but he didn't dwell on that too much because he had other things to worry about.

***

As Renault was in charge of all criminal matters in the colony, travel was integral to his job. He and Pierre had been in Montreal from mid-May to mid-July of 1746, trying to restore the city's judicial system, which had been compromised by a scandal. It appeared that some sort of bribery had been happening, and while the practice was commonplace at the docks, it was generally frowned upon in a court setting. Frédéric Picard was one of the top judges in the city and very well respected in the community. His older brother was a General overseeing the garrison stationed in Montreal. So when news had broken out that Judge Picard had accepted bribes in exchange for lighter sentences, the whole city was in an uproar.

Pierre marvelled at how well his mentor could soothe the rightly concerned citizens of the city. It took two months to complete the criminal investigation and to interview new candidates for Picard's former position, but in the end, Renault had largely reassured the people that the justice system had been restored to its former integrity. Picard had been dismissed, and those associated with him, whether guilty or not, carried the stigma of the investigation.

Pierre sat on the deck of the shallow vessel that was taking them home, enjoying the July sun. The new Chief Judge of Montreal seemed pleasant or at least eager not to spoil his career with bribery. It had been a remarkably exciting journey that had opened Pierre's eyes to the power his employer possessed.

"Could we not have taken a carriage?" Pierre asked as the boat rocked in the fast-moving river, making his stomach lurch unpleasantly. Renault sat beside him, re-reading the report Pierre had written concerning the investigation. It was to be submitted to the Intendant, Hocquart, upon their return. "This is cheaper, I've told you before, because it includes bed and board. If you wanted to pay for stays at inns along the route, we could have taken the King's Highway. I'm too old to sleep out under the stars."

What Renault said about his age was true. In the year that Pierre had been in his employ, Renault's fingers had started to bend and twist with arthritis. It was getting more difficult for him to use his hands for even basic tasks.

"You don't pay me enough to afford such things," Pierre reminded him.

"Vivienne could stop feeding you."

"You think I can cook for myself?" he laughed. "I'd starve in a week."

Renault smiled and looked out over the farms and villages that dotted the patchwork landscape. "When we return, I think it'll be time you started doing some business on your own."

Pierre was startled. "You want me to meet with Hocquart?"

Renault shook his head. "Leave Hocquart to me. I'm not ready to stop fighting my own battles yet, but this trip reminds me of how old I truly am becoming."

Renault had barely sat still for a moment during their time in Montreal. Pierre was exhausted just thinking about all that man had done in two short months. "You're not that old," he said. "Don't write your epitaph just yet."

The lawyer chuckled. "No, but part of the reason I took you on as my assistant was so you could run after people while I sat at home. It's one of the pleasures of old age."

"If you want it, I will do it," Pierre said. He recognized this for what it was. Though there was no mention of his title changing or of an increased salary, Renault was giving him a promotion and recognizing the value of the work he had been doing.

"By the way, do you remember Madame Demers?" Renault asked, not looking up from the report. "She had us over for that delightful dinner."

"You could call it that. I'm from Île-Royale; I'm used to my fish fresh."

"Yes. Well not everyone is Vivienne. Anyway, her daughter has expressed some interest in you." He said the words casually, but Pierre was well aware that Renault had been disappointed that Pierre had taken no interest in any of his daughters.

"Well, I'll be in Quebec for the foreseeable future. You can pass that along." It came out ruder than he'd meant, but he didn't particularly care. He was only eighteen and a lowly assistant. He was the first person up and the last person to sleep in Renault's house. Why did anyone think he had time for women?

Renault let the rebuff pass. "It is not a requirement that you live in the spare room forever, you know."

Pierre nodded but didn't say anymore. His thoughts were far away in France at that moment.

Little had happened in Quebec while they'd been gone. Caron's heart had finally given out, solving the problem of trying to convince him to retire. Hocquart had already filled the vacancy, much to Renault's annoyance. Technically, appointing judges was the Intendant's job, but Renault had been doing it for so long that he'd become used to viewing it as his task and his alone.

"I won't miss being accused of treason all the time," Pierre said when Renault aired the news about Caron's passing.

Renault snorted into his nightly glass of brandy. "Accusations of treason are the least of your problems."

Pierre looked at him, confused.

Renault leaned back, placing his feet on the polished surface of the desk. "If you stay at this long enough, you'll receive death threats, accusations of corruption, and attacks on your character, and eventually no one will want to speak to you at parties." He chortled at the look of concern on Pierre's face. "I wouldn't worry about it. How many decades have I been doing this? I'm still alive."

***

It was a late night in September 1746. The Superior Council had been meeting for hours to discuss tariffs. At one time, Pierre wouldn't have had any thoughts on the subject, but after a year of working with the government, he was developing some strong opinions. Unfortunately, since he was only an assistant, no one wanted to hear them. Sometimes Renault would listen, but Pierre knew he was doing little more than humouring him. He was a long way from ever being able to participate in the smoky arguments that ran the colony.

Renault had already retired for the night, and Pierre could have been in bed too, but he'd accidentally smashed a bottle of ink, and its contents had spread in a wide area on the floor. That's what he got for cleaning after midnight. He'd never get rid of the stain. His only hope was that Vivienne might be excited about making a new rug for the office. With his back aching after scrubbing on his hands and knees for an hour and with his fingers stained blue, he finally collapsed on his bed, hoping sleep wouldn't evade him this time. But then he noticed there was something else on his bed other than himself and the blankets.

Rolling over, he pulled a crinkled envelope out from under his body. Renault must have put it there. He would have been too impatient to hand it to Pierre himself. Fatigue forgotten, he sat up, fumbling for the flint candle starter. The candle spluttered to life, casting its golden hue across the bare walls. Pierre recognized the tiny, tidy writing of Marie. It had always enraged him when the nuns held her penmanship up as an example. He ripped apart the outer envelope, took out the letter inside, and read it through very quickly. The knot in his chest relaxed a bit as he reached the bottom of the page. Then he rearranged his weight more comfortably on the bed as he read through it again.

The Displaced: Fall of a Fortress

Marie was in the French countryside, as his father had said, safe but miserable. She had nothing to do and hated the aristocrats at the Court of Versailles, who felt she was a stupid simpleton because she was from the colonies. He laughed as she described Annette's failed attempts at navigating Court life; his heart ached when she talked of her worry for Nic.

Until your letter arrived I was worried you hadn't survived the trip. Once the fortress fell, the stories from around the island came flooding in. The British were ruthless in their treatment of people they discovered in the countryside. I was sick with worry that you had met a terrible end. Your father deeply regretted sending you away. He was on the same boat as we were. I think he would have thrown himself into the deep if he had known for sure that he'd caused your death.

I miss you. I will feel very stupid writing this if there's some beautiful blonde looking over your shoulder. Your father told me that Renault has four daughters, but know if there is someone, I'm not upset. I'd rather be your friend than not be able to talk to you at all. I just wish I could talk to you in person. Every day I see things I want to tell you about. Yesterday, I had to explain to the local butcher that I had never eaten a rat. He was surprised that there is even livestock in New France. All the while, he was trying to sell me bad beef. He was amazed that I knew what beef was.

It took me a few months to remember that I couldn't walk down the road and find you, even though Augustus is so close. He comes over for dinner almost every day. I always wish you were coming with him. I'm going to keep writing to you. I hope you don't mind, but I need someone to talk to.

Love, Marie

Pierre read the letter over and over until he had it memorized. She'd included a drawing of his father's cottage that she had done. He smiled at her ability.

Eventually, he nodded off, Marie's letter still in his hands. For the first time, that night, the bombs of Louisbourg didn't echo in his sleep.

***

The next morning, despite his few hours of sleep, he awoke early. He got up and started the fire in the fireplace and prepared the office for the day. The ink stain on the floor didn't seem as bad now that he was seeing it in daylight. When he'd finished the morning preparations, he sat down eagerly at the oak desk, next to the offending stain, and wrote for an hour. There was no one else, and she needn't be worried. He told her how he had felt like an outsider when he first arrived in Quebec, with the violence of Louisbourg so far away and the effects of war barely felt in the capital. In his last letter, he'd already told her of the long days and hours of study that he was putting in, so in this one, he wrote about how he was learning so much and how Renault was beginning to give him some of his regular assignments. He told her about his Uncle Tomas and his cousins who he didn't have time to see often but who were always happy to see him when he did visit.

Pierre paused, unsure of how to continue. Marie had been honest with him as she always was, but he was terrified to tell her that she filled his dreams, that what he missed most about Louisbourg was her, that he was happy in Quebec but would be happier if she was with him.

It felt like too much to say. He had never told her his feelings during the last days of the siege. He should have, but with his departure and both their futures so uncertain, he had decided against it. What if the distance made her forget him? Obviously, it hadn't and now he felt like a coward. Unsure of how to put his feelings into words and anxious to have his response delivered before the snow flew, he procrastinated once again and hurried off to the docks.

***

The winter of 1746–47 was a long one, like every other winter in New France. A hundred years before, when the French government first tried to fill the land with people, they had extended contracts to tradesmen and labourers to come and work in the developing country for a few years. It hadn't worked. The climate was so harsh that most contractors packed up and left after their agreements had expired. The same went for the soldiers who were stationed there.

Sitting in the office every morning, looking out at more and more snow coming, Pierre couldn't blame them. While his own bedroom was small enough to retain some heat, one of his jobs from the months of October to April was to break the ice that had formed over the ink pots on all the desks. He usually started his days wrapped in his thick, wool blanket waiting for the heat of the fire to fill the office.

No letters came from France during the winter months either. Of course he'd known that, but he wasn't happy about it. All the same, it seemed that he needed the time to decide what to write next. By the time the spring thaw came, he still hadn't figured out what he wanted to say. Considering that he spent most of his days drafting and polishing correspondence for Renault, he thought he should have been able to write a note to Marie with ease.

Renault kept him as busy as ever. There were unsettling murmurings among the military stationed in the Valley. Food was becoming scarce, as were other basic supplies. The rank and file were growing disgruntled with their treatment at the hands of the military hierarchy. While the Louisbourg garrison was the only one that had ever revolted in New France, there were concerns that their attitude may have spread to other regiments.

However, unlike the case in Louisbourg, or perhaps because of it, the Superior Council was quick to accommodate the army's requests. Vivienne complained bitterly to her husband that there was no more beef because all cattle not being used for milk were now the property of the soldiers. Pierre assured her that the sacrifice was worth it, to keep the fighting forces happy.

April 1747 came and with it, the rains that reduced the city to rivers of mud. It was almost impossible for anyone to travel between the Upper and Lower Towns. When the rain fell, the already steep roads turned into waterfalls.

As the river thawed, ships began to arrive, although the sailors complained bitterly of the dangers they had faced during the journey from Europe. One group of merchant vessels had been travelling together but were captured before they were even clear of Viveiro, Spain. Merchants were having to pay higher and higher wages, just so men would be willing to cross, so the sailors who did survive the crossing were becoming rich. This state of affairs was eating up most of Tomas's profits and he was becoming anxious for the war to be over.

But one day, more letters came. Six of them. Apparently, Marie had written one every month and had kept them in a drawer until she was able to send them. He laughed at (and admired) her efficiency. Marie still hated France despite the lack of snow. Annette's headaches were worse during the dismal rainy months of the French winter, and Marie found little relief from her constant complaints. Apparently, Annette had decided to marry her niece off to the richest eligible bachelor at Court, but Marie was not at all enthusiastic about the prospect, and she was doing her best to prevent it.

So Pierre finally realized there was no time to lose; he needed to act.

At the time that he had this epiphany, he was waiting for the Bishop in one of the corridors of the government building, to explain that a priest needed to report illegal activity even if it was described during confession. Pierre pulled a spare piece of paper out, put it on his knee, and started to scribble as quickly as he could.

Dear Marie,

I should have told you this years ago. There's no reason other than that I'm a coward. I kept putting it off for a better time, but I can't put it off any longer, not with Annette trying to marry you off. I don't want you to marry some stuffy aristocrat and spend the rest of your life in France. I have nothing to give you. I live in a closet attached to the office. I make a meagre amount of money that is barely enough to feed myself. Luckily,

Renault's wife, Vivienne, has made it her personal mission to see that I don't starve. I'm no longer mistaken for a twig, but my salary isn't enough to live on. And it won't be enough for at least two more years.

But I miss you. I miss you more than I miss the island and life before the war. For a long time, I thought I missed home, but I don't. I'm happy here because I'm building a life and a future, but it's not the same without you.

I don't want to stop you from marrying some viscount with a family estate and acres of land, not if that's what you want. I have no life to give you, at least not yet. But I love you and will be working the hardest I possibly can to give you everything I can.

I just want you to know that before Annette makes her plans.

Love, Pierre

It seemed inadequate now that he watched the ink dry, the paper crumpled from being set down on his thigh. But he couldn't risk losing her if there was a chance she would wait for him to get his life together. After his meeting, he went to the docks, his heart in his throat, and paid the exorbitant sum to have the letter taken across the Atlantic.

He didn't receive a reply for the rest of the summer. Augustus sent a letter but mentioned nothing of his neighbours, or not in the way Pierre was hoping.

The winter came, his third in Quebec, without any news from France. He tried to confide in Daniel and Jean during one of his few moments of respite, but neither could understand him. Jean spent most of his free time at the whore houses down near the docks, a frequent enough visitor that he had become a favourite. And for all of Daniel's talk of the Renault girls, he seemed in no rush to settle down. Instead, he teased Pierre mercilessly for waiting for a woman living on the other side of the world.

After these reactions, Pierre decided to keep his concerns to himself.

***

That winter, a problem arose that almost pushed Marie from his mind. Almost.

As 1747 drew to a close, reports of disappearances began to reach the capital. They had started not far from the city limits in a hamlet an hour outside of the city. It was reported that two young women there had gone missing. Both had gone to the well a week apart from each other and never returned. No trace could be found of them except for the wooden pails still sitting beside the well's stone walls. Snowshoe tracks leading to the forest had been discovered, but they disappeared once they reached the uneven surface of the undergrowth.

A month later, a young nun was abducted from the hospital just beyond the city walls. Her body was found a week later by a trapper, frozen in the woods. The following day, another woman was violently attacked as she was returning home from the butcher's. She had survived, at least for now, but still lay in the hospital, hovering between life and death.

Gilles Hocquart had gone back to France. His replacement was François Bigot, the former Finance Commissary of Louisbourg. Pierre had mentioned how Bigot's tact had helped smooth over the garrison's mutiny, and that made Renault eager to sit down with the man.

Two days after the most recent attack, Renault got his wish.

Bigot was a large man with a portly stomach that couldn't be completely hidden by his waistcoat and jacket. He was always well dressed, had an air of authority, and never left home without his powdered wig. That morning, he arrived at Renault's office, covered with snow, which he shook off in as dignified a manner as he could before he sat down across the desk from the Procurator General. He had no memory of Pierre, nor should he have had, but he was pleasant when introduced to the young assistant.

"There is no proof that any of these incidents are related to the others," Renault said quietly, rubbing his eyes with his gnarled hands. "Murders are a fact of life. While terrible, it is the truth."

"How long do we have to wait before you're willing to deal with these incidents as possible evidence of a murderous fiend on the loose?" Bigot asked heavily. He had been in Quebec only a short while and was still trying to get a handle on the city. The main thing he'd observed, though, was that the citizens of Quebec were beginning to grow extremely uneasy. He wanted to deal with the matter before uneasiness became outright panic.

"What do you want me to do?" Renault snapped after they'd been going in circles for over an hour. "The police are looking. There is nothing more that can be done."

"There have been two disappearances, one murdered nun, and one woman severely wounded."

"I know the numbers, thank you," Renault replied tartly, "but if this is the work of one prowler, and there is no proof of that, there is nothing more that can be done."

Bigot glared at Pierre, who had been silent so far, listening and taking notes. "What do you think?"

Pierre's jaw began to work, and he started chewing the inside of his cheek. "Well," the Intendant persisted. Pierre glanced at Renault and knew from the look on his face that if he agreed with Bigot he was out of a job. "I agree that it's concerning, but I don't know what else you expect the law enforcers to do, even if this is a fiend."

Bigot continued to fidget. "Then what do you propose we do?"

"We've already doubled the patrols and warned the population not to travel alone. I don't think there's much more we *can* do unless more information is forthcoming." Pierre answered.

"May I ask who you are?" Bigot said, looking at him suspiciously. "I was under the impression you were a clerk."

Renault leaned forward on his elbows. "This is my assistant, Pierre Thibault. The older I get, the more difficult I find travelling to all the appointments that are required of me. Pierre has been with me for three years now, and I've been teaching him. He is my eyes and ears for most things. You'll find him quite capable."

"I didn't realize you were having a difficult time. Should I write to Louis to release you?" Bigot said with concern.

Renault waved a twisted hand. "I'm allowed to train a replacement, you know. My mind's as sharp as ever. Pierre actually came to me from your part of the world," Renault said pleasantly.

"Bordeaux?"

Pierre laughed. "Louisbourg."

Bigot looked surprised.

"Born there. Escaped before the fortress fell."

Bigot continued to stare at him open-mouthed. Realizing what he was doing, he tried to recover. "Thibault, you said?"

"Augustus Thibault, the merchant, is my father. My best friend's uncle is Claude-Jean des Babineaux."

That name obviously meant something to the Intendant. He nodded, impressed. "You don't say. Well, welcome to Quebec. I daresay it's a tad less violent than the fortress."

Pierre shook his blond head. "The pirates and smugglers made life more interesting on the island."

Bigot snorted. It had been his job to try to stop those activities from draining money from the legitimate economy. However, after his interchange with Pierre, Bigot seemed far more interested in coming to a resolution about how to handle the case at hand.

The extra police presence didn't stop the attacks. Two more took place during the following fortnight, both ending in fatalities. A third had been underway when the police, drawn to the scene by the victim's screams, finally apprehended the man. The people of Quebec celebrated in the streets now that they thought the terrors had come to an end, but Pierre's role was just beginning.

With such a high-profile case, Renault was expected to prosecute the accused. It was a simple case, as the man had been caught in the act, but a trial still needed to take place. To Pierre's surprise, Renault declared that Pierre would be in charge.

"I've never been to law school," he pointed out over dinner when Renault made the announcement.

"Neither have the majority of judges and officials in this country. Your point?"

Pierre picked at his food. "I don't know if I'm ready."

"Are you implying that my training has been lacking?"

Vivienne rolled her eyes.

"Of course not. But I've never done anything like this before on my own." He felt himself getting hot under his collar.

"The man's guilty, caught in the act. You cannot mess this up."

***

With Renault's vote of confidence, Pierre set out for the prison the next day. The building wasn't particularly large, holding only six cells, but its thick grey stone walls and small barred windows were an imposing sight. As Pierre opened the thick iron exterior door, he felt as if he was entering a cave. It was always damp and chilly no matter the weather outside. Pierre never expressed his opinions aloud, but he did feel badly for any poor soul who had to exist in such dreary conditions.

Émile Michel was being kept in solitude in the basement of the prison. Most of the prisoners were housed together, shouting and yelling as Pierre passed. For his own safety, Michel was alone, separated from the rest of the world.

The dungeons felt more like tombs than actual rooms. The young jailer, barely older than Pierre, led him through a maze of corridors, using a torch for light, until they reached the dungeon that housed Michel. Pierre wasn't sure what he was expecting. He had never met a murderer before. The man sat in the far corner of the cell, both of his legs fastened to the wall by a long chain. He didn't stand up or make any signs of recognition when Pierre greeted him.

Asking the jailer to hold his torch up so he could see into the corner of the cell, Pierre observed that Michel was wearing the rags of a beggar.

"Is that what he came in?" he whispered to the guard.

"Won't let any of us touch him since we brought him in. Bit two of the guards as they were locking him up."

The man was of medium build, and despite his torn clothes, he didn't appear to be starving. On the contrary, long ropes of muscles covered his bare forearms. He had a massive black beard that could easily be tucked into his belt, and his dark hair was wild, with twigs and leaves tangled throughout. How they had got there when the ground was covered in snow was anyone's guess.

Pierre took a deep breath. "Monsieur Michel, my name is Pierre Thibault. I work for the Procurator General. May I ask you some questions?"

Michel didn't move or give any indication that he had heard. Pierre glanced at the guard, who shrugged.

"Monsieur Michel, I'm here to try to find out what happened. To hear your side of the story." Pierre spoke louder than normal, his voice ringing off the stone walls.

Michel blinked but continued to stare straight ahead.

"If you could tell me your side of things, it might help you in the long run. If we could maybe come to some form of an understanding of what occurred the other night—"

Michel grunted and turned so his back was facing Pierre and the guard.

Pierre retreated a few steps to where the guard stood. "Has he been seen by a doctor?" he asked. "Do you know if he can hear?"

The guard looked over Pierre's shoulder to where the prisoner was now watching them intently, his eyes gleaming from the darkness. "He can hear all right. Talk too. Cursed us all and put up a violent fight when we brought him in."

"What do you know about him?"

The guard shrugged again, unconcerned. "Found out his name and that's about it. From Nicolet apparently." Nicolet was a tiny community some eighty miles away from the capital. "How he got here is anyone's guess. Had nothing on him save for a few *livres* and a massive dagger. Those are upstairs if you'd like to see them."

Pierre spent another quarter of an hour trying to get Michel to acknowledge his presence, but for all the good it did, he might as well have interviewed the wall. He eventually gave it up as a bad job and followed the guard back upstairs to inspect the prisoner's possessions.

***

The trial wasn't set until March of 1748. Justice was usually dispensed within a few days, but Quebec was without an executioner when Michel was taken into custody, and the trial was postponed until one could be found. While there was no proof that Émile Michel was the sole perpetrator of all the attacks that had occurred, there were no others after his capture. That was enough for guilt to be assumed.

Pierre set to work, researching and preparing as many notes as he could. Once a week, he went to the prison, but Michel continued to ignore him. It wasn't his problem, Pierre reminded himself. If the man had no story, he was only hurting himself. A defence official had been provided, since it appeared that Michel was a lunatic and incapable of finding his own defence, but Michel refused to talk to him as well.

Renault also decided that Pierre would now be his official representative. Until this point, Pierre had always started meetings apologizing for Renault's absence. Now no one expected to meet with Renault, as they knew Pierre was coming. While Renault would continue to hold the title of Procurator General, his only jobs were to sign official documents and meet with the Superior Council.

Taking over for Renault came with a pay raise and Pierre realized that soon he would be able to eke out his own living.

"Is there someone you would like to share this news with?" Renault had asked one night not long after the announcement was made.

"She hasn't written back. Last I heard, her aunt was trying to marry her off to some rich nobleman." Pierre didn't look up from the document he was writing.

"What ship did it go on?"

He had to stop and remember. "*Orion*, I think." He was trying his best not to think about the letter, the ship, or Marie.

Two days later, as Pierre sat scribbling a note to the mayor of Montreal, Renault came bursting into the office looking very excited. Pierre looked up. Since he had taken on the majority of the workload, Renault was having far too much fun with his free time.

"I found the *Orion*," he said proudly.

"What?"

"The boat that you sent your last letter on. It was harboured in Spain for a time, hiding from the British fleets. It only arrived in France in October."

Pierre continued to look up at him blankly, the ink slowly dripping off the end of his suspended quill, pooling on the paper beneath.

"She may not have married a rich nobleman or a poor clerk. You may still have a chance," Renault said impatiently.

Pierre refused to get excited but continued to work away. "Thank you," he mumbled after a while, "for finding that out."

March came, and the date of the trial loomed closer. Every night, Pierre looked over his notes before going to bed. Michel had refused to speak to anyone for the last month, including the priest who had visited him the night before the trial.

On the day of the proceedings, the sun was shining brightly off the glittering snow, and Pierre headed for the courthouse early in the morning. He had bought a new blue jacket for the occasion and had spent a quarter of an hour trying to wrestle his hair into a braid. It was a wasted effort. But before Pierre took his place in the spartan courtroom, Renault slammed a powdered white wig on his head, ignoring Pierre's protests.

Pierre had watched and even helped Renault play this role, but now it was his turn to act as prosecutor. He stared at the plain maple cross that hung at the front of the room. He wasn't God, but today he was going to do his best to send a man into the great hereafter. It was a sobering thought, and he worried he might be sick.

Pierre was surprised when the prisoner was brought in. Michel had been cleaned and shaved, and new, or at least clean, clothes had been put on him. He looked less like the monster he was accused of being and more like a labourer Augustus would have employed near the docks of Louisbourg. But Michel seemed diminished somehow, as if the months he had spent incarcerated had drained him of his life force.

Pierre sat in his hard, wooden seat and waited as the Judge introduced the parties involved. There was a prayer and then the spectacle began. Pierre wished this wasn't such a famous case and that less of the city had turned out to see it. Scanning the crowd, he did feel a pang of regret for the prisoner. Everyone in attendance had come to see him hang; not a family member was in sight. With a jolt, he realized that both Jean and Daniel were sitting at the back, waving jovially at him as if they had bumped into him at a card game and not at the trial of the year.

His name was called and Pierre stepped forward to present the evidence against Michel. It was known that Michel had been caught stabbing a Madame Claire Girat. While Madame Girat had survived, there was little doubt that Michel had been trying to kill her. There was also proof that Madame Girat had been assaulted in other ways by Michel before the police arrived to rescue her.

The more he spoke, the calmer Pierre became. Soon he was striding up and down the courtroom, speaking as calmly to the Judge as if he were talking with Renault back at the office.

While there was little more than coincidence to tie Michel to the six other murders and disappearances of young women, the lack of further attacks once he'd been apprehended strongly suggested that he was also behind them. Three of the bodies had been recovered, all the victims having been stabbed to death by a weapon matching the measurements of the blade found on Michel. All the women had been similarly assaulted and the chances of another man running around the area doing the exact same thing were very unlikely.

Madame Girat was not called to testify. It was felt that it would be too traumatic for a woman who had already been through so much. Instead, her husband took her place.

Monsieur Girat was a quiet man, a tanner with six children. The attack on his wife was brutal and senseless. He recounted taking his children to the hospital to see their mother and the pain the family had endured as she had struggled to heal. Madame Girat no longer left the house alone and kept the windows and doors locked at all times.

There was little that the defence could present. Poor Félix Poirier didn't look very happy, but he made a valiant effort. He was careful not to villainize any of the victims. One had been a nun, and clearly the Girats were productive members of society.

A verdict was reached in less than half an hour. No one was surprised by it, and the Judge seemed to find a great deal of pleasure in handing it down. Michel remained as stone faced as ever, as he was pulled from the room to meet his fate. For one brief moment, his eyes locked onto Pierre's, and immediately Pierre felt a shiver go down his spine. He had never seen eyes like that before and was sure he had just met Lucifer himself.

Pierre didn't wait to see justice being served. A large crowd was already gathered around the gallows, but he had no interest in being there. Pulling off the ridiculous wig, he packed up his belongings and turned to go home, but a gnarled hand on his shoulder stopped him.

"You cannot leave after a performance like that," Renault grinned up at him.

His legs still felt weak from the effort it had taken him to stride around the room, but now that the trial was over, he wasn't sure why he had been so nervous.

With Renault on one side and Jean on the other, he was steered to one of the taverns down the street. It was a step above most of the taverns frequented by sailors, but that wasn't saying much. It was a dark, dingy place with a bar that ran the length of the room, cutting it in half. The wood floor looked as if it had last been cleaned when it was installed, but no one but Pierre seemed to mind.

Jean had obviously picked the place, as he was on a first-name basis with the owner. Jean was also never concerned about appearances. After placing orders, he started a card game and proceeded to challenge anyone in the vicinity.

A massive tankard of ale was placed before Pierre. With little practice in the last three years, he had some doubts about his ability to hold alcohol, but he wasn't about to express those concerns. Even Renault had replaced his usual brandy for a glass of something pale green.

Uncle Tomas eventually joined them, as did the clerks. Jean continued to supply Pierre with a steady stream of drinks, completely oblivious to the latter's protests that he couldn't handle anymore. More people were arriving, and Pierre had the vague sense that he should know who they were, but it was becoming more and more difficult to remember names.

The last thing he remembered was Jean challenging him to a fight. He couldn't remember why. He knew Jean wasn't mad at him. He lay in bed trying to pull the details back into focus, but that only made his head hurt. He tried to open one eye, but the light streaming in through the window made it feel as if it was burning. He threw his pillow over his head and rolled over. The movement almost made him vomit.

"Good morning," the all-too-happy voice of Renault announced a short while later. "How is the newest prosecutor doing this morning?"

Pierre just groaned. His mouth tasted as if something had died in there. "Keep it down."

"But why? It's a lovely day. The sun is shining," Renault chirped, pulling back the drapes. "You won your first case." He was purposely stomping around the room, making as much noise as possible.

"Just let me die."

Renault laughed. "Then you'd never get to read your letter."

Pierre's eyes snapped open. Bloodshot as they were from the night before, he squinted, trying to see the writing on the envelope Renault was dangling in front of him.

"Are you sure you want to read this?" Renault held the letter up. He was having far too much fun to stop goading Pierre now.

Pierre sat up and snatched the letter away. Not very steady, he collapsed back on the mattress, his head pounding.

"I told you she never married."

Pierre flipped the envelope over. It was still sealed. "How do you know that?"

Renault grinned. "Married women do not write to single men. Especially ones who live on the other side of the world." Still chortling, he stepped out of the room and closed the door behind him.

Pierre lay in bed, trying to get his eyes to focus. When he could finally see straight, he ripped the letter free from its casing.

Dear Pierre,

I thought you'd forgotten about me. When your letter came and I realized the Orion had just been delayed, I felt rather foolish for doubting you.

The war will be over soon! Claude has written from Versailles to say that the leaders are speaking, trying to come to terms that they can all agree on. He also says that Louisbourg may be one of the bargaining chips that is used. We may be able to go home. I realize home to you now is Quebec, but I hope I can see the island again.

I don't want to marry any stupid nobleman and I told Annette that. She finally seems to understand that I'm serious. There was a lot of whining and crying, but what else is new? I don't want to have to stay in this country any longer than I have to.

I hope you know that I've never loved you because of your father's money. Nor did I ever once think about it. I love you because you listen and you make me laugh. You never ran away from me when I was upset. I think you're the first person after my parents' death who actually cared about what I had to say. I know Elise, Nic, and Madame Badeau did, now that I think about it, but that spoils the mood. I didn't want you to leave Louisbourg. I would have gone with you if you had asked.

Know that you aren't forgotten, but I'm glad you're happy in Quebec. If I do return to Louisbourg, I expect a visit.

Love, Marie

Pierre stretched, his head still pounding. He wished more than anything that he could see her right now and tell her about the trial. He could write to her, but it wasn't the same. There would be other trials, he reminded himself. Maybe she would come for those.

Chapter 6

THE WAR OF THE AUSTRIAN SUCCESSION, as it would come to be known, ended in October 1748 with the signing of the Treaty of Aix-la-Chapelle. After two implementation treaties were signed in December of that year, Louisbourg was given back to the French. Louis XV gave all the territory in the Netherlands conquered by the French back to the Austrians. Of course, the French people weren't happy about this state of affairs, since it appeared that the war had been a complete waste of lives and money. However, the people of New France celebrated the return of Louisbourg, and they admired Louis for securing Île-Royale.

By early April, the news of peace had arrived in Quebec with the first ship of the year, and François Bigot called on Pierre personally to give him the news before the official announcement was made. Then the information was made public, and fireworks and parties broke out in the street. An entire week went by before life returned to any sort of normalcy. In the midst of the festivities, Pierre received another letter from Marie—just a few weeks after the first. She was finally going home, she wrote, and she couldn't be more excited, though Marie and her family wouldn't be leaving until July, as Claude had unfinished business at Court. She'd been away four long years, but the fortress was waiting for her, and that was all she cared about. She promised to write once she arrived in September, but she said nothing about what would happen once she was home.

Pierre had celebrated with the rest of the colony, but he knew he wouldn't be returning to Louisbourg with the other displaced residents. His life was in the capital now. His father had sent word that he too was going back to Louisbourg, but he'd said nothing about wanting Pierre to visit.

Pierre carried on with his work, but he had trouble focusing. Renault never mentioned Louisbourg unless Pierre brought the subject up, but Pierre rarely did that. He felt as if his entire life hinged upon whether Marie successfully crossed the Atlantic, and he didn't want to reveal his deep anxiety to Renault or anyone else.

Summer and autumn went by with no word. The river froze, and the city was covered in its usual blanket of white. The snow was so deep this year that it was impossible to navigate even the main arteries of the city without snowshoes.

Pierre knew he should have been accustomed to Quebec's winters by now. It was his fourth snowy season in the capital, but somehow, he was never prepared when the freezing winds came.

***

It was another snapping cold night in January 1750. Pierre sat by the fire in the office, the only one still working at that late hour. To fight off the chill, he kept his hat on and was wearing a pair of fingerless gloves. Renault was out late at another meeting of the Superior Council. He'd been gone for hours, but Pierre was waiting up, hoping to meet with his mentor before they both retired for the night.

Pierre now ran the business completely, travelling when needed. Renault was greatly enjoying his much-reduced responsibilities and was keen for Pierre to take over on paper as well as in practice. However, because Pierre had never attended law school in France, he could not officially take over as Procurator General. Renault was fighting to have that law changed, but in the meantime, he was the one who continued to deal with the Superior Council. Pierre had no complaints about that. The meetings dragged on far longer than they needed to, since each man's ego had to rear its ugly head before any actual decisions were made.

It was well past midnight when the door blew open, snow swirling into the room and up to the oak desk where Pierre was sitting. Renault shut the door quickly, cursing the weather as he took off his coat. I'm getting too old for this climate, he thought miserably. If he could get Pierre to officially take over, he could retire to the sunny hills of Southern France.

"What are you still doing up?" Renault wiped the snowflakes from his greying goatee. "Whatever projects you have can't be that important." It was true that Pierre's days of working perpetually long hours, morning and night, were long behind him. One of the upstairs maids now cleaned and organized the room in the morning, and Gagné, the clerk, prepared the next day's work.

Pierre shrugged and continued writing. "Do you ever read a case and think the victim deserved his punishment?"

Renault's bark-like laugh filled the dark room as he pulled off his thick overcoat. "Are you referring to Gaston Laflamme? I'm surprised no one killed him sooner." Renault peered over Pierre's shoulder. "However, it was still murder. Did you get the statement from the brother-in-law?"

"It wasn't hard; the man was sitting in prison awaiting his trial. Unlike Michel, this man was eager to talk, trying to justify his actions." Pierre rubbed his eyes. He never enjoyed a trip to the prison.

"You should retire," Renault clapped his twisted hand on the shoulder and chuckled. "Not as young as you once were."

Pierre stretched and yawned. "I had a question for you."

Renault stopped and pulled up a chair. He was dead on his feet, but he had a feeling he knew what this was going to be about.

"Most of the people are back in Louisbourg now, trying to rebuild their lives."

Renault nodded. He was surprised it had taken Pierre this long to bring up the subject.

"Have you heard from your father?"

"Yes, he's settling in fine, though apparently the British did a terrible job of rebuilding during their occupation." Pierre stared into the firelight. "But that's not it."

"That girl." Renault's yellow eyes twinkled. Pierre looked surprised. "You received another letter from her today. Vivienne told me. Are you ever going to tell me anything about her?"

Pierre felt a little embarrassed. "Marie Lévesque. She's a friend from home."

Renault mused for a moment. "She's not related to Caleb Lévesque, is she? the officer?"

Pierre laughed. "Her father. She moved to Louisbourg after Caleb and his wife died."

Renault leaned back in his chair. "Small world. I remember him from years ago. He came here on assignment and met Colette, his wife, while he was here. Refused to go back to France. Said they could shoot him or give him a new posting. Always liked his daring." He stared off into the distance, lost in memory.

Pierre allowed him a few moments, then interrupted. "I was wondering if she would come here."

"You don't need my permission for that."

Pierre looked up. "Really?"

Renault chortled, rapping his knuckles on the wooden desktop. "You're twenty-two. I think it would be healthy for you to move out. I could turn your chamber into something useful." His eyes twinkled. "You can walk to work."

Renault had never understood the spell this girl from home had cast. Pierre was young, good looking, and well educated, and with his job as Renault's assistant, he made a desirable companion, but he had no interest in the women here. "I look forward to meeting her."

Pierre fiddled absentmindedly with a spare quill. "Could I go there?"

Renault thought for a moment. He was enjoying his semi-retirement, and if Pierre left, even temporarily, his card game would suffer. "She wouldn't follow you here?" he asked, stalling his moment of decision making.

"Yes, she might. After all, she was born here, though ... you know how that ended. I sort of already asked. But I'd like to see the fortress again. Feel the ocean breeze."

Renault's knuckles picked up speed as they beat a steady rhythm against the table. "A fortnight," he said eventually. "But ask her first. That is a great amount of money and time to spend if she were to reject you. When is the Laflamme trial again?"

"Three days from now."

"Fine. Once the river thaws. Take one of Tomas's boats. He'll get you there in good time."

Pierre tried very hard not to grin. He knew it was a sacrifice for Renault to let him go because he'd have to go back to spending hours doing paperwork and interviewing people who were lying through their teeth. It was a young man's game, Renault had often said whenever Pierre complained.

Later that night, Pierre sat in his room, which, as usual, was just as cold as the office. Snow had piled up high against the glass windows, and the lone candle sputtered against the night air. Wrapped in a heavy woollen blanket, Pierre stared at a blank piece of paper he'd placed on the desk in front of him.

That morning, he'd finally received the long-awaited letter from Marie. It had been delivered by some intrepid explorers who had snowshoed across the frozen land between Louisbourg and Quebec. Pierre thought they were an odd bunch for travelling in such weather, but he admired their courage and was grateful to them. He learned from the letter that Marie had arrived back in Louisbourg in September—on one of the last boats carrying the former inhabitants of Louisbourg back from France. They'd made the trip safely and in relatively good health, and Marie was now back in the manor house overlooking the harbour. Nic had survived, having suffered no lasting physical damage from his time in Boston, although she said he refused to talk about the experience.

Pierre had always wondered if Marie would come back to New France. Despite her reassurances, a shadow of doubt had often crept into his mind. That's one reason why he'd waited until she was on the continent again before fully revealing his feelings for her. Since he'd been so churlish, deserting her in Louisbourg before he'd left for Quebec, he couldn't be sure that she'd trust him now. Not for the first time, he wished he hadn't let her go but had just helped her escape with him through the wilderness to Quebec.

He continued to stare at the blank piece of paper, knowing that morning was coming fairly soon, and if he didn't get some sleep, tomorrow was going to be painful. Finally, he picked up his quill and scribbled a few lines.

Marie,

Would you come to Quebec? I know you've just come home, but I miss you so much. I can find a place to rent. It won't be anything grand, but it would be enough for the two of us. I can take care of you now. Renault is trying his best to have me officially take over all of his duties. There's an issue because I never went to law school, but even if he doesn't succeed in convincing the French government to waive that requirement, I can still work here as an official or judge. It would be a stable life. I know you have no connections here except your uncle, and I don't think he's presently stationed here. But I have family and you would find people soon enough.

I love you,
Pierre

He wanted to write more, but he was too afraid. He put the letter into an envelope, sealed it, and locked the missive in his bottom desk drawer, where no one would find it.

Pierre eventually found an eccentric pair of trappers travelling to Acadia in the dead of winter, who promised to see the letter delivered for a fee. Pierre didn't completely trust them but felt it was worth a try. In the worst case, he'd have to re-send the letter when the river thawed and boats were travelling again.

The nearby region of Acadia wasn't peaceful, though. Since the Treaty of Utretch in 1713, the Acadians, located on the mainland west of Île-Royale, had been under the rule of the British. The Acadians tried their best to remain neutral. They'd promised to not raise arms in support of Louis XIV, but they'd refused to pledge allegiance to King George II. They did not want to disown their French roots. For forty years, they had successfully balanced these two contradictory positions, but things were now becoming serious for them. The British ruling government was growing impatient, and the fate of these people was becoming a matter of intense debate. There was talk among the British officials of just getting rid of the entire population.

In early April, a reply arrived, carried by one of the first boats coming from Île-Royale.

He didn't open it until late that night when he was alone in his room.

The piece of paper bore only one word: *Yes.*

He wrote a letter to Marie and then another to his father, telling them he was heading out to Louisbourg and would see them in a few weeks. Daniel then helped him find a small apartment not far from Renault's offices. It wasn't difficult. Quebec was a city full of transients, and rooms of one sort or another were always available. He then booked passage on the *Gloire*, said his goodbyes to Uncle Tomas and his cousins, and set off for Louisbourg to bring back his bride.

***

Marie stood in the corner of the de la Rocque's large ballroom in mid-May of 1750. Augustin de Drucour, the new Governor, had replaced Louis Du Pont

Duchambon. Duchambon and his family, including Charlotte, had stayed in France. They had no desire to continue living in the difficult conditions of the colony. Governor Drucour had held a party of epic proportions at the end of the summer in 1749 when most of the residents of Louisbourg had returned to the fortress from France. Paper lanterns had been hung in the gardens, a huge feast had been laid out, and the dancing had lasted until dawn. The city's clergymen had not been pleased.

This year, 1750, the de la Rocque family had decided to hold a ball as part of its continuing tradition of reminding the rest of Île-Royale that their family were of importance in France. Marie found him insufferable, but his connections were enough to keep the rest of the upper class simpering at his feet. She knew vaguely from Pierre's letters that the rest of New France wasn't quite like this. Less cut off from the rest of the world, the Valley of the Saint-Laurent wasn't nearly as impressed by a relative of a remote Duke and focused more on the leaders who actually contributed to society.

All the same, Marie was relieved to be back in Louisbourg. It was as much her home as it had been in her mind when she was missing it so desperately in France. It looked exactly as it had when she'd last seen it, but that was a problem. The walls were in ruins, since the British soldiers and civilians hadn't bothered to fix most of the damage that had been done during the siege. Some repairs were complete, but even those were just quick fixes for the military that had been stationed there. Drucour had ordered massive renovations for the fortress, and 3,500 new soldiers were stationed there. The Swiss regiment had not returned, nor had they been invited.

But it was still Louisbourg. Most of the old inhabitants were back as well as several new ones, and the place felt like home, even though she was standing in a corner of the ballroom, wishing desperately that someone she knew would show up. She'd received Pierre's letter a few days previously, and her stomach had been in knots ever since she'd read it. Almost five years had passed since she'd last seen him. Five years could change a lot, but she hoped what he'd said in his last letter really was true and that he hadn't changed his mind since writing it.

Marie had put extra effort into her appearance. Her hair had been carefully curled and set so the curls hung artistically around her face. Her pale-blue dress fit her perfectly, and she'd borrowed simple earrings from Elise and had allowed her friend to do her makeup. But still she worried. She'd made herself sick yesterday wondering what if, what if, what if.

A moment later, Sophie de la Rocque walked in on the arm of her new fiancé, Philippe Eurry de la Pérelle. She walked among the guests, ebony hair held high, accepting their greetings and congratulations. Philippe was the son of the city's major and therefore had some prominence.

Marie knew that Sophie was only too thrilled about her upcoming marriage because of Philippe's high position in Louisbourg society. Her wedding to Philippe would also mean that she would no longer have to be terrified of being single for the rest of her life. Her fear of never marrying was how, in the past, she'd found herself in a few compromising positions with Nic. Sophie was doubly elated because the marriage had been jeopardized by the siege. Only when peace returned and Philippe's father had been reinstated as major in Louisbourg did the actual wedding become a reality.

Sophie spotted Marie and made her way across the room alone, her green eyes dancing. "Guess what I did today?" she exploded without any introduction.

Marie eyed her acquaintance with amusement and some disgust. During the deportation, Sophie had been stuck in southern France, hundreds of miles away from Marie, and that geographical distance had not brought them any closer together in their personal non-relationship.

"Today I convinced Philippe we should have a Christmas wedding."

"Where will you go afterwards if everyone is covered in snow?"

Sophie waved her hand dismissively and bounced her dark curls. "I don't care. He can figure it out. I just think that getting married in winter will be so romantic."

Marie laughed. Sophie didn't have a practical bone in her body. "And it's bound to be all the more romantic, since it will take an hour to get to church because everyone will be snowed in."

Sophie threw Marie a dirty look. Before she could respond, Marie spotted Elise and her cousin Diane across the room and waved them over. They happily obliged. Marie hadn't seen Elise very often during their exile. Though she lived only twenty miles away in the next town, Annette was too nervous to let Marie take the carriage. It was a long time to be without her best friend. They'd spent most of the last few months talking late into the night when Marie went for sleepovers at Elise's home. Marie was only too happy to escape the cavernous manor house, where Annette and Claude had resumed their frosty relationship now that they were no longer bound together by the common British enemy. After several late-night conversations, it felt as if she and Elise had never been apart. Elise knew all about Pierre's impending visit and Marie's nerves.

"He's here," Elise whispered in Marie's ear. Marie looked around quickly but didn't spot him. She thought she might sweat through her gown if she didn't calm down soon.

"Who's here?" Sophie snapped. "Is there a Duke visiting?"

"Pierre," Elise said with an eyeroll.

"Why didn't you tell us?" Diane demanded.

"I didn't think you cared?" Marie asked, faltering under the glare of her companions. Marie had the distinct impression Sophie still had a soft spot for Pierre.

Elise nodded toward the far door, where a thin crowd of people had gathered. Diane and Sophie followed her gaze.

He must have grown, if that was possible. He'd let his hair grow longer so even though it was pulled back, some still hung over his eyes, framing his face. He carried himself differently too—with great confidence. His broad frame had filled out, and his muscles were packed tightly around his bones. He no longer looked at all like the scrawny teenager who'd caused so much trouble. He stopped in the doorway and looked around, trying to spot someone.

"Go and talk to him," Elise whispered to Marie, prodding her in the back.

"He has other people to talk to," Marie said.

Elise was growing impatient. "Yes, because he came back to see a bunch of people he hasn't spoken to in years," Elise huffed. "Don't be silly! He came to see you."

"Have you been writing to him?" Sophie asked. She didn't look at Marie for an answer but stared at Elise instead. Elise picked at her nails.

"We're *friends*," Marie snapped, but no one believed her. Pierre turned in the direction of where Marie was standing. Reluctantly, heart hammering in her chest, Marie waved her arm in the air nervously.

Pierre spotted her and grinned. Then his face suddenly changed to a look of confusion and something else—something Marie couldn't identify. He started toward her, and because of his size, he easily made his way through the crowd as if he were Moses parting the Red Sea.

"I don't think he wants to be friends anymore," Sophie said, making Diane and Elise giggle. Marie barely had time to hiss at them before Pierre drew up in front of her. He must have grown. Either that or she never really appreciated how tall he really was.

There was a time when she would have teased him for standing awkwardly at a dance in an ill-fitting jacket, trying his hardest to catch the eye of an attractive debutante. But those days were obviously over.

"Hello, beautiful," he laughed. She'd forgotten what his voice sounded like, how deep and husky his laugh was. For a moment, her brain forgot how to work. "You're more gorgeous than I remember." The awe in his voice was clear.

"I don't know if the surprise is really complimentary," she chided. However, she had grown and matured in the last five years, and now almost twenty, with her thick, chestnut hair and creamy complexion, she now knew she was attractive to others.

"It's not," he admitted a little breathlessly, "but you've always been beautiful. I guess I just didn't remember."

Marie wanted to get off this subject. "Have you grown?"

He had to bend slightly to make himself heard. "About three inches."

"Three inches?! You'll soon have to duck to get through doorways."

"I've been doing that for years," he laughed. "Just have to bend over a bit more now."

The musicians were beginning a new piece. "Come and dance with me," Pierre said, holding out his arm.

Marie didn't really want to dance with him. For one thing, she was a terrible dancer. For another, she'd decided to borrow shoes from Elise that were slightly too small, and she was already losing circulation in her toes. But even more important, all Marie wanted to do was talk to him, find out all about his life in Quebec, the stuff that hadn't made it into the letters.

And she said as much to Pierre: "We have so much to talk about. How can we do that when we're dancing or when you're dancing and I'm falling over?"

Pierre's blue eyes twinkled. "There'll be time for talk, I promise."

Grudgingly, Marie accepted and went to take her place in the line across from Pierre. He smiled reassuringly. "I know you hate dancing with an audience but just a few sets and then no one will pay us any attention."

Marie doubted that. She could almost feel the eyes of Lady Isabelle, the town gossip, burrowing into the back of her skull. The dance was a simple one, and Marie was grateful for that because she wouldn't need to think too hard and could focus instead on her companion. Her hands were still sweaty with nerves, though, so she tried to wipe them surreptiously on her skirts.

"You look well," Marie said to Pierre between dance steps. That was an understatement to say the least.

Pierre laughed. "I could say the same to you. France obviously agreed with you even if you hated it."

Marie smiled. "You paid attention when you read my letters."

"I hope so. You're the only one who wrote to me."

Marie stopped in surprise, and the woman next to her crashed into her, sending them both toppling into a nearby table. The music stopped, and with cheeks glowing, Marie stammered a hasty apology. She wished the floor would open and devour her. She'd spent the last fortnight counting down the days to Pierre's arrival and now she wanted to run away.

Pierre was trying not to laugh, but he wasn't succeeding.

"Really? No one else ever wrote to you?" That was a rather unfortunate revelation. She was thrilled that she was the only woman to write him but it put more pressure on all the letters she had sent him. Pierre shrugged, unconcerned. She looked behind Pierre to see Diane, Elise, and Sophie gossiping and giggling behind their fans. Diane blew them a kiss. Throwing caution to the winds, Marie grabbed Pierre's arm, dragged him away from the dancers, and steered him toward a door leading to a garden. He was guffawing intermittently all the way and didn't stop until they'd found a quiet spot to sit.

Elise, Diane, and Sophie and an embarrassed Philippe tried to follow but were waylaid by the Governor, who was quite pleased to find himself surrounded by three attractive women. He completely misread the situation and launched into a lengthy dialogue, giving Marie and Pierre a chance to escape.

"It's not funny," Marie said crossly once they were in the safety of the garden.

Pierre tried to control himself. "I'm glad you haven't changed."

Marie crossed her arms and ignored him while he regained his composure. Her face was on fire.

"Surely I wasn't the only one who wrote to you."

"No," he admitted. "But even the letters from my father were sporadic at best. You wrote me every month. Sometimes six of them would arrive at once. It was nice."

Pierre found a decorated wood bench tucked between a bed of roses and some rhubarb, and he beckoned her to follow him. Still supremely self-conscious, Marie sat beside him. His hand brushed hers. For a moment, she thought it was an accident. Then his little finger gently intertwined with hers.

It was time to say something. "I missed you," she said, barely above a whisper. "Annette and I stayed in the country while Claude attended Court. We were less than a mile from where your father was living. It made me sad thinking of the trouble we could have stirred up and the fun we could have had if you'd been there."

He laughed again, a great belly laugh that filled the garden. "We could have raised some eyebrows." He pushed one of the curls that fell across her forehead out of the way. "Tell me about France."

There wasn't much to tell that she hadn't already told him. Her letters were always twice the length of his. She told him about going to Paris and visiting the Court of Versailles—how people looked down on her for being a lowly "Canadian" even while they were wrapped in furs from the colony. She told him how Annette had tried more than once to set her up with an eligible bachelor of the Court who was willing to look beyond her "wildness." She had refused everyone. She couldn't imagine spending the rest of her life in such a boring world with no ocean or wilderness, where people created their own drama to distract themselves from the meaninglessness of their own lives.

Pierre listened attentively, but she could tell that the world she was describing was as foreign to him as the West Indies were to her.

"You really don't want to spend your life with all that finery?" It seemed easier than constantly fighting against the wilderness here.

Marie rolled her eyes. "At Versailles, people actually fight for the chance to watch the King relieve himself. It's the most ridiculous thing ever. I couldn't live there another moment."

Pierre didn't believe that piece of information. It was too bizarre to be true. So he told her about Quebec, the family he had met there, his cousins and his work. He told her about Renault and their adventures together and the wars he had fought in the courtroom. Marie had never seen him so at peace as he described the world he had built for himself. For his part, Pierre was surprised by how much there was to tell. He thought he'd communicated everything in his letters, but the words just kept spilling out of him.

Other people walked through the garden, seeking a reprieve from the heat of so many bodies packed together in the house. Marie and Pierre ignored them all, focusing only on each other. And the butterflies in both of their stomachs began to slowly dissolve.

"Is Annette here tonight?" Pierre asked eventually. He was surprised she hadn't come to interrupt them yet.

Marie shook her head, the tight curls bouncing around her face. "No. Two days ago she developed another one of her headaches. Possibly the worst she's ever had. I've never seen her so sick. She's still in bed."

"That's a shame."

"All sorts of people have been coming in to see her to try to solve the problem, but so far, nothing has helped." Marie was beginning to worry. Annette may have enjoyed drama, but this was beyond her usual actions.

"Want to go for a walk?" Pierre stretched his large frame. Sitting for long periods of time wasn't that comfortable for him, since the world hadn't been made for someone his size.

They took a turn around the garden, pausing to let others go ahead of them on the narrow stone pathway. As they neared the shadow of the house, Pierre led her off the path toward a secluded spot under a bent and gnarled fruit tree.

He pulled her close and bent his head to kiss her. She wrapped her arms around his neck, trying to close the space between them. His tongue was sweet and restless in her mouth, and her fingers tangled in his hair. His hand began to creep up her bodice when the sound of footsteps broke them apart.

Breathless, she leaned her head against his jacket, feeling her heartbeat return to normal.

"I've wanted to do that for a long time," he sighed, resting his chin on top of her head.

Marie giggled and wrapped her arms around his middle. "I hope I didn't disappoint."

He scoffed. As the footsteps faded, he lifted her into the air, spinning her around as she shrieked. He let her down gently to her feet before bending to kiss her again.

"Oy!" They broke apart. Nic stood a few feet away from them, his arms folded tightly across his chest. He appeared to be contemplating a murder.

Pierre looked slightly ashamed. "Hey, Nic."

"Long time," Nic replied, his dark features stony.

Marie rolled her eyes. "Do you need something?" she asked pointedly.

Nic ignored her. "I see you found my sister." He gave his friend a significant look. "Want a drink?"

Marie wanted to throw something at her brother, but Pierre put an arm around her waist and led her back into the party, motioning to Nic to come with them. Pierre hadn't seen Nic in years either. Best to placate him before he did something regrettable like punch him.

The three of them picked up some drinks and sat down at a table at the edge of the ballroom. Nic spent the next hour talking animatedly to Pierre. It was the most Marie had heard him speak since his return from Boston. He carefully stepped around his incarceration but continued to produce new subjects of discussion. Every time Pierre tried to bring up the hour, Nic suddenly lost his ability to hear and barrelled into the next topic.

Marie was bored, and Nic was purposely excluding her. She was debating with herself about just going home when Pierre reached under the table and squeezed her hand. He hadn't forgotten about her but was just humouring her brother. After all, they were best friends, and Nic hadn't been permitted to send out letters from behind British lines.

The party dragged on into the early hours of the morning as Nic and Pierre talked on and on. Marie caught Elise's eye from across the room once or twice but was unwilling to abandon Pierre to fill her friend in on what was going on.

Eventually, Pierre was able to extricate himself from Nic, who headed back to the King's Bastion, cheered by the drinks and the talk. Pierre took Marie's hand, lifted her out of her chair, and got ready to walk her home.

The salty sea air mixed with the low-hanging mist brought comfort to them both. Pierre had to admit that even the smell of cod had a certain appeal after all this time.

"May I call on you tomorrow?" he asked as the great manor appeared out of the gloom. Despite the late hour, noises were still floating up from the docks. The heart of the Louisbourg harbour never really stopped beating. "Nic won't be around, he's busy making sure the cadets rebuild this place."

"Why would you be interested?" Marie smiled.

"Well, I have two weeks before I go back. I need something to occupy my time."

"I may be at home. You'll have to drop by in the morning and see."

"Nine o'clock? or is that too early for m'lady from Versailles?"

"M'lady lives in Louisbourg now. Nine o'clock is just right. Come in the kitchen way."

"Why, I'm not good enough for the front door?"

"Oh, don't be silly. Madame Badeau would like to see you and approve of you or not!"

"Nine o'clock it is, Ma'am."

Pierre grinned, the moonlight flashing off his teeth. He gently brushed Marie's lips with his and retreated back into the night.

Marie knew it was silly, but all she could think of was the last time he'd left her and how he hadn't come back. Not for years.

***

The physician arrived at the manor house early the next morning but still came up with no cure for Annette's ailments. Marie had risen at seven o'clock, after only a few hours of rest, unable to sleep because she was so excited to be seeing Pierre again. She met the doctor in the hallway and thought he might have a message of hope, but he just shook his head sadly. Marie went over to Annette's bedroom to check on her but the sight she saw just reinforced the doctor's pessimism. Her skin was grey and she seemed extremely weak. Marie had never seen headaches have this kind of an effect on her, nor did they last this long.

Seeing that she could do nothing to help Annette, Marie went downstairs for breakfast, trying to keep her hands from shaking with excitement as she took a mug of hot milk from Madame Badeau. Then she headed into the front sitting room and started working her way through a pile of mending that had piled up. In France, she had been surprised to learn that women of high birth there felt such chores were below them. Some of them didn't even know how to thread a needle. And that was only one of the reasons they would never have survived if they'd been forced to live in Louisbourg.

She checked the progress of the sun every few minutes. The aroma of baking bread drifted from the kitchen and all through the house, but even that enticing smell couldn't distract Marie from fixating on Pierre. She'd almost made her way through a bunch of stockings when a visitor was announced. Pierre! Marie threw the mending she was working on back into the pile and jumped up ... and then sat down again. She didn't want to look too eager.

She walked slowly toward the kitchen, smoothing her apron as she went. That lasted for half a minute. As she picked up speed, she ended up skidding into the kitchen, slipping on the smooth floor, and having to save herself by grabbing onto the wooden table. Out of the corner of her eye, she could see Madame Badeau trying hard to keep a straight face. Pierre hadn't been exaggerating; he really did have to duck noticeably to get through the doorway. He looked taller than ever, standing in the small entranceway. Marie tried not to laugh with relief that he was once again standing in her home.

"Want to go to the market?" he asked. He'd assumed rightly that whatever conversation they had wouldn't be private if they stayed at the house.

Marie pretended to mull this proposition over. "If it's the only thing available."

Pierre ignored that comment, let Marie take off her apron, and took her arm to steer her out of the house.

"I wasn't sure you'd show up," Marie teased.

Pierre chuckled. "I hope I never become predictable or boring. Madame Badeau looked rather interested to see me."

Marie shook her head. "That woman is the worst eavesdropper in the world. She's an expert housekeeper, but I'll be glad to be rid of her following everything I do and say."

"What makes you think you'll be rid of her soon?" Pierre asked in an innocent tone. Marie didn't answer, but her stomach flipped unpleasantly. Maybe he'd changed his mind after all.

The spring weather was as warm as it had been during that last meeting, in May 1745, when cannonballs were raining down from the sky. But the mood of the fortress couldn't have been more different. The streets were alive with sellers pushing their wares along the busy streets and toward the marketplace. Children ran through the crowd, chasing each other as their mothers ran their daily errands. The market was bustling and full of the sounds of cattle gently lowing in their enclosures and chickens cackling in their cages. The sounds of the reconstruction of the walls mixed with the breeze coming off the ocean.

"Did you miss this?" Marie asked.

Pierre surveyed the once-familiar scenes, which were now foreign to him after so many years away. "It's much the same in Quebec ... just bigger and no fish. I sure didn't miss the smell of cod or the barrels of cod liver oil that always line up along the docks. And Quebec was more exciting, since it's full of people from all over the world."

"There are people from all over the world here too," Marie pointed out as they passed by a group of Spaniards just landed from the West Indies.

"Not just from around the world, from everywhere else in the colony: Montreal, the bayous of Louisiana, Ohio, even Lake Ontario. And there aren't as many pirates or smugglers," he said, noticing the gold glinting in one man's ear. "Or maybe they just hide it better."

Marie stopped to admire a bundle of fine merino wool, running her fingers along the delicate fibres.

"I've booked passage back to Quebec a week Tuesday," Pierre said slowly. Marie's breath caught in her throat, but she kept looking at the table of wool so Pierre wouldn't see the disappointment in her face. "The *Cassard* is one of my father's ships," Pierre continued, "so it shouldn't be too terrible on board." Pierre looked over at the wool. "There are two spots," he added slowly, "if you would still like to go."

Marie tried to stay composed but couldn't help grinning like an idiot. Pierre looked as nervous as she felt. "I already told you."

"You might have changed your mind." Pierre was serious. "Once we're married, you can't get out of it."

Marie took a step closer to him. "I haven't changed my mind. I don't want to get out of it! The answer is still yes."

With a roar of delight, Pierre picked her up and crushed her in his arms. People were starting to stare as he finally set her down. Marie was breathless but led him away from the crowds to find a less populated spot. The man might not care about decorum, but Annette certainly would if she learned that Marie was being embraced by the merchant's son in public.

"When?" Marie asked, her blood bubbling with the happiness of the decision made between them. She paid no mind to the world around them and almost toppled over a small boy carrying a bundle of wood.

Pierre shrugged. "Whenever you like. I really don't care as long as it's before the boat leaves."

"Tonight?" Marie asked seriously.

He laughed. "Why are you in such a rush?" he asked, curious. Renault had warned him that women made plans for weddings far ahead of time that men knew nothing about.

Marie linked her arm through his. "Why wait?"

"I could think of a few reasons—mainly Annette and Elise. You wouldn't want to deny them the opportunity to make a big deal out of this. It is a once-in-a-lifetime event," he teased, his blue eyes dancing.

Marie made a face, thinking of what Annette and Elise might plan if they were given the chance. Elise always wanted Marie to be fancier than she was. "They'll just have to be disappointed. If we ask nicely, Father Allard might marry us on short notice. Otherwise, we'll do it in Quebec when we arrive."

Pierre laughed again, rolling his eyes. "Well, I'm not willing to wait until then. I booked only one cabin. Maybe it's a good thing Annette is sick in bed."

As they continued to stroll around the city, Pierre was amazed by the extent of the damage the last few days of the siege had inflicted.

"Do you have a place in Quebec?" Marie was curious. She assumed he had found somewhere for them to live, but she wouldn't put it past him to forget.

"Are you worried about staying with the Renaults?" Pierre teased.

She'd heard enough about his employer to trust that he'd taken great care of Pierre, but she wasn't thrilled about the idea of living in a drafty spare room.

"Don't worry," he said, seeing the concern on her face. "Daniel and I found a place near Renault's office. It's not what you're used to here, though. It's pretty modest."

"Why are you so worried about that?" Marie asked. "I don't care. Really, I don't. As long as we're not in the spare room. Claude and Annette want for nothing. They have all the money in the world, but they're miserable, absolutely miserable. But I'll be with you for the rest of my life, and that is all I want, even if we have to count our pennies."

"France didn't solve Claude and Annette's problems?"

Marie snorted. "He spent all his time at Versailles, and she spent all her time in the countryside."

Marie and Pierre decided that he would speak with Claude that evening when the man finally returned home for the night. They didn't actually need his permission, but both felt it would be polite to ask. Claude wouldn't like it, but eloping in the middle of the night would have caused more of a spectacle. Neither of them cared much about the ceremony as long as it happened, and Augustus had space for them until their departure date.

Before then, Pierre had business to attend to. Renault had asked for a report on the current state of the governance in Louisbourg to present to the rest of the Superior Council. The information wasn't vital, since Louisbourg was a political entity of its own, but since his assistant was going there anyway, he thought it might be useful to gain some insights into what was going on at the fortress.

Marie floated home, unaware of her surroundings. Everything looked beautiful, and it felt as if nothing in the world would ever go wrong again. Even the crumbling stone walls held a certain charm. When Madame Badeau met her at the door, her suspicions were quickly confirmed just by the astonishing radiance emanating from Marie's face.

"But why else would Pierre come back after all this time?" the housekeeper asked.

"Well, maybe because he was working so hard and couldn't afford the fare?"

"Oh, now really," Madame Badeau snorted. "You never did stop waiting for him, so that must be love. Go and tell Annette; she could use the lift."

Annette was awake but still in bed, the window curtains closed tightly against the light of day. Taking a closer look at her aunt, Marie could see that she'd lost a great deal of weight and her skin had the unhealthy, paper texture of an invalid who'd been in bed for too long.

"How are you?" Marie asked.

Her aunt groaned in response, her eyes closed against the dim light. Marie settled herself on the chair facing the bed, which was usually filled by one of the servants. That groan seemed as good a response as Marie was going to get. "Pierre asked me to marry him." There didn't seem any point in launching into a preamble. Besides, Marie thought she might burst from excitement if she didn't get the words out.

Annette's eyes snapped open. They were bloodshot and swollen. "What?"

Marie couldn't disguise her disappointment at this reaction. She assumed that if anything could get Annette out of bed, it would be the opportunity to plan a party. "Isn't it wonderful?"

Annette grimaced, and worry lines appeared between her eyes.

"But he works in Quebec. You don't want to go there."

Marie looked uncertain. "Of course, I would live in Quebec. What would be wrong with that? I would be near Uncle Joseph."

Annette seemed very uncomfortable with the whole idea. For the first time in days, she pushed herself up into a sitting position, though the effort left her breathless. "But, my dear, you would be away from me."

Marie stood up. She knew Annette always struggled with understanding another person's opinions, but this was ridiculous. "I told you I've been writing to him since he left, so this can't come as a complete surprise."

Annette leaned her head against the rough wooden headboard. "I don't think it's a good idea."

"Why?"

"Your uncle wouldn't like it."

Marie couldn't care less what Claude thought and she said so. But Annette refused to budge, and Marie stomped out of the room. Madame Badeau had been listening in the hall, tutting quietly to herself. Annoyed at them both, Marie packed a bag and went to visit Elise.

Elise was as thrilled as Marie knew she would be. She'd known her friend was in love with Pierre long before Marie had realized it herself. The two stayed up late into the night, tucked into Elise's large feather bed in the attic, talking about Marie's future. The slanted roof with its wide crossbeams made it impossible to walk upright except in the centre of the room, and it was always either too hot or too cold. Elise also shared the space with crates of root vegetables and cured meats. So at first glance, it was a strange place to sleep and talk. But Marie found the room cozy. And no one could eavesdrop in this house.

"I wish you would find someone," Marie said to her friend as the moon rose above the rooftops. "Then our children could play together."

To her surprise, Elise's pale, freckled face turned beet red.

"What is it?" Marie asked.

Elise bit her lip. "There's something I haven't told you."

"What?" Marie rolled over to face her friend, stunned.

"Please don't be angry. I just didn't know how to tell you." Elise took a deep, steadying breath. "Your brother asked me to marry him."

Marie sat up. "He what? When did this happen? What did he expect you to say? What *did* you say?" She exploded her way through her questions. Elise couldn't possibly marry Nic. He was too rough for her.

Elise continued to lie on her back, her hands clasped calmly across her chest, staring at the rafters. "I said ... yes."

It took Marie a minute to find her voice. "Why?" It was a rude question, but Marie had never seen any interest between the two of them. She wracked her brain, trying to think of something that would have given her some indication that this was coming.

Elise blushed and pushed her pillow up so she could rest her head on it more comfortably.

"I'm sorry," Marie said. "That wasn't kind."

Elise gazed at Marie, her wide eyes looking even wider. "This is why I didn't tell you."

Marie felt slightly betrayed. She thought of Elise as a sister, and she wasn't aware that they were capable of keeping secrets from each other, especially not something like this.

"When did he ask you?" Marie asked, trying to keep her tone light.

"Two weeks ago."

"And you want to marry him?" She didn't ask whether Elise was pregnant. She wisely calculated that such a question would not be well received.

Elise sat up and fiddled with the end of her long, copper braid. "It took me by surprise. I didn't see it coming. But he was always nice to me when he wasn't busy wreaking havoc on the world." She paused to make sure Marie was listening. Marie understood but still had her reservations.

"I guess it really started during the mutiny. He would send me short notes, like the ones he sent you, but the purpose of mine was always to ensure that my mother and I were all right. When I could, I would send Pierre with food. I knew the mutineers were starving him." She sighed. "My parents and I came back to Louisbourg in June of last year. We were on the first boat that came from France. Nic was here with the rest of the garrison that had survived Boston. We ended up talking. It sounds silly, I know, but he told me about the mutiny and Boston, things he hasn't told anyone else about."

Marie was silent. Nic refused to tell anyone about the New England prison. He needed someone to talk to, someone who could listen without judgement. She wasn't that person. It was some relief to know that Elise had filled that void.

"He's not the idiot he was in school," Elise grinned. "He is loyal and responsible. More loyal than I ever realized."

Marie smiled. "I'm glad you found each other." She really meant it, even if it was a shock.

"My mother isn't happy about the marriage, though. She always had higher ambitions for me than my being a military wife like herself. But I don't care." Elise was growing braver as she spoke. "It's not the love story that you have with Pierre, and please don't judge me for that, but we'll be happy and stable. Nic has just bought us our own small house, and I'll take care of him."

"I know you will," Marie said quietly. "I just never expected this."

"When he came back from Boston, he said he realized how fragile life is. He said he'd always had feelings for me but never knew how to express them. He figured I was too proper to waste my time with him."

That sounded a bit more like her brother, but it would take Marie a while to overcome the shock. "When is the wedding?"

Elise shrugged. "I was waiting to hear when yours would be. Yours will be a farewell of sorts as well as a wedding. I didn't want to eclipse your day."

Marie suddenly felt guilty for doubting Elise's friendship. "You didn't have to do that."

"I know, but I wanted to. You'll really be my sister after this."

Marie nodded. "If you really want to spend the rest of your life cleaning up after my brother, you may need to come visit from time to time, for your own sanity."

"He's not that bad."

"He once didn't wash his face for three months."

Elise laughed. "I won't let him in bed unless he does!"

"Could we get married on the same day?" Marie asked. "But I'm afraid mine won't be the fancy affair you may want."

"That's what you think," Elise grinned.

For hours, the two young women stayed up talking about their futures as the fire glowed low in the hearth. Only as the sky lightened did they succumb to some much-needed sleep.

***

The girls awoke late the next morning and went down to the kitchen for a breakfast of brown bread and milk. They had the place to themselves, since Elise's mother had left long before to sell her bread at the marketplace. But suddenly, as Marie was thinking of how long it would take to sew herself a wedding dress and whether she really wanted to attempt it, Nic burst into the room without even knocking on the back door.

His dark eyes were wild with emotion, his chest heaving as if he'd just run a mile.

"Darling, what is it?" Elise stood up. Marie tried to keep her face expressionless at the word "darling." She didn't succeed.

But Nic wasn't looking at Elise; he was speaking directly to his sister. "You need to come with me."

Marie looked at him, concerned. "What happened?" Did Nic know something about Annette's condition that she didn't know?

Nic didn't stop to explain but grabbed his sister's hand and dragged her from the house. Elise followed uncertainly behind.

"What's going on?" Marie asked over and over again as Nic pulled her through the streets. He didn't stop until they'd reached the Thibaults' house. It looked cheery with spring flowers planted out front—quite the opposite to Nic's mood—but Marie couldn't understand why they were there.

Nic opened the door without knocking and ushered Marie and Elise inside. Augustus was waiting in the parlour for them looking distinctly worn, his shoulders slumped, a rum in his hand despite the early hour.

He looked up as Nic and Marie entered. He drained the remainder of his glass without making eye contact with either of them.

"What's going on?" Marie asked again, panic beginning to rise in her chest.

Augustus stayed silent and refilled his glass. She had never seen him look so miserable.

"Pierre was arrested last night," Nic said, stepping closer to his sister. "For desertion."

Marie backed away from him. What he was saying didn't make sense. "What are you talking about? He's not in the army." She could hear Nic's knuckles pop as he cracked them. She looked wildly at Augustus, hoping he would contradict the story, but he stared, broken-hearted, at the floor.

"Last night, two officers came here," Nic continued. "They had papers saying he was a part of the army stationed in Montreal and that he had been reported missing. They arrested him before he could board a boat out of the colony."

It had to be a joke. Marie looked around the room, waiting for someone to shout, "Just kidding!" But no one did, and the pain in Nic's eyes was too real.

The room began to spin around her. "But he's never been anywhere near the army."

Augustus made a noise somewhere between a grunt of assertion and a sob.

Nic nodded. "I know." He laid a hand on Marie's arm, but she pulled it away, refusing to believe him.

"They'll sort it out," Marie said, regaining a measure of confidence. "Renault can vouch for him. He can explain where he's been, that he was never in the army. They can check with the garrison in Montreal; none of them will ever have heard of him." It was all like a bad dream. A mistake had been made, but it could be sorted out.

Nic just shook his head. "I don't know if they'll wait that long," he said quietly. "These things are usually handled with a lot of speed. Wherever they got those papers, they were official."

Marie collapsed into a chair beside the fireplace. She was dimly aware of Augustus staring at her through his own haze of pain. "What do they do to deserters?"

Nic didn't look at her but fiddled with the dust on top of the oak mantle.

"Answer me!" She shouted, but she already knew the answer.

"They might send him to the West Indies, but usually deserters are shot."

Marie tried to gasp for air, but her lungs weren't working. She heard a terrible sound, like the shriek of a wounded animal, and realized the noise was coming from her. Nic ran over and put his arms under her before she collapsed in a dead faint.

PART THREE: LOUISBOURG 1750

Chapter 7

AUGUSTUS LEFT THE MORNING AFTER PIERRE'S ARREST. He'd tracked his son's whereabouts to the *Implacable,* a ship headed for Montreal. Pierre had been alive when the ship left Louisbourg, and Augustus hoped to meet the vessel in Montreal and deal with the situation.

The *Implacable* had indeed made it to Montreal, but there was no trace of Pierre being on board. The ship's logs had no record of him, and those could not be viewed a second time because after spending only a day in port, the *Implacable* had set off for the West Indies. None of the harbour officials had heard of Pierre either. With so many people coming ashore, one man would not be remembered, and there was no mention of Pierre in any of their official logs. The army, unsurprisingly, reported knowing no one by the name of Thibault, and the prison in Montreal also had no record of him. After going through all of these possibilities, there had been no one left for Augustus to interrogate.

Dominique Renault arrived in Montreal from Quebec, as did Tomas. They'd found no record of the ship stopping in Quebec or anywhere else along her journey from Louisbourg to Montreal. Nonetheless, Jean began to search the capital, searching through his connections with the seedy underside of the city, but no one had seen or heard of a blond giant walking among them.

Renault scoured Montreal, combing the prison and checking with all his contacts. Renault knew every law enforcement supervisor in the colony, but no amount of pressure gave him any answers. With the military, police, and shipyards searched—and everywhere in between—Augustus and his brother and nephews were running out of options.

Augustus returned to Louisbourg in July, exhausted and broken. Cut off as the fortress was, it would never give him the answers he sought.

"He can't have just disappeared," Marie insisted. She and Nic had gone to Augustus's house the day Pierre's father returned to hear the news, good or bad. It couldn't have been worse.

Augustus sighed. He seemed to have aged ten years. Since he'd left Montreal, he hadn't shaved or changed his clothes much. He'd lost weight, and his hair and beard were wild against his pale face. "There's no trace of him anywhere." The man ran his hands across his haggard face and took a deep drink from the whisky bottle in his hand. "Renault will keep looking, keep an eye out for any developments. I don't know what he'll find, though."

"But he has to be somewhere!" Marie yelled. She'd been going in circles for close to an hour, refusing to accept that no one knew where Pierre was.

Nic tugged on her arm. "Thank you for telling us, Monsieur Thibault." He bowed formally to the merchant and unceremoniously pulled Marie from the house.

Once outside, Marie yanked her arm free and rounded on her brother. "What did you do that for? He's given up. We can't just give up, not when Pierre's still missing."

Nic sighed and kept walking away from the house. The streets were teeming with people carrying out the regular business of the day. The noise from the reconstruction of the walls made eavesdropping impossible. "There's nothing anyone can do now," Nic said in exasperation.

"You're giving up too?" Marie felt completely betrayed.

"Look," Nic said, steering her around two young workers carrying a pallet of bricks toward the walls. "We know that Pierre got on the ship, but there's no evidence of where or if he ever got off the boat."

"You think he's heading to the West Indies?"

"Possibly." Nic kicked a stone lying in the middle of the road. "It makes more sense than keeping him in Montreal or Quebec."

"Why?" Marie's nerves were raw and she was trying to keep her emotions under control, but she could feel the tears pricking at her eyes.

"He worked there for five years. He knows Renault, Bigot, all the men in the Superior Council. He's known by most of the high-ranking officials in the colony. He would have had no problem proving he wasn't a deserter or even a member of the army for that matter. This wasn't a mistake."

"Of course it was," Marie countered angrily. "He was never in the army."

"I know that, but the paperwork was all there. I saw it. Whoever drew it up knew what they were doing. Someone wanted him arrested and disposed of. Someone with enough clout to do it." He gave her a significant look.

"He doesn't have any enemies."

Nic cracked his knuckles. "Yes, he did. He was the assistant to the Procurator General."

Marie winced at the past tense. Nic spotted her reaction and quickly squeezed her shoulder.

"In the five years that Pierre was in Quebec, he personally reviewed the cases of nine people who were executed. And there were many others thrown into prison for all sorts of things: theft, assault, conspiracy, corruption."

Marie was silent while she thought this over.

"No one ever thinks they deserve what they get. You think I'll ever thank Father Allard for pointing out the error of my ways when he strapped me? Of course not. People blame the justice system for ruining their lives."

They walked on in silence. Marie didn't want to believe her twin and she said so. Nic seemed to be expecting that.

"I know it's hard to hear, but you need to start thinking about that as a possibility. If it was a mistake, someone would have found him by now."

"You think he's dead then?" Marie glanced at a hog being led through the streets.

"I think there's a chance that he's at the bottom of the Saint-Laurent, thrown overboard before they reached land." Marie folded her arms tightly across her chest. "I'm sorry. That came out badly. But you need to consider all the options."

"But if he's still alive?" It felt like a blatant betrayal to simply abandon the search.

"I don't know, Marie. I don't know. The West Indies are an option but only one of a few. He wouldn't be able to escape indentured servitude." He glanced at her. "But if he's still alive, he'll find a way to contact you. He's never been one to care about the rules."

The ghost of a smile crossed her lips.

They reached the large oak door at the front of the manor house. Marie didn't want to go in. She felt imprisoned and ignored in the large home. To her surprise, Annette and Claude were both deeply affected by Pierre's disappearance. Marie understood Annette's sorrow but she was shocked at Claude's grief. Marie had expected him to be relieved that he no longer had to deal with Pierre. His anger, already always just underneath the surface, was increasing too, and that was another surprise. The result of their shared grief was that neither of Marie's guardians seemed aware that she was carrying her own impossible burden—that she had just lost Pierre to an uncertain and likely horrifying fate. Nic wrapped his arms around her and held her tightly for a moment. She couldn't remember a time when they had ever shown affection like this before.

"I'm so sorry," he said softly. "I don't know how we're going to move on, but we must."

Marie didn't share his optimism. She felt as if the sun had fallen out of the sky, never to return. For the next two days, she stayed in her room, not talking to anyone and refusing food. She thought the grief would crush her permanently. She felt entirely empty, as if her insides had been replaced by a void.

Annette had come in once to see her but was so upset herself that she was no comfort to Marie. Since Pierre's disappearance, her headaches had become an almost daily occurrence and she was constantly close to tears. Whenever she pulled herself out of bed, she just made things worse, spreading her anxiety wherever she went. Marie couldn't stand it. It was her mother's death all over again.

Madame Badeau came up to visit Marie on the evening of the second day after Augustus's return. The bedroom was in a state of turmoil. She'd begun packing for her move to Quebec, and a trunk stood open with dresses and keepsakes neatly folded inside. The two long lists Marie had made still sat on her writing desk, both untouched since the news had broken.

Marie herself lay on her bed, her back to the door, ignoring the world. Madame Badeau sighed and settled herself on the edge of the bed. The frame creaked loudly as her considerable weight was added to the mattress. Marie remained motionless.

"You can't stay in here forever." Stony silence filled the room. "I had to get one of the servants to tend to the garden, and she doesn't know anything about plants."

The fact that the maid was in the process of killing the garden didn't really concern Marie, but she realized Madame Badeau wasn't going to leave until she said something. She rolled over, her face red and swollen from crying. She said nothing and avoided Madame Badeau's inquiring eyes.

The housekeeper put her considerable hand on Marie's shoulder. "I know it seems dark now, but it will pass eventually."

Marie looked up at the kind, round face. She suddenly realized that she didn't know very much about Madame Badeau's life. The woman knew everything about the lives of her employers and their household, but Marie, at least, knew very little about her.

Madame Badeau smiled sadly. "I came here to the fortress as a young bride. My husband and I were married in Normandy two weeks before we set sail. He was a cooper, just finished articling. This was back when the fortress was still being established and they needed all the tradesmen they could get. Someone had to make the barrels to keep the supplies of cod liver oil moving."

She looked off into the distance, remembering a happier time. "Life was good here, at least for the first few months. But Félix caught a high fever during that first winter. He had never experienced such bitter cold. None of us had. He died within a fortnight."

Madame Badeau stroked the loose hairs away from Marie's face. "Broken hearts do heal; it just takes time."

They were both quiet, lost in thought.

"I can unpack for you if it's too painful." Madame Badeau's deep voice was soft with tenderness.

"I just wish I knew for sure. There's a part of me that still hopes he's alive." Marie felt silly admitting it out loud, but she knew Madame Badeau wouldn't laugh. She couldn't understand how she was expected to "move on" if Pierre was still somewhere on earth.

"I know." Madame Badeau stood up, making the whole bed shift. "You don't have to forget him, and you don't have to find someone else. I never did. It didn't seem fair to always compare someone to the man of my heart. Annette will want you to, but I'll put her in her place. Meanwhile, lying around here isn't going to solve your problems."

Marie sat up slowly. She had been so focused on what had been taken from her that the possibility that marriage was still expected of her was terrifying.

"I don't know if I'm ready to live again," she said slowly.

"It's not about being ready; it's about doing, and the sooner, the better." Madame Badeau headed for the door. "Also, Elise has postponed her wedding. She knew how distraught both you and Nic are. But at some point, you need to reach out to her, even though it will hurt." The housekeeper exited the room, her wide hips swinging.

***

The few weeks that Marie had spent working at the Hôpital du Roi during the siege of 1745 had been hectic, but in some ways, fulfilling. The worst part of the siege, for her, had been fear of the unknown. The days and nights of starvation, punctuated by roaring cannon fire had been enough to break even the strongest of spirits. She had signed up mostly just to get away from Annette, who spent every morning predicting their impending doom.

Elise hadn't been able to deal with the trauma and injuries that came with the job, so Marie went on alone. She had few skills to offer. Though she could clean and cook and wrap a bandage, that was where her abilities ended, and the regular staff were so busy that there had been no time for effective training.

Near the end of August 1750, Madame Badeau suggested that Marie apply to the Frères de Saint-Jean-de-Dieu who ran the hospital, as they and the Ursuline nuns who worked there would have more time to devote to her training now. The housekeeper had learned that they needed another *ramancheur*, or bonesetter. Learning how to re-set broken bones would give Marie a practical skill that she could use for most of the rest of her life. When Madame Badeau told her about the opportunity, Marie was willing, but Annette baulked at the idea.

"You can't become a nun," she hissed when Marie announced her intention.

"I'm not going to be a nun." Marie's exasperation was barely in check. "I just want to help."

"You have to be a member of the cloth to do that."

"No, I don't."

"They're going to try to make you take vows," Annette continued on stubbornly.

Marie sighed and just walked out of the room. Joining the Ursuline Order was an option, but not one that held any power over her. It didn't seem fair to promise her life to the church when Pierre filled her thoughts completely.

The hospital at Louisbourg was the largest building of its kind on the northeast coast of North America. Two storeys of large rooms were filled with over a hundred neatly organized beds. With its white-washed walls and high slate roof, the hospital was an impressive sight from the outside too. The spire that topped this second-largest building in the city was the tallest point in the whole fortress, easily visible above the stone walls for quite a distance.

The Hôpital du Roi served mainly sailors who had fallen ill at sea and the soldiers in the garrison, where the poor diet and close living quarters often resulted in minor but recurrent illnesses. The hospital also served the entire civilian population, with a handful of doctors trained in France and a greater number of surgeons who had apprenticed in the colony. The welfare of Louisbourg's population was in the good hands of the Frères de Saint-Jean-de-Dieu.

The main building stood on one side of the property, with two smaller buildings jutting out from either end, the entire compound surrounding a courtyard on three of its four sides. A large garden took up most of the courtyard itself, a peaceful place to rest within the sanctuary of the property's low stone walls.

Marie was nervous about going back to the hospital, but on the September day when Marie was preparing to go, Madame Badeau practically kicked her out the door. The weather was already starting to cool, so Marie had put on her grey, woollen cloak and held it close around herself to keep warm.

The clean, white interior walls of the hospital corridors were lit by large windows spanning almost the full length of the space between the rafters and

---

---

the floor. That was a familiar sight from the time Marie had spent here earlier, but the place was strangely quiet. During the siege, bombs were falling and the rooms were spilling over with the sick and injured. It was so peaceful now, it hardly seemed like the same place.

Sister Agatha was standing at the end of the hallway. She was ancient, and Marie guessed that she probably had a memory of when Louisbourg was first founded, in 1713. The old nun was short and bent over with age, and a thick chunk of shockingly white hair poked out from under her wimple. Despite her petite frame and age, however, she was a woman of great energy.

Marie wasn't sure if anyone would remember her. She'd been one of many volunteers who worked at the hospital during the siege. The facility had been filled to bursting point, and chaos reigned no matter how hard the staff tried to keep the place running smoothly.

Sister Agatha leaned forward, her eyes squinting in the bright light flooding the corridor. "Monique!" She exclaimed and limped forward with remarkable speed.

Marie tried not to laugh. "It's Marie."

The nun's face was as wrinkly as an old apple, lined with service both in Louisbourg and on the mainland. The sister patted Marie's cheek with her leathery hand. "So it is, dear. So it is. You must forgive me. Memory isn't what it used to be. What brings you here today?"

Marie explained her desire to work as a *ramancheur*, giving as few details as were needed. She didn't know any of the staff here well and didn't feel like talking about Pierre with those who wouldn't miss him.

Sister Agatha seemed far too excited about having a new recruit to be concerned about Marie's motivations for applying for the job. The nun practically bounced down the hall as she led Marie to the administrative offices.

191

A solitary priest was sitting there behind a plain, worn desk, bald except for a dark fringe that circled the back of his head. He was tall, middle aged, and generally thin, but he had a pot belly that was obvious when he stood up, poorly concealed by his black robes.

Sister Agatha explained the situation and introduced the priest as Father Maneau, emphasizing the fact that Marie had no desire to become a member of the cloth.

"Well, we can always use another helping hand," he smiled kindly at Marie. "What is your experience with healing?"

Marie described her work during the siege, which seemed to be enough to qualify her for long-term service.

"Sister Agatha, do you have time to train Mademoiselle Lévesque?"

Sister Agatha laughed. "I'm afraid not, young Maneau. I've barely enough time to finish my own chores."

Father Maneau looked affronted. "Are you sure?"

"I'm old enough to have changed your diapers, young man. Don't give me that attitude. I do the best I can with the body the good Lord has blessed me with." With that, she turned on her heel and marched out of the office.

"Bit of a firecracker that one," Marie commented, trying to smooth over the awkwardness.

Father Maneau nodded in a resigned sort of way. "Brilliant healer, but as she says, she's been doing this for a very long time. Let's go to see Sister Miriam. She'll show you the ropes."

He walked out into the hall with Marie and led her to one of the wards and into a room where a middle-aged nun was bending over a gruff-looking sailor, clearly laying down the rules. The sailor began to look bashful when he saw the priest and Marie entering the room and meekly pulled the covers around his chin.

Once introduced to Marie, Sister Miriam stood up, smiling sweetly. She had a round, red face that made her look as if she was in a perpetually good mood.

Apparently, the sailor had been refusing to stay in bed. Sister Miriam had just caught him attempting to walk around for the third time that day. He'd dislocated his knee falling off a rope ladder, and, as Sister Miriam had just told him, it wasn't going to heal if he continued gallivanting around the corridors.

Marie hid a smile and followed Sister Miriam around the building. She was a bubbly woman who obviously took great pride in her work. The hospital had two floors, each one regularly scraped and then cleaned with vinegar. The lower floor usually housed patients with injuries, while the upper level was reserved for people with illnesses and well-off patrons who paid for a private room.

Down on the first floor, Marie and her new mentor passed the largest kitchen Marie had ever seen, with seating for the staff as well as a laundry room almost the size of Claude's main floor. Water pumps had been installed in both rooms, a convenience that most people in the fortress did not have.

"So," Sister Miriam said when the tour was over, folding her arms across her ample chest, "there's not much to it. We use the apothecaries in town and herbs from our garden. Once you've learned the uses for the various plants, you can start gathering for us."

Marie nodded.

"In the meantime, however, I'll train you."

Marie was more than happy to begin. She was given a large, grey smock with deep pockets and then began to follow the nun around. Sister Miriam didn't mind having a shadow and patiently explained things twice if Marie didn't catch what she'd said the first time.

There was a lot to take in. Most of the patients were sailors, ill or injured after so many days at sea. They were being constantly reprimanded for their language. Marie found the sight of burly sailors being disciplined like school children quite amusing. There were farmers and soldiers as well, injured while in their line of work. Many of them found the hospital a welcome break from their regular duties.

Marie felt particularly squeamish when a labourer was brought in, his foot crushed by a falling barrel of cod liver oil. His bones were badly crushed, the muscles were torn, and ligaments were dangling from the flesh. There was no hope for it, so the foot would have to be amputated. Marie had to steady herself as she watched the procedure, the man's screams mixed with the sound of the saw's blade. She was told that it only took thirteen cuts for the foot to be separated from the ankle, but the whole operation seemed to take a very long time. Sister Miriam promised Marie that most days did not see such excitement, for which Marie was grateful.

Marie left the hospital as evening was sweeping in over the fortress. She was exhausted and famished. Sister Miriam and some of the priests felt that given enough time, Marie would be able to amputate a limb, but Marie herself shuddered at the thought.

As she lay in bed that night, thinking through the day, she realized that one of her goals had been accomplished. She hadn't thought of Pierre at all while she was at the hospital. The realization was bittersweet.

***

A week after she began at the hospital, Marie went to the Sarrazins' home. She still felt overwhelming envy and resentment whenever she thought of Elise's wedding but knew that wasn't fair to either Elise or Nic. It wasn't their fault that marriage had been stolen from her. The fact that Elise had postponed all planning or mention of her nuptials was a testament to how true a friend she really was.

The Sarrazins' modest wood-framed house, flanked on either side by larger stone buildings, looked merry with hanging baskets of white and red flowers below the windows and their green shutters. Marie knocked, hoping she could keep her emotions to herself.

She had purposely avoided Elise as much as possible since Pierre's disappearance, but today, Elise greeted her with such warmth and tenderness that Marie felt deeply guilty.

Elise was the only one at home. Her mother was at the market selling her loaves of bread, and the rest of her family was helping to repair the defences of the town. It was a massive undertaking that would take a few years to complete.

Marie was ushered into the sitting room where a pot of tea sat waiting.

"Do you want to talk about things?" Elise prodded, offering Marie a cup.

Marie shook her head. "What is there to say really? I'm sorry it disturbed your plans. You didn't need to postpone your day."

Elise waved the comment away. "It didn't seem right." She sipped her tea. "I didn't want my wedding to be painful, and I thought it would be easier if you had some time ... but I realize it's still all going to be incredibly difficult for you."

Elise's family was not wealthy, but because of her father's position within the garrison, appearances were important. The sitting room was filled with the good furniture, including a carpet imported from France. The rest of the house was more sparsely furnished with just the basics, most of which had been handmade by a carpenter in the city.

Elise always wanted to entertain Marie in the sitting room. It usually wasn't used except when the Sarrazins held formal teas or drinks.

"Is your mother coming to terms with your marriage?" Marie asked, downing some of her warm, comforting tea.

Elise shrugged. "Not really, but everyone else is pleased with it. My mother's dreams of my marrying into a wealthy family have evaporated, so she can't help but be disappointed. I don't know why she was always so bent on my marrying up. She says she's happy with my father, so military life can't be that awful."

Marie chuckled. "When is the big day?"

"Nic hasn't told you, has he." She shook her head in frustration. "Honestly. Saturday, October 6th. You know I want you to come. It might be one of the hardest things you ever do, but you are my best friend and I would be so sad if you weren't there."

"You're going to be my sister, Elise. I wouldn't miss your wedding for the world."

***

Marie felt as if she was putting in time until the wedding. The one good thing about the hectic schedule of trying to get a wedding ready was that the preparations overshadowed Marie's birthday. No one mentioned it, and she was grateful for that. She didn't want to think about being twenty-one and alone. Madame Badeau quietly slipped her a cup of coffee during breakfast, with a small smile, but Marie was able to pretend it was just another day.

No matter how much Marie reassured Elise and herself that the wedding would be a happy event, when the day finally came, she shed a lot of tears before going down for breakfast. She had helped sew the wedding dress, and she'd cut and arranged the flowers that Elise would be carrying, but thoughts of her own missed wedding kept coming into her mind. Try as she might, it was difficult to push them away.

The morning was bright and clear, with the autumn's first hint of chill in the air. The leaves were beginning to turn into a rich tapestry of scarlet and gold and gently graced the ground with their beauty. Some birds had not yet left for the south, and they serenaded the guests as they entered the Chapel.

Elise looked radiant in her pale-green silk dress. Her bodice was covered in tiny embroidered gold flowers that seemed to flutter as the bride breathed. Lace cuffs fell dramatically from her elbows, and her auburn hair was set about with tiny white wildflowers from Rochefort Point.

Marie sat uncomfortably watching her brother and friend in front of the altar. She would never have put the two of them together, but Elise's pale face shone with happiness as she exchanged her vows with Nic, and Nic looked happier than Marie had seen him since his return from Boston. Gazing at Elise in her radiance, Marie could think of no one who deserved such joy more than her kind and gorgeous friend. But as for Marie, she wondered if she would ever find someone else, someone who could fill the ever-present void in her chest. She doubted it. She couldn't see herself ever getting married now, promising herself fully to someone other than Pierre.

Annette's thin hand wrapped around Marie's and squeezed it gently. For a moment, Marie felt overwhelming gratitude toward her aunt for realizing her conflicting emotions, but when she glanced over at her mother's sister, she saw Annette's grey eyes filled with her own tears of grief. Annette was miserable in her marriage, but Marie didn't understand why she didn't do something about it. After sixteen years, could she not have made her peace with it?

***

After an early wedding luncheon, the newlyweds retired to their small wood cottage near the edge of town. Nic's career was just beginning and money was tight, but the young officer was already making a name for himself, so appearances had to be maintained. The appearance factor meant that they had to buy their own home, but the money factor meant that it had to be modest.

Marie felt desolate after the wedding. Nic and Elise lived within walking distance, but with her own home to run, Elise now had a different standing in society than Marie. Most of Marie's friends were married or were planning to marry soon. Marie was one of the few who was still living at home.

Jean eventually returned, sunburned, from the West Indies. He'd seen no sign of Pierre. Jean had even spent time searching the sugar plantations and any other places where an indentured servant could be, but there was no sign of his cousin. He stopped in Louisbourg to meet with his Uncle Augustus, but then he was off. With him went Marie's last hope that Pierre was alive.

She returned to the hospital, throwing herself into the work. When she was busy, Pierre didn't overcome her mind as much, but he was always there, haunting the peripherals of her consciousness. She continued to shadow Sister Miriam, and fortunately, the nun had an apparently endless amount of patience even if the sick and injured that Marie was trying to help did not.

As winter set in and the French ships retreated to their permanent ports, sailors no longer filled the halls with their assortments of puzzling ailments. Broken bones and other injuries related to agricultural endeavours were down as well as the farmers in the environs hunkered down to endure the frozen months. When the snow and ice came, there would be different kinds of sicknesses and injuries to deal with, but for now, the rooms and corridors of the hospital were relatively quiet.

People with illnesses filled most of the beds. Common colds and fevers were usually treated at home, but a few hypochondriacs insisted on convalescing under the watchful care of the clergy. It was Marie's job to deal with them.

She kept the rooms warm and dry and administered a strict diet of light liquids to the patients. If a person's fever was caused by inflammation, Marie would do a bloodletting, making a small incision in the crook of the elbow and letting out six to eight ounces of blood. It didn't always work, but the medical staff thought it was still worth trying.

Marie was amazed by how calm the nursing staff were. Often people would come in panicking or in pain, afraid that they were entering the last few moments of their lives or that they would be unable to heal. Initially, Marie found their cries upsetting. It wasn't until Sister Miriam sat her down and talked to her about her emotions that she understood why the healers were so aloof.

"If we panic, the patients will panic," she explained while Marie folded linens used for bandages in a side room off the kitchen. "They cannot see fear in our eyes or they will think that their situation is hopeless. And if they think they're lost, often times they will be, even if they receive the most excellent care."

After that, Marie tried being more objective and found that the new approach did change things for the better. It wasn't too long before Marie's life fell into a routine. She'd spend her days at the hospital caring for the sick and injured and receiving further instruction from the nuns. As time went on, she became an extremely competent *ramancheur*, and she grew to like the hospital, feeling peace in the chaos that often reigned within its walls. The priests and nuns remained unshaken by their work, and their calm, patient air was contagious.

Once a week, Marie would visit Elise, and their friendship kept growing despite their different stations in life. Elise had fallen easily into the role of running the household, occasionally helping her mother with the bakery, and being an emotional support for Nic. Since it was peacetime, Nic was often home, making for domestic bliss and a much more agreeable brother. He encouraged Marie to visit as often as she liked, but his new position as master of the home, reaching down to his solitary sister, didn't encourage her to increase the frequency of her visits.

Not that the manor house was particularly hospitable. It was often empty now, as Annette was gone most of the day. Where she went, Marie had no idea. She still did her charity work, organizing various benefits for the community, but that wasn't enough to explain her prolonged absences. Madame Badeau either didn't know or wouldn't say where she was.

Claude's mood continued to darken after Pierre's disappearance. He became more and more furious, spending most of his free time in his study with a bottle. Whenever he saw Marie, he lashed out at her, screaming and raving about nothing in particular. It was her very presence that seemed to offend him. Marie couldn't understand what she'd done to provoke this reaction, but it was increasingly difficult to abide. So she began to spend as much time as possible at the hospital.

One day in early spring of 1751, a soldier was brought into the hospital. He'd broken his leg in Montreal, and the break was severe enough that his superiors decided to send him home to France. On the journey, however, his leg refused to heal, and the skin around it began to rot and stink. Fearing he would die, the ship's captain dropped him in Louisbourg before continuing on their journey across the Atlantic.

Sister Miriam asked Marie to take a look at the patient. He couldn't have been more than twenty. He had a fever and was clearly in excruciating pain. Marie poked the area of the infection, and stinking green pus flowed from the small sore.

"What happened when you broke your leg?" Marie asked, continuing her examination. The leg bone was well on its way to mending, but there was obviously a problem with the muscle or skin.

"I was fixing a barn roof. You know, for extra *livres*," the man gasped. "I lost my balance and landed on the ground."

"You're lucky to be alive," Marie commented. "Did you land on anything?"

"There were a few boards."

She continued to press at the area. "I think you might have landed on something when you hit the ground. Was the timber new or used?"

The man shrugged. "My leg was bloody, but that's to be expected."

Marie turned back to the patient. "I'm afraid that's not really the case. I'm going to need to do some poking around. It's going to hurt, but then it should feel remarkably better."

The soldier just grunted and gritted his teeth. Grabbing a scalpel, Marie drew the blade across the abscess at the highest point of the inflammation. More liquid green pus oozed out, staining the sheet below the leg. Marie switched the scalpel for a pair of tweezers and gently pulled the angry skin apart.

The poor soldier gasped as the tweezers plunged between the pieces of inflamed flesh. "Sorry," Marie whispered as she dug around. Finally finding the cause of the problem, she slowly pulled a broken fragment of nail out of the muscle. "Well, here's your problem." She showed the soldier the offending object. "I think you'll feel much better now that that's out."

The poor man's pain wasn't quite over. Marie had to spend several minutes cleaning the remaining pus from the wound. Once she was satisfied that the worst of it was gone, she stitched the calf up and bandaged it smartly.

Standing up, she wiped her hands on her smock. "Well, soldier, in a few days I think you'll find yourself back on a boat to home."

He smiled up at her slightly, but it looked more like a grimace, and his face was covered with sweat.

Marie went to check on him the next day. He was in a much-improved state, sitting up in bed and talking with the other patients in the room. Sister Miriam reported that if he continued healing so well, he would be heading for France by the end of the week.

"How are you feeling today?" she asked. The soldier was sitting up, propping his head against his pillows.

"Much better," he grinned, showing a few missing teeth.

"You were stationed in Montreal, correct?" Her hands were sweating and she wiped them on her smock.

He nodded. "I was there for three years before that barn did me in." His voice was wistful.

Marie licked her lips. "Did you know anyone named Pierre Thibault?" Her heart was hammering so loudly she assumed he must be able to hear it.

The soldier thought for a minute, scratching his unkempt chin. "The name doesn't ring a bell."

"He was a tall man. Sometimes he had to duck to get through doorways. He had blond, curly hair and blue eyes." She tried to keep the desperation out of her voice.

The patient continued to shake his head. "Sorry, Madame, never knew a bloke like that."

Marie nodded. "Thank you," she said hastily, turning to leave before the tears started.

Chapter 8

1756 MARKED EIGHT YEARS OF PEACE on Île-Royale and six long years since Marie had last seen Pierre. She had continued working at the hospital and had become proficient enough that she was now operating independently. Back in France, with so much time on her hands, she'd taken up sketching, and she still did drawing now whenever she had a moment. Sometimes, after work, she would take her charcoals and sketchpad and draw the boats in the harbour or the flowers on the bluffs overlooking the ocean. Annette was annoyed that Marie continued to reject any suitors who were suggested, but Marie didn't care. Her heart still had room for only one man, and he was gone. As for Claude, Marie and Annette both filled their lives with other activities, so they could stay away from him as much as possible.

Marie was largely satisfied with the life she had built for herself. Though she still talked to Pierre in her moments of solitude, the grief no longer consumed her. She could remember him and talk about him without ripping open the deep, initial wounds.

One day in mid-June, Marie was sketching some fishermen repairing their nets on the same bluffs where Pierre had appeared, full of mischief, on that hot July day when she and Elise were sitting there, trying to cool off. It was certainly not as hot as it had been that day, but spring had come once again to the fortress, and it was moments like this that made Marie's heart hurt. If she tried, she could still picture Pierre's blue eyes alight with playfulness as he teased and flirted with her. She smiled at the memory.

The following Sunday, the parishioners heading to the Governor's Chapel had noticeably lighter spirits than they had had all winter. The feeling of isolation that usually settled over the city during the winter was lifting. The harbour was busy with ship traffic again, and fresh supplies were coming in from France. It was always a relief to have the world flood in after so many months of seclusion.

Father Allard stood to give his sermon as he did every Sunday morning. But this time, he looked thinner and more drawn than he had when the winter started. His health had become poor, and it was rumoured that he was dying, but today he looked especially sombre.

"News came last night," he said, his voice so quiet that everyone leaned forward to hear him better, "that Britain, in an effort to secure her interests in the colonies, has declared war on France."

The people in the Chapel were completely silent for a moment, and then babbles of panic spread like wildfire around the sanctuary. Marie turned and saw Elise in the crowd only a few rows away. By the look of shock on her face, it was obvious that Nic hadn't told her. All around her, panic was spreading. The last war with Britain had ended fewer than eight years before. They had been home for only six years.

Father Allard made a half-hearted attempt to restore calm to the crowd. Apparently, the British had been at war with France for months, but news travelled slowly to the fortress. Land disputes had arisen in the interior, with French soldiers attacking British forts, and the British had finally had enough. After delivering the message, Father Allard sat down, exhausted.

Marie wasn't sure what to do, but most people didn't appear to be staying in the Chapel. Annette had stood up and fled the moment the announcement was made. Father Allard didn't look as if he cared. He was making no effort to get to the door to stop the exodus. Perhaps, in view of the devastation caused by the last siege, he felt the panic was justified.

In the terrified crowd outside, Marie found Elise. "Did Nic tell you?" Her voice shook slightly.

Elise's beautiful green eyes were wide with fear. Louisbourg had already fallen to the British once, and they would want to repeat the victory. To survive one siege was lucky; to survive two was impossible. "No. He never mentioned anything." Elise linked her arm with Marie's, and the two hurried down the street, away from the teeming crowd.

"Where *is* Nic?" Marie looked around wildly. The news was clearly spreading quickly throughout the city. People were leaving their homes, congregating in the dirt streets to confer with each other. They looked confused, but Nic would know what to do or he'd at least have more details about the situation.

"He had a meeting," Elise said, half-distracted. "Marie, what are we going to do?"

Elise let them both into her house. It felt cold and empty without Nic there.

Marie shook her head, chewing her lip in concentration. "I'm staying with you until Nic comes home. I need to hear what he says. Besides, I don't want you to be alone." And Marie knew she didn't want to be alone either.

It was a tense afternoon. Neither Elise nor Marie said much as the hours ticked by. Elise suggested a walk, in an attempt to take their minds off the crisis, but Marie refused. The streets were filled with people just as frightened as they were.

When Nic finally arrived, he looked deeply harassed. He had been stopped by almost every civilian he had passed on his way from the King's Bastion to the house.

"There's nothing to tell," he said after he'd collapsed into a worn armchair by the fire. "We're at war with Britain again. It started in the interior. Minor conflicts have been going on there for almost two years back and forth, but they were isolated to the Ohio Valley. The boundaries between France and Britain were never very clear. I don't think anyone thought it would end in all out war. But now the conflict's spread to Europe, which doesn't bode well for us. If Louis needs troops in France, he'll be sending less here."

The silence in the small space was deafening. Elise tried to comfort her husband, kneeling beside his chair and stroking his arm with her hand, but there was no one for Marie to turn too. Not wanting to impose herself on them any longer, she went home.

The news must have reached everyone by now. There seemed to be a sort of stunned silence in the streets. Perhaps nothing much would change. They'd apparently been at war for some time without knowing it, and no invasion had happened. But the British possessed the greatest navy in the world and might even be doing blockades already. Eventually, French ships would stop coming to Louisbourg, starvation would set in, and that would be a far more potent enemy than the British navy would be, if they arrived.

As she entered the house, Marie could hear Annette and Claude screaming at each other from somewhere in the belly of the home. She bypassed them by going straight upstairs, and collapsed into her bed, staring up at the brocade canopy. She had never felt so lonely in her life.

***

About two weeks after the news of war reached the fortress, on a cold evening in early July, Marie found herself taking the long way home from the hospital. It had been a tiring day. With the possibility of war interrupting the supply chain from the rest of the world, the priests were taking inventory of what the facility currently had on hand. They knew they needed to get those numbers now and order more supplies from Europe while the oceans were still passable.

But that wasn't the hard part. Two patients had died that day: one of sweating sickness and one from a fever of unknown origins. It didn't seem to get any easier when a patient died. Marie could now put on a brave face for them, but once they had passed over to the great beyond, her strength failed her. With all of this happening, she wasn't in the mood to go home and listen to Claude raging—this time at the threat of war—but she was hungry, so she left the hospital and headed for the manor house.

A cold, miserable rain began to fall. She hadn't worn her cloak, so her bodice was soon thick and heavy from absorbing the falling water. Once she arrived at the stone house, she went in the back door, into the relative safety of the kitchen, hoping that Madame Badeau had something to keep her busy and away from her guardians.

To her great surprise, Nic was sitting by the fire. Marie hadn't seen him in that spot since he'd lived at the manor. She couldn't help but compare his appearance now with the looks of the much younger Nic. His cheeks were less round now, and his body was broader from the muscles of adulthood, but with the firelight dancing in his eyes, the usually black disks looked younger and livelier than usual.

He stood up as she closed the door, trying not to drip on Madame Badeau's well-scrubbed floor. Madame Badeau wasn't there, so they were alone so far.

"What adventure were *you* on today?" he asked, smirking as she walked past him, her shoes squeaking and squelching as she went.

She didn't speak until she was in front of the roaring fire, trying her best to wring her hair dry with a cloth. "It was a busy day at the hospital. They're trying to get prepared for a siege."

Nic leaned forward as she continued to dry herself off. He looked extremely serious. His hands were clasped in front of him, resting on his knee, and he sat perfectly still while he waited for her. When she sat down on the chair across from him, still very damp but no longer creating puddles, he didn't even glance up.

"Are you all right?" she asked. He didn't look well. She had never seen him sit so still—ever.

Nic sighed and removed his hands from his knee. "I've received some news," he said, slowly and deliberately, "from Montreal." He looked up and into her eyes. "It concerns you."

Marie felt her stomach contract. "What?"

"Promise me you won't do anything stupid."

Marie balled her hands into fists. The news she'd waited so many years to hear had finally arrived. She bowed her head and braced for the worst.

Nic began to trace the pattern of the wood grain on the side of his chair. "Pierre's alive."

Marie's head snapped up. "What?"

Nic studied her carefully. "When he boarded the ship, he was given a different name, Charles Geroux. That's why we couldn't find him."

Marie felt as if she had just received a blow to the chest. She was speechless, though a million questions were exploding in her mind. Then the room went strangely out of focus. She grabbed Nic's arm to keep her balance, and he took her over to the kitchen table and sat her down on the bench in front of it. Now she could hang onto the table if she thought she was going to faint.

Nic sat down across from her.

"Where has he been?" Marie's voice was hoarse.

"He's been sitting in the prison in Montreal for the last six years. He was released when the war was declared. They need every man they can get." Nic's grip on his sister's hands increased.

"I thought you said deserters were shot," she accused.

Nic cracked his knuckles. "I don't know why he was imprisoned, but I wouldn't complain."

"If he was in prison, why didn't Renault find him?"

Nic shook his head helplessly. "Your guess is as good as mine."

Marie just sat there, stunned. No word for so long. Since Pierre wasn't dead, he must have suffered greatly. She stood up without thinking.

Nic grabbed her arm and pulled her back down to the bench. "Where do you think you're going?"

"Where is he now?" Marie demanded, ignoring his question.

Nic looked exasperated. "He's still in Montreal, but that's not the point."

"He wrote to you?"

Nic sighed. He'd been afraid of this reaction, but it would have been beyond cruelty not to tell her. "No," he explained patiently. "Because of the desertion charge, he isn't allowed to communicate with anyone except by speech. I only know because a friend I have in Montreal is an officer there. I asked him to keep an eye out in case Pierre ever resurfaced."

Marie felt too agitated to sit still. A giant bubble seemed to be growing inside her chest. "Does Augustus know?" she asked, barely containing her excitement.

Nic nodded. "I told him first."

"Then we can sort this all out." Her eyes were shining with excitement. She stood up again and paced around the kitchen. "He can come home, and we can get married."

Nic held up his hand. "It's not that simple."

"Why not?" she demanded, her anger rising. Did Nic have any idea what this meant to her?

"Sit down." She glared at him but sat down anyway.

"Pierre can't communicate with *anyone*—I mean *anyone*," he said slowly. "Anyone he's with believes he's Charles Geroux."

"But your friend—"

"My friend told me there was a blond-haired giant who'd just emerged from prison. This giant is also from Louisbourg. Who else would it be? In seven weeks, he goes south to the Ohio Valley."

"But he's not an actual solider—"

"You really need to stop interrupting me," Nic snapped. "Pierre Thibault is now a soldier. The paperwork exists; it was signed by a General Picard. It's completely legal and binding. There's nothing anyone can do. You can't just quit the French army, especially when there's a war going on."

Marie bit her lip to keep from crying.

"He might have been held as Charles Geroux so no one could find him. I don't know what name he goes by now, but either way, he's in, and there's nothing anyone can do about this."

"But it was faked! Renault, Bigot, they can get him out!"

"You need to listen to me!" Nic pushed his face forward so it was only inches from hers. "He's in the army, and with a war going on, there's no way he can be released. The desertion charge may have been faked, but now he's a soldier through and through. Maybe once the conflict is over things will change, but until then, he's going to the Ohio."

Nic watched as the tears formed in his sister's eyes. He tried to put a comforting hand on hers, but she pushed him away. "I'm sorry, Marie."

She just shook her head and stood up.

"I'll figure something out," he promised. "He's alive. That's one good thing."

Marie ignored him and ran upstairs to her room, slamming the door loud enough that the sound reverberated throughout the house.

Madame Badeau emerged from the cold cellar. She'd been waiting there for the exchange to finish before emerging with her armful of beets. "She's not going to stay put while she knows where he is," she warned sternly.

Nic stood up. "But she's not stupid enough to go after him alone. I'll think of something."

Madame Badeau shook her head, dumped the beets on the kitchen table, and began peeling.

***

The next day the rain finally stopped, but the mood around the fortress was still glum. Though the declaration of war had little impact on the everyday lives of people in the city, the memories of the last siege were going through everyone's minds. Just as bad, the walls weren't completely rebuilt, so the destruction the bombs had caused eight years before still stood in some places as a constant reminder of what was most likely going to happen again. So far, the ships were still coming. Maybe with the battles being waged in Europe, Britain would ignore the fortress. Everyone wanted to think that, but it was a desperate hope, not a likely eventuality.

Late that evening, Augustus was sitting behind his desk on the first floor of his house. The room was littered with papers. He never let the housekeeper to clean here; it was his own private place. The piles of paper drove everyone crazy, but Augustus found comfort in the clutter.

He took off his glasses and rubbed his eyes. His son had been found but was now heading into battle. After six years of waiting, with Pierre rotting in prison the whole time, the news came as little comfort. He was still unreachable and would continue to be, unless he survived the war.

The ships would stop coming too. When was anyone's guess, but the British navy was too powerful for regular vessels to contend with.

A quiet knock came at his door. "What?" he shouted. He had given very specific instructions not to be disturbed while he was working.

The sun-darkened face of Marie Lévesque appeared around the doorframe. Embarrassed, Augustus stood up, sending papers flying off the overcrowded desk.

"Marie. Good to see you." He tried to cover his awkwardness by offering her a drink but then remembered that young women didn't drink whisky.

"I'm fine," she smiled, unsuccessfully trying to hide her agitation. She stayed in the doorway as if afraid to enter the chaos of the room.

Augustus nodded. "What can I do for you?"

The man looked so much like his son. She'd avoided him as much as possible since the disappearance because the reminder of Pierre just caused her pain. "I'm going to Montreal," she announced.

Augustus nodded his grey-blond head, impressed by her daring. Despite her brother's belief to the contrary, he had been expecting this. "I'm not surprised."

She took a deep breath. "Would you come with me?"

Augustus sank back into his chair. He picked his glasses up from the top of one of his towers of paper and cleaned them with his handkerchief. He delayed his response until he'd placed the spectacles back on the bridge of his nose.

"I don't think so, my dear," he said sadly. "I don't think that would be a good idea."

"Why not?"

He didn't answer but drummed his fingers on the arms of his chair.

"I need a boat." She tried to sound more confident than she felt. "I don't have much money, but I can pay for passage there. Do you have one going to Montreal? preferably, one that will get there in the shortest possible time?"

Augustus studied her for a moment, trying to decide whether it would be wise to help her. He could see the pale-blue pattern that looked suspiciously like faded bruises on her chest that she had tried to hide. Annette would be furious with him when she inevitably found out, but it seemed a small price to pay for Pierre to have Marie again. It would help him appease his guilt for having neglected his son so much over the years.

Augustus rifled through the mountain of papers on his desk, finally finding what he was looking for. Marie glanced around the room. Every surface from the bookcase to the extra chair was covered in loose piles of paper.

"How do you ever find anything?" Marie asked, amazed.

Augustus smiled. "Surprisingly easily. My housekeeper, Madame Cloutier, has tried from time to time to get me to organize this mess, but I can never find anything once it's filed away. He pulled a crumpled piece of paper out from the bottom of a stack and held it up triumphantly.

"I don't have any boats going to Montreal—at least none that will get you there before he leaves. But I do have a captain, Côté, who isn't too busy at the moment. I could send some things on the *Meriette*. I have some rum and claret the capital would probably enjoy." He continued to mumble to himself as he pulled more lists from the stacks.

Marie waited patiently but eventually cleared her throat to remind him she was still present.

"Oh, my dear. I'm sorry. Yes. As long as Côté is willing, I think I could have you on your way by tomorrow afternoon."

That was better than Marie had hoped for, and she thanked him profusely. He waved the gratitude away. It was the least he could do.

"I need to ask one more thing of you, though." She paused as if worried that it would be too much. "Please don't tell anyone, especially Annette, where I'm going."

Augustus looked at her sharply. "You know I can't hide it from her forever."

Marie nodded. "But at least give me a few days' head start. I need to find Pierre before anyone can find me."

There was a bit too much understanding in the look that Augustus gave her. Evidently, he knew more about what went on behind the doors of the Babineaux household than most.

"I will do my best to make sure that Claude does not find out where you have gone."

***

Everything was settled, and the *Meriette* was on the open water as night fell the next day. The ship would travel around the north shore of the island in order to avoid Acadia and the British as much as possible. They would travel through the Gulf of the Saint-Laurent, past the Madeleine Islands, before reaching the safety of the Saint-Laurent River. Augustus had seen her off, giving Côté specific instructions to keep an eye on Marie. Knowing how rough and rude sailors could be and despite his justifications to himself, he still wasn't sure he'd made the right decision. If anything happened to her, he would hold himself responsible.

He retired to his home and waited for the fireworks to begin.

Sure enough, the next morning, as he was preparing to leave for the warehouse, a visibly distraught Annette barged into his bedroom. Madame Cloutier stood helplessly behind the woman, clearly upset that the visitor had made it past her to such a private part of the house.

Annette's usually well-set, dark hair was wild, standing in bunches around her puffy face. Her eyes were red after what Augustus assumed was a night of hysterics. He knew he should feel slightly bad about the night she had obviously spent pacing around the house, but he didn't.

"What's the matter?" He continued to tie his cravat.

"Marie is missing!" Annette wailed. "She never came home last night."

Augustus tried to look surprised, but acting had never been his strong suit. "Do you know where she is?"

"No! She's missing! How could I know where she is?" Annette stomped her foot in frustration. "Nic hasn't seen her, and the hospital has no idea where she is. What if she's dead?"

"I'm sure she's not dead." Augustus began to comb his hair. "When was the last time you saw her?"

Annette glared at him, furious that he wasn't taking this as seriously as she was. "Yesterday morning. We need to do something!"

"My dear, why do you think I would be able to do something? Isn't Claude the one with all the power?" He ducked as Annette threw his snuff box at him.

"Don't you dare bring Claude into this. He doesn't care about her. Never has."

Augustus straightened up and walked out of the room. There were far fewer things for her to throw at him in the hallway. She let him pass without argument, following as closely behind him as possible.

"Don't you walk away! I need your help! I have to find her."

Augustus stopped at the top of the stairs. He watched Annette with a wary expression. It was hard to want to help her when she was in such a screaming state. "You need to calm down." If he told Annette where her niece was, there was a chance Claude would find out as well. He very much doubted that Claude would go to Montreal to chase his niece down but he still didn't like the idea of it.

"I *am* calm!" she exploded.

"Give it a few days. I'm sure she'll turn up." Augustus headed down the stairs. Annette followed him, worming her way between him and the front door.

"You know where she is, don't you?" Her voice was very quiet.

Augustus shrugged. "How would I know that?"

"I know they found Pierre. Nic told me. Has she gone after him?"

Augustus shifted his huge frame. He had never been able to lie to Annette. And he knew that despite her failings, she loved her niece deeply.

"Did you help her?" She was pleading.

"You have to promise this will never reach Claude." Annette nodded. "She's on her way to Montreal." Annette let out a cry of despair. "How could you?"

His anger finally kindled, Augustus rounded on her. "How could I? How could I not? She wants to go. Let her. She's an adult. She can make her own decisions. I put my best captain on the job. She's in good hands." He was so loud he was sure the neighbours could hear.

Annette swelled indignantly.

"Save your breath." Augustus spat. "They deserve to be happy."

"Why didn't she tell me?"

"Probably because she knew this is how you would react."

With the anger out of her, Annette seemed to shrink, stepping toward him and wrapping her arms around his middle. "I'm sorry," she said in a small voice.

Augustus patted her head, trying to control his temper. "She should be fine."

Chapter 9

BY THE MIDDLE OF AUGUST, THE *MARIETTE* HAD REACHED Montreal, and Marie was looking out at the place from the ship's deck. It certainly didn't hold a candle to Louisbourg or Quebec with their heavy fortifications and thick walls, jutting up to protect their citizens from attack. Montreal was surrounded only by a crude, wooden palisade made from sharpened logs. A stone steeple and many tall buildings soared above the palisade, giving an impression of power, but the city still seemed vulnerable in the face of the encroaching wilderness.

Marie had spent the entire voyage second-guessing herself. Once she was out on the ocean, she realized no one in their right mind would just quit a job at the hospital and run away to find (or not find) a man she had not seen for six years. She didn't doubt that it would be wonderful to see Pierre, but would he be happy to see her? She just assumed that prison wouldn't have changed his opinion of her, but she became more and more afraid of his reaction as the ship rocked along the Saint-Laurent.

Augustus had made sure she had a cabin, a place where she could be alone, away from the prying eyes of the crew. It was clear to everyone on board that this voyage was just a ruse to get Marie to Montreal, and that didn't generate any extra respect for her. As long as she kept to herself, though, the crew largely ignored her, and she was prudent enough to know that she shouldn't go out and roam the decks of such a large ship without a chaperone. Most of the sailors believed it was bad luck to have a woman on board, so that was another reason for locking herself in her minute cabin most of the time.

As soon as the ship dropped anchor, Marie quickly scrambled ashore. Her heart was hammering and she thought she might be sick. She debated trying to find a room in a nearby inn to freshen up, but she thought she might lose her nerve if she didn't start her search immediately.

She wasn't sure what the best course of action was. There were no barracks in Montreal, since the garrison was billeted with the civilian population. Pierre could literally be anywhere. So she decided to search for the military offices and found them after asking various merchants and passersby where they might be. This took less time than she thought, since Montreal was smaller than Louisbourg and Quebec. The last city before the wilderness of the interior, it also had a frontier feeling that Louisbourg, with all its isolation, did not possess. Nic's officer friend was not at the military offices, since he'd already left to join his battalion in the Ohio Valley.

The officers that she spoke to had no idea where Charles/Pierre was stationed at the present moment, nor did they know where he was bunking. They did know that he was to be sent to the Ohio Valley in a few days, but that was the only information they could give her. Marie felt they were being purposely unhelpful. Exhausted, she found a small inn, somewhat cleaner than the vessel she had just left, and cried herself to sleep. The morning didn't offer much more promise, as Marie had no plan. She had hoped the military would give her all the help she needed, but that obviously wasn't going to happen. She had money but didn't want to offer any bribes, at least not at this stage. She had a week to find Pierre.

Montreal was bustling with activity. Marie spent her first day carefully checking every tavern, warehouse, and construction site she could find. She even hired a trustworthy-looking farmer to take her beyond the palisades in his oxcart as he was leaving the market, so she could go outside the palisades to check some nearby farms. There was no one in any of those places who looked remotely like Pierre. She realized she might not recognize him right away after six years. He could have lost weight or cut his hair. And he could have permanent injuries from beatings he'd probably received during his incarceration.

The people who ran the inn were concerned about her. Young women of good reputation did not travel alone in Montreal. The plump, matronly innkeeper tried to befriend Marie and give her advice, but Marie had other things to do. The owners made sure she ate and knew her way around the city, but Marie couldn't bear to tell them why she was there. The longer the search took, the more pathetic she felt. As she lay in bed the night of the second day, she started to feel afraid. Even if Pierre was here, she was running out of time, since he'd soon be marching to Ohio.

The next day, Marie awoke feeling as if there was nowhere left for her to look. However, she made the rounds of various drinking establishments and began asking people if they had seen anyone matching Pierre's description. To her initial delight, a few people seemed to recognize who she was talking about. But they refused to elaborate and just gave noncommittal shrugs or averted their eyes. No amount of begging, pleading, or offers of bribes got any more information out of them.

Wherever she inquired, she left her name and where she was staying. If someone had a change of heart or did see Pierre, maybe he would find her.

Dejected, she went back to the shores of the Saint-Laurent. It wasn't the ocean, but the sound of the rushing river water helped calm her down. She watched the setting sun sink low behind the evergreens on the opposite bank.

But none of the beauty around her helped give her any hope of finding Pierre. And even if, by some fluke, she did find him, he would be leaving in a few days. Then she'd have to find one of the ships' captains whose names Augustus had written down for her and sail back to Louisbourg alone.

Was Nic's officer friend right when he'd said Pierre was in Montreal? Could he have confused another man for Pierre? It was possible, and that would mean she was here on a fool's errand. Pierre may never even have made it to prison. He could have been pushed overboard anywhere along the route and ended up at the bottom of the ocean.

Evening was closing in, and sailors and labourers were slowly trickling into the heart of the city, looking for food and drink. Marie got up and followed them, but in the gathering dusk, she could hardly make out the features of anyone, let alone Pierre's.

Marie knew she had to get indoors before night fell entirely. Montreal had the highest crime rate in the colony, partly because anyone wanting to make a quick escape—*coureurs de bois*, *voyageurs*, or petty thugs—could easily melt into the surrounding forests and escape detection. She didn't want to add to the crime rate. Marie hurried through the streets, paying extra attention to her surroundings, afraid of getting lost in the semi-darkness. There was no point in going missing herself, and if she was late getting back to the inn, she knew the innkeepers would be in a state. All of this was nothing, though, compared to the fact that she had not found Pierre. Had Nic's officer friend betrayed Nic—and her? Would someone lure her to Montreal for nefarious purposes? She shook her head to get those paranoid thoughts out of her mind.

Suddenly, she heard a laugh coming from an alleyway she was passing. She recognized the deep, husky noise and almost swooned. Then, as she walked back and looked into the alley, she was faced with a sight she would never have imagined.

Pierre was there. It was clearly his laugh that she had heard. He was painfully thin, the tendons in his hands standing out sharply from what little flesh was still around them. His cheeks were sunken and the skin was stretched tight against his cheekbones. His blue eyes seemed extra large compared to the rest of his face. But his appearance wasn't what frightened her. He had his arm around a beautiful, buxom blonde, wearing a bodice that barely contained her chest. A wine bottle swung freely from his other arm. There was another woman there. Just as beautiful but raven haired, she was definitely a part of the other two's plans.

Pierre leaned against the stone wall of the building, bending his large frame to reach both of them, his hands roaming over their tight dresses.

For a moment, Marie couldn't move, and she felt as if the breath had been knocked out of her. She covered her mouth to stifle any sound and fled into the night.

How she made her way back to the inn she couldn't remember. Once in her room, she tried to takeoff her boots, but her hands were shaking so badly, the laces tangled. Then the room started spinning around her as she fought not to be sick. Over and over again, the image of Pierre flashed before her eyes.

She eventually gave up trying to undress and collapsed onto her bed in a fit of tears. The pillow was soon soaked through. This was even worse than when he'd first disappeared. At least then, she'd believed he'd died loving her, but now she knew that wasn't the case. So all this time, she'd been duped. He'd just made a supreme fool of her. Maybe he had signed up for the army himself and hadn't even been thrown in prison. He may have been scared off by the thought of committing to her for the rest of his life and had taken the next ship out of Louisbourg. And under an assumed name—so she wouldn't be able to trace him. Marie felt as if her insides had been removed. She was hollow and couldn't properly process what was happening.

Around dawn, her tears spent and her body exhausted by the anger coursing through it, she finally felt the first pulls of sleep. She was more furious and humiliated than she had ever been in her life. Furious at Pierre, at those stupid whores, and at herself. She should have listened to Nic and just stayed in Louisbourg. A deep shame was beginning to flood over her. Pierre had been gone for six years, and he didn't want her anymore. How was she supposed to go back home now?

She had to talk to him—if only so she could vent her anger. And somewhere in her consciousness, as insane as it was, she felt he might be able to give her some reason for his outrageous behaviour. As her mind slowly slipped into oblivion, she decided that she would find him again and not go home disgraced until she had at least demanded some form of an explanation.

***

Her eyes were swollen shut and refused to open. For a moment, she had almost convinced herself that yesterday was a dream, but as the bird song outside the window brought her to clearer consciousness, she knew it had not been a dream but a nightmarish reality.

She lay in bed, trying to find the strength to move. Most of the anger had abated while she was sleeping, and she just felt empty now, devoid of any feeling. Her resolve to confront Pierre had also evaporated with sleep. She just felt stupid for thinking he would still want her after all this time. There was nothing to do but go home and somehow try to move on.

She pulled her eyelids open and stared at the wooden ceiling. At that moment, she suddenly became acutely aware of someone else's breathing. For one mad moment, she thought it might be Pierre, but then her brain caught up to her circumstances. Terrified, she turned to see the dark form of Claude sitting perfectly still in the corner, his face completely bloodless and full of rage.

Marie froze. His dark eyes stared menacingly from the gloom of the corner. He didn't say a word but continued to glare at her. How he had got there so quickly was anyone's guess. Though Annette wouldn't have kept the information to herself if Augustus had told her.

She backed up against the wall, terror coursing through her veins. There was no use in screaming as he advanced on her, horse whip in his hand.

***

Marie always knew that Claude lived in a near-constant state of anger, either suppressed or expressed, but she never knew the depth of his rage until that day. Of course, he had to be a lunatic to use a whip on anyone, but the rage also manifested itself in his screams and growls and manic pacing around the floor. He wasn't angry that she'd left Louisbourg; he was furious that she'd gone after the grandson of a *habitant*. She had dared to cross him and was now paying the price. "You thought you could just run away?" Claude growled. "Just pack up in the middle of the night?" The whip cracked across her back. "Do you have any idea how worried your aunt has been? The scandal that you caused?" Another crack left Marie gasping for breath, and blood started oozing through her bodice.

"Running after the grandson of a *habitant*?" The whip came down again. "Your aunt's a vixen, but I think you've bested her." The whip cracked with every word. "You and your brother ruined my life! After everything I've done for you, you destroy my reputation!"

Marie couldn't breathe. She tried to cover her face, but Claude dragged her arms away from her head. "That's right. Cower, you bitch!" His fist smashed into the side of her head.

Marie couldn't focus on the raging anymore. The screaming and shouting was coming from a great distance. Her vision went to black and she fell to the floor.

***

Claude paid for the passage home—on a different ship. Whatever safety Captain Côté might have provided was gone. He probably thought she'd found Pierre and things had ended happily.

As Claude strode onto the ship, pushing Marie in front of him, the sailors knew better than to question him. So he had full control of the situation and locked Marie away in a small cabin with only her thoughts and the pain of her wounds for company. She felt as if she'd been broken in two and part of her was destroyed beyond repair. And then there was Pierre. She didn't realize how much she'd depended on Pierre, albeit in her thoughts, over the past years. She believed she'd accepted that he was gone, but she was wrong. He was really gone now and had left her in disgrace and inconceivable pain.

There was nothing to stop the final scenes of Pierre from poisoning her brain, and nothing was done to heal the wounds in her body. She was given hardly any food—only a thin soup in the mornings and evenings. Meanwhile, Claude prowled the ship, ignoring her for the most part, though every other night, and sometimes more often, he would appear in Marie's cabin to remind her of the evil she had done.

There didn't seem to be a part of her body that wasn't injured, and the rocking waves made the wounds even more painful. She couldn't balance. Instead, her body constantly rolled from side to side, angering whatever sores were there.

After a month, Marie could no longer stand. She felt hot and dizzy. She couldn't see them, but some of the wounds must be festering. Claude noticed and finally stopped visiting her. Alone in the belly of an unknown ship, Marie began to wonder if she would ever see Louisbourg again.

***

As Marie was going back to Louisbourg, broken in mind and body, Pierre was marching to the Ohio Valley. The region was only thinly populated, and it was covered with thick forests full of hemlock and sycamores. The rolling hills and tightly packed trees reminded him of the landscapes of home. The French had originally settled the Ohio Valley, but the boundaries were never firmly established, and when British colonists started encroaching on what the French considered to be theirs, hostilities boiled over into all-out war.

Though it had taken weeks, Pierre was finally being called by his real name, not Charles, but that was the only thing he insisted on. Six years in prison had broken him. He no longer claimed his innocence or tried to explain that he had never been a soldier. No one had believed him in the past and they wouldn't now. Whoever had orchestrated this plot had been successful. Pierre had been wiped from the face of the earth. The distance between Montreal and Ohio was 180 miles. It was a slow march, taking the better part of a month. The French were travelling with their Huron allies, which made navigation easier, since the Huron knew the land better than the French—but traipsing through the wilderness carrying seventy pounds of clothing and equipment was no easy feat, especially for Pierre. Starvation had robbed him of any muscle he had. No one expected him to live once the fighting started.

After a full week of downpour, Pierre decided that whoever the French were fighting for it wasn't God. Fighting through knee-deep mud made everything harder. Eventually, Montcalm, the General from France, told them to make camp and wait out the elements. Pierre didn't see the point. Sitting in the rain with nothing but a canvas sheet between you and the precipitation wasn't much better than walking through the forest.

The Hurons had their own camps. It could be Pierre's imagination, but the Natives didn't seem to be suffering so much. They could hunt in the forest better than the rest of them and never seemed bothered by being constantly wet.

There was little food for the French soldiers, and the only water they had was found along the way. There was alcohol, but since Pierre, as a deserter, was considered to be the worst of the battalion, he never saw it. Pierre remembered being angry at the Louisbourg garrison for the mutiny of 1744, but now he understood. He was tired and famished, and the fighting hadn't even started yet.

No one paid him much attention, since his perceived desertion made him the lowest of the low. If anyone did speak to him, it was only to sneer and throw insults. Often, he had to throw his food away untouched because someone had slipped some inedible substance into it.

He also had no contact from anyone outside the battalion of soldiers he was travelling with. There was no way he could plead his case to Renault or tell Marie he was still alive. He was a ghost now. Not really existing but still walking the earth.

The Displaced: Fall of a Fortress

Pierre crouched next to a tall ash tree, waiting with the rest of his battalion. His officer, who'd stripped off his French uniform in exchange for Huron war paint, was hidden a few yards away in a grove of ferns. They were all silently waiting for some British soldiers, who were scheduled to pass through the area on their way to the nearest British fort, Fort William Henry. So far, the French had been winning the war in the interior. Since the French had allied themselves with the Huron and had assimilated their fighting style, the British stood very little chance against the guerrilla fighters.

The valley was silent; even the birds sensed that danger was present. Pierre hated the tense moments before battle, and his hands were slick against the barrel of his musket. All around him, the men waited for the flash of red to appear. This wasn't his first battle, and it wouldn't be his last. The thought made him want to stay in the thick undergrowth of the forest forever.

Soon, the sound of voices drifted on the wind to where the guerrillas were hidden. The red of the British uniforms were visible long before the enemy actually came close. They were moving single file through the underbrush of a small valley, unaware that they were incredibly easy targets for their opponents, who were hidden all around them on the hills.

Pierre's muscles tensed as he aimed his musket. All around him, his compatriots silently moved into position. The Huron moved closer, their footsteps barely making a rustle in the leafy terrain.

The sunlight glinted off the tips of the British bayonets held high in the air against their owner's shoulders. Pierre glanced left and the signal came.

The cries of the Huron were fierce. They fell on the front and back of the caravan while the French muskets attacked the centre. The British scrambled around, fumbling for their weapons and trying to discern where the attack was coming from. The air was thick with the white smoke of

230

gunpowder, making it difficult to see, and the thick forest made escape difficult. The French and Huron knew the land better than the British, most of whom had arrived straight from Britain for the war.

The skirmish was over in a quarter of an hour. The British who were still alive had scattered, leaving the dead and wounded behind. The call came not to pursue. Food, ammunition, and other provisions had been left behind, and in the wilderness, these were far more important than following the escaped British soldiers.

Pierre shouldered his musket, his upper chest throbbing from the force of the butt of the gun slamming into him repeatedly. Walking among the dead and dying, he was trying to find the ones who needed to be put out of their misery.

He came across one soldier, no older than seventeen, face still round with the chubbiness of youth, pimples standing out against the white pallor of his face. The boy didn't say anything. He just looked up at Pierre fearfully. Pierre could hear the gurgling breath escaping from the bullet wound in the boy's chest, and crimson bubbles of blood were spreading from the small hole.

"You won't survive," Pierre said in the English he had learned from one of his cellmates in prison. The boy began clawing desperately at the wound, his lips already tinged with blue from lack of oxygen.

Pierre bent down and pushed the boy's face away from him. Drawing his knife, he slit his throat, waiting until the convulsions stopped. He wiped the blade on the grass, refusing to look at the corpse before he moved on to the next scarlet-covered body.

That night, he sat a distance away from the fire, leaning against the trunk of a large evergreen. The others sat close to the flames, happily sharing the fermented bouillon and ale that had been lifted from the British stash. They sang and laughed, relieved to have survived another battle.

This had been his third battle on the way to Fort Ticonderoga, the closest French fort. He had taken off his white shirt, the front peppered with the blood of the boy.

After the first two battles, he had scrubbed the bloodstains off his uniform as much as possible, but the other soldiers in the battalion mocked him. Most wore the stains on their uniforms proudly.

The blood didn't bother Pierre now. That frightened him. It was becoming easier to snuff out life, to watch the light go out of a man's eyes. He hated it. Hated that it was getting easier. Hated that he wanted to be included in the singing and joking after the battle. He was beginning to not recognize himself. He was becoming a monster, killing without thinking much of it afterward.

Once upon a time, he had been a man of education and social standing. He had loved once, had a bright future ahead of him. That man was gone. Who had taken his place he didn't know. He sat watching the flames of the fire shooting up against the dark sky. He had spent six years not seeing the sky, locked away from humanity. His hands no longer shook after he killed, but he wished they would.

Louisbourg was a long way away, and he doubted he would ever see it again.

PART FOUR: LOUISBOURG 1758

Chapter 10

THE MONTH OF MAY 1758 was unusually warm. The sea air floated up from the water, covering the city with the undeniable stench of fish. The ever-present fog rolled in off the North Atlantic, its tendrils slowly groping their way past the buildings near the harbour. Closer to the middle of the city, however, Léonard de la Rocque's elegant home was flooded with the best of society, wine, and food. He'd made the ball an annual affair, giving the bourgeoisie of the city a chance to mingle with the local aristocrats and prestigious military figures. A comment or suggestive look could effectively alter one's social standing in the coming year (for better or for worse). Though de la Rocque's gatherings were not overly lavish, they were generous—as was suitable to his station.

The war changed all that.

Two years of British blockades had depleted the stores of the colony. Supplies were scarce and food even scarcer, so this year's ball featured cod served five or six different ways. There was plenty of beer and liquor, though. In fact, those kept all the people of the colony going, not just the upper crust.

Marie leaned against a richly papered wall at one side of the ballroom, staring into space, furiously grinding her teeth together. At twenty-nine, she was considered an old bride. There was no other way to say it. All her friends were married, and some had little families of their own. Most of them had written her off, condemning her to spinsterhood.

However, eighteen months before, in November 1756 (about three months after Marie's return from the disastrous trip to Montreal), she had finally accepted a proposal from Jacques-Xavier de Charlevoix. Jacques, recommended highly by Claude, was a young lawyer trained in Paris, and he was the nephew of a Duke in France, with excellent connections to the fur trade and the political sphere in Louisbourg. He was also the city playboy. But Marie could hardly say no, given Claude's vicious threats and Annette's hysterical begging.

Reports had recently been brought in from the Mi'kmaq that the British were mobilizing in the colony of Halifax with Louisbourg as their target. In a fit of dark humour, Marie said to herself, as she kept leaning against the ballroom's elegant wallpaper, that she hoped the British would arrive before her marriage could occur. Claude had made it clear he wanted this marriage to take place. Still not completely healed from the trip to Montreal, Marie wasn't stupid enough to cross Claude again. Besides, she needed to get out of his house. (Claude had arranged the marriage as a personal favour to Jacques's uncle, the Duke, in exchange for patronage at Court, and he'd also given money to Jacques, who was happy to take the funds, along with the connection to Claude's aristocratic blood.) Now that she was engaged, however, she was beginning to see that Jacques was never going to change, and she knew she'd give almost anything for the wedding to be postponed—forever. While society was rejoicing at her upcoming wedding, Marie was obviously under no silly romantic notions that this would be a happy or even a civil union.

Elise was standing beside Marie, her hair gleaming elegantly in the candlelight, but the effect was spoiled when she started nervously twisting an auburn curl around her finger and tapping her toes in anxiety.

"Have you seen him at all?" Marie whispered out of the corner of her mouth, her eyes combing the crowd of swirling silk.

"Not since you came in." Elise glanced around the room over her fluttering fan. "I don't know where he is, but I'm sure he'll be back soon." She didn't believe that Jacques was doing anything innocent, but she didn't want to emphasize that.

Marie snorted. She had already done her part, playing the blushing bride as she and her fiancé walked into the ballroom together. Though she'd put up a good front, she was well aware that behind the smiles and best wishes was a furious wave of hateful gossip. Marie knew the marriage was a sham, and it was frustrating that people thought she was too stupid not to know what she was getting herself into.

In the last quarter of an hour, three people had congratulated Marie on the upcoming nuptials and pointedly asked where the groom was. "What am I supposed to tell them?" Marie complained, pulling at her bodice. Her green silk dress was starting to feel constrictive. It had been made before the war started, and surprisingly, she had been thinner then. A diet made up almost exclusively of salted cod had caused her, and everyone else in the city, to retain water. The boning in the stays were poking painfully into Marie's ribs, which wasn't improving her mood.

Elise sighed. "Tell them he's indisposed at the moment."

"With his mistress." Marie stared miserably at the dancers.

Elise threw her a look.

"What? Everybody knows it. Why do you think they keep drawing attention to the fact? He's never been discreet." Marie twisted the stem of her wine glass anxiously between her fingers.

Elise hung her head. She knew only part of what went on behind the doors of the Babineaux house, but she knew the situation must be worse than she'd imagined for Marie to agree to this arrangement. "It's not perfect, no," Elise went on, "but what are you going to do about it?"

Marie smirked.

"Oh, no!" Elise hissed. "You're not about to do anything stupid."

Marie harrumphed and took a large sip of wine to try to cover her frustration. Marie still loved Elise dearly, but Elise's enthusiasm for Marie's upcoming marriage had caused some friction between them.

Marie gazed around the room, looking for a distraction, when her eyes fell upon a squat form waddling toward her. "Save me!" she hissed in Elise's ear. "Here comes Lady Isabelle."

Lady Isabelle was the fortress's chief gossip. With no children and a husband too busy with politics to notice her activities, she spent her time sticking her considerable nose into other people's business. Marie was well aware that Lady Isabelle knew exactly where her fiancé was but wanted to gloat over Marie's misfortune.

She was a short, plump woman who came up only to Marie's collar bone. To make up for her challenge in height, she wore a powdered wig that protruded at least a foot above the top of her head. It wobbled precariously whenever she moved. Elise and Marie tried to manoeuvre their way behind a nearby clavecin to get out of the elderly lady's sight, but she reached them before they could hide themselves.

"Oh, my dear," she cooed in her high-pitched, birdsong voice. "You must be so excited!" Lady Isabelle always stood slightly too close for comfort. Marie could see the shallow scars from smallpox on her face, expertly hidden under several layers of makeup.

Elise put a supportive hand on Marie's arm. Marie plastered a horribly forced smile on her face.

"How many more days is it now? twenty-two?" Lady Isabelle continued in her sickly-sweet voice, moving slightly closer so her perfume filled Marie's nostrils.

Leave it to Isabelle to count down the days to someone else's wedding, Marie thought darkly. "I'm not sure. About three weeks."

Lady Isabelle laughed her horrible, high-pitched laugh. "Oh, my dear, you're not counting down the days? I most definitely would be if it was me. Although I never thought the day would come that you would be married. Never thought it would happen." She waved her hand dismissively.

Elise squeezed Marie's arm. Despite her best efforts, Marie could feel her blood rising as Isabelle prattled on.

"But where is the happy groom?" Lady Isabelle asked with a nasty glint in her eye. "I thought I saw him earlier."

Marie unclenched her jaw long enough to make a stiff reply. "He's momentarily indisposed, but I'm sure he'll be back shortly."

Lady Isabelle chortled. "Best keep your eye on him. Don't want to lose him to some sweet young thing." She elbowed Marie knowingly in the ribs and waddled off, white wig swinging dangerously to one side.

"Well, that could have been worse," Elise muttered, relaxing slightly.

Marie said nothing but downed her glass of wine as quickly as possible. "I need something stronger." She eyed the table across the room, laden with bottles of whisky and rum from people's cellars.

Elise pursed her lips together disapprovingly as she watched Marie navigate her way through the crowd.

***

Marie waited until she was out of sight of her sister-in-law and then ducked into the corridor where the air was slightly cooler. Nic had given Elise strict instructions to stay as close to his sister as possible. He knew Marie was getting cold feet.

Still out of sight of Elise, Marie stood in the hallway for a moment, thinking hard. She was tired, humiliated, and angry. She felt trapped in a corner, with no possibility of escape. The wedding was only three weeks away, and already she could feel the weight of matrimony heavy on her shoulders. She pulled at the bodice of her gown again, trying in vain to rearrange the folds of fabric so she wasn't stabbed every time she inhaled.

The sound of Elise's voice drew closer, breaking through Marie's thoughts and moving her into action.

The de la Rocque's property was the largest private home in the city, with multiple rooms covering the second floor. Even with the sounds of the festivities drifting up the staircase, Marie could still hear both of them before she entered the room. How Jacques could invite himself to use another man's bedroom was beyond her. She didn't knock but just threw open the door to shrieks of terror from within.

Jacques-Xavier was tall and thin, with black hair and dark features that endeared him to almost every female he met. He was an influential man with a powerful family, but at the moment, he was sitting completely naked, red as a tomato, staring up at his fiancée much like a toddler caught with a biscuit in his mouth.

Laure, Jacques's mistress of the moment, fled into the corner of the room, shielding herself as best she could with the bed sheet. She seemed absolutely terrified to find herself in a situation where her lover and lover's betrothed were in the same room with her.

"Hello, darling," Marie spat wickedly. "People are starting to wonder where you are." Jacques turned a dangerous shade of purple as he struggled to retain some form of dignity. It was difficult, since Laure had taken most of the bedclothes with her.

"Shall I tell them you're busy fornicating?"

"Get out, you little bitch!" he snarled.

"Going to make me?" Marie was feeling reckless. Pushed to her limit, she no longer cared about the outcome. "It's going to take a while for the two of you to be presentable again." She sneered at the woman cowering in the corner.

Jacques started to lunge toward her but then thought better of it. She yanked her engagement ring off her finger. It was expensive, sapphire, and from France. The ring alone had caused almost as much gossip among the members of upper society as the betrothal itself. Few people in the military town had ever seen anything so luxurious. She held the ring at arm's length over the open fire.

"You want it?" Worth a small fortune, it was far more important to Jacques than she would ever be.

Jacques glared at her from under his curtain of black hair. With some satisfaction, Marie saw a glint of fear in his eyes. As much as everyone in the fortress was more liberal than their colonial counterparts, this particular incident would create quite the scandal within the community. Being found in bed with the daughter of a prominent Louisburg official, who was also another man's wife, might be a large enough scandal that even the great House of Charlevoix might not recover from it. Jacques certainly never would.

Marie threw the ring into the fire. "You can make the announcement." She turned on her heel and headed out the door.

***

Marie made it through the square garden plots and almost to the stables before Elise caught her arm. Puffing and panting, she pulled Marie to a stop and held her hand firmly, her chest heaving as she tried to catch her breath.

"What is your problem?" Elise huffed when she could speak again. "You can't leave!" Her pale, freckled features were bleached in the moonlight.

Marie glared at her. "Yes, I can!" She pulled her hand away.

Elise drew her petite self up to her full height and squared her shoulders. It was a posture Marie had often seen her take when she was cross with Nic. "What did you do?"

"Nothing," Marie turned away. She was almost at the gate that led to the street.

"Yes. You did something!" Elise caught her hand again. Though tiny, her grip was enough to prevent Marie from leaving. "You confronted him, didn't you?" Her voice was growing louder with panic. "He'll kill you! You know that, right? Why? Why are you so stubborn?!"

Marie glanced nervously at the house behind them. The music and laughter were loud enough to cover the argument, but if anyone noticed them, her situation was going to become dangerous.

"Shut up or they'll hear you." With a tremendous effort, Marie yanked her arm free and headed toward the street.

"You can't do this," Elise hissed, following as closely as she could. A few goats in a nearby pen poked their heads between the wooden slats. "Where will you go? What will you do? You can't just abandon your life because Jacques has mistresses."

"Mistresses?" Marie spun around. "There's more than just Laure?"

Elise bit her lip, looking furious with herself.

"And everyone knows?" Marie muttered to herself. An ugly look crossed her face. "I'm not marrying him when the entire city knows about his extramarital affairs." She turned and walked out of the garden, letting the gate stay open behind her.

Elise hitched up her skirts and followed, trying to keep up. "He's not coming back, you know. He's gone. Just accept that!"

Marie froze and turned, an odd expression on her face. "Don't you think I know that?"

Elise fumbled for an answer. "I didn't mean that. It's just ... you ... stop holding out for a happy ending. It's not coming ... He's gone ... Don't run away from a good life because you wish it was something else."

"That's not what this is about!" Marie cried, panic and exasperation rising in her chest. "I know he's gone for good! But getting back to the point: Would you like a life like this? a husband like Jacques? All of society laughing at you because they think you're too stupid to know what's going on? Just leave me alone!" Close to tears, she ran as fast as she could into the night.

She kept going farther and farther into the solitude of the darkness. The streets were unlit, but the glow of the moon illuminated the dirt streets ahead of her. Fog was still creeping up from the harbour, swirling around her ankles. She was consumed with thoughts of the argument. Anger and frustration at Lady Isabelle, Claude, Jacques, and herself overwhelmed her. She stormed through the streets, rage blinding her vision, not watching where she was going, blood pounding in her ears.

A small knot of men was standing just ahead of her. They were laughing uproariously, but she didn't think much about them. There were plenty of taverns and inns around, and most soldiers and sailors spent their free time with a bottle. She was too concerned with who might soon be following her to think about what might be lying ahead.

Despite the military patrols, the street was empty, except for the men. Shadows fell in strips on the unpaved road as the moon was blocked by the buildings. The men were standing by an alleyway created by the surrounding structures. Marie glanced behind her nervously. The road was empty.

Suddenly, they were all around her. Breaking fully from her thoughts for the first time since she'd left the ball, she found herself surrounded, the men larger and older than she'd first guessed. She tried to step around the group, but her arm was then abruptly twisted behind her back. One of the men bent down and leered at her, showing gums with many missing teeth.

"Well, hello there," he laughed. Marie turned away from the fumes of raw spirits coming from his mouth.

"Help!" Marie shrieked. A closed fist smashed into her stomach, and her arm was twisted farther up her back. She gasped in pain. The men guffawed around her. A hand pinched her. She lashed out to kick the offender but fell sideways, unbalanced. She screamed again as her arm was wrenched in its socket. She thought it would break from the force of her captor's grip, and her sides burned from the bones of her stays, which were still jabbing into her. A dirty hand clamped itself against her mouth, making it difficult to breathe.

The louts were pulling her into the alley. Eyes wide with panic, she looked desperately around for some form of assistance. She saw a shadow advancing from a nearby street. Friend or foe, she didn't care. It was worth the risk. She stomped her heel down on the foot of the man holding her. He jerked her arm upward, but his grip on her mouth loosened. She bit the hand, tasting blood and grime, and screamed at the top of her lungs. The dark shadow yelled something indistinguishable and ran to meet her captors with fists raised.

The man holding her swore and let go. Marie stumbled to the dirt, her arm throbbing painfully, then clambered as fast as she could from her attacker. Her assailant was walking toward her, large hands clenched. She could see blood dripping down his hand, minute circles of blood sinking into the sandy ground. Marie continued to scramble backwards, and as he advanced, she noticed a glint of gold in his ear. Pirate.

A shout for assistance came from the pile of writhing limbs behind him. Glancing behind her adversary, she saw that both of his companions were entangled with her champion. With a roar of frustration, the pirate aimed a kick at her, missed, and launched himself into the fray.

Marie knew she should run, but something kept her rooted to the spot.

Whoever this fighting man was, he was huge. One of the louts already lay unconscious on the ground, and she could see the other two tiring quickly. After a hard uppercut to the chin, the second man folded to his knees, and his companion backed away, hands held up in supplication before disappearing into the darkness.

Finally, victorious, her champion stood up, hands on his knees, trying to catch his breath. He was a soldier, his muted white uniform dirty and lopsided from the fight. He bent down to retrieve his hat.

Marie felt a shiver run down her spine as the soldier stepped into the moonlight. He was as tall as she remembered, although more muscular, especially through the shoulders. His golden hair was swept back from his face, but it was still wild and unruly, despite the leather lace holding it in place. When he turned to face her, she saw the blue eyes, with a splash of yellow, widen in surprise.

Her own shock was mirrored in his face. She stepped back, afraid of what to say or do next. For a moment, the two stood staring at each other, unconcerned about the unconscious bodies sprawling not far from their feet. Worry was etched in every line of his face. "Are you all right?" His voice was no more than a whisper.

Marie's brain seemed to have jammed. "What ... what ... are you doing here?" she finally asked, her voice hoarse with emotion. She would have been less surprised if a ghost had materialized in front of her.

The soldier looked at her uncertainly, as if he was unsure what the right answer was. "I was transferred back here ... six months ago." He rubbed the back of his neck.

"Six months?!" She could feel herself beginning to tremble, both from the ordeal she had just suffered and from her anger at his reply. Her eyes began to sting, and she brushed them impatiently. "You've been here for *six months*?"

He nodded silently, standing a few steps back as if he was afraid of getting too close.

Emotion overcame her, and she turned from him, racing through the streets. She heard him shout but ignored him. She wasn't moving as fast as she usually did. Whoever invented raised heels was an idiot, she thought viciously. The two-storey whitewashed stone home came into view just as the heel of her left shoe gave way, and she tumbled to the ground, swearing as she went.

Pierre had been following her all the way, and he now stopped and bent to help her up.

"Are you all right?" he asked for the second time. Marie picked herself up, brushing dirt from her voluminous satin dress. She wobbled as she tried to find her balance on her broken shoe and grabbed his proffered hand. Once steady, she ignored him as she pulled off her footwear.

"Talk to me," he pleaded.

Marie glared at the ground, unable to look at him. "What do you want, Pierre?" She was embarrassed to be found in such a state.

"Give me a chance to explain."

"Explain what?" she yelled more loudly than she meant to. "What can you possibly say? You've been gone eight years! Eight years! You think we've all been just sitting around waiting for you to come home?"

He looked alarmed. "No. Not that. Just—"

"Just what? You think you can walk in here after so long and find everything the same?" Marie felt irrational anger bubbling up inside her. For years, she'd wanted to have this conversation. Wanted to see him again, touch him again, hear his explanation for all the time gone by with no word from him. But now that he was here in front of her, all she felt was bitterness and anger that threatened to overwhelm her.

Pierre reached gently for her hand, but she snapped it back. "Go! Get out of here! I don't want to see you. You left before. It shouldn't be so hard to do that again!"

Pierre's head snapped up, his jaw clenched. "You've just been assaulted. I want to make sure you're not hurt."

"Well, it's too late for that. Too late. You think everything is the same? It's not the same! Things have changed!" She glanced over her shoulder toward her destination. The stately house stood just across the street. She was so close but running dangerously out of time.

"I know that!"

"No you don't, you bastard!" The tears were far too close to the surface. Swallowing hard, she turned toward the house. Pierre shifted so he stood between her and her destination.

"Get out of my way," she whispered.

Marie stared at Pierre. His face was a mere few inches from hers. The lines around his eyes were deeper than they used to be. "Goodbye, Pierre." The finality in her voice frightened him.

"Marie ... please."

Marie was just opening her mouth to reply when she heard the sound of hooves on the sun-hardened road. Her time was up. Terrified, she pushed past the wall of muscle and disappeared into the house.

Pierre stood still, in the middle of the street, shivers of disappointment coursing through his veins. He turned as the horse drew nearer and recognized the compact rider as the horse came closer. He ducked into the shadows and hurried off the way he'd come. He turned his face away from the road. The last person in the world he needed to recognize him right now was Claude-Jean des Babineaux.

***

He hadn't made it very far when a wild, chestnut horse came tearing around the corner. It came to a halt—mere feet from him. Nicolas Lévesque pulled the reigns violently as the horse bucked. Nic looked angrier than Pierre had ever seen him.

"What the hell, Nic?" Pierre yelled, jumping away from the panting beast.

"Have you seen Marie?" he demanded.

Pierre rubbed the back of his neck. Nic had given him explicit instructions to stay away from his sister.

"It's important!" Nic hissed. The horse pawed the ground, imitating its rider's agitation.

Pierre looked up. "She's at home," he muttered.

"Damn it!" Nic cursed. "Has Babineaux been this way?"

Pierre nodded. He had known Nic a long time—known him to goad the nuns at the school and take on men twice his size under the influence of liquor. He'd also heard the stories of the fearless fighter he was on the battlefield. But he had never seen fear like this in his eyes.

"What's wrong?" Pierre grabbed the horse's bridle.

Nic swore under his breath. "Claude's going to kill her."

"He's what?"

Nic paid him no attention. He dug his spurs into the horse's flanks and tore off down the deserted road.

Pierre stood, torn for a fraction of a second, and then ran after the horse.

***

Later that evening, Augustus Thibault was sitting in his study, looking over his shipping logs. The British were planning another invasion of Louisbourg—

that much was common knowledge—and the situation was already affecting business. The failed naval attack of Louisbourg in 1757, only a year before, had been but a minor setback for the British. France's attempt at sending reinforcements from Toulon had been blocked in Cartagena, Spain. Augustus's own ship captains were already being very cautious about coming from and going to Louisbourg, for fear of British bombardment.

As long as France controlled Île-Royale, the Saint-Laurent was supposedly safe for French ships bringing the supplies that kept the colony alive. During the last siege, some boat traffic had managed to get through, but almost nothing was getting through now. In some ways, Augustus was looking forward to the inevitable invasion. At least whatever came of it would make it clear whether he should keep his business going or just retire.

Pierre had returned, but things were not going well. He had heard about Marie's engagement, and Nic had warned him not to bother her. He was also angry and sullen, refusing to respond to the efforts his father was making to repair their fractured relationship.

Suddenly, Augustus's peaceful evening was interrupted by a commotion outside his study door. Reaching the front entrance of his house, he found his son in a state of great agitation and excitement, holding a bleeding, moaning, grey bundle that appeared to be a woman.

"What the hell is going on?" Augustus roared, blinking rapidly to make sure he wasn't imagining the macabre scene. "What are you doing here?"

Pierre just ignored his father and started to order the servants around. That part wasn't out of the ordinary. The strange part was the wounded woman. Without a backward glance, Pierre marched purposefully up the stairs with the moaning woman in his arms and strode into one of the spare bedrooms.

"Just a minute," Augustus yelled up the stairwell. "What the hell *is* going on?"

Augustus went up the stairs two at a time and walked right into the bedroom. Now he could see the face of the young woman his son was holding in his arms. The beautiful face of Marie Lévesque, covered in blood and bruises, was pressed against his son's chest. While not surprised by her broken condition, Augustus was amazed that Pierre had finally involved himself in her problems.

"She needs the hospital," Augustus said, finally appraising the situation. "She can't stay here. What can we do for her?"

"She can't go. Claude will be looking for her." Pierre threw his father a look of deepest loathing. "Nic's already gone for a physician." He turned from his father and shut the bedroom door, leaving his father standing helplessly in the corridor.

***

Pierre tried to lay Marie on the bed, but she clung to him with her hand wrapped into his shirt folds. The bedroom door opened, and two maids came in to light candles and start a fire in the empty hearth. Another brought in towels and linens and yet another, a steaming bowl of boiled water, garlic, and witch hazel. Madame Cloutier, the tall, willowy, and formidable housekeeper, supervised the operation. No one asked questions.

Pierre felt helpless. No one met his eyes as they dashed around, completing their duties. Then, after a last burst of activity, all the servants left the room, with Madame Cloutier going last, shutting the door smartly behind her.

The sudden silence of the room was unsettling. Marie still clung to Pierre with alarming strength. "Please don't go," she whispered so softly he could barely hear her.

He gave up trying to extricate himself from her grip and sat down on the bed with her cradled in his lap. She didn't say anything, but he could feel her shaking—from shock, pain, tears, or all three, he didn't know, but he rocked her gently as her small body kept trembling. He reached for one of the quilts that had been piled up on the bed and clumsily wrapped it around her slender frame with his free arm.

He'd been a soldier for two years and had fought in fierce battles all over the continent. He'd seen men shot, killed, scalped, and ripped apart by cannon fire. Nothing, however, had prepared him for the sight that had met him half an hour before.

He had followed Nic through the dark streets back to the manor house. Light was flooding out from every window. When Nic knocked on the front door, Madame Badeau opened it for him and Pierre walked in behind. The housekeeper said nothing to Nic but stared in amazement at the sight of Pierre. He couldn't blame her for being shocked; it had been a long time since he'd darkened the doorstep of the Babineaux mansion. Once inside, Pierre looked around and saw no sign of Claude. That was a relief. Hopefully, he'd left before Marie arrived. But that didn't explain the fact that the house was in a state of panic and confusion.

"How bad is it?" Nic asked without waiting for an answer.

"She'll live," Madame Badeau replied grimly, moving her large weight behind Nic as he crossed the foyer, heading for the stairs.

Nic glanced toward the top of the stairs. "Get Thibault a horse. He'll transport her," he said as Madame Badeau continued to stare at Pierre.

Pierre, unable to follow the conversation, had followed Nic's gaze up the stairs and saw there a sight that made his heart stop. Marie was lying on the floor, on her side, completely unconscious, blood slowly oozing from her head. Pierre rushed up the stairs, stopped just before her body, and bent down to gently brush some of her chestnut hair away from her face. The damage was horrifying. How could this have happened? He had left her only a short time before.

Nic came up and stood beside him. Pierre then gently turned Marie over to see if she had other injuries. She did. Her left arm lay at an odd angle, and he could see the bone of her left forearm sticking out. A small, crimson stain was slowly blossoming across the intricate bodice of her green silk gown. Her face was already beginning to swell, one eye and a split lip ahead of the rest of it, every inch of her usually flawless skin now covered in bruises and lacerations.

Pierre's shoulders slumped. "What happened?" He felt that all his strength had left him.

"Claude," was all Nic said, distracted in conversation with the servants who had come to where Marie was lying.

"Claude did this?!" Pierre spluttered. He had always been told that Claude hit Nic only because Nic egged him on. If that was true in the past, it definitely wasn't now. Things had obviously escalated to a terrible level.

"Yes." Nic looked down at his sister, then glanced at Pierre with pity. Claude would never forgive Marie for loving Pierre or for going to search for him in Montreal. He wouldn't be humiliated by a *habitant*. Worse, she had defied his orders once again tonight and shamed him by rejecting Jacques.

"She can't stay here, Pierre," Nic said, "and she can't stay with Elise and me because Claude would find her there. She has to go somewhere else where there's a possibility she'll be left alone."

Pierre looked up, struggling to understand. His fingers were beginning to tremble.

"Can she stay with your father?" Nic bent down to survey the damage more closely. He seemed detached from the situation, as if he had seen this sad tableau many times before.

"You think Augustus wants to get entangled with whatever this is?" Pierre dismissed the idea with a shake of his head. He balled his hands into fists to try to stop the tremors that had spread to the rest of his hands.

"He will," Nic said simply, and with authority. "I'm going to get a physician. I'll meet you at your father's." He had grasped Pierre's broad shoulders and stood to leave.

"You don't understand," Pierre called out, anxiety rising in his chest. "She doesn't want anything to do with me. I saw her earlier on patrol, and she told me so. I can't take her anywhere."

Nic looked at his friend with a mixture of amusement and exasperation. "You really think she meant it?" No matter what Marie said, or suffered, Nic knew Marie had never stopped loving Pierre. He knew her too well to believe her when she said otherwise. She'd take Pierre back in a heartbeat if he could somehow explain Montreal.

Pierre stared. "Of course, she meant it."

Nic shook his head and started walking down the stairs. "No, she didn't," he called over his shoulder.

Apprehensively, fearing he would wake her or otherwise cause more damage, Pierre gently wrapped Marie's body in a thick blanket and took her downstairs. He called for Madame Badeau to bring her grey cloak. Ferdinand was already standing outside the front door, his hand on the bridle of one of the Babineaux horses. (Nic had ordered that transportation, confident that Pierre would be convinced to take Marie to Augustus's home.) Pierre wanted to make that steed gallop as fast as it could, to get Marie to safety before anyone could pursue them, but he knew they had to move slowly enough not to wake Marie up. She did wake up, though, about five minutes into the journey, shaken into consciousness by the jostling of the horse on the uneven ground. While she said nothing, her good arm clung tightly to Pierre's body, and he could hear her gasping in pain when the horse hit rough ground. Luckily, they encountered no one on the dark roads. No one to report to Claude what they had seen.

***

Pierre looked down at Marie now, cradled in his arms in his father's house, wondering how things had degenerated to this point. Marie lived in his memory, strong and healthy. What lay in his arms was a stranger. He was terrified. He rocked her slowly and whispered reassurances into her ear, but he didn't know what else to do. Her head had finally stopped bleeding. Her intricate hairstyle was matted with sticky, congealed blood. He could feel the dampness where her blood had seeped through his uniform.

"Marie?" he whispered tentatively. It was his first attempt to speak since she'd awoken.

She opened her eyes and gazed steadily at him. "Nic is coming with a physician," Pierre said. "He'll be here soon. Can I help?" Her large, hazel eyes still looked as deep as the ocean, and her thick black lashes were still intact.

But one eye was almost completely swollen shut, while the other stared at him. She blinked solemnly and leaned her head against his chest again without saying a word.

He knew it wasn't important, but suddenly Pierre became very concerned about the last time he'd washed any part of himself.

Nic arrived shortly after that, followed closely by Father Weber, a priest who ran a small mission home that served the poor in the less desirable area of the city. While not a qualified doctor, he was a part-time physician who made a great effort to help any poor soul who came into the sanctuary. Marie had met him years before when she was working in the hospital. When Nic needed someone to help who could be counted on for discretion, Father Weber happily filled the job.

Father Weber was a small man both in height and girth. His wiry white hair stood up on his head as though it were trying very hard to escape from his skull. Although stooped with age, he gave off an air of someone with great amounts of energy. Weber had been born in Prussia but as a young man had joined a merchant vessel headed to New France to avoid some legal trouble at home. He found himself stranded in Louisbourg harbour after a serious bout of illness sent him to the hospital there and the ship he was travelling on kept going, unable to wait for him to get better. He had simply decided to stay there. While he'd been a devout Catholic since birth, he became a priest in the colony and happily lived the next forty years serving in whatever capacity the rest of the clergy refused to be involved with. He'd spent the occupation in Quebec but preferred the isolation of Louisbourg and returned with the French.

Father Weber gently pulled back the quilt. Marie refused to let go of Pierre, but the priest was able to make a cursory examination while she rested her head against the soldier's chest. She moaned as the little priest prodded her side and shoulder. Finally, Father Weber straightened up and surveyed Marie seriously.

"My dear," he spoke kindly in thickly accented French. "I am afraid that I am going to have to ask your lovely companion to leave." He glanced at Pierre. "Madame Cloutier and I need to dress your wounds." He nodded at the housekeeper.

Marie's grip on Pierre's uniform increased, her one good eye wide with fear.

"What's wrong with her?" Pierre asked quickly.

Father Weber looked at him sharply. "I need you to leave."

For a moment, Pierre thought of arguing, but a quick glance at Nic told him it was useless. He gently shifted Marie to the bed, forcibly untangling her fingers while she groaned from the pain of the slight movement. He bent as he laid her head on the pillow and whispered, "I'll come back for you, I will." He squeezed her hand. Nic continued to glare at him as they both went out into the hall.

Pierre met his father pacing at the bottom of the stairs. Neither of them said anything to the other for a minute, the silence billowing between them.

"You knew Claude was doing this to her." It wasn't a question. Augustus had shown too little surprise at Marie's condition when Pierre had carried her into the house.

Augustus nodded.

Pierre walked out of the house and vomited onto the road.

***

Pierre returned later that night after finishing his military patrol. The house was dark and quiet. As he passed by his father's study, he noticed a light coming out from under the crack at the bottom of the door. He would have gone on, but he heard voices mentioning his name. He knocked softly and went in.

Nic sat across the desk from his father, a bottle of whisky half drained between them. Despite the late hour, Nic seemed restless, his long fingers drumming on a tiny area on the polished table top that had been spared the clutter of the rest of the room. Augustus leaned back, his eyes red under his wire-rimmed glasses.

"Since when are you two friends?" Pierre had never known them to have held a conversation.

Augustus ignored him and fiddled with his glass. Nic laughed unpleasantly. "You've been gone a long time, Pierre." Augustus and Nic were, strictly speaking, not friends. However, they had come to know each other during the search for Pierre, and their mutual concern for the girl upstairs made meetings such as this necessary.

Pierre collapsed into a spare chair, poured himself a healthy measure of whisky, and drained it in a gulp. "What happened?"

Augustus removed his glasses and began to polish them with his handkerchief. He didn't speak until they were replaced comfortably on the bridge of his nose. "Nothing life-threatening, although it could have been. She was lucky." Pierre snorted in disbelief, but Augustus carried on as if he hadn't heard.

"The head wound is stitched up, and she isn't showing any signs that the blow to the head caused any lasting damage. Her ribs are bruised, maybe cracked at the worst. Some of the boning in her stays must have broken and pierced the skin, but luckily, they didn't go too deep. Her shoulder was dislocated, but it was fixed easily enough. Then there's the broken arm. It's unclear how that will heal," he finished heavily.

"Her arm wasn't amputated?" Pierre asked in shock.

Augustus shook his head. "Father Weber is an experimental man."

Pierre bent his head as he tried to compose himself. Hot waves of shame and guilt rolled over him.

"There's nothing you could have done," Augustus said quietly. The look on Nic's face seemed to suggest the opposite.

"What the hell is going on?" Pierre asked finally. He had been stationed back at home for six months, and no one had told him anything about this. He had been told that Marie wanted nothing to do with him, but they should have told him about the danger she lived with every day.

Nic sighed. "Claude beats her."

Pierre felt very much like hitting him. "I gathered that. For how long?"

"After you left."

There was a pregnant silence.

Pierre rounded on his father. "Since I left?! Do you realize what you've done?"

Nic stood up. "It's not his fault, you idiot. It's yours!"

"What did I do?"

"Six years after you left, after no word from you, she decided to go find you."

Pierre's eyes grew wide. "To find me? I was in a prison in Montreal."

Nic glared at Pierre. "I told her where you were after you were released. An officer friend of mine told me about your situation. But I never dreamed she would go after you. A woman making that kind of trip alone. I didn't think it was possible. But she went, after your father here found her a ship." By his tone of voice, he clearly hadn't forgiven Augustus for assisting her.

Pierre was numb with shock. His face was completely drained of colour. "She never found me. I never saw her!"

Augustus smiled sadly. "She found you," he said quietly.

Pierre stared, horror-struck, around the room. He felt his chest tightening. "No, she didn't. I never saw her!"

"She saw you," Augustus repeated, looking up from his drink.

Nic glared at Pierre with a look of disgust. "Do you remember that night or were you too drunk to remember what happened?"

Pierre thought back. After his abrupt enrolment into the French army, he had rotted in a prison in Montreal for six years. He had professed his innocence, but no one ever listened to him, and he hadn't been allowed any communication with the outside. Instead, he spent six years locked in an isolated dungeon, with other forgotten prisoners.

The disdain that the prison guards had for him, supposedly a deserter, left him starving and beaten on a regular basis. He was released from prison when Jumonville Glen and his battalion were attacked by the British in Pennsylvania and the subsequent war had been declared. The army needed every able body they could get. Pierre had spent the first few weeks after his release angry, despondent, and sick. He spent every night steadily drinking himself into oblivion, usually with the company of less than reputable women.

He felt sick realizing that knowledge of his sins had been spread far beyond the confines of Montreal. Nic then told Pierre how Claude had found Marie and whipped her and taken her back to Louisbourg. Since that day, she'd been the target of his rage, living in fear. Both Nic and Augustus had tried to remove her from the situation, but they'd been unable to get her out. Claude always found her.

Pierre sat stunned. Waves of shame, guilt, anger, and despair washed over him. He felt the room spin and thought he was going to be sick again. After several minutes, he eventually gained control of his emotions long enough to speak. "I need to go and see her," he whispered.

"She's sleeping now," Augustus said kindly. "Father Weber gave her laudanum before he set her bones. She'll be out for several hours. Let her rest."

Pierre wasn't listening. He stood up, knocking his chair over. "I need to see her. I need to explain—to tell her I'm sorry."

Augustus came around the desk and grabbed his shoulder. "Son," the gesture of familiarity shocked Pierre back to the present. "She can't talk to you. Wait until tomorrow."

Pierre shook off his father and headed up the stairs. The room was lit only with the fire now burning low in the hearth. The windows were closed and the room was stifling. The willowy form of Madame Cloutier rose when he entered, and she offered him her chair. He took it and waved her away.

Marie looked worse than he remembered. Her face had swollen even more, purple and blue with the bruises. He could barely recognize her features under the damage. The quilt was pulled tightly up under her chin so he couldn't see the rest of her injuries, but he could feel her broken left arm bandaged against her chest.

Eyes stinging with tears, Pierre tried to think of when she would have seen him in Montreal, but too many nights spent in a drunken haze ran together. He couldn't imagine her being there; the very thought of it made it difficult to breathe.

The door opened and Nic stepped in quietly. For a moment, neither of them said anything but focused on the beaten girl between them.

"She didn't want to see me," Pierre muttered. "I ran into her on the street tonight completely by accident. She didn't want to even look at me." He seemed diminished. His face was pale and his hands shook in his lap.

As angry as Nic was, he could see that the man before him was writhing in his own personal hell. As much as his pride made him want to blame Pierre for the situation, he knew very little of it had anything to do with his friend. "She should be safe here for at least a few days," he offered. "Claude won't think to look here."

Pierre nodded, blinking quickly.

"Just don't draw attention to yourself."

"I need to talk to her—to explain—if such a thing is possible," Pierre babbled.

Nic nodded. "She needs someone to watch her tonight and give her more laudanum if she'll take it."

Pierre said nothing.

"Talk to her when she wakes up, but then you need to leave and go back to the barracks." It wasn't a suggestion. Nic nodded to himself and then let himself out of the house.

***

Pierre hardly moved at all as he started his vigil. Marie slept lightly in her drugged state, groaning if her body shifted even slightly. Each noise felt like an iron fist clenched in his heart. He couldn't remember if he had ever endured a longer night. She had gone to Montreal, seen him, and tried to find him, and he never realized it. If he had known, would he have risked desertion and come back? Probably.

Up and down the room he paced, too agitated to stay still. The fire had long since died, but the full moon cast silver highlights over the cozy room.

Just as the moon began to sink beneath the horizon, he heard a moan from the bed. This one was different. Marie was trying to sit up. He rushed over. "Hey, don't do that. You're going to hurt yourself more."

Marie stared up at him with her one eye, thoroughly confused. She reached out with her good hand and poked her finger at his forehead, dragging the appendage heavily down to the tip of his nose. "You're real." She sounded uncertain.

Too full of emotion to say anything, Pierre just nodded.

"I thought I dreamed you." She continued to stare at him groggily through the haze of medication and pain. "Although, in my dreams, the conversation usually goes better." She looked worried. "Did I really scream all that stuff at you?"

The corners of his mouth twisted. "Yes."

She looked around the room. Nothing in the semi-darkness looked familiar. "Where am I?"

"You're at my father's house." Her confusion didn't dissipate. "Nic feels that Claude won't find you here, or at least he won't cross Augustus. You should be safe for a few days."

Marie gave an involuntary movement at the sound of Claude's name and let out a gasp as her body protested. "I want to sit up, but I need help." A faint sheen of sweat glistened on her forehead as she struggled to move.

"I don't think that's a good idea." He was afraid of touching her for fear of hurting her more.

Marie muttered rebelliously under her breath.

To try to placate her, Pierre grabbed the extra pillow on the bed and carefully tucked it behind her.

"Thanks," Marie said as she shifted her weight painfully.

Pierre bowed his head and stared at the floor. He wanted to speak, but the lump in his throat was growing exponentially. He couldn't bring himself to look at her now.

"I'm sorry." The words were quiet, as if spoken from a great distance.

His head snapped up. "For what?"

"I'm sorry I said those things. I was angry." She spoke slowly, with great effort.

Her apology made him feel even worse. "It's all right. I deserved it."

She looked confused again. "No, you didn't. I was afraid. Afraid of what I was feeling, so I got angry. That's no excuse."

Pierre was starting to worry that the blow to her head may have done some serious damage. He wasn't sure if this was the best time, but he needed to talk to her before he was entirely consumed by his guilt.

"Nic told me," he began and then stopped. He cleared his throat. She looked at him, her eye sharper than it had been since she had awoken. "He told me about you coming to Montreal. That you saw me with those women. That you were so close but I missed you. That I ..." It was becoming difficult to speak. Hot tears were blurring his vision as he tried to articulate what his actions had cost him. It was important that he tell her, that she understand that he had been drowning his sorrows the only way that was available to him.

That it all meant nothing. If he had seen her and had known, he would have taken her with him that moment. She wouldn't have had to suffer Claude's scorn and beatings. They could have started their life together.

He felt something gently squeeze his hand. He looked down to see Marie's slender fingers wrapped around his. Marie smiled softly from the bed.

"I don't hate you," she said, finally with clarity, sounding much more like herself.

His shock must have shown on his face because she continued. "I mean, I did. A lot. For a long time. But when I woke up today ..." She glanced out the window. "I mean, last night when I saw you there, I didn't care what had happened. For the first time in a long time, I felt safe. I just wanted you to stay." Her voice was starting to sound rather far off.

"I'm sorry. I am so sorry." Pierre's voice was cracking. "I was angry ... I was miserable ... I thought I'd lost you." He paused, trying to compose himself before he went on. "Had I known ... seen you ... I would have kept you there. I would have fought Claude for you ... protected you from all of this." His voice broke. "I've never tried to replace you."

Marie gave him an odd look and studied him for a moment. "I did," she said very softly. "I tried very hard."

She leaned back into the pillows as if the effort of her confession had exhausted her. She didn't seem in a hurry to say anything else, but her grip on his fingers was strong and sure.

"Is that who Jacques is?" he ventured after a while. The answer would potentially be painful, but he needed to know.

Marie laughed bitterly and then winced as her ribs moved. "No. He was a means of escape, but it wasn't worth it." She closed her eyes to hide the tears that were forming. Awkwardness was beginning to grow between them.

"I'm not marrying him, you know," she said conversationally.

"I thought you were. Nic wrote me a year ago to tell me about the engagement. He told me you were happy." He noticed her inquiring look. "As an officer, he was allowed a letter."

A long string of unflattering names came out of Marie's mouth. "That's what this," she waved a hand over herself, "was for. I just couldn't stand him anymore. I was never happy with him. I never even liked him. I found him with another woman, again. I told him I'd had enough."

Pierre squirmed uncomfortably. "I'm sorry." He reached out tentatively to touch her cheek but then thought better of it.

She smiled sadly. "Me too." He noticed the moisture clinging to her lashes. "Why are you back here?"

"My father paid a large sum of money to have me transferred. Nic used his influence as well, but he didn't want me anywhere near you," he sighed. "How are you feeling?"

"I hurt in places I didn't even know I had."

Pierre winced at the dark humour. "There's more laudanum if you want it." She nodded, eyes still closed.

He passed her the small vial containing the dark liquid and helped her take it.

She looked at him dreamily as the painkiller began to take effect. "Please come back."

"I promise."

She squeezed his hand again with all her strength, and then she was gone.

***

Marie awoke in the early afternoon, feeling much more like herself, at least mentally, than she had the last two times she'd opened her eyes.

It was the first time she looked at her surroundings properly. She had been to Augustus Thibault's house many times but never to this part of the house. She assumed she must be on the second floor, a level that as a guest she had never been to. The feather bed that she was reclining on was warm and soft, and the thick velvet bed hangings were parted to let the sunshine in.

She sat up slowly. No matter how gently she moved, her ribs screamed in protest and her head throbbed. Nic was sitting by the window, sheafs of paper spread in his lap. He carelessly threw them on the table when he saw her stirring.

"How are you this morning?" he asked, shifting his chair closer to the bed. "Well, it's not really morning anymore, but I'm glad you've made it back to the land of the living."

Marie looked at him without expression. He tried again. "How are you feeling?"

Marie grunted as she tried to prop herself up on the pillows. "Sore."

"I assumed. Do you want anything to eat or drink?"

Marie shook her head but stopped. Moving made it throb.

"What happened?" Nic asked seriously, leaning forward, his elbows resting on his knees.

Marie didn't say anything but stared at the patchwork quilt. She wasn't afraid of her brother, but he wasn't going to be happy with her. She had a feeling that Elise had given him a general idea of how it all started.

"What happened this time?" he repeated, resigned.

"You haven't seen Claude?"

Nic sighed and shook his black hair. "No, I haven't. Although he must be out in public because someone stopped me at the office and asked me how my sister was. Apparently, he'd heard you had fallen terribly ill and might not be better in time for the wedding."

Marie gazed at him. "And what did you say?"

"Just because someone speaks to me doesn't mean I have to answer."

"That would explain why your mother-in-law hates you," Marie replied tartly.

"My relationship with my wife's mother has nothing to do with the present situation." Nic paused. "Did you really tell Jacques you wouldn't marry him?"

Marie looked defiant. "I did."

Nic let out a hiss of frustration. "And where does Pierre fit into all this?"

Marie looked at him blankly. "What about Pierre?"

Nic glared at her as if she was being stupid on purpose. "What about him? You broke off your engagement with Jacques because you two finally managed to get together again! You put your life in jeopardy again for this idiot. Marie, it has to stop!"

As bruised, sore, and embarrassed as Marie was, she did her best to pull herself up to her full height. "Excuse me?" Her eyes blazed dangerously. "You're implying that Pierre has something to do with the events of last night?"

"Pierre always has something to do with your life," Nic spat impatiently. "Why do you think I told him to stay away from you?"

Marie looked hurt and offended as a memory from earlier came to her mind. "You told him I was happy with Jacques."

"Of course, I did. I didn't want you to know that Pierre was stationed here. You would have just gone looking for him."

Marie stared up at the bed canopy, trying to decide what to say. Finally, she turned to her brother. "Then why did you help him come back?"

Nic cracked his knuckles, glaring at a spot on the floor. When Augustus had first asked him to help bring Pierre back to Louisbourg, he had refused. It took several months of nagging from Augustus before Nic sat down to think about the situation. Pierre had been his best friend, the closest thing he ever had to a brother. Nic couldn't begin to imagine what his friend had endured over the last eight years. He had heard the stories of what happened to deserters; he had doled out the punishments himself on more than one occasion. Whatever Pierre's faults, Augustus's plea to have his son return home, even for a short while, was valid. "I have never been able to envision a future with you and Pierre where Claude didn't end up doing something like this." He pointed to the state she was in. "I couldn't begrudge Augustus wanting his son back, but I knew if Claude had the faintest idea you were in contact with Pierre, all hell would break loose. Even if nothing came of any conversations, even if all you did was scream at him for Montreal, I knew Claude would do *something*. He's not exactly rational."

"You think I was happy with Jacques? Last night had nothing to do with Pierre. I found Jacques with Laure and I'd finally had enough. It was the last straw. I'm not going through with the marriage. It's humiliating, the way he parades these other women around."

Nic looked unconvinced. "Jacques has position and influence, and he wouldn't beat you—"

"Is that your idea of a happy marriage?" Marie asked cuttingly. "As long as your physical needs are met, that's enough? Love, happiness, and amicability have nothing to do with it?" She had to bite her tongue before she started comparing Nic's marriage to the situation.

Nic glowered at her. "No, but the last few hours haven't exactly proved me wrong."

"I didn't know Pierre was transferred back until last night as I was leaving the party. I was trying to get home and grab some things before Claude found me. I was hoping to hide at the hospital. It didn't work, though," she finished quietly.

"So Pierre was a coincidence?"

Marie smiled sadly. "I doubt you'll believe me, but it's true."

Nic leaned back in his chair. "Why did you do it, though? Why last night?"

Marie lay back on the pillows. "I don't know. I just couldn't take it anymore. Anyway, it was better to do that now than in a month when it would have been too late," she said simply.

"But marrying Jacques would have been better than this." Nic pointed to her ruined body. "That was the idea behind agreeing to the engagement. What are you going to do now?"

Marie shrugged her shoulders and then gasped as the movement jostled her left forearm. "I'm just going to stay here and heal."

Nic shook his head. "Marie ..."

"Please stop blaming him, Nic," a voice muttered from the recesses of the pillows. "This isn't his fault."

Nic ignored her. "Uncle Joseph is still stationed at Fort Saint-Frédéric at Lac Champlain. But he had offered you his home."

Silence greeted this announcement.

"If we hurry, it can happen before the siege. The British blockade is not yet as effective as it has been. The entire island isn't surrounded. If you got to Baie des Espagnols, the rest of the journey should be fairly straightforward."

Marie was moving again, trying to sit up and pull herself off the bed. Nic scrambled to help her.

"What are you doing?"

Marie grasped his forearm so tightly it hurt. "I want to get up and walk."

Nic knew better than to argue and helped her manoeuvre out of bed so she was standing upright. He stayed within arm's reach as she slowly shuffled around the room.

"That feels better," Marie sighed. She moved slowly to the window and looked out at the afternoon sun.

Nic followed her in case she suddenly felt weak. "Going to Quebec would spare you from the coming siege and get you away from Claude, and you would have more independence," he continued on as if she wasn't trying to avoid the subject. "You could work at the hospital there. Joseph would happily support you."

Marie turned from the window, scowling. "I don't want to go."

"And why do you suddenly not want to go?" He couldn't keep the sarcasm out of his voice. This had always been Plan B before the engagement had happened. He was beginning to seriously regret helping Pierre come back to Louisbourg. At the moment, he didn't care about anyone's feelings; he just wanted Marie to be safe. Joseph had agreed to take Marie on as his charge. And Augustus and Nic had arranged, several times, for her to leave for Quebec. However, every time Marie had actually packed and left the manor, Claude had found her before the ship left.

Marie didn't answer but began moving slowly around the room, not looking at her brother. It felt good to stretch her muscles.

"Marie, Claude will find you if you stay here too long."

Marie suddenly felt her legs buckle. The room was spinning. She grabbed the back of a nearby chair, trying to steady herself before she fell over. Nic's arms wrapped around her and scooped her up as easily as if she was a bag of flour, setting her safely back on the bed.

Embarrassed, Marie settled back into the warmth of the bedding. "Thanks, little brother."

Nic shook his head. "Only by five minutes."

"Six."

Nic smiled despite himself. "If you want to see Pierre again, that's fine, but I need to make plans for you to leave. We've been trying to do this for years, Marie. For all we know, tomorrow Claude will be breaking down the door. And if you're set on avoiding Jacques, this is the only way."

"Fine," she sighed. "How long do you think it will take to find a ship?"

"Not much more than two weeks. Father Weber says no travel for a fortnight."

Marie nodded and stretched out her hand. "Thank you for taking care of me, Nic. I'm sorry it happened again."

Nic grabbed her offered hand. "Don't say that. It's not your fault."

"This time it kind of was. I was feeling reckless."

"Still ..." Nic cleared his throat. "Get some sleep, sis."

***

True to his orders from Nic, Pierre had gone back to the barracks and spent the night in his bunk surrounded once again by the smelly, belching men of the Louisbourg garrison. The barracks housed rows of bunks suspended from floor to ceiling. Some bunks accommodated up to three soldiers a night, but Pierre, through a rigorous routine of pretending to kick in his sleep, had managed to get a bunk to himself. Even so, he was too tall to properly stretch out on the thin mattress.

During peacetime, there wasn't much to do in the fortress. Most men spent their free time doing labour for extra pay on the farms surrounding the fortress or in the city. Now, however, with the knowledge that the British forces would eventually leave Halifax, the garrison began training in earnest. Artillery was moved and ships were armed. Trenches were dug outside the walls, and men were stationed in the fields, trenches, ramparts, and within the city, looking for signs of trouble.

All the same, these activities didn't take up the entire day. It was a waiting game. Nerves were stretched to the breaking point, and time off was encouraged to keep the soldiers sane. Having lived through the last invasion, Pierre knew roughly what was coming, although he didn't plan on living through it this time. That wasn't why he'd been stationed here.

Pierre usually went down to the warehouse to help his father when not on duty as a soldier. While he was paid less than his colleagues, who did manual labour, it did help him feel more like a human being again after years as a soldier running around the countryside killing anyone who opposed him.

The morning after he brought Marie to his father's house, Pierre was back, walking into his father's first-floor office. It was difficult to be in that place, which he had once thought would be his. Most of the clerks who had been employed before he had been sent to Quebec were still there, but he wasn't the owner's son anymore. He could see it in their eyes. He was just another soldier trying to make extra pay.

His father was in the office surrounded by his usual mounds of paper. There wasn't as much current paperwork to do now, though. There were rumours of blockades starting in the summer, and no merchant ship wanted to go head to head with a British warship. Most of the clerks came in only once a week now because of Augustus having mercy on them and paying them a bit while they looked for other part-time employment.

Augustus looked up, nodded in recognition, and continued with his paperwork.

"How is she?" Pierre tried to make the question sound conversational, without success.

Augustus sighed and shook his thick, grey-blond mane. "Madame Cloutier has taken over as the chief attendant. Marie will recover."

"You say that like you've seen worse," Pierre accused.

Augustus didn't raise his head but nodded into the papers he was writing on. "In Montreal, Claude whipped her. On the trip home, some of the wounds became inflamed. She had a terrible fever. I'm not sure how she survived. She spent several weeks in the hospital, and somehow they were able to mend her."

Pierre clenched his fists and turned away bitterly. Augustus saw the emotion and stood up and moved toward his son. "What's done is done, Pierre. You cannot change it."

Pierre snorted in dismissal. "Is that how you live with yourself?"

Augustus sighed but didn't rise to the bait. "Focus on now. You are both alive. She will recover, and for the first time in a very long time, you are together in the same place."

Pierre stared out the window at the mostly empty harbour.

"She has asked not to see you for two weeks," Augustus said, quietly turning back to his desk.

Pierre spun around. "Why not?" Fear that she had reverted back to her original attitude gripped him.

"I would guess that she's embarrassed. She's in a great deal of pain and wants to heal more before she sees you again," he replied calmly.

"Is this her idea or Nic's?"

"I would hazard Nic's, but I wouldn't fight him about it."

***

It was a long two weeks. While Marie finally felt well enough to wander around, she was forbidden to leave the house during the day for fear that someone would see her. She was permitted to walk around the garden behind the house after darkness fell, but she still chafed at having to spend so much time inside. She understood the concern for her safety, but she felt as cooped up as a chicken in a cage. She had no clothes, having escaped from the house with nothing but what she was wearing the night of the ball. The green silk gown lay blood stained and crumpled in a corner. She had borrowed a chemise and thick shawl from one of the maids downstairs. She could possibly have borrowed more, but her injured ribs prevented her from wearing her stays.

The coming conflict seemed unimportant at the moment, her world having been turned upside down with the reappearance of Pierre. As far as she could tell, the British were doing nothing. Her only information came from the servants and Augustus, however, none of them wanted to cause her more stress.

Elise visited a handful of times during the fortnight that Marie was convalescing. She had the ability to see past the injuries and baggage they carried, treating Marie as if their times together were just more visits in Elise's front room. Marie appreciated those interchanges more than Elise would ever realize. The two women would just sit on the bed, drinking tea. Elise refused to bring up Pierre and the chain of events that had led to this particular beating. Marie would bring it up when she was ready. Besides, the British invasion and the reality of Nic going into action was now consuming most of Elise's energy. So it was better for her not to delve too deeply into Marie's problems but to be there for her as a kind presence.

***

The two-week recovery period had been Nic's idea, but Marie hated it. Nic would secure some sort of passage off the island for her as soon as she was considered well enough to travel.

Meanwhile, Pierre and Nic met every night in the tavern. Since Pierre's return to the fortress, they had had little to do with each other. But now that Pierre knew Marie had seen him at his worst in Montreal, he could no longer blame Nic for his anger. Pierre felt as responsible as Nic believed him to be.

Nic now seemed resigned to the fact that Pierre was back in his sister's life. He knew, when he signed the papers to have Pierre stationed at Louisbourg, that he was also leaving open the possibility that Pierre could reconnect with Marie. He felt deeply conflicted. Marie was happy that Pierre was back, a feeling she hadn't had in years. However, Pierre's proximity to Marie put her in danger. Though they were both adults and could do what they wanted, Nic was the one who had picked up the pieces after Pierre had left, and he couldn't stop resentment from boiling up in him. All the same, now that they shared deep concern for Marie's well-being, they went out for drinks from time to time to discuss her condition. At first, their conversations revolved around Marie and her injuries, but they eventually morphed into a resurrection of the friendship they had once shared.

"Have you been to see her?" Nic asked one night out of the blue, the smoky tavern around them teeming with drunken sailors unable to leave the harbour.

Pierre choked into his tankard. He thought they were talking about fishing. Eyes streaming, he eventually muttered, "I thought two weeks ended tomorrow."

Nic gave Pierre a shrewd look. "Counting the days?"

The cadet wiped his face and glared across the room at the tavern owner, who was pouring ale at a long counter.

Nic's dark eyes danced with mischief. "She's bored. I think she'd like to see you now."

Pierre's neck snapped around so quickly he pulled a muscle.

Nic snickered as Pierre massaged his left side.

"I was there two days ago." Nic paused to take a drink. "She's bored out of her mind and could use some company."

"I thought you visited her every day."

The black locks waved in disagreement. "I don't want to go too often. Claude might be watching."

Pierre arched an eyebrow. He hadn't thought of that. "Aren't you being a tad paranoid?"

Nic shrugged his shoulders. "I don't know. I have no idea how he keeps finding her." He rubbed his eyes with the heels of his hands.

"Is it the priest? Weber?"

"No, she hasn't needed treatment every time. I've ruled out most of the servants too. I trust most of them but I don't tell them where I take her. Except for Madame Badeau, whom I trust completely."

Pierre sat back and scratched his chin. He knew Marie considered the heavy housekeeper a surrogate mother. No, it wasn't Madame Badeau.

"I wouldn't worry about it, though," Nic said, trying to be reassuring. "You have every reason to go to visit your father's house."

Pierre looked dubious.

"And even if Claude figures it out this time, he's no match for Augustus. Augustus would knock him senseless before Claude got anywhere near the house."

"Would he?" Pierre said darkly, standing and heading toward the door.

"Say 'hi' for me," Nic called to the hulky, retreating back.

Chapter 11

A HEAVY MIST HAD BEGUN TO RISE AS PIERRE made the trip across town. Others who were out walking or doing errands were dodging the raindrops, trying to reach their destinations as quickly as possible. Pierre flipped his collar up against the wind. He refused to wear his uniform when not on duty. It helped him feel more human.

A solitary candle was burning in the window of the second floor. Pierre watched as Marie moved around, silhouetted against the light. He paused, staring at the slight figure. His heart was pounding against his ribs. Eight years was a long time to be without someone you loved so much your life depended on her. The house was quiet. Servants skirted around him as he made his way upstairs.

The bedroom door was open a crack, and he knocked softly. Marie was still by the window and turned to see who the visitor was. She looked infinitely better than she had at their last meeting. The swelling had gone down, and she appeared to be much more like herself again. Purple and green were still marbled along the corner of her jaw, but otherwise, she looked like his sweet but feisty Marie. Marie gave a shy smile as Pierre peeked around the door. She suddenly wished she'd put more effort into her appearance. She tried desperately to smooth her hair back into the braid she'd slept in.

"I didn't know you were coming." She was moving toward one of the chairs very carefully, afraid to jar her body.

Pierre slid the chair closer and motioned for her to sit. Marie slowly lowered herself into the offered chair. The intimacy of their last encounter had evaporated with the passage of time. They were both feeling awkward.

"How are you feeling?" he asked, sitting down on another chair and drawing it up a bit closer to her.

Marie glanced up quickly, colour flushing to her cheeks as she caught his eye. "Much better than the last time I saw you. Still sore, though."

"You look a lot better."

Marie laughed and he grinned.

"I'm afraid I don't remember much of it."

"You were on a lot of drugs."

A nervous laugh escaped her. "I just wanted to thank you. For everything you did." She moved her fingers nervously along the top of the small table in front of her.

Pierre shook his head dismissively. "I'm sorry I couldn't have done more." His voice was soft with regret.

Marie looked up at him. "There's nothing to be sorry for."

Pierre shifted his weight uncomfortably.

Silence fell between them again. Marie was at a loss for something to say. She didn't want to talk about the past. If he dug too deeply, he wouldn't want to stay.

Pierre set two battered books on the table. Marie's face lit up.

"Where did you get these?" She pulled them toward her eagerly with her good hand. Books were scarce and expensive—a luxury few could afford in the frontier city.

Pierre smiled at her reaction. "I borrowed them."

Marie opened the top book, fanning the pages with her thumb. "*Merci.* Your father doesn't have any books. Since my headaches went away, I've been so bored."

Pierre's husky laugh filled the room. "You're right!" he said eventually, still wheezing. "All he owns are nautical charts and maps."

"What does he talk about at social gatherings?"

"Boats?" Pierre grinned.

It was Marie's turn to laugh. "Good thing he doesn't go out much." She put a hand on her side as her muscles protested the movement.

Pierre quickly reached across the table and held her upper arm. "Are you all right?"

Marie smiled weakly. "I'm not used to laughing."

The silence deepened. Marie felt acutely aware of the warmth of his hand through the thin fabric of her shawl. Catching himself, he removed his hand hastily.

Unsure of what to say next, Marie picked at an imaginary spot on her nail. "Did you know that I didn't want to leave?" The question was little more than a whisper—as if he hadn't meant to ask it. Marie nodded.

"You know that I didn't choose to join the army, right?" This was the question that had tormented him the most. Had anyone told her what had happened or had she thought he abandoned her and enlisted of his own volition? Marie raised her head slowly and rested her bandaged hand on the table. They were back at the past, exactly where she didn't want to be.

"Of course, I knew," she admitted. "I really thought it was an accident at first. But Nic showed me the papers. Who is General Picard?"

Pierre's angular features hardened. "He's a General stationed in Montreal. The only connection I can think of is a trial Renault and I prosecuted. Picard's younger brother was a judge caught accepting bribes. It was a scandal that ended the judge's career." Pierre's bitterness was clear.

"I thought I would hang," he said eventually. "I think Picard wanted me to, but Captain Robert, the head of the prison, was suspicious of my lack of military record. I don't think Robert trusted Picard, but since Picard was his superior officer, Robert couldn't confront him about it. All the same, Picard must have known that Robert suspected something was amiss, so I think that's why, instead of being hanged, I was left to rot.

A haunted look came into his eyes, and he stopped, staring at his hands. Marie had never seen that kind of pain in his strong features and instinctively reached her hand across the table. Without thinking, she gently began to stroke the back of his hand.

He smiled at her touch. "It was a long time ago."

"Was it terrible?"

He nodded. "I was beaten and starved on a regular basis. I was kept with some British prisoners. Became good friends with some of them. Or as close as criminals can be. No one cared what happened to us."

"But you got out."

"Once war was declared, they needed every able-bodied man."

Marie started to draw circles on the back of his hand. Because his hair was blond, it was hard to tell from a distance how hairy he was, but up close, it was obvious that his body was covered in soft fuzz. Marie smiled. She'd forgotten that detail.

"Where did you go?" asked Marie.

"Everywhere."

She gave him a look.

"I'm serious. I even went south to La Balize in Louisiana. It's between the ocean and the Mississippi River. Flat, marshy land for as far as the eye can see."

Marie paused, intrigued. "Really?"

He grinned. "I did." He sat up a little taller. "It's amazing down there. So much different than anything I've ever seen before. Boiling hot, though. I don't know how anyone can stand living there all the time."

"What else?" She was enthralled now. La Balize was about as far south as anyone could go before reaching ocean water again. She had never met anyone who'd travelled to that remote outpost.

"And the bugs," he grimaced comically. "I thought they were bad here, but you can't even piss down there without mosquitoes sucking you dry."

She bit her lip to keep from laughing.

"I saw an alligator."

"You're joking." An alligator was almost as mythical as a unicorn in the imagination of French colonists.

Pierre was really enjoying himself now. "Not just one. Hundreds—in the swamps. They weren't afraid of us either. During the day, they would stay in the water because of the heat. All you could see were their eyes. But at night, they would wander around on land on these tiny, stubby legs. You wouldn't think they'd be fast, but they could outrun a man."

Marie leaned forward, her good arm resting on the table. "Did they attack you?"

"They tried. If one gets a hold of you, you're done for. We had to set up sentinels just to watch out for those beasts. Once, we shot one and ate it."

"Now you're just telling stories."

"On my honour, it's true. It tasted a bit like raccoon."

Marie was holding her sides, trying not to move as her body shook with laughter. "How on earth do you know what raccoon tastes like?"

There was a mischievous glint in his blue eyes that she hadn't seen in years. "You've never had raccoon?"

"Not knowingly."

"Then tell me what you've been doing for the last eight years."

Marie hesitated.

"Just because you haven't wrestled alligators doesn't mean I'm not interested," he said gently.

So she told him, slowly at first, avoiding key subjects, then building momentum when she started talking about how she had trained with the nuns at the hospital to be a *ramancheur*. She became more animated as she talked about assisting the priests and setting bones. She told him about patients and surgeries. As one of the largest hospitals on the continent, the Hôpital du Roi had visitors from all over the world. Her hands moved with excitement as she talked about the royal doctors who had visited to train the surgeons and staff.

Pierre gazed at her in wonder. The light and passion that were radiating from her gave him a feeling of peace. She was still the same woman, strong and independent underneath the bruises.

"Are you still working at the hospital?" he asked when she finally paused for breath.

Her shoulders slumped, and the light immediately faded from her face. "No," she said sadly. "When the engagement between Jacques and me was agreed upon, he insisted I give it up. He didn't want a bonesetter for a wife."

Pierre felt a flash of anger rise in his stomach.

Marie nodded as if she knew what he was thinking. "I wanted to fight him about it, but then there was Claude."

Pierre made an involuntary movement toward her. He hadn't thought it was possible to hate Claude more than he did, but now he realized the man must be a sadist.

Just then, Marie and Pierre could hear Augustus's heavy footsteps on the stairs. The silvery-blond head of the master of the house appeared in the doorway. Seeing the two of them engaged in conversation, he quickly retreated with a hasty apology.

Pierre glanced out the window. "It's very late. I should be going."

Marie stood up slowly. "Thank you for coming," she smiled at him from under her thick lashes. He felt his heart skip a beat.

"Can I come tomorrow?"

Marie nodded.

"Until tomorrow then." He squeezed her hand in farewell.

***

Marie sat at the fire in her room trying to fight off the chill of the stormy night. It was May, but with the howling storm that battered the fortress, it felt more like a cold night in April. She preferred the quiet of her room to the busyness of the house. She hated how the servants stared at her and muttered behind their hands. She knew her arrival had started a most delicious scandal that they could not repeat outside the walls, but she hated feeling like an exhibit and so stayed alone in her room as much as she could, waiting for her body to heal.

She spent the day reading and waiting for the sounds of Pierre on the stairs. She knew that she'd missed him, but she'd forgotten just how much she enjoyed his company. There were no barriers when she was with him. At least there hadn't been in the past. She shivered at the thought. Eight years. A lot could happen in eight years. He would have to know everything that had happened. But she doubted he would stay after he knew the truth.

Despite the drafts coming in through the window, she was wearing only her chemise and a light robe because she was tired of the heavy night clothes she'd been wearing when she was in bed almost all the time. The cut on her head had scabbed, and Madame Cloutier had removed the stitches, but the place where the wound had been itched fiercely. She wore her waist-length hair braided to try to deter herself from scratching the scab off in a fit of frustration. Marie had definitely made an effort to look her best today. She had no wardrobe to change into, but she'd cleaned herself up, and Madame Cloutier had helped braid her hair. She'd avoided looking in a mirror ever since her arrival at the house. Glancing in one this morning, though, she felt she could definitely have looked worse.

There was a soft knock at the door, and Pierre's large frame appeared. He let the door stay open behind him.

She must have forgotten how large he was. While the room was fairly big, he seemed to take up most of it. He had to duck slightly as he came in through the doorway. Seeing that sight again made Marie want to laugh.

He sat down across from her in the spare chair, the same spot he had occupied the night before.

He saw her staring and grinned at her. "How are you?"

"Better than I have been," she replied truthfully. "The books have helped immensely. But I do miss going outside."

"If it makes you feel any better, it's raining non-stop. Everyone is staying inside anyway—if they can." He stretched his long legs in front of him.

Marie laughed. "I'm not sure if that should make me happy, but it does."

He leaned forward across the table. "What did you get up to today?"

"I read," Marie said. "And I slept and I tried not to think about the British. That's it."

Pierre smiled, a grin that lit up his entire face. The lines around his eyes were deeper now. "Just to reassure you about the British, the trenches around the fortress are looking pretty good. Better than the walls at least."

Marie wrinkled her nose. "The walls still aren't complete?"

Pierre shrugged. "They're trying to finish them, but they've been trying to do that for nearly a decade. There's only so much that can be done in this amount of time." Pierre could see that his attempt at reassurance wasn't working. What was the use of having good trenches if the walls were still a mess?

"So the siege is imminent?"

"Not necessarily, but the higher-ups believe so. Once the British leave Halifax, it will be only a few days." He sighed, remembering the last siege. Despite being in the militia, he had visited Marie as often as he could. He'd found great comfort in just sitting on the floor beside her, listening to the bombs fall.

Marie stared into the depths of the fire, watching the flames dance in a fury of orange and gold. "Do we have a chance?"

"Less than last time."

She nodded. "That's what I thought." Silence fell between them, both thinking of 1745. Suddenly remembering something else, Pierre pulled a small package from his coat pocket. "I brought you this. Thought it might help with the boredom." He pulled out a bundle of paper and charcoal and placed it on the table between them.

Tears sprang to Marie's eyes. She brushed them away impatiently.

"I don't know if you still draw but—"

Marie interrupted. "Of course, I do." Without thinking, she stood up, swooped down, and pecked Pierre on the cheek, feeling the stubble against her lips.

He turned his face toward her and pulled her in for a longer kiss. She began to squirm and pulled away.

"What's wrong?" he asked blankly.

She shook her head and retreated a few steps away.

"Do you want me to leave?" he asked uncertainly.

She glanced at him for a moment and then realized he was serious.

"No! Of course not. It's just ..."

"Just what?" Frustration was creeping into his voice.

Marie paused and looked around the room desperately for a distraction. She could feel her face flushing with anxiety.

"Is it Jacques?" he asked quietly.

"No, it's not Jacques!" Her voice was climbing.

"Then what is it?"

"Things have happened."

"All right ..." He was still very confused. "What things?"

He stood, staring at her with such concern and tenderness that she wanted to run from the room screaming. She felt as if she was breaking apart. The panic was bubbling up inside her, threatening to burst out, and the thin layer of armour that she held around herself was slowly cracking away. She wrapped her arms around her chest, trying vainly to keep the emotion from exploding out of her. The time had come, but she wasn't ready.

"Please stop," she whispered. "Go. Just go. Leave me alone." Her body began to shake with the emotion she could no longer control. "I'm ... I'm not that girl you loved so many years ago." Tears were beginning to roll down her cheeks.

"I'm ... not the same ... I'm b-broken ... I-I'm damaged." She was gasping for breath. "You d-don't ... want ... me."

Pierre moved toward her, but she retreated to a corner of the room, arms still locked around her torso, staring resolutely at the wooden floor.

"What happened?"

She glanced up. Pierre was still standing in the middle of the room, looking terrified at the scene before him. She shook her head violently.

"I can't tell you." Her voice was shaking. "I just ..." She swallowed. "Pierre, things have happened."

"I know that."

She shook her head furiously. "No, you don't! You don't know!" She was shouting.

"Then tell me." His voice was patient, but that made her feel even more trapped.

She retreated until her back was against the wall and slowly sank down to the ground. She wrapped her arms tightly around her knees.

Very slowly, Pierre walked across the room and sat down on the floor in front of her. He stayed motionless for a few minutes. She avoided his eyes.

"What happened?" he asked again softly.

"You wouldn't understand," she mumbled lamely.

"Maybe not, but I'm not about to leave. No matter what happened."

Marie snorted in disbelief.

"Marie, since the last time I saw you, I've killed people. More than I can count or remember."

"It was war." She mumbled.

"Do you think that makes it any easier to live with?" he asked fiercely.

She flinched at the edge in his voice. Reluctantly, she had to agree with him. She mumbled something as quickly as she could.

"I didn't catch that."

Marie felt a sickening swoop of embarrassment. "I'm not a virgin anymore," she mumbled, slightly louder, staring at her knees.

Silence. She glanced up at Pierre quickly and saw confusion on his face. "I think you're aware that I'm not either," he said slowly.

She shook her head. "It's not like that. Six months ago." She swallowed hard, the word sticking in her throat. "Six months ago, Jacques and I got into a big fight. I was angry that he had said he'd be bringing his mistresses everywhere. Literally everywhere. Everyone knew. It was so humiliating. I was screaming at him, telling him he couldn't do it anymore. He asked me what I was prepared to do to stop him." She could feel Pierre stiffen a few feet away. "I didn't understand at first. But then ... then ... I did ... I refused ... but ..." She closed her eyes against the memory, trying to block it out. She could feel the heat radiating off her face.

"I tried to fight him off." The tears leaked out of the corners of her eyes faster than she could stop them. "I really did. But ... but ... but I couldn't." She dissolved into tears completely.

Gently, careful not to anger her injuries, Pierre's strong arms encircled her, and he pulled her onto his lap. He held her as tightly as he could, as if trying to hold her together, to prevent the evil that had happened from ever touching her again. Marie wept bitterly, her head pressed tightly into his chest, afraid of ever leaving the safety of his arms. She could feel Pierre around her, shaking too, weeping for what had happened, for what had been lost.

Marie felt as if they would sit there forever, but eventually, her tears were spent. They stayed tangled on the floor, simply listening to each other breathe.

"I'm so sorry," he whispered finally.

"It's not your fault." Something in her voice made it clear who she felt was responsible. "I've never told anyone," Marie whispered.

She felt his lips on the crown of her head.

He shook his head. "Not your fault."

She hung her head.

"No, listen to me!" He placed his rough hand under her chin and tilted it upwards. His eyes were puffy, but they still flashed dangerously. "It wasn't your fault. You did nothing wrong." She tried to pull away, but he kept his arms tight around her. "Why would the evil he did to you change who you are to me?"

Marie still avoided Pierre's gaze, but she felt a tiny spark in the pit of her stomach. Rape was something that could destroy a reputation just as easily as loose morals could. She had seen it happen once before, and the woman in question had joined the convent in disgrace. No one ever came out and explicitly blamed the victim, but she was no longer desirable—as if she had chosen that life.

Marie looked at Pierre, unsure of what to say. They sat in silence for a while, the fire burning lower in the hearth, casting long shadows across the room. "I feel as if it's all my fault. My fault that Claude hit me. My fault that Jacques used me ... I feel as if I deserved it."

Pierre laid his cheek against the top of Marie's head. "You didn't deserve that. No one does." He looked at her sharply. "No one."

Marie didn't know what to say. She didn't quite believe Pierre, and she knew that he knew that.

"Do you remember when my mother died?" he asked quietly, gently stroking her head.

Marie hesitated. "Yes."

"I remember sitting alone up on the bluffs, not sure of whether I was ever going to leave that place and go back home. I hated the world. I remember when you suddenly showed up and refused to leave." She could hear the slight smile in his voice. He looked down at her. "I was so angry. But I never realized how much I loved you until that moment."

Marie sat up and stared at him despite herself. "You what?"

Pierre smiled down at her. He smoothed her hair away from her face. "That's the moment I started loving you. I didn't realize it for several more years, but that's when it started."

Marie couldn't meet his gaze. "You were thirteen," she mumbled.

"Like I said, it took a while for me to realize it."

He traced the plains of her face lightly with his finger. "What do you do when you get shot?"

She was startled by the question. "I don't know, I've never been shot." Then a horrifying thought occurred to her. "Have you?"

He smiled at the look on her face. "Two years ago, I was shot in the thigh."

Marie shuddered involuntarily.

"It was an ambush. Nothing more than a skirmish with the British, but somehow, I was shot. I was the only one." He shook his head at his own ineptitude. "We were in the middle of nowhere. No fort or village for miles. They had to dig the bullet out. It was in deep." He paused and glanced down at Marie, who looked slightly revolted. "It was the most painful thing I've ever been through. But I didn't really have a choice in the matter. Not unless I wanted to die slowly from lead poisoning."

Marie understood what he was trying to say and nodded.

"So I can't imagine what *you've* been through ... I start to shake and I want to hit something very hard when I think about it ... But I want you to know you can talk to me about all of it ... You need to talk to someone."

Marie let out a deep breath. "I think you're the only one I can talk to."

Pierre squeezed her gently. "I think I feel the same way. You have quite literally seen me at my worst and can still look me in the eye." He sighed heavily. "I wish I'd been here so I could have protected you from all this."

Marie shifted her weight. "At some point, you need to forgive yourself."

"Someday maybe I will, but right now my legs are asleep."

Marie laughed as she scooted away from him. He stretched and tried his best to help her get up off the floor without causing too much pain.

The rain was beating louder against the window panes, increasing the feeling of security Marie felt in the room. She yawned, exhausted from the emotion of the evening. Pierre bent down and kissed her forehead. "I'll come back tomorrow if you'll have me."

Marie blushed. "Of course, I want you to. I can't believe you still want me after all this." It seemed too good to be true.

"I never wanted to leave you, beautiful."

***

The next day brought more rain and saw Pierre trudging through it on his way to the offices of the military at the King's Bastion. Nic had summoned him to a meeting there. As he stomped through the mud and rain, he remembered that various soldiers in the garrison had told him that inclement weather like this had saved the fortress from a British invasion the previous year. But it seemed unlikely that Louisbourg could be saved by weather two years in a row.

The conversation Pierre had had with Nic two nights before about Claude was making him paranoid. Every few minutes, Pierre glanced behind himself to make sure he wasn't being followed. Nic met him at the door of the great government building, and they made their way silently to a small room off the main hallway. Nic settled into one of the flimsy wooden chairs that were clustered around the table there. Nic motioned for him to sit down.

"So, Captain, to what do I owe the honour?" Pierre asked.

Nic glared at Pierre. He hated to be reminded of his position over a childhood friend. Ordering your subordinates around was one thing. It was vastly different when you'd shared many a strapping with one of them.

Nic sighed. "How is Marie?"

"Physically, she's on the mend. But emotionally, Claude's done quite the number on her." He tried to keep the blame out of his voice but felt he was doing a poor job of it.

Nic tapped his fingers on the table. "It's been two weeks. Do you think she can move?"

"Where do you want her to go?" Pierre asked. He knew that a move away from Augustus's house had been the goal, but his personal feelings were getting in the way of being objective.

Nic didn't answer but rubbed his hands across his face. "As far away from this war and Claude as she can get."

"France?"

Nic laughed darkly. "Not with the British patrolling every square inch of the ocean."

Pierre sighed and leaned back in his chair. "How long do we have?"

Nic shrugged. "This is all confidential. You know that?"

"You really think I want to start a panic? Besides, who would I tell?"

Nic ignored him. "The Mi'kmaq say the British left Halifax yesterday. As long as the weather is bad, they won't be able to land. But the weather will change, so we have days."

Pierre nodded. He knew what was coming. "But where is she going to go?"

"So far, I have arranged travel for her to Quebec. If this place falls," he gestured around the room abstractly, "Uncle Joseph's home is open to her. He's aware of the situation and knows that she could arrive if the stars ever align."

"Claude found her once in Montreal. What's going to stop him from finding her in Quebec?"

Nic paused. "I've arranged for her to enter a convent there."

This was new. Pierre tried to cover his surprise. "You really think a convent is the answer?"

Nic shrugged. "Even the British won't kill a bunch of nuns."

"I don't like this convent idea."

"Not everything is about you," Nic snapped.

Pierre chewed the inside of his cheek. "Why can't she just stay at Joseph Dumas's?"

His Captain threw him a significant look.

"You still don't approve of me," Pierre sighed. "So why did you help me come back here?" Nic paused, weighing his words. "You're a soldier now. There's nothing either of us can do about that. If you survive, then what? You go to the next battle and the next until you're too injured or dead. You'll never be promoted with the desertion record. What kind of life is that? I was the one who wanted you to come home so you wouldn't spend the rest of your life as a wandering soldier—but not to my sister. If Claude ever caught you with her, she'd be dead."

Pierre stared at his hands, his blue eyes clouded with disappointment. Unfortunately, he couldn't argue with Nic's logic.

"Maybe at one time, it would have been appropriate for you to marry her, but she deserves more than life with a disgraced soldier."

Pierre sighed. "But she won't want to become a nun."

Nic cocked his head to one side, appraising his friend. "That's where you come in."

Pierre shook his massive blond head of hair. "I'm not going to lie to her."

"That's fine. But it's not like you can marry her either."

***

Though she wasn't doing very much during the day, Marie felt as if she was in a state of perpetual exhaustion. Her scalp itched fiercely, and the throbbing in her arm still hurt badly when there was nothing to take her mind off it. All of this meant that Marie was spending most of her time sitting. She kept to her room, as instructed, and though it was a bit dark, there was one large window that let in what natural light there was.

Marie was sitting by the window, careful that her profile could not be seen, reading one of the books that Pierre had delivered. May was supposed to be warm, she thought ruefully as she pulled the shawl closer around her. All the rain and lack of sun was making her feel gloomy. A knock at the door roused her from her reading.

It took her a while to get across the room. Elise stood in the doorway, arms laden with clothes, looking very pleased with herself.

Marie ushered her in. "What are you doing here?"

Elise dumped the contents unceremoniously on the bed. Straightening up, she surveyed Marie. "You look better than I thought you would."

Marie rolled her eyes. It had been five days since she'd last seen Elise. Beside her breathtakingly gorgeous and well-dressed friend, she felt especially woebegone in her linen chemise. "I guess I'll take that as a compliment."

Elise sat down beside the mound of fabric and began sorting through it. "How are you feeling?"

"Much better than I was." Marie looked over the pile, trying to determine what it contained. "Where did you get this stuff?"

"Some of it's mine and some of it Annette smuggled out for you." She saw the look of concern on Marie's face. "Claude has no idea where you are.

He's been over to our place a few times, ranting and raving, but now that Nic is a Captain, he's too afraid of him to do anything too drastic."

"I'm sorry about that," Marie mumbled.

"Not your fault. Maybe this time he won't actually find you." She looked up at Marie expectantly, her well-set copper hair gleaming in the sunlight. She could no longer contain her curiosity. "I've heard Pierre has been here."

Marie nodded and sat down on the bed next to her friend. "Did you know he was back?"

Elise frowned. "Nic told me, but he made me promise not to tell you. He's still terribly angry with Pierre for drawing you into his sordid life and provoking Claude. I don't think he realizes the abuse started before you left."

"How did you know?" Marie had tried her best to hide the bruises with clothing and powder.

Elise smiled sadly. "Powder doesn't hide everything. I didn't say anything because I was waiting for you to say something. I thought you were embarrassed."

"I was." Marie lay back slowly and stared up at the beige canvas that acted as a canopy over the bed. Augustus might be as wealthy as Claude, but his furnishings (and bed hangings) were plain and rough compared to the tapestries and ornament at the manor house. "Do you think I'm pathetic for still wanting Pierre?"

Elise didn't say anything immediately but fished a pair of plain leather shoes from the pile and placed them on the floor. "No, I don't," she said, straightening up. "And even if I did, you shouldn't worry about what I think."

Marie gave her a quizzical look.

Elise moved toward the foot of the bed and leaned against one of the bedposts. "I admire how hard you've tried to be happy and create a life for yourself," she said. "I really do. I don't know if I could do that if Nic died. But," Elise paused, thinking, "I know you're not really happy. I can see it in those moments when you think no one's looking. And it's more than Claude and more than Jacques. If they were the only problem, you would have gone to Joseph in Quebec. I always thought you stayed here because part of you wanted to be in Louisbourg so Pierre could find you."

"Did you tell Nic that?"

Elise laughed. "Of course not. I've told him you won't leave now, but he doesn't believe me. I love him, but he can be rather obtuse."

Marie smiled. "Even after I saw him with those women, I still wanted to talk to him. I wanted to confront him and scream and yell, but then I hoped he'd have an explanation."

Elise studied her friend's profile against the pale quilt. "What *is* the explanation?"

Marie filled her lungs up as far as they would go without hurting and let the air out slowly. "He spent six years in prison, starved and beaten. He'd been labelled a traitor—well, a deserter when he hadn't even been in the army—and he was about to be shipped off to the Ohio Valley to fight, with no way of contacting anyone he loved. He was angry and lonely and drunk."

Elise mulled it over. "I can accept that. And if that information is enough for you, I accept it even more."

"You really don't think I'm pathetic?"

"No, but I think you're a mess." She stood up and offered her hand. "We need to get you cleaned up."

297

It felt wonderful to finally shed the borrowed clothes after so many days. With her good hand, Marie washed the last of the sweat and blood from her body, behind the screen near the fire. Elise passed some clean undergarments around the screen. It took longer to dress than usual. Bending and stretching still made her ribs scream, but after a while, she'd put on her undergarments and a layer of petticoats.

Elise had organized her cargo of clothing on the bed. "What do you want to keep?"

"Without my stays, there isn't much I can wear." Marie came out from behind the screen to look.

"Remember, you'll eventually heal—most likely before you get new clothes."

"Fine. I'll keep them all then." She reached for a basic blue wool skirt and bodice that would fit without bending her ribs and started to put them on.

"I'm beginning to feel human again," she said as she slipped her hands into the pockets of the skirt.

"You look so much better too," Elise said, "except for your hair. Now sit down, so I can do something with it." Marie sat on her chair by the fire and tried to relax as Elise carefully began untangling her long, chestnut locks.

"Are the stitches still in here?"

"Madame Cloutier took them out."

Elise found the scab and tried to avoid it. Marie passed hairpins to her with her good arm.

"How did you feel when you first realized Pierre was the soldier who rescued you from the drunken men in the street?"

Marie winced as a particularly difficult knot was attacked. "I don't know if I've ever been so angry in my life. I carried on for a bit and then ran back to the manor. But when he showed up there after the ... the ... When I woke up with my arms around him on the horse ..." Marie paused, trying to think of how to explain it, "I never wanted to let him go again."

"You know, Nic is going to do everything he can to make sure you go to Quebec."

Marie snorted. "I'd like to see him try."

Elise sighed as she patted the last few strands of hair into place. "That's what I said. Why doesn't he ever listen to me?" She sat down on the chair beside Marie. "I don't know if I'll be able to come back. The rumour going around is that you're ill. But Nic's worried Claude is following people. I don't really have any other reason to visit here except to see you."

"It breaks my heart," Marie said, "but I don't want to put you in danger. It's done me so much good just to see you today. Who else would be thoughtful enough to bring clothes and help me get cleaned up? You're the greatest friend anyone could ask for."

Elise waved her hand dismissively and wrinkled her freckled nose. "Think nothing of it. I expect that you're going to give Nic plenty of reasons to be angry over the next little while, so he'll keep me up to date on what's happening with you."

She gave Marie a warm hug.

"Are you leaving before the British arrive?" Marie asked quickly.

Elise shook her head. "I go where Nic goes. Everyone I know is here." Elise left shortly after that, leaving Marie feeling very envious that Elise at least knew what her future held.

***

Marie was sleeping badly. Her arm hurt, her ribs still prevented her from sleeping in any position she wanted, and her lack of physical exercise during the day made her restless despite her fatigue. She had finally fallen into a light sleep when the door of her room banged open.

Light blazed in from the corridor, blocked in part by the gigantic figure of Pierre in the doorway. Marie sat bolt upright in bed, then grasped her side as it protested such movement. Grabbing the flint box, she lit the candle on the bedside table just in time to see Pierre collapse into one of the chairs by the fire.

"What the hell is this?" Marie yelled, her heart still pounding. Pierre gazed up at her through half-closed eyes.

Marie looked at the clock on the wall beside the fireplace. "It's three o'clock in the morning!" she exploded.

Pierre shook his head absently and stared at her in a daze. "You're so beautiful." He smelled strongly of liquor.

Marie glared at him. "What have you been doing?"

"I was at the tavern."

"I gathered that," she huffed.

"I went with some of the cadets." He grinned absentmindedly over at her. "I'm getting too old to keep up with them."

"Clearly," Marie sighed, exasperated. "Well, you can't stay here." She got out of bed gingerly, walked over to him, and put her good arm under his shoulder. Then she tried to help him up. Pierre heaved himself onto his feet and took a step toward the door, but then he staggered and collapsed onto the bed.

"I'm definitely too old for this," he groaned.

Marie rolled her eyes. "You're thirty, not twenty. At least move over so I can fit." A deep snore issued from the dark recesses of the blankets. "Of course," she muttered.

Marie carefully pulled off his boots and undid his sword belt, laying it on the table. She sat on the bed for a few moments staring down at the unconscious figure. He looked peaceful with the weight of his life momentarily erased from his mind, much more like the boy she remembered. His golden hair lay sprawled over the blankets. She pushed back the few shocks of blond hair that had fallen over his face. His cheeks felt like sandpaper, with their day's worth of invisible blond growth.

She reached over and poked him in the ribs. "Pierre?" Absolutely no response. She poked him again, but he simply rolled over and spread out across the bed even more. Sighing, she grabbed her pillow and the candlestick and made her way down to the couch in the sitting room.

***

The muffled sounds of the house slowly waking up brought Marie back to life. The servants working that early in the morning were making their way around the house, starting fires in the fireplaces, opening some windows, and starting the work in the kitchen. There was little food to prepare, but it was important to everyone to keep up the daily routines.

She opened one eye and spotted an extremely young maid peeking around the corner, trying to decide if it was safe to come in. Marie waved her forward and carefully raised herself off the couch.

It was early, the June sun was only beginning to rise, and Pierre wouldn't be awake yet. Marie smiled to herself as she gathered up her belongings and made her way back to her room.

She was right. Pierre lay sprawled across the entire bed, snoring lightly. She poked him experimentally in the ribs again, but that produced absolutely no effect.

She stood beside him for a moment, thinking, and then grabbed her pillow with her good hand and began to beat him around the head with it as hard as she could without giving herself more pain attacks. With a yell, he tumbled out of bed onto the floor, scowling up at her in confusion.

"What was that for?" he growled, trying to pull himself out of the mess of sheets and blankets.

Marie smiled sweetly at him. "I'm just repaying you for last night."

Pierre glared up at her, eyes swollen and rimmed with red. He ran his hand through his tangled hair and then swung himself back onto the bed. "I'm sorry about that," he mumbled, pressing his fingers into his eyelids. "I was very drunk and may have had some ideas that were much less than honourable."

She laughed. "I assumed as much."

"Luckily, I was too drunk to carry them out."

The sound of drums carried through the window. "Aren't you supposed to be responding to that?" Marie asked.

Pierre threw one arm over his eyes. "Not today. I have connections with the Captain. I can be late."

Marie rolled her eyes. "Nic was one of your drinking partners last night?"

"Only for the beginning. Then he left, but he knew I wouldn't be in any shape to come in this morning." He sat up. "I need more sleep, or I'm going to be very sick."

"I'd like some too," Marie said conversationally. She was enjoying herself. "The couch isn't exactly comfortable."

He pulled himself out of bed with great effort. "Good, but don't talk so loud." He headed to the door slowly. His entire body ached. "Once you're up and dressed, come and find me."

Marie laughed. She crept back into her bed, pulling the quilt around her. She could faintly make out the smell of him in the fabric. She closed her eyes and drew the quilt tighter around her body.

***

It was almost midday by the time Marie pulled herself out of bed. The water on the washstand was as cold as always, but she scrubbed her face and chest as well as she could before dressing.

Augustus spent most of his day away from the house, either at the docks or in the warehouse beside the home. Marie's presence had made it such that he was no longer able to bring people to the house, and therefore did most of his networking at the tavern. He wasn't happy about the arrangement, but Marie was appreciative.

The house was silent except for the sound of servants scurrying around. She wondered how much Augustus was paying them to remain discreet about Marie's presence. Most of them knew who she was, the ones who'd been on hand to see her dramatic arrival (with Pierre) in the middle of the night. Evidently, the news had not made its way to Claude, since he hadn't banged down the door yet. She shivered at the thought.

She found Pierre sitting at the scrubbed wooden table in the kitchen, a bowl of soup in his hands, his back to the door. Madame Cloutier was moving around the dark room, talking to Pierre adamantly about something. Then, in the middle of the conversation, her dark eyes spotted Marie, who was standing in the doorway. She nodded in her direction, drawing Pierre's attention away from his food.

Pierre grinned and motioned for Marie to join him. He looked slightly the worse for wear after his late night, but he was happy to see her nonetheless. "Good to see you finally awake. The day's almost over," he teased.

Marie plopped herself down beside him on the worn bench and happily accepted a very watery but steaming bowl of onion soup from Madame Cloutier. "*Merci*," she said, inhaling the aroma. It wasn't much, but any food was appreciated at this time.

Marie hadn't bothered to tie her hair back, and it fell down over her shoulders in waves, almost to her hips. Pierre pushed one side of the cascade back so he could see her profile. Whatever conversation had been going on between him and Madame Cloutier was now over. Marie glanced sideways in concern, but nothing seemed to be bothering Pierre.

"How are you, Marie?" Madame Cloutier asked, frowning with worry. "I heard someone decided to make a scene last night." She threw Pierre a disapproving look. "I don't know where I went wrong with that one."

Marie smirked. "You shouldn't blame yourself, Madame. You did your best. I think he just got in with a bad crowd."

The subject of their banter glowered up at them.

"That's true," the elderly dame chortled. "Pierre here was something else as a young man. I can't believe he turned out as well as he did—though that's not saying much."

"I don't know," Marie mused, scraping the last morsels out of her blue and white porcelain bowl. "I wouldn't exactly call him well adjusted."

"At least he never broke anyone's nose," Pierre piped in, looking pointedly at Marie, his eyes twinkling.

"Oh, that was you, Marie!" Madame Cloutier was delighted. "He never admitted what happened. Now I know why."

Pierre's face was bright red. "I was twelve. No one wants to admit they were beat up by a girl when they're that age."

Madame Cloutier's reedy laugh drifted across the room. "Would you want to admit that at thirty?"

Pierre appraised the woman sitting beside him. "I don't think she could do it now."

"You were a lot smaller then." Marie leaned over and squeezed one of his considerable biceps.

"What did he do to deserve a broken nose?" Madame Cloutier asked. She picked up the used dishes and deposited them in the scrub basin.

"Why do you assume I deserved it?" Pierre asked indignantly.

Madame Cloutier arched an eyebrow and put her hands on her hips. "Did you?"

"Yes," Pierre conceded, a light pink colour creeping onto his cheekbones.

Marie glanced at him.

Pierre nodded as if to say "If you must." "She knows about far worse things I've done," he said out loud.

Marie laughed. "Pierre, Nic, and a bunch of other boys, including two of my friend Elise's brothers, were swimming in the harbour. Elise and I were there too because our parents had sent us to tell them to get out of the water and go home. But the boys were having such a good time they didn't want to leave."

Pierre gazed down at the table, looking very much the part of a guilty young boy.

"Anyway, we finally got them out of the water, but then they started teasing us and generally being unbearable. They reduced Elise to tears. I tried to get them to stop, but they wouldn't. Eventually, I just lost my patience and punched the closest one, who happened to be Pierre. That shut them up."

Pierre stood up and stretched as Madame Cloutier roared with mirth. "I never would have thought you were strong enough."

Marie was a little embarrassed. "I'm sorry about that now. I'm not sure I ever apologized for what I did."

Pierre waved his large hand. "It's not really important anymore. I'm sure I've paid you back with interest."

The young maid that Marie had seen earlier that morning came into the kitchen looking for Madame Cloutier.

Pierre gestured to the door and Marie followed him into the sitting room. Pierre settled his long frame on the couch. He seemed preoccupied, but it could just have been the hangover's lingering effects. Marie sat carefully beside him, smoothing her skirts.

"I need to talk to you," he began reluctantly, not making eye contact.

"That sounds ominous."

Pierre rubbed the back of his neck.

"Please just tell me what is going on," she sighed. She had a feeling she knew what was coming.

Pierre ran his fingers through his hair so the short pieces at the front stood on end. He continued to avoid her eyes. "Nic wants you out of here as soon as possible, before the British arrive," he said in a despairing tone.

"Where does he want me to go?" she asked, trying to sound detached. "And why isn't he telling me this himself?"

"He wants you to go to Quebec under the guise of living at your Uncle Joseph's. However, he's making arrangements for you to join a convent."

Marie said something rude.

Pierre tried again. "The British are coming, but reinforcements from France are not. The estimate from the gathering in Halifax is that we'll be outnumbered five to one. We can't win, and when we lose, I don't know how safe Quebec will be, but it will be safer than here at least." He paused to draw in breath.

Marie didn't say anything for a moment. She now understood the reason behind the late-night binge. "Is Nic sending his wife to a convent?"

He had known this was how the conversation would go, but he wasn't sure what he was supposed to do about it.

"The British have been mobilizing in Halifax. The Mi'kmaq say they've already left. They should be here any day now. When they get here, no one will get in or out until the siege is over. There's a ship, probably one of the last to leave, going in three days for Montreal. It will stop at Quebec. If you leave now, Claude won't be able to follow."

"I gathered that," Marie said bitterly. "But why does Nic want me to become a nun?"

Pierre sighed and looked at her for the first time. "You can't think of any reason why he wants that?"

Marie tilted her head to one side, thinking. "If I go now, you also wouldn't be able to follow until after the war is over. If he gets me into a convent, you definitely won't follow." She could feel herself trembling with indignation.

"Exactly," Pierre said, grim-faced.

The blood was pounding in Marie's ears. She knew Nic had planned to send her away from Louisbourg, and she appreciated the need for her safety. But who did he think he was, purposely trying to separate her from Pierre. She stood up and began to pace around the room.

"No," she said finally.

"Excuse me?" Pierre asked warily.

"I said, no. I'm not going."

Pierre had expected that. He shook his head and walked over to her. "And why the hell not?" He'd meant to respond more diplomatically than that.

"I don't want to go."

"You have to go, even if you don't join the convent." Despite his promise to Nic, he didn't know if he had the resolve to win this argument.

Marie set her jaw stubbornly. "No."

"There's nothing for you here!" he exclaimed, exasperated.

Marie glared at him. For a moment, he was afraid she was going to slap him.

"Really? Nothing?" She was shouting.

"What do you want me to say?" His voice was rising as well. "There's war, hunger, bloodshed, and a madman trying to kill you. You need to get out of here. The sooner, the better."

"Is that what you want?"

"What I want doesn't matter. What matters is that you get permanently out of harm's way. Harm from both Claude and the British."

"Does what *I* want matter?"

Pierre hissed in frustration. "You want to spend the rest of your life hiding in a bedroom? Want to spend the rest of your life inside, hiding from daylight, only coming out at night? Do you want to wait until we're conquered and then shipped back to France like the Acadians? 'Cause you can if you want. You can keep on being a prisoner of this house until the British break down the door and then go back to Europe with whoever else survives this. But you won't be free from Claude."

Marie stormed out of the room, heading back to her refuge. But she paused a moment, at the door. "If you just wanted to send me away, then why have you come back here? Why? Why not just leave me to get better alone?" She turned on her heel and slammed the door behind her.

She made it to her room before tears of anger started burning in her eyes. She was a fool. A damned fool for not having seen this coming. Of course, it was no surprise that Nic expected her to leave. That had always been the plan. The fact that Pierre's explanation of his behaviour in Montreal had changed her mind would be unimportant to Nic. She wanted to stay in Louisbourg as long as Pierre was here.

She heard the door open quietly. Pierre stepped in. They stood facing each other awkwardly for a moment.

"I can't marry you," he spoke quietly, uncertainly. "You know that, right?"

Marie froze. Yes, she knew that. Pierre was a colonial French soldier and needed permission to marry. Permission that Claude would clearly use his influence to prevent.

Pierre stepped toward her, his blue eyes blazing. "I need Claude's permission to marry anyone, and he certainly won't give me permission to marry you."

Marie stood quietly for a moment, twisting her hands violently.

"I haven't seen you for eight years. There hasn't been a day that I haven't thought of you. Somehow, you've come back into my life. I have you back again."

Pierre reached out a hand and squeezed hers gently. "I love you so much. I want you so badly, but I can't marry you. I have nothing to give you. There was a time when I did. I could have given you a good life. But that's all gone now."

He paused, and she looked up into his eyes. "That's the first time you've said that in a long time," Marie said.

"What?"

"That you love me."

Pierre paused for a moment, reflecting on what he'd just said. "It's true, but you've been terrorized for all these past years," he said softly. "You were beaten again two weeks ago. You've been locked away, hidden, unable to go outside, blocked off from the world. You can't make major life decisions now. This is the worst possible time for that. Nic has your best interests at heart. Leaving will keep you safe."

"And what do you want?" she repeated, staring fiercely up at him.

He looked away. "I told you, it doesn't matter. You need to get away to safety."

"It matters to me," she insisted. "Do you want me to go?"

He swallowed and bowed his head for a moment as if in prayer. "Yes, I do. I want you to be safe more than anything else."

"Tell me the truth," she demanded.

"The truth?" He laughed bitterly. "I want you to go."

She slapped him hard across the face.

"Fine," he snarled, his blue eyes on fire, stepping quickly across the room to close the distance between them. "I want you to stay here. I want to marry you. I want to take you to bed now and never let you out of it. I want to leave the army and this forsaken island and never come back."

"All right. Let's do that then."

Pierre cocked his head, surprised by her answer. "Excuse me?"

Marie looked up, determined. She was squaring her shoulders, preparing herself for a fight. "I said, let's do that then."

Pierre laughed darkly. "You're telling me that you don't care if I can't marry you? You're willing to stay in a war zone with the threat of Claude, just so you can stay and wait to see if your husband—well, your sort-of husband—doesn't die?"

"Yes."

Pierre threw his head back and laughed again, but this time, the edge of bitterness cut deep. "If France beats the British, and I somehow make it out in one piece, it doesn't change anything! Claude will still hunt for you. I still can't marry you, and you'll still have to spend your days hiding from him."

"So what? Shut up!" Marie shouted. "I don't care. I've waited years and years for you. I'm not leaving you again. I would have married you eight years ago on the night you first asked me. I asked you to ... I asked you to take me to a church right then, but you wanted to wait and look where that got us!"

"You don't think I'd marry you if I could?" he roared. "Of course I would, but my life isn't my own anymore! I go where they tell me to. I fight who they tell me to. I eat what they tell me to, and I have to marry who they say I can! ... After Louisbourg, I'll go somewhere else, probably a New England prison. That's no life for you."

"And I say I don't care!" Their faces were inches apart. "I'm tired of waiting! I'm tired of other people telling me I can't be with you! I haven't done anything wrong except love you!" Her hands began to tingle unpleasantly. She balled them into fists to prevent them from hitting anything. The nerves in the arm that had been broken started to send out jabs of pain.

Pierre pounded his fist on the table by the fireplace. "I can't take you to a church and call you my wife! Though I've wanted to do that since I was seventeen." His voice was dangerously low, cracking with the strain of holding back his fury. "You hate me for having my way with a whore but expect me to do the same thing to you and call it marriage?"

"I expect you not to abandon me again just because my precious brother asked you to."

Pierre glared at her, furious. "Fine," he said in a voice that he wanted to sound calmer. "Fine." And he stormed out of the house.

Chapter 12

MARIE SPENT THE REST OF THE DAY SWINGING from confusion to anger to despair. As always, she did not leave the house during the daylight hours but paced listlessly from one room to the next, trying to understand what had happened earlier that afternoon. After avoiding servants and Augustus's inquiries for several hours, she eventually shut herself back in her room. But alone in her room, she had nothing to distract her from her thoughts and her fears for Pierre. Where on earth had he fled to?

It was a relief to finally retreat to the dark garden. It was on a large plot of land directly behind the house, surrounded by a wooden fence that divided it from the neighbours, and it was extensive enough to support many of the home's food needs. It was her favourite part of the Thibault estate. When she wasn't hiding in her room or pacing around the upstairs, she spent her time in the garden, taking refuge from the frightening and frustrating realities around her.

It was the first day of June, and the rain had temporarily abated. The cool but calm weather was a welcome change from the blustery storms of the previous week. The smell of damp earth and stone calmed her. The dark mist pressed around her like a blanket. There were no nosy questions here. No odd looks. She settled herself on the wooden bench facing the onion bed and rested her back against the cool stone wall. A thick, leafy grapevine snaked above her head. It never produced any fruit, but it was sumptuous. She stared up at the few stars peeking out from behind the clouds as she slowly twisted a poor clover flower between her fingers.

He appeared silently as he always did, frightening the life out of her. The moon gave off enough light that she could see his face. At least he had the decency to look ashamed.

"Hello, beautiful."

Marie stared down at her hands. Embarrassed, angry, and unsure of what to say, she continued to look carefully at the clover flower as she twisted it around and around.

Pierre knelt down in front of her and put his hand under her chin. "I'm sorry I left."

Marie sighed and stared at the ground. "Are you one of those people who just walks out whenever you get angry?"

"Not usually. I was angry, but that's not really why I left."

Marie stared resolutely at the clover. "Then why did you leave?"

Pierre shifted his weight on the stone slab under his knees. "I talked to some people, tried to figure out what to do. I even asked Father Weber if he would marry us without permission from my commanders. He didn't like that very much."

Marie shut her eyes and ground her teeth together. "I don't understand why this is so complicated. What happened? What did we do?"

Pierre sighed. "We didn't do anything."

Her eyes snapped open. "You know why this is all going on?"

He nodded and pulled himself onto the bench beside her, leaning his head against the stone wall of the house. "When I was younger, I used to joke that my parents didn't like each other very much. I'm an only child. There were no others. No pregnancies that didn't make it to term, no children who died of terrible illnesses—just me. It wasn't until I got older that I realized that was true. After me, my mother felt that she had done her duty to my father by providing him with a son."

Marie's mouth fell open. "I always just assumed that there were problems that weren't discussed."

"There were." He laughed bitterly. "But not the kind most people think of. My father swears he never wandered while she was alive. He doesn't think she ever did, considering she was always so busy helping everyone else. So it was just the three of us in this house. They never fought, but I don't think they ever interacted much." He paused and rubbed his face as if washing away some memory.

"After she died, things between my father and me were ... strained. He worked all the time. I knew he was a busy man with lots of ships that had diseases and pirates and all sorts of issues. So I just accepted that this was normal life. We never talked to each other about anything of great substance, but I didn't understand why. Then he started seeing someone. For years, I didn't know who it was. He sent me to Quebec partly so that he could be with her. I was an unwanted distraction. He swears he loved her in a way he never loved my mother, but he spent his time with her, not me." His tone was unbelievably bitter.

Marie put her hand on his arm. "Oh Pierre, I'm so sorry."

"Not as sorry as you will be. Do you remember when I asked you to marry me?"

"Yes." Her lips twisted at the corners. It was a moment she had brought back to mind many times, to give herself some peace and joy during the darkest moments of the last few years.

"Do you remember when Annette was sick in bed?"

"Yes, she had a fever. She almost died," Marie whispered uncertainly.

Pierre shifted his weight uncomfortably. "No, Claude threw her down the stairs."

"What?! Why?" But she had a feeling she knew the answer.

"She was pregnant. She and Claude couldn't have children, so she thought she was barren. When she told my father what had happened, Augustus convinced her to trick Claude into going to bed with her. Claude refused. I don't know why. Maybe that's why my father and your aunt bonded: having spouses who didn't want them.

"I didn't know any of this. Augustus didn't tell me until after it all happened. But I literally went and asked Claude if I could marry you the day his wife had the miscarriage of my father's bastard child. How could that not end badly?"

Marie was stunned. Unsure of what she had been expecting Pierre to say, it definitely wasn't this. Thinking back now, though, it made sense. Annette's absences from the house, Augustus's concern for their welfare. And she had suspected nothing.

"Is that why Claude never hits Annette?"

Pierre looked surprised. "He doesn't?"

Marie's long hair waved around her head as she shook it from side to side. "Except for that one time when you said he threw her down the stairs. I always wondered what I did to deserve his outrageous hatred and his beatings, while he never lifted a hand against her. He screamed at her all the time, but he took most of it out on me after Nic left the house." Marie sighed and squeezed Pierre's hand. He looked down at their joined hands and smiled.

"Claude will never, ever give permission for us to wed," Pierre said, "and unfortunately, he has enough power that people listen to his wishes."

They sat in silence for a while.

"Does Claude ruin the lives of everyone who upsets him?" Marie asked, not really expecting an answer.

Pierre scratched the back of his head. "Claude had a Bishop sent back to France because the Bishop suggested Claude try to work on his marriage."

Marie had forgotten about that event; she was only eleven at the time. Suddenly, she didn't feel so isolated. Glancing at Pierre, she reached out and brushed the moisture that clung to the corner of his eye.

"I lost everything. For those six years in prison, all I could think about was you, but once I got out ..." His voice cracked. "I-I can't believe how close you were. How close we were two years ago. But I messed it all up. Marie, I'm so sorry. I'm ..."

Marie put her hand on top of his mouth. "It doesn't matter anymore. It doesn't matter what you did, what I did. What matters is that we're here." She wrapped her arm around his and laid her head on his shoulder.

He closed his eyes and enjoyed the feeling of having her so close. Then he extricated himself and lowered his body to the ground again. The moon shone off her skin, the ghost of the bruises now completely invisible in the inky night.

Pierre pulled out a simple silver ring from his pocket. "This was my mother's—Camille's. I want you to have it. I can't marry you in a church before a priest, but I promise you and God that I will love you until the end of my life. I will do everything I can to protect you from anything or anyone who may want to harm you. I'll honour you and cherish you, and I promise that someday, when this is all over, if I can ever be my own man, I will marry you properly."

Marie covered her face with her good, right hand for a moment. She was grinning like an idiot and giddy with excitement. She took her hand away from her face and extended it. Pierre then slipped the band over the knuckle on her third finger. "I love you," he whispered and kissed her hand gently, mindful of the bandages on her left arm.

"Do you still want me to leave?" Marie asked hesitantly.

"Yes and no. I want you to be out of harm's way, but I'm so afraid that if you leave again, I'll never find you."

"Me too," Marie said.

"So I'd like to be selfish and keep you here if you'll have me. I'll keep you as safe as I can, and when this is over ... I don't know." He sighed heavily. "I don't know what's going to happen. Maybe I need to stop thinking about it."

Marie ruffled his hair. "If Louisbourg falls, we'll all go back to France."

"You say that as if it was all so simple. Besides, you hate France." He stood up slowly. "I think my knees are broken."

Marie laughed. She was in such a buoyant mood that everything seemed hilarious. She touched the ring on her finger. She never wore jewellery. It felt odd to have it there, feeling far heavier than it actually was. "Do you have one?"

He chuckled and pulled her to her feet, arms wrapped around her slender waist. "No, my father claims he never had one, though I suspect he just thinks rings are unmanly."

Marie giggled. "That seems like something he would think." She paused for a moment. "What can I promise you?"

He bent down and kissed her more roughly than before ... and for longer. "Nothing," he said at last, releasing her for a moment. "No promises needed. You're still here, and that's all that matters. After everything, you're still here. Heaven knows why we're finally with each other again, but I'm glad of it."

Marie leaned her forehead against his. Her long hair tumbled all around them. "I don't want to live without you. I've done it. For a while I hoped that somehow you would magically appear, that against the odds, you would come back, but eventually I gave up."

"I didn't know about Claude. Please believe me. If I had known, I would have come back. Done something to try to stop it ..."

Marie smiled sadly. She didn't doubt him. He wrapped his hands around her fingers, completely covering them.

"Will you come with me?" Pierre asked.

She smiled shyly and nodded.

Pierre helped her get up from where she was sitting, and they silently made their way back into the deserted house.

"Where is everyone?" Marie asked. It was late, but usually at this hour, the house was still filled with the soft hum of end-of-day chores.

A faint blush crept up the back of Pierre's neck. "I may have told my father what I was planning to do. I think he told everyone to be scarce tonight, so we can have some privacy."

Marie's eyes widened in surprise. "And your father? Where is he?"

"Out drinking, I expect, with some of his less reputable partners." Pierre glanced down. "You don't have to do anything you don't want to."

The room was warm and inviting after the chill of the dark garden. Marie sat down on her bed, but Pierre stayed by the door. "I realize this might not be easy for you," he said awkwardly, a fierce crimson rising in his cheeks.

Marie shook her head and walked back toward him. "Don't worry about me."

He leaned against the wall and pulled her closer. "But that's my job—worrying about you."

She brushed the short hairs away from his eyes. "I just don't want any comparisons. I'm not as experienced as you are."

Pierre scoffed. "You think I'm stupid? Besides, there's no comparison."

He gathered her in his arms and held her tightly against him.

***

Sometime later, Marie lay in his arms. Cradled between his muscular arms and chest, she felt a security and satisfaction that she had never felt before in her life. She wiggled as close to his warmth as possible.

Pierre smoothed her hair away from his nose. "Can I call you my wife now?"

Marie grinned. "I like the sound of that."

"My beautiful wife," he whispered into her hair. "Madame Thibault." He pulled the bedclothes over them both.

Marie giggled happily. "How long do we have?"

"Forever."

She slapped his arm. "You know what I mean."

"Yes," he sighed, unwilling to go back to reality. He rolled onto his back but kept his arm tightly around her so she moved with him. "We have tomorrow and then I have to drag myself away from you and back to the army."

Marie sat up, startled. "How on earth won't you be missed for another day with the British fleet on their way? You didn't do anything today."

"Speak for yourself." He grinned and pulled her back down so her head rested on his chest. "I did a few things. But my Captain told me personally that he didn't want to see me for at least a day."

Marie laughed in amazement. "You didn't tell him, did you?"

"As a matter of fact, I did. I figured if I can't ask your father because he's dead or your uncle because he's a madman, then I should at least ask your brother."

"What did he say?"

"A lot of terrible things that I will never repeat to you," Pierre said, staring at the canvas canopy above them. "He blamed me for a lot of things, but I think he knew he couldn't convince you to leave if we'd reached a decision, so he finally conceded. He's not happy about it, of course."

"I'll bet he's not."

Her fingers traced a raised outline of scar tissue on his left breast. She felt a sickening wave of revulsion as she recognized the letter "D."

"Always a deserter," he muttered.

"They branded you?" He grabbed her hand and intertwined his fingers with hers.

"Yes, so I'll never be able to forget." His eyes were sad.

She traced a small scar near his temple. "What did they do to you?" She suddenly realized how long they really had been apart. He had lived terrible things that she would never know.

Pierre placed a large finger at the top of her shoulder and began to follow a long, thin, white line downward, over the curve of her breast, and across the nipple to her stomach. There were other thin scars too—some only the thickness of a hair strand, carefully crisscrossing over the pale skin of her torso. The scars of a horsewhip.

"I could ask you the same thing."

Marie looked down. "He usually just used his fists but not that time in Montreal."

Pierre shuddered at the matter-of-fact tone of her voice. "I want to kill him."

Marie smiled sadly. "I know, but that would accomplish nothing but vengeance followed shortly by more heartbreak after they hang you. I would prefer that you spend the rest of your life in bed with me."

He smirked. "You like it?"

"Yes," she whispered, turning a brilliant shade of red.

He rolled onto his back, moving her with him so she was on top of him. Her long hair fell to her waist. She felt much less self-conscious than she had the last time. He pushed her hair behind her shoulders and admired her for a moment, reaching up to kiss her lightly.

"Your hair keeps getting in the way," he laughed.

"I could cut it if it's a distraction to you."

Pierre pulled her head down so he could kiss her. "No, it's beautiful. It just keeps smothering me."

Marie collapsed in a fit of laughter.

"What? It does!" he said indignantly.

"All right," she wheezed, reaching for a hair ribbon on the bedside table. "I know you hate short hair." She quickly fastened most of her locks behind her head. "Happy?"

"I've never been happier," he grinned as she moved toward him.

***

He stared at her sleeping form as the moonlight shone off her slender body. She lay there so beautiful beside him, her face turned toward his chest, looking completely at peace. He ran a hand down her smooth back as he tried to fight off the feelings of guilt that were overcoming him.

She was here now, and she wasn't going to leave. He could have sent her away, fought harder to convince her that her safety was the most important thing. He could still recall Nic's look of betrayal as Pierre had explained that she wasn't leaving but staying here with him. The possibility that they would both be killed in the coming conflict was great. Was it really worth the few days they would have together until then?

Marie stirred and gazed dreamily up at him.

"I'm not used to sharing my bed," she said, stretching sleepily.

"Me neither."

"Can't sleep?" She touched his face gently with concern.

"I'm just wondering if I made the right decision keeping you here."

Marie smiled and curled closer into him. "It wasn't your decision to make. It was mine. You can't make me leave."

"Would you leave now, even if I promised to find you afterwards?"

"Of course not."

He pressed his lips against the top of her head. "I didn't think so."

***

The sun was well up in the sky before Marie asked, "Aren't you hungry?"

"Of course." He pinched her bottom, making her jump. "But there isn't very much to eat. The last of the wheat stores have already been opened."

"I still want something, even if it's stale bread. Maybe it's time we went back into the real world." Marie eased her way off the bed and began to rummage around the floor, looking for her clothes that had been strewn here and there during the night.

"Will anyone still be here at this time?" Marie asked.

"Do you mean do you have to get dressed?" Pierre laughed. "Probably be a good idea. You don't want to distract anyone from their duties."

Marie reached back to the bed and tossed a pillow at him.

The rest of the house was silent except for the deafening pounding of rain on the windows. Marie had given up on finding all her clothes, so Pierre got dressed and went to the kitchen in search of some food. Marie walked to the window, leaning her forehead against the cool glass. It had been raining heavily for so many days that it felt as if it would never stop. Hopefully, the constant downpours would keep on delaying the British, but the rain was turning the city's streets into impassable rivers of mud.

Marie was so transfixed by the droplets of water clinging to the glass, watching them dance and swirl on their journey to the ground, that she didn't hear Pierre come up behind her until he'd wrapped his arms around her waist.

"I have some soup for us to eat here. With the amount of excitement I caused showing up in the kitchen, I think I'd rather starve than go back there."

Marie giggled and turned around, leaning her head on his chest, breathing in his scent. It was so calm here in the house that the coming war seemed very far away.

"Want to go outside before we eat?" she asked suddenly.

Pierre frowned. "No. It's pouring rain and the soup's going to get cold."

"I know, but I love the rain." She let go of him and moved toward the door. Pierre sighed. She had a tendency to do things like this. He stepped between her and the door.

"It's daytime. You're supposed to stay inside."

"Who's going out in this?" she pointed to the downpour. "I just want to feel the rain on my face."

Pierre rolled his eyes.

Marie crept down the stairs, avoiding everyone, and pushed open the side door leading to the garden and stood in the doorway, smelling the sweet scent of rainwater, damp earth, and plants. She stepped out into the storm, face turned up toward the heavens, letting the water wash over her. She closed her eyes and sighed contentedly.

Pierre appeared beside her with his cloak spread wide over his head. He knew better than to offer something to keep her dry, but he wasn't about to stand in the rain soaking himself. She smiled up at him, her hazel eyes bright. She leaned up to kiss him, her lips and skin chilled from the rain. She was drenched all the way through her clothes, which wasn't especially comfortable for Pierre, but as he pulled away, she wrapped her good arm around him, soaking his shirt around his middle. He moved his cloak so it covered both of them. They stayed joined together in the garden, blissfully unaware of anything else until lightning cut across the sky, forcing them inside and back to their now tepid bowls of soup.

***

Pierre lay on his stomach, dozing peacefully, his body sprawled across their marriage bed. He was so tall that his legs hung off the bed by at least a foot. Marie smiled as she watched him. She wanted to touch him, to run her fingers down the indent in his spine and hold onto the bubble of contentment where they were temporarily suspended. But she was afraid of waking him. The terrible fear of the unknown was beginning to boil inside her. The invaders were coming. What would happen to them then?

Marie reached for the paper and charcoal Pierre had given her. She wanted to capture him as he was at this moment: completely at peace, unburdened by military duty or the collapse of an empire.

She drew quickly as the daylight slowly crept from the room. The long curve of his back, the slope of his shoulders, the mess of golden locks dancing around his head, his lean legs extending beyond the mattress. Then there were the scars on his body. She knew the origin of some of them but not of others. It looked as if a bullet had gone clean through his right shoulder, though he'd mentioned only the one in his leg. A thick, shiny, white scar ran the length of his upper left arm, and she didn't know what had caused that either. She hoped there'd be time for Pierre to tell her where they'd come from.

Her eyes travelled to his muscular calf. She almost laughed out loud when she spotted the faint outline of the wound that Madame Lavis's dog had left there. Pierre and Nic had decided to spend an afternoon goading the poor canine, thinking they'd have no trouble because it was safely behind its fence. That illusion collapsed when the dog leaped over the fence and chased after them.

Marie was startled when her eyes moved up to his face and she saw him staring at her, a look of deep serenity on his features. His blue eyes twinkled as he watched her hand move over the paper. He continued to stay perfectly still.

"How long have you been awake?" Marie asked, startled.

"Awhile. I like watching you draw. You look so peaceful and full of determination. I haven't seen you draw in so long."

Marie laughed. "I felt I had to make a greater effort after you gave me the supplies."

Pierre rolled over. "I used to keep the drawings you sent me in Quebec. My cousins used to tease me about that fiercely."

"I've never drawn you before, you know."

Pierre sat up and took the paper from Marie. "I like it."

She looked at him, suddenly afraid for their future. "You're leaving tomorrow."

He squeezed her hand. "Yes. I don't want to spend anymore time away from you than I have to, but they're sending me to the trenches and I won't be able to come back until they transfer me somewhere else—if that somewhere else is closer to you. Hopefully, they'll post me at the ramparts. I'll at least be in the city, not far from here."

Marie nodded but didn't trust herself to look at him.

Pierre pulled himself closer to her and wrapped his arm around her. "Don't be afraid."

The tears were far too close to the surface, but she laughed at the absurdity of the situation. "That's ridiculous. You'll be right in the thick of it." She kept trying in vain to blink back the tears that were slipping over her lashes. "How badly are you outnumbered?"

"Five to one at least. The last report from the Mi'kmaq was around fourteen thousand, but we won't know for sure until the army arrives." Pierre pulled her onto his lap. "I'll send back word as soon as I can."

"What did you tell them at the barracks? And why aren't you sleeping there anymore?" It was an unimportant question, but she thought if she focused on the invasion anymore, she might explode.

"The truth." She looked up at him sharply.

"Or a version of it anyway," Pierre said. "I told them I had met someone and was spending my nights with her because it was better than being with them. During the mutiny, I couldn't understand why the soldiers were upset. I mean, the King's Bastion is huge. But now that I live there, I understand. Drafty fireplaces, leaking roofs, men in close quarters, farting and burping all night long."

Marie laughed. "I love you."

He kissed the tip of her nose. "I love you too."

"I'm glad I rank higher than a bunch of stinking soldiers when it comes to bedmates."

"You might snore a little, but not as much as a hundred men."

"I don't snore," she pouted.

He snuggled into her. "No, you don't, but you do steal the covers."

Silence fell between them, both thinking about the next day. "I can't promise that everything is going to be all right. Terrible things are going to happen," Pierre said at last. Marie held him as tightly as she could. "But I got you back, and I'll take these few days in exchange for whatever comes next."

***

The next morning broke cold and rainy. Marie curled closer into Pierre's back, lying peacefully in the pocket of warmth under the quilt. She could feel the steady beat of his heart and sighed, knowing he would be gone soon.

The steady beat of the military drum carried through the windows. Pierre sighed and rolled out from their sanctuary. He moved around the room quickly, looking for his discarded clothing. Then he came back to the bed and kissed her lightly.

"Be safe," Marie whispered.

"They haven't even made it here yet. Don't fret yourself until that happens." Pierre gave her a quick smile and kissed her forehead before heading out silently into the sombre day.

PART FIVE: INVASION

Chapter 13

THE FORTRESS WAS IN A STATE OF FRENZIED PREPARATION. The British fleet had arrived. Four hundred men-of-war ships carrying over fourteen thousand men were waiting in Gabarus Bay for the weather to improve enough for landing. Three miles was all that stood between the fortress and the invaders.

Outnumbered though they were, the inhabitants of Louisbourg were not going down without a fight. No one had said it, but everyone knew that the longer the fortress could defend itself against the British, the less likely an attack on Quebec would happen that year, giving the French government a greater chance to send reinforcements.

Deep trenches had been dug around the fortress, and the ramparts, still not completely repaired despite the efforts of the last nine years, were being hastily patched. The trenches covered the plains in front of the fortress, avoiding the marshland to the southwest. Cannons had been painstakingly rolled to the front lines. Mortars, with their explosive shells that could be shot high in the air, were moved into position, and the five French warships that were in the harbour prepared themselves to be the last stand between the British navy and the citizens of Louisbourg. Sailors, whether in the navy or not, became a part of the defence. And as a mark of just how desperate the situation was, the army and naval leaders were conferencing together, though both famously detested each other.

The thick fog that had enveloped the island's coast for so long finally dispersed on the morning of June 8th. The British General, James Wolfe, had tried to make a landing the day before, but the waves had prevented any craft from reaching the rocks. Today, the water was calmer, Pierre thought pessimistically.

The French soldiers were lined up in the trenches above the water, the higher ground a tactical advantage even though they were sorely outnumbered. Pierre had spent a week in those trenches, randomly firing at the British to remind them that the French were still alive. Food was scarce and substandard at best, and there was little shelter from the pounding rain and driving winds. It had been a long week, and some of Pierre's companions in the trenches had already been taken to the hospital sick after being exposed to the elements for so long.

They were all exhausted and starving. No matter what form of attack the British would launch, the French soldiers, who had spent a week or more standing knee-deep in mud, were prepared for little except to meet their maker.

Pierre lay on the wet grass, above the trenches letting the dampness soak through his coat and staring at the dark clouds rolling above his head. A couple of cadets were wrestling behind him. He ignored them and tried to bring Marie's face to his mind's eye. Her creamy complexion, with a hint of rose across her cheekbones, swam into view. His fingertips ached, unable to touch her.

A shout rang out through the damp air. Pierre opened an eye, annoyed that his daydream had been interrupted. The cadets behind him stopped playing, and men were running and shouting. Pierre sat up and looked toward the harbour. The last of the fog was vanishing, revealing innumerable British warships. The sight was enough to make any man's blood run cold. The five warships in Louisbourg harbour could not withstand the British indefinitely. Victory was not possible.

"They're coming," Pierre muttered, picking up his musket. Small figures could be seen swinging over the sides of the boats. The offensive was mounting. A lanky boy of seventeen lay sprawled on the ground beside him but didn't move. Pierre smacked him on the back. "Gérard, the Redcoats are coming."

A grimace spread across Gérard's spotted face. "Well, I'm not getting up until they land."

"Like hell you will. Best to be standing when they start shooting at us." Pierre reached a massive hand around the boy's worn collar and pulled him onto his knees.

"All right, all right. Let go!" Gérard shouted. "I'm not a damn kitten."

Pierre laughed and turned back to the battle preparations unfolding before him.

The soldiers stood silently, watching the enemy soldiers jump from the sides of the ships and into the boats that would ferry them to soil.

Gérard swore under his breath. "We're dead."

Pierre agreed but thought silence was the better option. The French officers began the defensive. Fires were set to prevent the enemy from seeing the position of the soldiers and the cannons. But as the fires grew, the wind direction changed, making the smoke blow back onto the French army.

Pierre fell to his knees, coughing as the smoke sank into the trenches. The men scrambled out of their positions, trying to find clear air. Gérard rolled onto the grass above the trench, eyes streaming. Pierre looked toward the water. The landing boats were filled and starting the advance.

From somewhere behind him, the order was given to fire, but chaos reigned. The cannons sticking out of the sides of the British ships roared, but the French weren't ready to shoot back. Pierre ducked against the incoming volley and readied his musket. Beside him, Gérard's musket was jamming.

The British were stuck near the coast, unable or unwilling to advance under the barrage of bullets from the French soldiers in the trenches. Some British soldiers fell; Pierre could see the unmistakable red wool of their uniforms floating in the surf.

Then, above the barrel of his gun, Pierre spotted one of the British commanders riding at the front of one of the boats. With a screaming shout, he leaped over the front of the bow, wading in the thigh-deep water until he reached shore.

Pierre had never seen anything like it. Suddenly, the British force began to pour over the sides of their vessels, splashing and yelling.

The smoke from the fires continued to swirl around the French, mixing with the white discharge of their muskets. It was difficult to see the enemy, but one thing was clear, the British were gaining a foothold.

A trained soldier could reload a musket in less than thirty seconds during a drill. During the heat of battle, however, with all the distractions of combat, that time inflated to almost two minutes. All the same, the French continued to pour everything they had at the invading red army. It did little good. Bullets rained all around them. A cadet near Pierre went down, a musket ball to the brain.

The cannons roared from their position beside the trenches, but for every British soldier they obliterated, another two took his place.

A bullet slammed into Gérard, knocking him to the ground. The boy crouched on the wet grass screaming, his thumb no longer attached.

The order came to retreat. Pierre wrapped his arm around Gérard's shoulders and pulled him to his feet. It wasn't clear how far back they were going until the stone walls of the fortress, about three miles away, were almost in front of them.

"We're just letting them come?" Pierre spat at Nic as the defeated troops trickled into the safety the fortress provided, carrying their ancient artillery with them.

Nic shrugged. He felt sick enough about the situation without this harassment. "The idea," he said, "is to defend the fortress, not get slaughtered on the plains."

Pierre opened his mouth to retort.

"You want to stop them? Be my guest." Nic pointed to the field that would soon be filled with British tents and artillery. "There's nothing left to do. We don't have the men or the ammunition." He glowered up at Pierre, waiting for a reply.

Pierre said nothing. Vindicated, Nic turned away.

There was nothing they could do now but wait for the siege to begin.

***

There is only so much time one can spend darning socks and mending before the tediousness of the task takes over. For the past two days, Marie had tried her best to keep busy with duties like these while the explosions in the distance echoed through the house. Since the young maid, Sabine, had come back with the news that the British were anchored off shore, unloading their artillery, a knot had developed in the pit of Marie's stomach. Eating was difficult, she couldn't sleep, and she had nothing to do to keep her mind off the numbing fear that those she loved at the front weren't going to come home.

Augustus had left four days before to fight with the militia. Now that the British had landed, he and some of his fellow militiamen were assigned the duty of harassing the Redcoats. Shooting at the British while they tried to make camp, stealing supplies, and burning tents that were left unoccupied wouldn't stop the British, but it would make life more difficult for them. The only ones left at Augustus's home were Marie, the two maids, and Madame Cloutier. The maids avoided Marie at all costs, but Madame Cloutier found some time to talk about the battle and give empty reassurances. Marie found these unrealistically optimistic predictions just infuriating. Some of her fellow citizens of Louisbourg were not going to survive this battle, and it was pointless to pretend otherwise.

It was late in the evening of June 10th, and the setting sun was burning the sky crimson and pink after finally showing its face after so many rainy days. There had been no word from Pierre to say he'd made it through this first battle, and Marie didn't press for news. She knew better than to expect her brother to keep her informed.

She was walking around the lower level of Augustus's house, locking windows and extinguishing candles. That was normally the maids' job, but most of them had left to return to their own families, so there weren't enough people to do all the housework. Helping out gave Marie something to cut the oppressive boredom of waiting, waiting, waiting. As she was putting out the candles in the front entrance, the heavy front door swung open, bringing with it a wave of warm, salt air. Pierre stepped into the hallway soaked and covered in dirt and grime. His exhaustion was obvious as he leaned his musket against the wall. With a cry of relief, Marie flung herself into his arms.

"I'm all right, I'm all right," he whispered softly, stroking her hair. His voice was weak, but he looked unharmed from what she could see.

Relief washed over Marie as she stepped back to inspect him. "What happened?"

Pierre didn't reply but moved slowly, shrugging out of his blue coat and pulling off his boots. Then he unbuckled the belt that held his pistols and knife before sinking into the nearest chair. "We couldn't hold them off," he said finally. "There were too many of them. We were tired and starving and cold. We've retreated all the way into the fortress. They've started to make camp."

Marie bent down in front of him, caressing his face in her hands. "You're freezing," she muttered. "When was the last time you had something to eat?"

Pierre smiled at her. "This morning."

Marie called for Madame Cloutier to bring warm water and clean clothes. Turning back to her husband she asked, "Can you walk upstairs to bed?"

Pierre laughed quietly. "I'm not hurt, you know. Just tired and hungry."

Despite his protests, she wrapped her arm around his waist and walked with him up the stairs to her bedroom. He took off his shirt and sat down as Sabine and the other maid brought in brown bread, liquor, soup, towels, and water. Silently, Marie began to wash the blood and battlefield grime off his aching shoulders.

"Talk to me," she whispered. His torso was covered with bruises.

He sighed and rested his head on her chest for a moment. "They left us out in the trenches for a week before the British finally landed. A week with little food and no shelter. So many of the boys got sick. Men can't fight properly when they're starving and exhausted."

Marie nodded. She'd been afraid of that. It was the first siege all over again. The fortress didn't have enough supplies to keep the fighting force healthy and still sustain the citizens.

"In no time at all, they'd made it to the beach. We couldn't hold them off," Pierre continued, a haunted look in his eye. "We fought them. I fought as hard as I could, but they still made it here. We had to retreat."

Pierre had said that already, but now wasn't the time to point that out. "But you're not injured?"

He shook his head. "Not yet, but so many of our men are already lying dead on the battlefield. Now there isn't much to do except try to stop them from surrounding the fortress."

Marie placed the filthy towel back in the basin and stood between his knees. She rested her head on his damp hair. "How long are you home for?"

He sighed and pulled her closer. "Just tonight. Someone finally had enough sense to pull out those who had been in the trenches for so long. Figured we needed a night indoors and a decent meal."

"What would you like first? whisky? bread?"

Pierre leaned his head against her chest. "I need you," he looked up, pleading. "The rest can wait."

***

Darkness had fallen by the time Pierre rolled off the bed to get some of the food the maids had left on the table by the fire. Marie lay on her stomach, watching him move around the room. The firelight dyed his skin a ruddy orange.

Pierre came back toward the bed and set a bowl of soup and a plate of stale bread on the bedside table. Then he got back in under the covers and reached over to get the bread. "What about you? What have you been doing all this time?" he asked between mouthfuls of bread, his cheeks round with food.

Marie smiled in amusement at him. "Nothing nearly as important as you. I've been darning socks."

"Socks are important," Pierre said.

"I'm going mad here," she admitted reluctantly. "It wasn't pleasant before, just hiding and waiting around, but now I'm here worrying about you all day. What if ..."

"You and your 'what ifs.'" He stretched a long arm over to the bedside table and grabbed the bowl of soup.

Marie gave him a look. "Thoughts just begin to race through my head."

Pierre leaned his broad back against the headboard. "Are you eating?" He was completely serious now.

Marie sat beside him and fiddled with a strand of hair. "Not really. I can't sleep, and I can't eat. I told you, I'm going mad."

Pierre was quiet for a while. She could see his jaw furiously moving back and forth. "Maybe you shouldn't be here anymore," he whispered to himself.

"I can't leave," Marie muttered, an edge in her voice. She wasn't about to reopen this conversation.

Pierre gazed across the room, his blue eyes looking at but not really seeing the window because he was so preoccupied. You can't leave the fortress ... ," he said. Marie looked at him, impatient for him to continue. "You worked at the hospital before, correct?"

"You know that."

"And you're a *ramancheur* now? You're actually healing people?" He wasn't teasing.

Marie nodded. "The nuns trained me. I'm quite the competent little healer now. You want me to go there?"

Pierre shrugged. "If it gave you something to do and took your mind off things. I'm not Jacques, you know."

Marie bristled at the suggestion. "Of course, you're not, but the hospital ... you've wanted me to stay inside so no one sees me."

Pierre sighed and put his arm around her, pulling her closer.

"You've had a lot of terrible things happen to you recently. It leaves its own scars, ones that aren't visible." Marie took one of Pierre's hands in hers and traced the lines on the palm with her fingers. "I'm worried that if you stay here alone until the British break down the door ... that those wounds will fester. It's already affecting you."

"But what about Claude and Jacques? It's so much more likely for someone to see me at the hospital and tell them where I am."

Pierre looked at her for a moment, thinking. "It's up to you. I can't protect you at the hospital, but I can't protect you here either. Not anymore. Although I wish I could."

Marie was thinking hard. She wanted desperately to be back at the Hôpital du Roi, helping and healing, contributing to the defensive effort. But if Claude found her, she had little doubt that he would kill her this time.

Marie bit her lip. "I'll go if the hospital will take me."

"That's my girl," Pierre said, drawing her toward him and kissing her on the forehead. "But we need to figure out how to keep you hidden from those brutes."

"And I'm terrified at the thought of you and Nic and even Augustus fighting against the British. You won't all come back."

Pierre nodded. They were too outnumbered and poorly equipped for any type of victory. "None of us are safe now. If the British win, it will be awful."

Marie looked at him intently. She knew he had more information than he was revealing. "Last time, we were given the honours of war," she said slowly. "Though we were defeated, the British allowed our army to march out of the city, flags flying, drums beating, and bayonets fixed. It was symbolic, but it was important. At least it showed that the enemy acknowledged our army's valour."

"It won't be the same this time," Pierre said. He got out of bed and started pacing around the room, clenching his fists in frustration. "The French have done too much in this war for the British to be merciful this time."

"Merciful?" Marie shuddered. Back in 1745, the conquering army had been largely peaceful and had simply gone about the business of establishing a new government, but there had been stories. Rape, beatings, and looting had happened in the early days. The British commanders did what they could to prevent the violence, but the city was large and the situation chaotic. It hadn't helped that the French soldiers were furious in surrender and had done what they could to riot and stir up trouble.

Pierre shook his damp hair out of his eyes. For the first time, Marie saw a look of fear in his eyes. "France started this war. Whatever happens to us is our own fault."

"Why are you so cynical?" Marie reached out and grabbed his arm, pulling him back onto the bed. She could feel his agitation, so she started to rub his broad shoulders.

"Did you hear about what happened at Fort Oswego and Fort William Henry?"

Marie shook her head. "No. That never made it back here."

Pierre sighed. "I was at Fort William Henry. We attacked, they surrendered, and everything was straightforward at first." Marie continued to knead Pierre's muscles, but that didn't help take the despair out of his voice. "On the mainland and everywhere else actually, except here in Louisbourg, the Native allies fight alongside us. I mean they fight with us here too, but there are a lot more of them on the mainland.

"When the fort fell to us, Montcalm agreed to a peaceful resolution. The British soldiers and everyone else were supposed to leave the place in peace. That should have been simple, but something went wrong. There can sometimes be a language barrier between us and the Huron. I don't know if Montcalm or any of the other officers knew what the Huron were planning— if they were planning anything. I don't even know. Actually, I don't think they were, and it wasn't the entire group. I asked my Huron friend Moxus afterwards, and he said he didn't know it was going to happen."

Pierre lay down on the bed, resting his head on Marie's thigh.

"After the soldiers left, a group of Hurons went in and massacred the sick and injured left behind. I got there partway through the attack, and the French officers in the fort there did nothing to stop them. As the people of the fort left, the Huron killed more. Men, women, and children were scalped where they stood. Others were harassed, stripped naked, their only worldly possessions stolen from them. Montcalm tried to stop it, but a lot of the other officers didn't care. Just turned a blind eye. Some even helped. They say 1,500 people were killed."

Marie felt sick. "What happened at Oswego?"

"Montcalm refused to grant them the honours of war, which on its own is quite an insult. Some of the British tried to escape, but most of the escapees were hacked to death with tomahawks by drunken Hurons and French soldiers."

Marie stared at Pierre, horror-struck. Seeing the look on her face, he sat up quickly and rubbed her back until she felt in control of herself again.

"We won't be given honours of war," he continued quietly. "Most of them out there are looking for revenge. Maybe we'll be shipped off like the Acadians. Hopefully, that will be the worst of it—though I doubt it."

Marie looked at Pierre, her eyes wide with panic. She didn't see the fate of the Acadians as positive. They'd been stripped of their land, their possessions, and sent into exile and not to places of their choice. Families had been split apart. They would never get back home, never have their lives back.

"What can we do?" Marie asked after a long silence.

"There's nothing we can do, love." Pierre rolled over and pulled her down beside him. "Hope against all odds that we win and if not, that we can just get on the boats as quickly as possible and get out of here."

Marie rested her head on his chest, noticing, again, the "D" branded onto his skin. "Would you leave now? desert them?"

Pierre was silent for so long that she thought he hadn't heard the question. She repeated it. "I heard you. I'm just thinking. There's nowhere for us to go. If we didn't desert to the British our only other hope would be to make it across the island and find someone with a boat. I did that journey once. It was suicide at the time. We made it only by sheer, dumb luck."

Marie felt as if an iron fist had gripped her chest. Pierre stared down at her as if he knew what she was thinking. "There's no use fretting now." She buried her face in his chest and curled her body around him.

He gently stroked her bare back as they listened to the rain.

***

The next morning broke clear and calm, but the atmosphere within the fortress was bleak. The garrison had taken to running small raids among the British camps, but there was little else they could do. The British were too far away to launch a major offensive with the men and supplies they had. Harassment and waiting was all they were capable of. Life had stopped; survival had taken over.

Even with few patients, the hospital was filled with activity. Pierre looked around for someone who could be in charge, but eventually settled for anyone who didn't seem to be a patient. An elderly nun with her arms full of linens smiled when he introduced himself.

"I'm Sister Agatha, dear. You say that your wife would like to serve here with us?"

Pierre nodded. She was so short, he felt he almost needed to bend over in two to talk to her. "Yes, Marie Lévesque. She worked here for some years—until a year ago."

Sister Agatha's face lit up. "Oh, Marie. Of course, I remember her." She smiled and patted Pierre's shoulder, which was the highest point she could reach. "Well, we can always use more help, dear, and she was a great deal of help. Follow me, I'll introduce you to one of the brethren."

Pierre followed Sister Agatha down a busy, whitewashed hallway, with doors leading off to other rooms.

"We're trying to get ready for when the order of battle begins," she explained unnecessarily. He nodded politely. He glanced into rooms and hallways that broke off from the hall he was in and noticed the neat row of beds. Pallets were being organized for even more patients, should the need arise.

Sister Agatha stopped at a plain wooden door and knocked sharply. A muffled voice called her in, and she went in, leaving Pierre standing alone in the hallway. He could hear excited murmuring coming through the door. When she reappeared, she ushered him into the office and left to deliver the linens still clutched to her chest.

Pierre walked in and was surprised to find himself face to face with Father Weber.

"I didn't know you were acquainted with this hospital, Father," he said, trying to cover up the uncertainty that had suddenly invaded his consciousness. He was still grateful to Father Weber for everything he'd done to save Marie's life, but the priest had refused to marry them without the permission of Pierre's commanders. Pierre didn't completely trust him. Father Weber shared Pierre's surprise. "I'm not usually here, but being a member of Les Frères de Saint-Jean-de-Dieu, and the events being what they are, I have found myself reassigned."

Pierre nodded. He felt rather uneasy.

"When Sister Agatha told me a soldier's wife was willing to offer assistance, I must admit I didn't think of you immediately. I wasn't aware that you had recently married. May I offer you my congratulations?"

Pierre gave him a sour look. "I guess not," the priest appraised him over the tips of his fingers. "Please sit. What can I do for you, Thibault?" The little priest was so short that his feet swung freely under his desk.

Pierre shifted uncomfortably. "Marie would like to assist here at the hospital if you are willing. She needs a safe place to spend the siege as both my father and I will be part of the battle."

Father Weber nodded. He leaned back in his chair and folded his hands across his flat stomach. "You realize that none of us are 'safe' anymore."

Pierre nodded. "She helped here until eighteen months ago."

"I am aware of that."

"However, with her broken arm, she still isn't able to do a great deal."

Father Weber inclined his head. "I am also aware of her injuries. As I recall I had something to do with attending to them. However, within a fortnight, she should be able to use the arm, whatever use that may remain. We would benefit very much from her help. I assure you, you may count on the discretion of everyone here."

Pierre nodded. "I appreciate it. Would she be able to stay here with the nuns?"

Father Weber paused for a moment. "Will you be staying with her?" There was a slight sneer in his voice.

"No." A soft pink rose above his high cheekbones. "I will be at the battle."

"Of course," Father Weber inclined his head toward the soldier, his wiry white hair appearing to be even wilder than ever. Since you told Sister Agatha that she is your wife, am I correct in assuming that the two of you are now living together at your father's house?"

"I'm not here to confess, Father."

"No." A pause again. "However, the welfare of all souls in this city are my concern.

Pierre glared at the tiny man. "If you'll recall, Father," anger creeping into his voice, "I did ask you to find it in your heart to marry us. However, you refused. I'm not about to take judgement from someone who is more afraid of the wrath of man than the wrath of God."

The priest bristled and pulled himself up to his full diminutive height behind the desk. "We will happily accept your wife, Monsieur Thibault." He put a nasty emphasis on the title. "Bring her tonight if she is willing to come."

Pierre pushed himself roughly away from the desk. "Thank you, Father," he mumbled and left without a backward glance.

***

"I didn't want to leave immediately," Marie lay naked beside Pierre. Her heart was gradually returning to its regular rhythm. She twisted one of his chest hairs around her finger, still damp from the recent exertion.

Pierre chuckled low in his throat. "I know you didn't, but I, unfortunately, ran into Father Weber, and since he knows the truth behind our arrangement, I think he wants to save you from the evils of my bed."

Marie laughed and snuggled closer into his arms. Their time was limited. A little less than a fortnight was all they had been given, all they might ever get. Once she left, who knew when they would see each other again? She ran her fingers gently across Pierre's cheekbones, trying to memorize how it felt to caress him.

"I will find you at the end of all this," Pierre promised.

Marie nodded but didn't trust herself to speak. The odds were slim that they would both walk away from the battle unscathed. The hospital was the best option for her, but now that the reality of permanent separation was in front of her, she was filled with dread.

"In this life or the next?" she asked. She was angry that, once again, they had to separate, and it also wasn't fair to fill their last moments together with thoughts of that cruel reality.

"Whichever comes first," he said, smoothing away the hair from her face. The scars on her chest gleamed silver in the candlelight.

"How did all of that start anyway?" he asked hesitantly as his fingers traced the lines. He had never asked about the abuse because he hadn't wanted to force a conversation that she wasn't ready for, but there were no secrets between them now, and he wanted to know.

"You don't have to talk about it if you don't want to," Pierre added hastily.

"I don't, but I guess you deserve some sort of explanation." She rearranged herself so she was more comfortable. Pierre rested his head on her stomach. She combed his hair absentmindedly with her fingers.

"After the siege of 1745, he went to France with the rest of us. Annette wanted to live in the country, which I never understood, but your father was there, so I guess that explains it."

Pierre nodded.

"Claude spent all his time at Versailles, trying to champion the citizens of Louisbourg. He had wanted Louis to try to get the city back during the war, but, of course, that never happened." She sighed. "Something happened during that time. I don't know what it was, but it made Claude even more moody and volatile than he already was.

"He didn't come home until we were preparing to come back here. And once he was back at our place in the country, he locked himself in his study and didn't come out until we boarded the ship for Louisbourg. He was in the worst temper the entire trip back. He wouldn't talk to anyone, not even Annette. At first, I thought he was angry with her for not coming with him, but it was deeper than that. Everything bothered him: the noises, the smells; it was always too hot or too cold. And as soon as we arrived back here, he threw himself into his work. I don't know if those he worked with ever noticed a change in him because he could still be charming. But overall, he was almost always horrible. He drank almost all the time, and when he drank, it made everything worse: the moodiness, the irritability, the silence.

"After Annette's illness, or I guess miscarriage, the situation deteriorated. He would go into rages where he would throw things and scream and rave. It was terrifying. Absolutely terrifying." She paused, unsure of how to continue.

Pierre looked up. "War can change you. Watching people die, killing people, fighting for your own life."

"But Claude never saw action, and he was already a volatile bully."

"More than I thought he was," Pierre breathed.

Marie thought for a moment, her fingers absently pressing on the base of Pierre's neck. "You saw horrors in Ohio, but I don't think it made you awful. You're more serious, though. And I think you needed that. You're not the pranking jester you used to be."

"Miss him?"

Marie smiled wistfully. "A little. But I wouldn't have wanted to marry you if you still thought adding live fish to stew right before it was served was a good way to entertain people."

Pierre doubled over laughing. Marie jabbed him in the ribs with her elbow. "It wasn't funny!"

Eyes streaming, Pierre slowly sat up, wheezing. "I forgot about that," he gasped. "Lady Isabelle went hysterical, she was so angry."

Marie giggled too, despite herself. "Her wig fell off, remember?"

They lay for a time slowly letting the laughter evaporate from their veins, watching the stars appear through the window. Pierre traced the thin white scars across her chest again.

"Right after you left." She answered the silent question that hung in the air. "That was actually the reason I ran away. He and Annette had a huge fight. She was throwing plates, and he was saying all sorts of things to her. I was in my room and after it was over he came in and beat me. He took all of his anger at her out on me. I guess he felt I was disposable."

Pierre shook his head in frustration. "I want to kill him for what he did."

"But you won't," Marie said. It was more an order than an observation.

He rubbed the back of his neck. "I can't promise I wouldn't do it if the opportunity presented itself."

Marie ignored this and looked away.

"No one knew what had happened to you. Your father went and searched for you. Renault was involved, and he searched all the prisons. I guess they hid you from him. Jean even went to the West Indies. I thought you were dead. When you were released, Nic received word of your whereabouts. So I packed my bags and left the next day. When Claude found me, he whipped me and then it became a regular thing at home. Nic tried to hide me in certain places— his house, friends' houses, inns—while he arranged passage for me out of the city, but it never worked. That's why Nic hated you. He blamed you for the abuse. I never told him how it started. I was too ashamed. He just assumed it was because I ran away to find you."

"I always wondered." Pierre gazed at her seriously. "I won't ever let him touch you again."

Marie smiled and ruffled his hair. "I know. I'm not nearly as concerned for myself now as I am for you."

Pierre looked down at her and kissed her. "Don't worry. I've made it through many a battlefield."

Marie slapped his thigh. "You're far too cocky."

"It beats going to pieces." He looked out the window at the darkened sky. "I need to get you to the hospital before Father Weber comes and knocks down the door."

"I don't think he's about to do that."

"I wouldn't put it past him. He definitely doesn't like me. I'd prefer not to have another encounter."

***

The hospital spire rose high above the homes and shops of the city. Marie and Pierre walked quietly through the streets. Few people were out; even the never-sleeping harbour was silent. Marie kept her hood over her head for the entire trip. Pierre carried her few possessions. She wouldn't need much where she was going.

Soft candlelight streamed from the many windows, as the patients in the wards were resting for the night. The calm before the storm, Marie thought grimly. She reached out to Pierre, who had stopped at the foot of the stairs leading to the front entrance. He smiled sadly and shook his head. He wasn't going in with her. Suddenly, Marie was overwhelmed by the realization that this might be the last time she would ever lay eyes on him. She crushed herself against his body and held tight, not wanting to ever let go.

"I love you," he whispered and squeezed her tighter. "You can do this. It will begin soon. The British will want it to be over as soon as possible. So stay here. Take care of yourself."

"I'm not worried about myself," Marie replied thickly, still not wanting to let him go.

He smiled, disentangling himself from her grip, and held her at arm's length. "I know you're not. But I'll worry about me." He didn't laugh now or offer any empty reassurances. He bent to kiss her one last time. "I'll come visit if I can. Off you go. They're expecting you."

Marie nodded. She tried to speak, but her throat was too constricted for words. Pierre stepped back into the shadows and nodded for her to go on. With a huge effort, she turned into the hospital, leaving Pierre standing in the darkness.

Memories flooded her mind as she walked back into the long, whitewashed corridors of the hospital. It still smelled the same, she thought ruefully, wrinkling her nose. Dirt, blood, death, and vinegar were mingled with the faint smell of the fresh flowers and herbs that the nuns had placed around to try to combat the less desirable odours.

Sister Miriam was waiting for her. Marie had missed her most of all after Jacques stopped her from working at the hospital, as he felt it was below the station of a woman he was courting. The nun greeted Marie in a rib-splitting hug.

"How long it's been! Much, much too long! I thought your fiancé didn't approve of you working here. Has he changed his mind? Either way, I'm very excited to see you again, even in the circumstances as they are."

Marie smiled. "Actually, I ended up marrying someone else."

Sister Miriam was tactful enough not to say any more on the subject, although her eyebrows did disappear under her wimple for a minute.

She took Marie's arm and led her down the hall. She had quite the grip. "I know I've trained you in everything you need to know, and you were always excellent at following instructions, but Father Weber has informed me that until your arm has healed, you can't do anything too difficult. You have one more week, am I correct?"

Marie nodded. Hopefully, the bandages would be coming off in six days. She was eager to get rid of them and put the memory of the beating behind her.

"Well, until that's all healed up, you aren't to be doing anything too strenuous. Hopefully, we'll have a bit more time before things get out of hand."

Marie's stomach flipped over, thinking of Pierre.

Sister Miriam led Marie through the courtyard to the nuns' apartments. The wide vegetable garden was the only source of food for the compound during this time of war. They walked in silence to the second floor, where Sister Miriam nodded toward a small room at the end of the hall. "You may stay here for the time being," she said kindly. "Tomorrow, we'll see just how much you remember."

Marie shook her head at the idea. "Probably not very much."

Sister Miriam smiled as she walked Marie into her room. "You'll be surprised how quickly it comes back. If you need anything, let me know."

She left Marie alone in the spartan room. A cot stretched along one wall. It was the only furniture apart from a table that held a candlestick, a flint, a basin, and a pitcher of water.

Marie sighed and sat down on the bed. There was no fireplace, but the open window let in a warm breeze. Marie undressed, put on her night shirt, and crawled into the bed. Here, alone in the huge hospital, the upcoming siege was more real to her than ever before. Was it truly better to be here than back at Augustus's house? She drew to her mind the image of Pierre standing in the semi-darkness at the foot of the hospital steps, and how he'd said, "I love you" for maybe the last time. The idea caused her physical pain. She curled into a ball, trying to wrap herself around the feeling of hopelessness. Now that she was away from him, she was more frightened of the future than she wanted to admit. She wrapped the blanket around herself, not for heat but simply for the comfort of something to hold onto.

***

The King's Bastion was filled with the tight energy that precedes battle. A large number of men were now in the colossal building, awaiting the order to defend King and country with their lives. Most of the soldiers posted at Louisbourg came from the rural towns of northern France. Voluntary enrolment in the army took them to the colonies, and most spent the rest of their lives there. Difficult as life was in the army, it was better than toiling in the fields as a peasant and still never having enough to eat.

Most of the young men didn't enjoy this new world of harsh and frozen conditions. It was an alien, primitive place with only the basics of civilization and culture—and with very few people to defend. Many men were so demoralized by their new situation that they simply deserted. If caught, they were shipped to the West Indies as forced labourers. Desertion eventually became such a common problem that the government gave orders to shoot any soldiers they found trying to escape. Pierre wasn't the only one to carry the desertion brand, but he was the only one on Île-Royale. The entire garrison knew it and treated him accordingly.

Every settlement in New France had a militia: civilians who were trained, albeit minimally, to defend the area. Louisbourg's militia was one of the largest in the colonies, made up of men born and raised in New France.

Pierre was an exception. Most military men of his age were in some form of leadership position. But at thirty, he was still just a soldier, who, after two

The Displaced: Fall of a Fortress

years of patriotic service, was still sentenced to the life of a cadet, sleeping in shared accommodations, the least of all servicemen, but the first to meet the enemy. His colleagues were still teenagers, and his superiors were younger and sometimes less experienced than himself. Being in the French army was not a service; it was a life sentence.

In the twelve days they had had together, Marie had helped him forget the humiliation and injustice that had become his life. But she was gone now. Safe or at least as safe as any civilian was at this point, but still gone from his life. Leaving the hospital had been one of the hardest things he had ever done, abandoning her to an unknown fate, unable to be there to protect her anymore.

He ran his hand idly along the rough stone walls as he walked back to the barracks, realizing there was only one good thing in this whole situation. Whatever happened now, she was his again. She was his, and whatever sacrifice he had to make was worth it because he was now fighting for her.

The barracks were quiet. The bravado and confidence of the day was quietly slipping away as sleep came. And the snoring, farting, and grunting that usually filled the dark night air in the barracks had been replaced with silence. Every soul was preoccupied as the reality of battle and death loomed.

Pierre found his bunk and swung his large frame onto the mattress, folding his limbs to fit in the small space. Gérard lay in the bunk beside him, staring up at the ceiling. He was an orphan from Normandy—part of the last boatload of soldiers from the mother country. He had been enthralled by stories of frozen winters where a man could skate on mighty rivers that were frozen solid. Now the likelihood that he wouldn't live to see such a sight weighed heavily on him. He may now be missing a thumb, but he was still expected to fight.

"She finally kicked you out, eh?" Gérard asked with a trace of bitterness.

Pierre flung his boots to the ground and lay back. "You could say that," he sighed.

***

The grey smock Marie had been given to wear was comfortable if not flattering. It fit easily over her clothes but made her look as if she'd wrapped herself in a sheet. There was one good thing about the uniform, though; it had two deep pockets in front. Years before, when she'd first worked at the hospital, she discovered that those pockets allowed her to carry a loaf of bread, cheese, medical supplies, and a roll of bandages comfortably with her at all times. This time around, though, she kept only her supplies and Camille Thibault's silver ring in a tiny pocket pinned inside one of the large pockets. It was slightly too big for her finger, and she didn't want to lose it among the blood and bile of the hospital. It wasn't safe to leave it back in her room either. In these days of war, anything could happen.

On the morning of June 13th, she washed and dressed quickly, putting an apron on top of the smock. She knew that she needed to be ready for work early. It was going to be a long day.

Once she'd reported for duty, she was introduced to Sister Berenice, a middle-aged nun with iron-coloured curls that didn't fit completely under her wimple. Sister Berenice was the daughter of the Commissaire-Ordonnateur, the ordinance officer in charge of keeping the financial records of the city. She'd joined the convent at sixteen and had begun to work in the hospital the following year. At this point, she was in charge of the new recruits. Marie had worked with her before and was always impressed by her ability to organize just about anything. While the Frères de Saint-Jean-de-Dieu were in charge of the hospital, it was really Sister Berenice who kept the institution running. Nothing went on within the grounds that she didn't know about.

While related to Jacques, she was the complete opposite of him in every way. She was also one of the few people whom Marie had confided in about her treatment at Claude's hands. Sister Berenice would keep Marie's secret. She was also well aware of the kind of person her young cousin was and had been very vocal in her opposition to Marie's union with him. The nun knew the marriage was happening for all the wrong reasons, and Marie knew without asking that Sister Berenice was thrilled that things hadn't worked out.

The portly sister wrapped her arms around Marie's thin shoulders.

"Oh, my dear, it's so good to see you," she exclaimed. "I've missed you so much. You look lovely."

Marie laughed. "I'm happy to be back." The longer she was in the hospital, the more comfortable she felt. While her stomach ached with homesickness for Pierre, the familiarity of the smells and sights of the hospital hallways made her feel comforted despite the siege looming on the horizon.

"I heard you were married," Sister Berenice jabbered on. "Congratulations. I'm so glad your husband allowed you to come back and you didn't marry my good-for-nothing cousin."

Marie bit the inside of her cheek to keep from laughing.

"Who is this lucky young man?" Sister Berenice turned and led Marie down another hall.

Marie hesitated, unsure if it was wise to connect herself to Pierre publicly, but then she remembered that her very presence here was being kept a secret. "He's actually a friend from childhood. We had hoped to marry years ago, but then the war started."

Sister Berenice nodded. "I'm glad things worked out for the two of you." She meant it.

The hospital was quiet, as the staff had no problem caring for the patients already admitted. Most of them had become ill from exposure to the elements and the effects of starvation, and most of them were soldiers. When the siege began, the hallways would be filled not just with soldiers but with civilians. The British would spare no one.

"I want Father Weber to examine your arm one more time," Sister Berenice announced, leading Marie toward the priest's office. Once he's given me an update, I can assign you the appropriate kind of work. I don't want to be responsible for causing you further discomfort."

Marie groaned inwardly. She wasn't looking forward to talking with Father Weber, but there seemed to be no way out. Sister Miriam left her at the bench outside the priest's office door, where she waited uncomfortably. She contemplated running away, claiming a clean bill of health, but then thought it would be unwise to lie to a nun.

Father Weber eventually ushered Marie into his cramped office. He didn't say anything at first but simply glared at her from across the desk. Not feeling intimidated, Marie glared right back. It wasn't her first choice to be living in sin.

"I'm concerned about your welfare," Father Weber began gravely.

"Not enough to actually perform the ceremony and eliminate the need for said worry. Sir," she added hastily. She wasn't going to accept his illogical admonishments, but she also didn't want to be banished from the hospital.

Father Weber kept glaring at Marie. "You realize there are laws I am expected to follow." For such a short man, he could look very intimidating.

"I thought your laws came from God."

More scowling. "Mademoiselle Lévesque, I realize that this man has convinced you to elope with him, but it is a very serious offence before God."

357

Marie cut him off. "I can assure you that this is not a case of Pierre convincing me to do anything. I am very capable of making my own decisions." She swallowed hard. She couldn't let him see any vulnerability. "Seven years ago, Pierre and I became engaged, with plans to wed as soon as possible. We have known each other since we were children. Pierre was falsely charged with desertion from the military before we could marry." Father Weber's eyes widened for a fraction of a second before he rearranged his face into a more neutral expression.

Marie continued, her heart beating wildly. She could feel her face flush with anger. "There is a General in Montreal who we suspect orchestrated the whole thing. I actually went to Montreal to try to find Pierre. That's when Claude's abuse became worse. I have wanted to marry this man for many years. I would have married him long ago if I could have. I am well aware that you have rules that you must abide by here, but I have done nothing wrong. Neither has Pierre. If we could marry in a church before you and God, we would. I don't believe the offence lies with either of us."

Father Weber said nothing for a long time following this speech. He merely looked at Marie in a calculating way as she sat there quietly. She refused to be the first to break the silence, hoping her speech had made him uncomfortable. Finally, Father Weber spoke. "I see that there is no convincing you otherwise, my dear."

Marie smiled with relief.

"Then I shall leave the subject for now." Father Weber rose from his chair and walked around the desk. He sighed heavily as though it was causing him a great deal of pain not to continue on the subject. "How are you feeling?"

He examined her head carefully, announcing it to be completely healed and then proceeded to her ribs. "They no longer feel tender?"

"No, they stopped hurting completely about a week ago." The priest nodded approvingly to himself.

"Then we shall see what has become of your arm." He slowly unwound the bandage, removing splints as he went.

It looked better than she had expected it to, but that wasn't saying much. A thick, red scar about four inches long ran along both sides of the limb. The arm was also no longer completely straight. Under the ugly scar tissue, the bone poked up a little. Marie examined it critically, wiggling her fingers. It could have been much worse. She was well aware that injuries like this usually resulted in amputation. So she felt it was a miracle that hers was still attached and functional.

"I'm afraid that's as good as it will get," Father Weber observed. "I'm very pleased that I could save the arm, though, and that there doesn't seem to be much muscle damage. How does it feel?"

Marie moved her wrist experimentally. "It feels fine." She poked at the scar. "It doesn't feel nice to touch, though. In fact, it feels numb."

Father Weber smiled in an understanding way. "It will feel numb for a while, and the longer it has to heal, the better it will feel." The priest passed her a number of objects, ranging from a light quill to a heavy flower pot and asked her to hold each one in her left hand. After she put each object down, he asked her how her arm felt. "Odd" was the answer that kept coming to her mind. She'd been using her right arm almost exclusively for so long that she'd almost forgotten the left could work.

When he was finally satisfied, Father Weber resumed his position behind the desk. "Well, Marie, I think I can call you cured. However, I want to make it very clear that you are not to be doing any heavy lifting, moving patients, or exerting great force. No setting femurs."

Marie nodded meekly, running her thumb over the uneven scar.

"And," Father Weber continued, "I want you working only on things that will not tax you physically: stitching, bandaging, washing—the boring jobs. If we can hold the enemy off long enough, then maybe you can teach the men just how powerful a woman can be, but until then, only easy jobs that place few physical demands on you."

Marie happily agreed. "Am I going to become one of those mad old women who can feel the storm coming in their bones?"

Father Weber laughed. "Probably. But do me a favour and never let Sister Berenice know. She's convinced she can control the weather, as well as everything that goes on in here."

Marie stood to leave. "Is there anything else, Father?"

The little Prussian paused as if teetering on the edge of speech. "No, my dear. I've taken up enough of your time."

***

The days blurred together as Marie's life at the hospital fell into its routines. Every morning, Marie got up with the sun, dressed quickly, and went down to the main building to eat what few rations were available. Then she went to check on the patients.

She was one of only a few volunteers and the only one with as much training as the nuns. Even in peace time, the nuns of Louisbourg were a small, close-knit group, and most sisters in the convent ran or taught at the school. Marie secretly wondered if the sisters would be as pleased about her "marriage" if they knew who her husband was. Pierre was strapped almost every day for his inability to behave himself, and he'd caused more than one sister to go prematurely grey.

But now that the school was closed because of the war, all personnel were at the hospital, where the nuns became even closer to each other. But Marie wanted to contribute to the group as much as she could, so after her meeting with Father Weber, she made it clear that she wanted to participate fully. Sister Berenice had tried to put her on bed rest—that is, mopping the brows of patients with fever. Marie had no intention of spending a week fending off handsy soldiers who used their illness as an excuse for molestation. It was a job that one of the priests could do.

As a compromise, Sister Berenice paired Marie up with the newest member of the convent.

Sara Clarke was not a nun yet, but she had been living with the nuns for nine months, trying to decide if she wanted to embrace this lifestyle.

Sara's parents had come to Louisbourg from Boston after the first siege in 1745 and stayed even after the fortress was handed back to France. They were the only British in the settlement—something they were constantly trying to explain. They had even converted to Catholicism and pledged allegiance to King Louis. They lived a block away, above her father's apothecary shop.

Marie was confused by this situation. She had been under the impression that all British citizens had been put on boats within days of the signing of the Treaty of Aix-la-Chapelle. No one had a choice in the matter.

"My mother lost three children after we came to Louisbourg," Sara said after Marie asked why she and her family were still at the fortress. "They're buried in the cemetery here, and my mother refuses to leave them."

Sara was at least ten years younger than Marie, but her large, pale blue eyes were always serious. The little hair that peeked out from under her cap was so blonde it was almost white. Overall, the girl was so pale that Marie was surprised she didn't glow in the darkness like the moon.

"But why would the French let you stay?"

Sara shrugged as if the answer was obvious. "My father bribed them."

Marie had to admit that was a valid point. While Claude was a favourite of the smugglers and pirates, he was not the only official who looked the other way if his palm was greased. Bribery was such a common problem that if an inquiry was ever performed, most of the criminal officers would have to arrest themselves.

"Are you safe here?" Marie asked, concerned. "It must be difficult. Especially now." While a great deal of trade was done with New England in peace time, since 1745 most of the French viewed the British as bloodthirsty barbarians and refused to trade with the British colony to the south.

"It's been terrible," Sara conceded. "My three brothers all went back to Boston as soon as they could. Although as long as I don't speak, no one can tell the difference." She pushed her white-blonde hair back under her cap.

Marie glanced at her nervously. "I'm sorry."

"It's not your fault," Sara sniffed.

"No, but it's still unfortunate," Marie sighed. "I doubt you're selling secrets to James Wolfe."

Sara laughed humourlessly. "He doesn't need my help."

That much was true. As the British were preparing for the upcoming siege, it was becoming clear just how outnumbered Louisbourg was. The British had already taken over the lighthouse and the Island Battery. True to her word, Marie didn't leave the confines of the hospital, but the reports that people were bringing in were frightening. They were surrounded and outnumbered. Once again, the British had bypassed the cannons stationed on the batteries overlooking the water and the handful of warships stationed in the harbour and settled on a land attack. The planners of Louisbourg had assumed most attacks would come from the sea. The crumbling ramparts and insufficient army wouldn't be able to compete with the British. Meanwhile, the French soldiers were stationed behind the ramparts in miserable weather. Every day, a few soldiers would trickle in, most needing nursing after being exposed to the elements for too long. Once recovered at least in part, they were sent back to the front. There were too few soldiers to allow for long-term convalescence.

Initially, whenever a soldier came in, Marie would ask if he knew Pierre and where he was, but after hearing of the minor conflicts he had been a part of, she realized she couldn't handle knowing the danger without the outcome.

Every night, she crawled into bed exhausted, terrified of what the morning would bring. She'd accepted that the French would never win this battle, but the fate of Pierre and Nic made her head spin with worry.

***

One week after her arrival at the hospital, on June 19th, the rumble of thunder woke her from a sound sleep. Rolling over, she pulled her quilt over her head, trying to drown out the sound. But then she realized that the sounds were coming too frequently for them to be thunderclaps, and there were no flashes of lightning in the sky.

Marie leaped out of bed and ran to the window. The sun was barely peeking over the stone walls of the fortress, its rays streaking the misty ground with pink. It would have been a beautiful sight if not for the unmistakable clouds of dust billowing from the ramparts. Marie shut her eyes in silent prayer. The roar of cannon fire and screaming of mortar shells were clear now that she was awake.

She scrambled away from the window and threw on her clothes. She twisted her hair on top of her head with the swiftness of years of experience and ran down the stairs and across the courtyard that separated the nuns' accommodations from the rest of the hospital, skidding to a halt in front of the hospital administrator, Father Maneau.

"Don't worry, you haven't missed the siege," he said sarcastically, looking over the rim of his glasses. He seemed unperturbed by the destruction going on elsewhere. He moved slowly down the corridor, checking in on wards as he passed, as if this was a regular morning.

Marie moved on.

The roar of artillery fire split the air, and the explosion of metal disintegrating its target reverberated through her bones. They had all been here before. They had all sat with bated breath, praying that the next bomb was not destined for them. The entire hospital was silent as the echoes of the past smashed into the present.

Marie felt her insides had turned to ice. Each shriek of artillery meant someone had become a casualty. She pressed her lips together, silently begging God to save them.

"It's all in God's hands now." Marie opened her eyes to see Sister Berenice only a few steps away. Marie didn't trust herself to speak but nodded numbly. The kindly nun didn't seem to expect an answer but carried on briskly down the hallway, whispering the same words to the other staff congregated in the corridors.

The bombardment lasted a few hours. By noon, the reports were trickling in, along with the injured. Homes and businesses had been destroyed. A fire had started when a tavern had been hit with heated shot from a cannon. The fire was still burning, though the owner and people from the neighbourhood finally had it under control.

The hospital filled quickly with patients and also with their families, who were unwilling to leave their loved ones.

Marie found Sara already stationed in the crowded room near the main doors. Chaos always took over after a bombardment, but the priests at the entrance did their best to make sure minor injuries found their way to Sara and Marie.

Sara's grandfather in Boston had been an apothecary with some rather unusual views. He had passed his beliefs on to his offspring, and Sara's insistence on following them was beginning to irritate Marie.

"We're wasting time," she complained as Sara cleaned her hands again in freshly boiled water before moving on to the next patient.

"No, we're not," Sara persisted. "This will help keep us and the patients healthy."

Marie shook her head and ground her teeth together. Sara was fanatical about keeping things clean. Before starting, she had insisted that a kettle containing water, garlic, and witch hazel be kept boiling at all times. Standing beside the fireplace, Marie thought she might faint from the combination of heat and overwhelming smell that had permeated the room. Every time a procedure was finished, Sara would wash the tools and her hands in the boiling water, a process that also ate up precious time.

"These people need medical attention before they bleed out," Marie snapped. This was not entirely true, since most of their patients had only minor injuries, but Marie was impatient because the people kept pouring in. "I can't help them if you're constantly removing everything I need to do my job."

"It prevents illness!" Sara repeated for the hundredth time and continued with her manic cleaning.

Marie grunted with frustration. There were so many people swarming around the hospital that every moment mattered. And Sara's obsession with cleanliness wasn't limited to herself and the tools. Every wound, no matter how small, had to be meticulously cleaned, something that caused more discomfort for those already in pain. After being shushed for the fourth time in as many minutes, Marie eventually gave up—though that didn't stop her from having nasty thoughts about apothecaries from Boston.

The work was slow and ghastly. Fragments of stones blasted apart by enemy fire had imbedded themselves deeply into the soft tissue of one man's body, and that type of wound was repeated in a great number of cases.

A young child, no more than six, sat cuddled in Sara's lap, his small arms wrapped around her slender torso. A dozen shards of rock were embedded above his left knee. He'd been standing outside his house with his mother when a cannonball had collided with the side of the building. His mother was being tended to by a nun, as her injuries had resulted in a broken leg and a nasty head wound.

"All right," said Marie, kneeling in front of the young boy and Sara. "I need you to be brave for me, okay?" Marie prodded gently at the wound. The little boy whimpered and buried his brown curls into Sara's bosom. Sara stroked his hand and softly sang lullabies to him in English. Marie gripped the splinters and squeezed the chubby thigh as hard as she could. Then she pulled as gently and firmly as possible, ignoring the boy's cries and extracting the half dozen stone pieces as quickly as possible.

"Oh, my brave boy, you did such a good job," she crooned as Sara pressed down on the wound. Marie squeezed his hand reassuringly, and he gave her a weak smile. "I'm just going to bandage you up and then you'll be as good as new." The boy nodded and wiped his nose on his dirty shirt sleeve.

As discreetly as possible, Marie cleaned a needle and threaded it. With a significant look at Sara, she began to stitch the gaping skin together while Sara did her best to distract the boy. Finally finishing, Marie patted his good leg and kissed his cheek.

"You were very brave, young sir," she smiled, saluting him.

The boy kicked his leg experimentally, then hobbled off to see his mother.

Marie looked around the room. There were a few soldiers supported by others staggering through the door. It was now early evening, and those who were injured were coming slowly to the hospital from the battle, supported by friends.

A burly militia man was placed on a blanket in front of the fire. One look told Marie all she needed to know. A tourniquet had been tied around the man's thigh just above the seeping bullet hole. Marie prodded the skin around the wound, gently trying to judge how deep the ball was.

"That's quite the wound there, soldier," Marie said conversationally.

"Damn Redcoats," the man muttered. He was incredibly pale under the mud splattered on his face. "Hurts something awful."

"I'm afraid it's going to get worse before it gets better," she said honestly but sympathetically as she reached for the whisky bottle nearby.

"Can you find something for him to bite down on?" Sara asked his companion.

The man's face went pale under his dark beard. "What's this?" he spluttered. "There's a British bitch here?"

"Yes," said his companion, "and you're in bad enough shape without a Brit coming to your rescue ... Hey, where are the French girls?" Sara ignored the companion and reached out to the wounded man to settle him down. "Don't touch me!" the patient snarled. Sara jumped back as if burned by a hot poker. Her face had grown, if possible, paler.

Marie froze for a fraction of a second. "Now really!" She spoke with as much authority as she could. "You're being ridiculous. Madame Clarke is a wonderful healer."

"She's a bloody British agent," the wounded man said. "That's what she is, and I'll be damned if I let that bitch touch me." People in the rest of the room were beginning to realize something was going on. Heads were turning.

Marie looked around for help. Father Maneau had heard the outburst and was working his way across the room, a look of panic on his face as he tried to prevent Sara's nationality from inciting a riot.

Sara melted into the crowd as the pair of militia men continued their verbal attack. More priests appeared by Father Maneau's side, so Marie fled after her companion.

She found Sara in a quiet corner of the kitchen, hastily wiping her eyes on her handkerchief, so Marie wouldn't see her tears. The young women working in the kitchen were tactfully ignoring her.

"I'm sorry about that." It seemed like an insignificant thing to say, but Marie didn't know what else to do.

Sara shook her head. "It's nothing. I was stupid for thinking this wouldn't happen." Her voice shook slightly. "No one ever thinks we belong here."

"What do you mean?" Marie sat down beside her, not sure how to extend any comfort.

Sara sighed. "There were always those who hated us for being here after the British left. My father had us all swear an oath to King Louis, but it wasn't enough. Since the war began, things have been much more difficult for my parents and me. Two weeks ago, the windows of my father's shop were smashed, and some of the shopkeepers will no longer sell to my mother because they know she's from Boston. It's getting very difficult to buy any food at all, not that there's a lot to be had anyway."

"That's terrible," Marie said in amazement. She felt incredibly guilty about her earlier joke about Sara not selling secrets to General Wolfe.

"That's one reason why I'm here. Trying to prove that I care about this place and the people. I'm not trying to destroy it."

Marie put a comforting hand on her shoulder. "Does everyone here know you're from Boston?"

"Everyone except the patients."

"And they're fine with it?"

Sara shrugged. "Not all of them. I've overheard things when they think I'm not listening. But they tolerate me."

"Then you're safe here," Marie said, firmly hoping she could meet some of these nasty people so she could put them in their place. "We'll just make sure you don't speak in front of the patients." Sara raised a skeptical eyebrow. "I'm serious," Marie went on. "You and I will work together. I know you're supposed to be monitoring me, but I'll talk to the patients and we'll both treat them."

Sara still looked dubious. "I don't know," she said uncertainly.

"It's only the first day," Marie pointed out, "and look what happened. We possibly have weeks of this ahead of us. Last time, the fortress lasted six weeks, but there wasn't any gunpowder. This time, they've been stockpiling it for years in case the British came back. So the battle might last longer this time."

Sara nodded reluctantly. "You'd be willing to stick with me for the rest of this?"

"Yes, but only if you lay off me about the cleaning."

Sara began to splutter indignantly.

"I'll do my best," Marie said hastily, "but if I forget, don't murder me."

Sara thought for a moment, then laughed nervously.

***

Marie retired to her room that night, exhausted both emotionally and physically. Hot and sticky, she stripped out of her clothes and stood by the window, embracing what little breeze there was.

It had worked, she thought ruefully. She was so busy she never stopped to think of anything other than what was in the present. But now, the thought of Pierre pierced her heart. She looked out at the darkness, breathing in air choked by gunpowder and smoke, and wiped the tears that slowly tracked down her cheeks.

Surely, he wasn't dead, she thought. He hadn't shown up at the hospital. Then she remembered that the dead never made it to the hospital. Would anyone tell her? Maybe no one would, since she wasn't officially his wife. She might be forced to search for his body or to find out what happened to him during the upheaval when everything was over?

She pulled the small silver band out of the pocket in her smock and slipped it onto her right hand, closing her hand into a fist so the ring wouldn't slip off. She held it close to her heart as she lay in bed, wishing with all her might that she could will Pierre to safety.

***

It was June 25th, six days into the siege, and the hospital population was swelling at an alarming rate. Soldiers, civilians, and sailors filled the beds and spilled onto pallets on the floors. During the previous siege, the enemy had seemed content to wait while the situation inside the fortress grew ever more desperate, at least at first. This time, the goal seemed to be utter destruction.

Sara and Marie had worked out a partnership even though it was an unusual one. Marie spoke to the patients, calming and soothing them and finding out information while Sara silently worked. No one ever questioned why there were two healers treating them. After a few days, they found that they could communicate without words: a look here, a nod there and soon both were tending to the wounded while Marie spoke for both.

As frustrated as Marie found the cleaning techniques that Sara still enforced with manic energy, she found that she herself was starting to use them without thinking. She began washing her hands after treating every patient. People laughed at her, but Marie found the exercise a much-needed respite between the madness of caring for one injured person and then another—a moment where she could catch her breath and compose herself before carrying on.

Marie sat in the kitchen, eating her sparse midday meal and enjoying the silence that came with a break in the bombardment. Every day, for hours at a time, the cannons and guns from both the British army and the British navy fired over the fortress. It was becoming so commonplace that the silence, when it came, was deafening. The idea was to break the spirit of the inhabitants, and that was an effective battle tactic. The forces that kept raining destruction down from above made it difficult to carry out daily routines. As the dust from each bombardment settled, the French engineers would rush in to try to repair the damage as much as possible. The buildings closest to the ramparts were the hardest hit. Those that were still standing and not made of stone were being dismantled for building supplies.

The hospital kitchen was filled with people eating and with cooks preparing the meagre rations for the patients. No one paid Marie much attention, and she appreciated the break. Her back ached from bending over all morning, and her hands were chapped from the continuous washing. An exhaustion that Marie had never felt before had settled into her bones, and she knew it probably wouldn't leave until this war was over.

Father Laval, a tall, extremely thin priest who spoke little but was an excellent physician, entered the room. He dealt with the most difficult cases, those with little hope of recovery. Marie paid him no mind until he stood in front of her, looking down his hook nose at her.

"Can you follow me, Madame Lévesque?" The lines of his face deepened with concern, his voice quiet.

Marie felt the hairs on the back of her neck stand up. She bent to pick up her dishes, but the priest motioned for one of the kitchen staff to take care of them.

He said nothing as Marie followed him, her heart in her throat, to a crowded room packed with those who had just arrived. The floor was covered with blood and bile, making navigation difficult. Father Laval made his way through the maze of bodies with the ease of a man who had seen such carnage before.

That morning, a British ship had hit a warehouse where several sailors had taken shelter. The fire was still burning, and men were being brought in with varying degrees of burns. There was little to be done for most of them. It was a waiting game: either they would recover or they wouldn't.

Marie followed the priest, and they exited the mayhem into a narrow corridor which was almost as full as the room they had just left. Sailors carried men in and out, soldiers were conferencing in small groups while they waited. The confused jumble of bodies and limbs was overwhelming, but the scene was frighteningly quiet.

Marie spotted Father Maneau walking slowly down the hall, pausing at every man propped up against the wall or lying on a pile of blankets. With a sob, she realized he was administering last rites. Breathing as deeply as she could, she tried to steady herself, absolutely terrified of who was waiting at the end of the corridor. Father Laval pointed him out, but that wasn't necessary. She would have recognized his face anywhere.

Two soldiers stood around him, but Marie didn't recognize them. He was wrapped in a blanket soaked with blood, and he seemed smaller now than he ever had in life. She bent down and stroked the midnight crown, matted now with blood and filth. She had seen bodies that looked as if they were merely sleeping, but Nic's was not one of them. His face was contorted with pain and caked with blood.

One of the soldiers spoke, but she wasn't paying attention. The information washed over her and made little difference. A grape shot had hit him in the chest, tearing his torso apart. Miraculously—or cruelly—depending on how you looked at it, the hit hadn't killed him. There was no help for such injuries on the battlefield, so the soldiers had brought him to the hospital, but the damage was too great and he had died on his way.

Marie's hands felt numb. An old woman on the streets of Quebec had once told her mother that Marie and Nic shared a connection, an awareness that others did not. Marie's mother had hurried them away as quickly as possible, muttering about witches. The woman's words, however, hadn't proven true. As children, they were almost indifferent to each other until their parents' death. However, staring at his corpse, she felt as if a part of her was trapped with him, gone forever, where she couldn't reach it.

Suddenly, she didn't want to look at him any longer. The idea of being near his body revolted her. Her hands were sticky with congealing blood. Disgusted, she pushed the corpse away, fleeing outside, heedless of the voices calling after her.

She leaned against the outside wall, her strength finally crumbling, and wept. Wept for her brother; for the countless wounded and dead she had tried to save; for Pierre, who might still be alive but for how much longer; for every sorry soul trapped inside this hellhole.

She wept until there was nothing left. She hadn't seen Nic in over a month. He'd been furious about her decisions, and she'd been annoyed at his interference. Their differences hadn't bothered her at the time, but now they seemed monumental. After everything he had done to fight for his country, to try to protect her, he had bled out, surrounded by strangers.

The distant rumble of cannon fire brought Marie back to the present. Standing up, she swallowed large gulps of air, trying to calm herself. Nic was gone, but he had died trying to defend them all and there were still hundreds who needed her help. She wiped her face with her apron and walked back into the hospital, wringing her hands, trying to rid herself of her brother's blood.

Father Laval was standing inside the door, not wanting to intrude on her grief. Marie looked up warily.

"I'm very sorry, my dear." Marie simply nodded. She wasn't in the mood for empty words. They meant nothing and could heal nothing.

"Your brother was married?" Marie's head snapped up. She hadn't thought of Elise. "She needs to know what's happened." Marie nodded numbly. She felt both an overwhelming need to see Elise and dread that she would have to be the one to break the news. "I can go and tell her myself," Father Laval continued, "but I was wondering if you would like to accompany me?"

Marie nodded. She felt that her voice had forgotten how to work. "Elise ... I need to talk to her ... She'll be all alone."

Father Laval nodded as if he understood what Marie was going through. "When you are ready, we will go and tell her."

***

It was late afternoon when Marie and Father Laval finally extricated themselves from their duties and made their way to the small stone house that had once been the home of Captain Lévesque. Usually, Marie would have welcomed the break from the carnage, but each step filled her with dread. She half-hoped that Elise wouldn't be home, so she wouldn't have to be the one to shatter her world. As soon as she thought that, though, she hated herself for being a coward.

Elise was home. At the sight of her sister-in-law and a priest on the doorstep, she sank to the floor in a faint. No words needed to be said. Father Laval stayed long enough to make sure that Elise understood the news and was in no immediate medical danger, but then he headed back to the hospital, leaving the two women alone in their grief.

Elise didn't say anything for a long time. She just sat huddled on the sofa, wrapped in a quilt that Marie had placed around her shoulders. Marie sat opposite her, completely silent, lost in her own thoughts as the sun sank beneath the horizon and darkness engulfed them. Two women tied by a grief that was beyond words. Marie waited because she knew that Elise would need to talk eventually, though she couldn't force her. Eventually, Marie roused herself long enough to light some candles. She began puttering around the kitchen, made some tea, and then sat down across from Elise again.

"He told me not to worry," Elise whispered as Marie placed a teacup in her hands. Elise was so quiet that Marie had to lean closer to hear her. "Of course, I always did, but he never wanted me to know how bad it was."

Marie nodded. Nic was stubborn like that. He would carry the weight of the world on his shoulders before he would let her see how bad the politics were in this place. He never wrote home in hopes that no news would be considered good news. It was something that had always bothered her. Although, looking back, she had done the same to Nic—not telling him about Claude beating her after Nic had enlisted and left the manor.

"He didn't want you to know how bad it was because he loves you."

"Loved me."

Marie winced. "I'm sure that, wherever he is now, he still loves you very much."

Elise threw a nasty look at her friend, and silence fell between them again. Despite the warm temperature of the night, Marie felt chilled and bent to light the fire. It felt good to have something to do with her hands.

"What am I going to do now?" Elise finally asked. Her face was snow white, and the panic in her voice was clear.

"I don't know," Marie replied. "You'll receive some kind of compensation, although I don't know what." She said the words delicately, but she knew that wasn't what her friend meant.

"My mother is going to be furious. It was partly for this reason that she didn't want me to marry him."

Marie had to agree. Elise's mother had been vocal about her opposition to the marriage. So she didn't blame Elise for not wanting to see her now. "What about Diane? Surely you can stay there until the siege is over." After that, was anyone's guess.

"Diane's pregnant again," Elise muttered, avoiding Marie's eye.

Eight years of marriage had produced no children for the Lévesques. Elise had always tried to make the best of it, but Marie knew how much the situation hurt her. She wouldn't go anywhere near her cousin, not when she was with child.

"I was angry with him right before he left," Elise suddenly shouted, tears continuing to course down her cheeks.

"It's a stressful time for us all," Marie said, trying to calm her down.

"I knew what could happen, but I was still angry with him. I can't even remember why."

That sounded about on par with what Marie knew of the last few years of their relationship. "We all do things we wish we could take back. But he knew you loved him, and he loved you very much." A fresh wave of tears greeted this announcement.

Marie wrapped a comforting arm around Elise's shivering shoulders. She wanted to confide in Elise that Nic had been upset with her too, about the guilt that was piling up in her as well, but her friend was in no shape to reciprocate with support. Marie also knew that Elise shouldn't be left alone.

"I'll stay tonight, but I have to go back to the hospital tomorrow morning."

"It's bad, isn't it?" Elise asked thickly, her usually porcelain face swollen and blotchy from tears.

"Yes," Marie sighed. "But you don't need to worry about that now."

Marie made a light meal of salted cod and stale turnip, encouraging Elise to eat, even though she only picked at the food herself. She tidied up while Elise roamed the house, unsure of what to do with herself.

Marie tucked Elise into her large feather bed and crawled in beside her. She held her sister-in-law while she wept, unable to think of anything to say. A small part of Marie had assumed Nic would walk away from this battle the way he always had.

Her thoughts turned to Pierre, who was still on the battlefield, still in the line of fire. While hopefully alive, she knew she could be in Elise's position at any moment. Even worse, she wouldn't officially be a widow, so the church wouldn't recognize her as next of kin. She would be a ruined woman, alone in the world.

She watched the moon rise while she stroked Elise's copper hair, thinking of Pierre lying under the same orb. It was oddly comforting to know they were both under the same sky. Elise finally fell into an uneasy sleep as the moon sank closer to the horizon. Marie slipped out of bed and silently took one last look around the house.

It looked as it always had: neat, clean, and sparsely furnished but now unaware that its master no longer lived. There was nothing of their parents in this house because nothing had been removed from the wreckage after the fire, so this was all that remained of Marie's family.

She lovingly picked up Nic's snuff box from the desk. Just like its owner, it put function over appearance, but it was attractive in its own way, with a hand-carved wooden lid depicting the *voyageurs* travelling over rapids. Nic had traded a beaver pelt for it when he was ten, the fur being from the first animal he had ever killed. Though he'd never tried snuff, he'd eagerly given the pelt to a fur trader just back from Europe in exchange for the box. He'd been so proud of it. He'd tried snuff shortly afterwards and hated it. Marie laughed at the memory and wiped a tear from her eye.

Whatever happened to them when the fortress fell, the snuff box, like Nic's body and those of so many other poor souls who had lost their lives here, would stay behind. And the lives of those who had lived and loved in Louisbourg would be forgotten in the echoes of history. Marie now understood why Sara's mother didn't want to leave the graves of her children. She placed the snuff box gently back on the desk, curled up on the couch, and slept till the first rays of the morning sun filtered into the room.

Chapter 14

AFTER NIC'S DEATH, daily life became even more difficult. The bombardment still rained fiery hell from the sky, and the wounded, dying, and starving were coming in faster than the hospital could handle. The bombs were falling more frequently, the accuracy of the targets ever improving. Supplies were running low and people were bringing in loved ones who simply couldn't take the bombardment anymore. Morale was low, even though everyone was fighting to keep the wheels of daily life moving.

Unable to leave the hospital, Marie had tried to write to Elise every day, but there had been no response, so she had no idea what her sister-in-law was doing. Father Laval had gone to check on her one night and reported that the house was empty. Nic's body had been laid to rest in the cemetery outside the walls, but Marie had been informed that Elise hadn't gone to the burial. Marie's anxiety about her just kept growing. Why was she being so absent and silent?

Marie awoke four days after Nic's death to the room spinning. After giving herself a few minutes, she felt a bit better, but she had to lie down again after she got dressed. She didn't feel feverish, but her stomach was writhing. Was it possible that she'd contracted an illness while working with the sick people at the hospital? She carefully made her way down the hallway, all too aware of cannon fire roaring through the air.

Breakfast was the usual bowl of porridge, but this morning, Marie could hardly get it down. Then, as soon as she finished, she had to run from the room to bring it all up again. It seemed like such a waste, with food in dangerously short supply. Her head still spinning, she accepted a sip of water from Sister Miriam and meekly went back to bed. "There's illness sweeping through the city," the nun had said. "Better to rest before you contract something worse." It was true that diseases were starting to become rampant in the city, as farmers and other inhabitants of the surrounding area had poured into the fortress seeking shelter and causing cramped living conditions.

Marie woke up an hour later, feeling better but exhausted. A deep tiredness seemed to have settled into her bones, and no amount of sleep could get rid of it. This overwhelming fatigue is not going to leave until the siege is over, she thought miserably. Everyone was working at capacity with minimal sleep, though, so she shouldn't treat herself as a special case. She stretched and got up slowly, waiting for waves of nausea to wash over her, but they didn't come. She debated whether she should return to the patients below but instead crawled back into bed. With luck, she would sleep it off and be fine in the morning.

The next day was the same except that the nausea and dizziness were worse than before. She stayed in bed until the feeling abated and then dressed slowly before going downstairs. She tried a bit of porridge, but again, she couldn't keep it down. Luckily, the kitchen workers were absorbed in their activities and didn't notice her. She wanted to go back to bed, but instead she went into the laundry room and started folding sheets until she was sure she wouldn't vomit. But an overpowering stench of fish then came drifting down from the kitchen, making her head spin.

Annoyed, Marie went looking for Sara.

She was working on a soldier whose leg had been blown partly off above the knee. Father Laval was in the process of sawing off the now-useless part of the limb, while Father Maneau kept the young man restrained by putting a knee on his chest. Sara was bending over the fire, heating a metal pan that would be used to cauterize the veins once the bone had been severed.

Sara nodded grimly as Marie touched her shoulder to let her know she'd arrived. The sound of the saw cutting through bone set Marie's teeth on edge. Luckily, the poor cadet had lost consciousness and was unaware of what was happening to his body.

"The priests are going to hold him down, but can you hold onto the stump while I do this?" The sawing had stopped, and they would need to move quickly. "Then we can start sewing this poor boy back together."

Marie nodded. She took her position, wrapping her hands around the thick thigh as best she could. She tried not to look at the bloody appendage but mistakenly glanced at the floor, where the remnants lay in a pool of blood. She closed her eyes and waited.

Suddenly, the sound of sizzling flesh filled her ears. As the smell of charred skin and blood hit her nose, completely overwhelming her, she sank to the floor.

***

Marie awoke some time later to find herself lying on one of the wooden tables in the kitchen. A cold towel had been placed on her forehead, and her feet were elevated, resting on a towel. She glanced over to see Sara looking quite amused by the proceedings.

"Welcome back to the land of the living," she chuckled. "You caused quite a stir."

Marie groaned and tried to sit up, but Sara pushed her back. "What happened?" Marie was all too aware of the kitchen staff gawking at her.

"You fainted, my dear." Sara sounded completely delighted. "For the first time, people have stopped talking about my ideas and are focusing on you."

"You're enjoying this far too much," Marie muttered. She wished the floor would open up and swallow her.

"Did you eat today?" Sara giggled.

"Of course, I did," Marie snapped. "But," she conceded after a moment, "it keeps coming up."

"I hope you don't have what's going around," Sara said sarcastically.

Marie glared. She was deeply embarrassed. "Thanks for the concern, but I don't have a fever and I'm sure I'll be fine by midday. Are you going to cure me now?"

Sara bit her lip to keep from laughing. "I don't think that's possible." She paused dramatically. "Father Maneau thinks you're pregnant."

Marie sat upright, pulling the cloth off her forehead. The room spun dangerously and she collapsed again, looking at her friend in horror.

"Is it a possibility?" Sara laughed at Marie's consternation.

Of course, it was. Just not a possibility that she had ever thought of. Between the war and her recovery from Claude's beating, she hadn't for a moment considered it. But she counted backwards quickly in her head and then stared at Sara, thunderstruck. Sara chuckled happily to herself.

"It's nice to know that the miracle of life continues even amidst all this destruction."

Marie nodded numbly. "Are you sure I'm not just sick?" she pleaded.

Sara gave her a dubious look. "How long has it been?"

"Six weeks." She counted again just to make sure.

"You're sick in the morning?"

"Only today and yesterday."

"Smells bother you?"

"Obviously."

"Are you tired?"

"Aren't we all?"

"You're pregnant," Sara said with satisfaction.

A feeling of dread settled into Marie's stomach. Suddenly, she felt trapped. Pierre. She needed to tell Pierre. But was he even still alive?

"Are you all right?" Sara asked quietly. "You look terrified." She sat down beside Marie. "You're not happy about this, are you?" she said, slowly scrutinizing Marie.

Marie looked at her. "Is that a terrible thing to say?"

Sara shrugged. "Not really. Every now and then, we get some poor girl who dies after trying to end a pregnancy. It happens. But you're married." She said that as if it settled the matter.

Marie looked down at her fingers, took the ring out of her pocket, and began to twist the silver band between her fingers. "Not really," she said quietly.

"What do you mean 'not really'?"

Marie looked around to see if anyone was paying attention. Now that she was obviously going to pull through, no one gave them a second look. "We didn't actually get married. We just eloped."

Sara gasped. "What on earth would you do that for?" she hissed, scandalized. "Marie, that's terrible."

"Calm down!" Marie was in no mood for a lecture on morals. As quickly and quietly as she could, she explained the situation to Sara. More than once, Sara seemed ready to bolt from the room as if the presence of sin was going to rub off on her, but Marie somehow convinced her to stay put until the story was complete.

There was silence for a while as Sara thought the situation over. Marie could see the internal conflict raging. On one side, Sara was in the process of becoming a nun and Marie was committing a most grievous sin. On the other, marriage was being withheld from them unjustly.

"Does anyone here know?"

"Father Weber knows. He's the only one. We asked him to marry us, but he said no." Marie felt suddenly as if she was on the verge of tears.

Sara placed her thin hand on top of Marie's. She looked both scandalized and deeply impressed at their daring. "I've never agreed with the rules regarding the government's involvement in a soldier's marriage," she stated in a matter-of-fact tone.

Somehow, hearing that lightened the burden that Marie felt was smothering her. It was a relief to finally be able to confide in someone.

"But now you're pregnant," Sara said softly, "and you feel guilty."

"Not guilty," Marie replied. "Just terrified. We're not married and there's a war. What happens when this is all over? What happens if Pierre doesn't come off the battlefield?"

Sara nodded sympathetically. "I don't know." She stood up. "But I need to go tell people what's going on before the worst conclusions are made."

***

Marie had slept all night, but that didn't seem to matter. When morning came, she was as exhausted as ever. It took her a moment to remember why she felt so uneasy, but when everything came back into focus, her anxiety returned in full force. Her stomach flipped over in protest as she pulled herself out of bed. The bombs were already falling. She stared out her window as the plumes of black smoke told of at least one fire raging somewhere near the ramparts.

After being sick, she lay back down, her throat burning from the acid, wondering how on earth she was supposed to last until February like this. She had met with Sister Berenice the night before, to explain the situation as far as she understood it. Just like everyone else who'd heard her news, the nun was thrilled, a reaction Marie didn't understand. She didn't even know if her husband was alive. She had kept her fears about Pierre to herself, and the nun had instructed her to stay in her room until the feelings of nausea passed. Luckily, in a little more than an hour, she felt fine.

Marie dressed as quickly as she could. Nothing had changed from the day before, but she couldn't help staring at her stomach, trying to judge whether there'd been some sort of growth. She nibbled on a little bread that she'd brought to her room the night before. After rinsing out her mouth with some water, she headed down to the chaos. Sara was seated in the kitchen, boiling needles, tweezers, and who knew what else. She seemed perturbed about something. Marie sat opposite her at the table and waited for her to finish.

"Oh good, you're here." Sara looked up quickly before turning back to the cauldron and scooping steaming needles out with a ladle. "Everyone takes me more seriously when you're around. I've been sent here to wait for you because everyone else thinks I'm a waste of time."

Marie made a noncommittal sound, picked up some linen sheets, and began to rip them into strips. "You know people have been treated for thousands of years without all this cleaning."

Sara ignored her and ladled more instruments out of the water. "How are you feeling today?"

Marie shrugged. "Same as yesterday. But the way Sister Berenice was going on, you'd think I was dying. She wanted me to leave."

Sara nodded as if this wasn't news. "She found me last night after she talked to you and spent a good while fretting about your 'condition' as she called it. She doesn't want you near any of the sick people."

"She told me that too."

"Yes, well, it's my job to make sure you stay away from the second floor. Otherwise, I'll probably be the one who gets in trouble." She gave Marie a severe look. Marie tried to keep a straight face and nodded obediently.

Sara scooped her boiled equipment up into a linen bundle and stood up. "Well, that should keep us going for at least the morning."

"Is it bad?" Marie asked—though it became obvious that the question was rhetorical as another mortar exploded close enough to make the windows rattle.

Sara nodded and headed into the hall. "About fifty bombs dropped last night, and they're getting more accurate. I heard one of the soldiers say that they're using the spires to gauge where everything is."

Marie lifted a pile of fresh bandages into her arms. Apparently, she'd slept through the bombardment last night. That wasn't a very comforting thought. "I guess that's one reason why everything was supposed to be only one storey high when they were building this place."

Sara shook her head, exasperated. "No one ever listens, do they." She pushed the door to the ward open, and they began their day.

For the first time since the siege began, the civilians in the hospital outnumbered the military men. The bombs were raining down with terrifying precision, and almost every time they landed, it was on a building. The flames would often leap from one building to the next, trapping the people inside and injuring the fire fighters.

Burns and crushed or broken bones were the most frequent injuries that needed treatment. Sara's pile of clean supplies lay forgotten as the hospital personnel battled the ever-increasing group of invalids. Even Sara wasn't concerned with sanitation when a person was on the brink of death. Broken bones could usually be set, but those crushed by the falling bombs and rubble were almost impossible to repair. It was slow, painstaking work. Worse, the hospital didn't have enough opiates for all the patients. The only available painkiller was liquor, which wasn't enough for a patient with a splintered knee cap. Amputation was becoming the solution of choice. It seemed cruel to doom someone to that fate, but with so many patients, if the wound festered, the victim would surely die.

*** *

As evening turned to night, a fresh wave of soldiers flooded in. The French had tried an offensive attack that had gone disastrously wrong. Outnumbered and outgunned, once the element of surprise was lost, there was little they could do except try to hold their own.

The night was stifling and the extra bodies packed into the hospital made the atmosphere even more oppressive. Feeling dizzy and exhausted, Marie excused herself and leaned against a wall in the corridor. She was sweating, and her hands were stained red from the blood of a poor boy whose hip had been crushed by a piece of rock in an explosion. His screams as he begged for his mother still echoed in her ears. *He won't make it through the night,* she thought miserably as she watched two soldiers help a man down the hall. His foot had been blown off. A tourniquet had been tied around the stump, but

Marie doubted that would save the man's life in the long run. He already had the grey-green look of a corpse.

Marie looked beyond the mangled body to the main door. She had a mad desire to run out into the streets and not return—away from the madness and hopelessness that was engulfing her. She took a deep breath, wiped her hands on her apron as best she could, and turned to go back into the mess of patients when something caught her eye.

Pierre stood at the end of the hallway, hidden in the shadows of the open front doors. She shook her head to make sure she wasn't dreaming. He was completely covered in blood, slightly bent at the middle from pain and exhaustion. A half sob, half scream escaped from her lips. She ran to him, wanting to embrace him and hold him as tightly as she could, but she was afraid of the damage that might do.

"What happened to you?" He lowered his head toward hers. She pressed her hands against his forehead and cheeks, trying her best to assess his situation. Under the mud and stubble, he was very pale.

"It's not my blood; it's Christian's." He nodded toward the man without a foot being carried down the hall. "I helped bring him in. Nearly did me in too."

Marie sighed with relief and wrapped her arms around his middle. He yelped, nearly jumping out of his skin.

"What is it?"

He lifted his shirt to show a deep gash running around his right side. Glistening white bone poked out in a few places.

"You said it wasn't your blood!"

"Well, it mainly isn't. A Redcoat tried to stab me." He tried to make light of the situation but grunted in pain.

Marie continued to assess the damage. "Tried to? I'd say he succeeded."

Pierre laughed weakly. "If he'd succeeded, I wouldn't have made it here."

Marie tried to laugh, but she sobbed instead. Her vision blurred by tears, she wrapped her arms around his neck and held him tight. Forgetting that they were in the hospital, that he was injured and battle weary, she pressed her body against his, revelling in the fact that he was there with her.

"I'm all right, beautiful. I'm all right," he repeated over and over again, holding her as close as his mangled side would allow.

"I've been so worried ... so scared ... after Nic ..." She could barely get the words out.

"Marie, I'll be all right. I promise. But if I stand here much longer, I'm going to collapse."

Marie yelped in embarrassment, grasped his hand, and led him down the hall. He stared around at the chaos. It was the opposite of the last time he'd walked these halls. Marie was also thinner than when they had parted, and she had dark circles under her eyes.

"Are you going to stitch me up?" he asked. He didn't want to be separated from her.

"You don't have much of a choice in the matter. There are a lot here who are far worse than you, I'm afraid. I wonder how there's anyone left on the battlefield when I see all the men in here. Obviously, it's not going well." Marie paused and shook her head, discouraged.

She left him sitting against the wall with others who were able to sit under their own strength, while she grabbed supplies and looked for Sara. Though she still thought Sara's practices were mad, she suddenly wanted to take every precaution possible.

"Is he all right?" Sara asked in alarm as she gathered her supplies. She'd been resting in the kitchen. She too was shaken after all they'd been through that day.

"He just needs stitches. He'll be fine. Maybe some whisky."

Sara grabbed a bottle and followed quickly behind Marie. "Have you told him?"

"About what?"

Sara let out an exasperated sigh. "About the baby, of course."

That brought Marie up short. She'd completely forgotten about the pregnancy. "No, and I probably won't. He doesn't need that distraction."

Sara made an impatient clicking noise but said nothing.

Marie returned to find Pierre laughing with the man beside him. He grinned when he saw her, although the pain in his eyes was clear.

"That's my wife," he told the elder militia man proudly.

The man laughed but looked impressed despite the fact that Marie was covered in blood and sweat. "The nun?"

Pierre snorted and then winced. "The brunette."

The man grinned mischievously. "Well, then, sweetie, if you ever want to change your life calling, I'll happily take ya."

Sara rolled her eyes and muttered something rude in English.

Unperturbed by this, the man turned back to Pierre. "I guess you're in good hands then."

"I doubt it. She'll be less concerned about my comfort than if she was treating a stranger. She's still mad at me for getting involved in this whole mess."

"Oh, shut up, you." Marie glared. "You'll be just fine. Now take off your shirt."

Both men howled with laughter. Pierre needed help getting his shirt above his shoulders, so Marie stopped the joking and gently pulled it off.

The wound was deep but fairly clean. Sara washed it with boiled water, and Pierre grunted as Marie pressed against the wound.

"Do you have any other injuries I should know about?" Marie asked, though she was afraid to know the answer.

"No. All good except for this one."

Then Marie realized that minor injuries were usually treated on the battlefield, and this one, bad as it was, would be considered minor. Pierre had used the need to drop off a comrade as an excuse to see her. She sat down beside him, preparing to stitch him back together.

"Yes, so far, I'm fine," Pierre went on. "More than I can say for most of the boys ... and ... I'm sorry about Nic." He gripped Marie's shoulder as he said that. "I wanted to come and see you, but I wasn't allowed. Almost punched my new commanding officer."

Marie fumbled with the needle but held her composure. "I went to tell Elise with one of the priests ... I haven't heard from her since."

Pierre leaned forward unconsciously. "Has anyone been to check on her?"

"The house was empty," Marie muttered.

Pierre leaned against the wall, trying to think of where Elise could be. "That's not good." He clamped his jaw tight together. No noise escaped from him, but Marie could see his hands clenched, the knuckles white with strain as the thread slowly pulled the flaps of angry, red skin back together. It wasn't neat, but he was in one piece again. Pierre then leaned forward so Marie could wrap the bandages around him, adding extra padding for protection. He leaned back again, sweat beading on his forehead.

"How are you?" he asked, grasping her hand, his eyes closed as he recovered. "I've missed you."

"I've just been here, saving the world." Marie handed him the bottle of whisky. A smile played on his lips as he took a healthy measure.

Pierre kept a firm grip on her hand and opened his eyes. "Are you all right?" It was clear that he'd spent as much time worrying about her as she had about him.

She nodded, not trusting herself to speak.

Sara glared at her from across the patient beside Pierre. Marie just shook her head. "Tell him," Sara mouthed. She looked as if she was ready to lunge across her charge if Marie didn't take action soon.

"Do you think you can walk?" Marie asked gently.

Pierre groaned and shifted his weight. "You're trying to get rid of me already?"

Marie laughed feebly. "No, I need to talk to you. Somewhere private if possible."

Pierre looked surprised but moved out of his chair, groaning as his feet took his weight. She helped him shrug on his shirt. Then he downed as much liquor as possible before saying, "Where to?" Marie pointed to the door that led to the garden and the nuns' apartments. She could feel Sara's eyes following her out of the building.

***

The air was hot but not nearly as stuffy as the atmosphere in the crowded hospital. It was wonderful to enter into the silence and feel the breeze. The British were evidently taking a break from the continual bombardment.

Pierre's massive form stood in the shadows. Marie took his hand silently and led him toward her room.

He came to a stop when he saw where she was headed. "I can't go in there. That's where the nuns are." She tried half-heartedly to pull him along, but injured or not, he was still incredibly strong and resisted her.

"All the nuns are at the hospital now. They aren't here."

Pierre shook his head stubbornly, the light from the hospital windows flashing off his golden hair. "A man in the nuns' apartments? I don't want to be blamed for that."

Marie sighed, defeated. "Fine, then. We'll just stay out in the open."

There were no seats in the courtyard. Obviously, the clergy felt sitting was a waste of time. Pierre sat down and leaned against the stone wall of the hospital building, exhausted. Marie stood in front of him, balanced between his legs. He placed his hands on her hips, stroking her gently.

"What's the matter, beautiful?" he asked softly.

"What makes you think there's something wrong?" She bent forward to kiss him, trying to put off the moment of truth.

Pierre stayed motionless, but she could see the muscles of his face tightening as he tried to endure the exhaustion and the pain.

She sighed. "I didn't want to tell you because you're out fighting. I was hoping for a better time."

He gazed at her through half-closed eyes. "What's the matter?"

"I'm pregnant." She tried to keep the fear out of her voice, but it quivered.

His eyes snapped open. "What?"

"I'm pregnant," she repeated, stronger this time. "About six weeks."

He was stunned. Shock was etched in every line of his face. "Are you sure?"

She nodded. Pierre held her at arm's length and stared at her in disbelief, his eyes bright in the muted light from the windows. "Pregnant," he whispered and then pulled her into a rib-crushing bear hug, laughing. "This is wonderful!"

Marie tried her best to pull away from him. "Are you sure?"

He stopped laughing, looking at her with concern and drawing her closer to him. They were both now sitting on the ground. Marie worried for a minute about someone seeing them in that compromising position, but then realized no one would care. Not in the middle of the chaos of pain surrounding them. "You're not happy about this?"

Marie paused, then shook her head.

"Why? Is something wrong? Are you terribly sick?"

Marie looked away. She felt like a traitor. Of course, he was happy. Everyone was happy about the baby. What was wrong with her?

"Talk to me," he pleaded gently, stroking her cheek.

Marie drummed her fingers on the ground. She probably couldn't articulate everything that was on her mind without causing offence. "We're in the middle of a war that we aren't going to win. You're on the front lines. Every day, I see the sick, wounded, and dying come in looking for help that I probably can't give them. If they survive, they'll never be the same. Nic's already dead, and you've just been stabbed. There's barely enough food. The hospital is running out of medicine. When we lose, what happens? I'll be sent to France, and you'll probably be in a New England prison somewhere if you're lucky. Will we ever see each other again? It could be years before we're reunited and then what?" She paused to take a breath, tears beginning to leak down her cheeks. She brushed them impatiently away. Pierre stood silently, looking stricken.

"And I promise I don't care," Marie went on. "I don't. But we're not really married. So what about the baby? It can't be a bastard. Not our baby!" It was all out, but she still felt a deep sense of shame, having ruined what should have been a happy moment.

Pierre didn't say anything for a long time. He just continued to stare at her, his arms limp at his sides. The door to the courtyard creaked open, and Sara became visible in the candlelight. She saw the two of them and quickly ducked back inside.

Very slowly, as if awakening from a dream, Pierre wrapped his arms around Marie and pulled her close to his chest. Marie tried to be mindful of the bandages, but Pierre didn't seem to care.

"Did you not realize that this was a possibility?" She could hear the hint of amusement in his voice, and anger boiled within her.

"Of course, I did," she snapped, her feelings hurt. "I just didn't think it would happen so quickly ... I'm old."

Pierre released her and made a face. "I forgot that expectant mothers can be touchy." Marie bristled. He sighed. "I'm sorry I laughed at you ..."

A cannon roared from the direction of the harbour. Marie felt Pierre's body stiffen beside her. The temporary peace was over.

After Nic arranged for me to be posted here at the fortress last year," Pierre said slowly, "I got on a boat and arrived in the middle of November. Ships usually don't travel at that time. The winds and storms were awful, and I didn't think we were going to make it. I remember one poor cadet spent the entire trip hanging over the edge of the boat." He smiled at the memory. "First time I saw someone sicker than me ... . Nic had told me to stay away from you. Told me you'd moved on. You already know that, but I kept my word. I didn't want to interrupt your happiness, but there isn't a lot to do when you're a soldier here in the middle of winter."

Pierre sighed and twisted his torso from side to side experimentally, wincing as the stitches caught against his skin. "So when I was bored, I sometimes just went out and walked around the city. One day, while I was on one of those walks, I saw you as you were going to church with Annette. You had a blue hat on and that huge grey cape you always wear that's so ugly." Marie smiled a little at this. "You were going up the steps to the Chapel and you looked happy or at least I didn't suspect any of the things that were going on. I just stood there and watched you until you went in."

Pierre fell silent, picking at a blade of grass beside him. Marie placed her hand on top of his. "Why didn't you say anything?"

He looked up, the yellow in his blue irises glowing in the moonlight. "I thought you wouldn't want to see me," he said sadly. "So I just stood in the snow, balls frozen solid, watching you like some creepy, pathetic sod."

Marie laughed. "You've never been creepy. But I wish I'd seen you," she finished seriously.

"I always looked for you whenever I went places. Louisbourg really isn't that big, but I never ran into you. That night I fought those men, I didn't know it was you. I just knew someone was in trouble. I couldn't believe it when I saw it was you. I thought I must be dreaming. You cleared that up for me quickly enough, though."

Marie placed her head on his shoulder, trying not to touch his wounded side. He smelled overpoweringly of dirt, sweat, blood, and manliness, but she didn't want to let him go. "I wish I'd known you were back. I would have sought you out as soon as I could have."

Pierre nodded. "I know. I wish I hadn't listened to Nic. He was always overprotective of you. But it doesn't matter now. Maybe this is all we get—the last few days of Louisbourg. But I'll take it."

Marie looked down and wrapped her slender fingers around his hand, feeling the calluses and blisters.

"I might be gone tomorrow," Pierre continued. "I don't want to be, but I can't promise that I won't. But I've had the chance to love you again. If I die on the battlefield, at least I don't have to die wondering what could have been. That thought had always tortured me."

The sound of cannon fire ripped through the silence. Marie pursed her lips together to try to stop the tears. "But I don't know if I can do this without you."

Pierre smiled as he looked down at her, brushing a few strands of hair away from her face. "I know you can. I want to meet my child, but if I can't, you'll be more than capable to give it the love it needs." He kissed her forehead. "But I'll see what I can do to help with the situation."

Marie didn't understand what he could possibly do to make the situation less bleak, but at that moment, the door opened again. Sara's incredibly pale head was visible, clearly sending a message.

"Do you have to go back?"

Pierre nodded.

"But you're injured. You need rest at least for the night."

Pierre looked around at the buildings surrounding them. "There isn't room for me here. You're up to your elbows with people in far worse shape than I am. I can go back to the barracks and sleep."

Marie stood up, placed her hands on her hips in the best impression she could of Sister Berenice at her sternest. "You will do no such thing. You are injured, and you need rest. I'm the *ramancheur*. I know what's best." She could see Pierre fighting valiantly not to laugh.

He struggled to his knees and accepted her help as he rose stiffly to his feet. "All right, Madame. But if my commander comes looking for me, you can deal with him. I'm following your orders." He wrapped his arm around her waist.

"Don't worry," Marie said darkly. "If your commander comes, he'll know his place."

"That's my girl," Pierre smiled.

As they re-entered the hospital, they could see that it was even more crowded than when they'd left. The families and loved ones of the admitted patients were slowly trickling in. In several hours, though, things would calm down—as long as tonight's bombardment didn't destroy too much of the city.

Marie found a pallet in a quiet corner of a room at the back of the building. Most of the other patients there were already taken care of and drifting into an uneasy sleep. Despite Pierre's protests, Marie helped him into bed, tucking the blankets around him.

"I'm not a little boy anymore, you know," he said crossly as she kissed his forehead.

"Are you sure?" she teased. "In that case, I won't come and check on you tonight."

Her husband grinned. "I think you'd better, once everyone else has gone to bed."

***

The bombardment was becoming more and more deadly. Every day, the shots became more frequent and more precise, and the hospital was filling up beyond capacity. Fires raged; food was scarce; and the dead, dying, and injured kept streaming in. Sister Miriam had taken ill and was confined to her bed, and Father Maneau had been killed by a cannonball, two days previously while travelling to see Governor Drucour, causing Father Laval to take over the hospital's administration temporarily. The remaining citizens of Louisbourg kept pressing on, but despair was getting the upper hand.

Marie walked into the kitchen at about midday. She felt terrible and hadn't been able to keep anything down. So she was getting thinner, and people were concerned. Heavily sugared tea seemed to be the only thing she could take in that wouldn't come up again. She was drinking it by the bucketful, but she still felt weak and dizzy. She kept working, though. Her suffering compatriots needed her.

Before she walked into the wards, she looked over and saw Sara standing alone by one of the kitchen windows, her back turned away from the world. At first, Marie didn't think anything of it, but then she heard the gentle sound of tears. Approaching slowly, she found Sara in a most distressed state. Her face was red and puffy, her hands were shaking, and her usually pressed uniform was rumpled.

"Sara, what's the matter?" She had never seen Sara lose control and thought that her friend was beyond letting the war disturb her professional conduct.

Sara sniffed dramatically but didn't say anything. The other women in the kitchen simply ignored the shivering figure and continued preparing the little food they had to work with.

Marie tried again. "Sara, talk to me. What happened? Is it your family?"

Sara looked at Marie through watery eyes as if just realizing she was there. She shook her pale head. "My family's fine," she said flatly.

"Well, that's good," Marie chided. Better than she herself was doing.

Sara sighed and wiped her face on her sleeve, a gesture Marie had never seen Sara make before. "I don't know if I can do this anymore, Marie," she said softly.

Marie was startled. "What do you mean?"

"I mean all of this. Trying to save all these people. It can't be done." She began to wail. "More and more people keep coming, and more and more of them are dying or losing limbs. Remember that little baby girl yesterday? She hardly even lived and now she's dead." She dissolved into tears once more.

It was true, Marie thought painfully. The bombardment wasn't stopping. In fact, it sometimes felt as if the British were just getting started. It was one thing to injure and kill sailors and soldiers who had signed up for combat, but to subject the civilians of Louisbourg to such destruction—it was inhumane. Marie tried to remember back to the baby Sara was talking about, then realized that she had simply walked away when the woman came in with her tiny, burned child, unable to handle the overwhelming horror that had engulfed her.

Marie laid a hand on Sara's thin shoulder. "I'm sorry I left you alone yesterday. That wasn't fair."

Sara looked up and laughed. A high, mad laugh that scared Marie more than the tears. "Of course you left. You're pregnant."

"Sara, maybe you should go and lie down. I'm sure we can manage without you for a while." But even as she said this, she knew it wasn't true.

Sara stood up, her thin frame shivering from emotion. "No. I can't leave—not when there's so much to be done." And with that, she marched purposefully out of the kitchen and into the waiting wards.

Marie turned to the kitchen workers. "How long was she in here before I came?"

One of the girls shrugged, but her companion thought a moment. "Maybe half an hour? She's actually calmed down quite a bit, but she probably shouldn't be near any patients."

Marie swore under her breath and marched toward the door, if Sara wouldn't rest, she would just have to find reinforcements and make her take a break. As she reached for the door handle, something huge crashed into the door and ripped it off its hinges. Marie was thrown to the floor, and the door fell onto her, covering the bottom part of her body. Ears ringing, she lay panting, trying to catch the breath that had been knocked out of her. She could hear screaming all around her, and the smell of smoke was thick in the air.

With a tremendous effort, she kicked the door off and scrambled to her feet. She felt herself swoon as the blood rushed from her head and leaned against the wooden table for support. Thick, black smoke was billowing in from the hallway. The kitchen maids behind her were screaming, and she could hear the sound of what seemed like hundreds of voices coming from beyond the doorway.

Ignoring the sensible voice in her head that told her to run, she pushed her way into the hall. The war had come to the hospital. Two craters gaped in the floors, and sunlight flooded in from the holes in the roof. Fires had started along the path the mortars had taken as those who could walk scrambled over the beds to get to safety.

Another mortar exploded in the courtyard, and Marie ducked as the force of the impact blew out the hospital windows. She felt as if someone had clubbed her over the back. Panting, she looked around for someone, anyone, to help. Two priests, their black coats catching around their legs, were rushing to put out the flames with buckets of water from the kitchen. More and more horrified patients were trying to flee. Marie ran to the closest door. It seemed that the choice for the patients was between dying in the chaotic confines of the hospital and losing their lives under the sky. Marie chose the sky. Throwing the door open, she began shepherding as many people as she could out of the ward and into the courtyard. Those too ill to walk were lifted by those who could. As the procession slowly made its way outside, Marie scrambled back in. One of the fires was out and the others were almost extinguished.

Gasping for breath, she looked around. Most of the patients were out, and those who still remained were safe from the fires at least. The bombardment had blasted out most of the floor, making craters large enough for Pierre to lie down in.

Bombs were still falling in the vicinity, and people were still screaming. Overwhelmed, Marie saw a small girl, no more than seven, crouched in the corner of the room, her arms wrapped around her knees. Marie crawled toward her before realizing that the child's torso had been burned by the impact of the mortars. Without thinking, Marie scooped the girl up into her arms and ran into the kitchen, one place that was still relatively unharmed. Paying attention to nothing around her, Marie laid the girl on the table, quickly cutting her scorched clothing away.

"What's your name, sweetie?"

"Anne," the girl sniffed. She was making a remarkably small amount of noise for the amount of pain she must be in. It probably hasn't hit her yet, Marie thought clinically.

"Okay, Anne," Marie said, grabbing some linen and pouring cold water on it, "I need you to be brave for me." She laid the cloth on the burn, hoping it would give some relief.

"I want my mamma," Anne sniffled, tears streaking down her round cheeks.

Marie's heart dropped. "Where is your mother?"

"She's at home," Anne wailed.

Marie's brain didn't seem to be working right. "If she's not here, then why were you here?"

Anne started to sob uncontrollably. Marie's heart was pounding. She needed to get Anne to her mother if she could, but she couldn't transport her in this condition. The burn wasn't serious, and it would heal if treated, but the poor girl's system had been immensely traumatized. How had this child got here without a parent?

Spotting a jar of balm of Gilead, Marie quickly slathered it on the girl's shoulder and chest before wrapping her up in a towel that was so dirty it would have made Sara scream. "Anne? Can you tell me where you live?" Anne rubbed her eyes. "I'm going to take you home to your mother, but I need you to tell me where you live."

Anne hiccupped and choked but nodded. As gently as she could, Marie picked her up and laid the girl's small body against her shoulder. For a moment, as she stepped out into the city, she thought she'd walked into a different world. Gunpowder and smoke filled the air, mortars had made gaping holes in the roofs of the nearby buildings, and rubble was strewn about the streets. People were running all around her, trying to get into the hospital to help. This wasn't the fortress of Louisbourg; it was hell.

With direction from Anne, Marie hurried through the ruined streets as quickly as she could. Anne, it turned out, had sneaked away from home to try to find a friend who she thought was in the hospital. Unable to find her, the young girl was about to leave when the mortar struck.

"Your mother's going to be sick with worry," Marie scolded as they rounded a corner. Anne pointed to a home that Marie knew very well. She froze, overcome by fear.

"Is your mother's name Sophie by chance?" Anne whimpered, "Yes." Marie suddenly wished she wasn't delivering Anne back home. "And your father will be Philippe," Marie mumbled under her breath. Marie hadn't had much to do with Sophie after Pierre's disappearance, but she had gone to the wedding. Searching back into her memory, she remembered that Sophie's oldest was named Anne. Now that she inspected the child, looking for a resemblance, she realized that Anne looked very much like her father, with her sandy curls and large eyes. Sophie, the gossip, was the last person Marie wanted to speak to right now.

She wanted very much to turn and leave the child on the steps, but the look of utter terror on Anne's face made her realize that wasn't an option. With a sense of foreboding, Marie knocked on the ornate oak door.

***

Sophie was as striking as ever, with her green eyes and well-coiffed ebony hair. Apart from the frantic worry crossing her face, she looked as if she'd been living in a world apart from the battle—at least until the bombs had started coming right into the city. Sophie pulled open the door, took one look at her daughter, and let out an ear-piercing screech. Without looking at Marie, she pulled Anne into her arms and held her tightly to her chest, tears of joy coursing down her cheeks.

"Oh, Anne," she repeated over and over again. "Where have you been? I've been so worried."

Hoping that she'd been overlooked during the joyous reunion, Marie tried to beat a hasty retreat.

"Wait!" Sophie cried.

Marie stopped and turned. She saw the shock on Sophie's face. Obviously, she hadn't been expecting Marie.

"Marie? What are you doing here?" Anne had snuggled, sobbing, into her mother's chest.

Marie smiled awkwardly. Sophie had not seen Marie since the night she'd broken her engagement to Jacques, and last she'd heard, Marie was too ill to receive visitors. "Hello," Marie said, stepping up onto the stoop. "I brought Anne back. She was at the hospital looking for a friend of hers. I'm afraid she's been badly burned. She'll pull through, but she's in pain."

Sophie looked down at her daughter, horrified. She retreated into the house, calling for Marie to follow. Leaving the door open, Marie reluctantly stepped inside.

Sophie laid her daughter on the sitting-room sofa. She bent over the little form, fussing over her and caressing her while trying to assess the extent of the damage.

Marie peered over her shoulder. Angry blisters were rising on the burn sites, but they would heal. "She'll be all right, Sophie," Marie said. "Just continue to apply salve to the burns. They should heal."

Sophie looked stricken. "What if it leaves a mark?" she asked hysterically. "No one will want to marry her then."

"Oh, for heaven's sake!" Marie exploded, completely losing her patience. "That's not important right now. She's a little girl, Sophie! Just be thankful she's alive and not maimed! Two mortars hit the hospital this morning! What was she doing there alone?"

Sophie's eyes grew larger in response. She called for one of her maids, and when she arrived, Sophie pulled Marie into another room—right off the sitting room.

"Two bombs fell on the hospital today?"

Marie wasn't in the mood to deal with Sophie's silliness. "Yes. Hit one of the wards."

"Is anyone hurt?"

Marie laughed, disgusted at the stupidity of the question. "Of course, people were. The hospital's filled to capacity. How did she get there?"

Sophie looked extremely uncomfortable. "She was friends with the older woman who lived a few houses down. The woman's dead, but I didn't want to tell her and upset her, so I told Anne she was sick and in the hospital."

Marie rolled her eyes. "Why wouldn't you just tell her the truth?" She pinched the bridge of her nose. It didn't surprise her that Sophie wasn't paying enough attention to her child. That made her even angrier.

Sophie crossed her arms defensively. "The woman killed herself, Marie. What was I supposed to say?"

"I don't know, but maybe keep a better eye on your daughter."

Sophie looked murderous. "Really? You're going to judge my parenting, are you? Annette's been sick with worry about you. She doesn't know where you are and thinks you're dying. What have you been doing, since it's now obvious that you're not at death's door?"

"It's none of Annette's business," Marie replied fiercely. "And it isn't yours either." She turned to storm out of the house, but Sophie grabbed her arm.

"Where have you been?" Marie tried to untangle her arm from Sophie's grasp. "Tell me or I'll tell Claude you're at the hospital."

For one brief moment, Marie realized that Sophie knew exactly what had been going on in the Babineaux home. "You little bitch," she breathed. She wanted to slap her. "All this time, you've known what Claude is and you've never said a word."

Sophie looked offended. "Of course, I said things, but what is anyone supposed to do? I knew you weren't sick. No one believes that story. I don't blame you for running out on the wedding—but disappearing completely? That's not fair."

Marie wanted very much to remind Sophie that her own daughter was lying in the other room, covered in burns, because her mother had lied to her and neglected her, but she bit her tongue. She looked at Sophie full in the face for a long, calculating moment. "You can tell Claude whatever you like."

Sophie shook her dark curls that had begun to fall out of the complicated arrangement on top of her head. "You weren't always at the hospital! Claude checked there."

Marie wanted to believe that Sophie knew this information out of concern and not because of her insatiable desire for gossip. She must have spoken to Annette. "I need to get back," Marie said quietly, pushing her way out of the room.

Sophie looked scandalized. "Does this have anything to do with Pierre Thibault? I heard he was back."

Marie stopped, amazed at how many people knew about Pierre when she hadn't.

"He wouldn't want you after a broken engagement," Sophie goaded, trying to get a reaction from Marie. A tiny cry came from the other room.

"Your daughter needs you. Don't tell anyone you saw me. Please. If Claude finds me, I'm dead." She doubted Sophie understood the gravity of the situation. She turned on her heel and ran out of the house, ignoring Sophie's protests.

Marie had given no thought to Claude when she'd rushed out with her little patient, but as she darted through the damaged city, she was suddenly very aware of how vulnerable she would be if she met him. Sophie knew now where Marie was. It was only a matter of time before word got out about where she was.

The fires were out when she returned to the hospital, and with most of the structural damage assessed, engineers and craftsmen were already working to repair the damage. Marie wondered vaguely if Claude and Annette's home was still untouched by the bombardment.

Only two mortars had hit the building, and most of it was still undamaged. Governor Drucour was standing just outside the entryway, having a heated discussion with a group of priests from the hospital and other officials. Marie paused behind a column at the entrance to listen. From what she could hear, Drucour wanted the hospital evacuated, the patients sent somewhere more secure. Unfortunately, no such place existed.

As Marie slowly stepped around the debating throng, she noticed the dark gleam of the head of Jacques-Xavier de Charlevoix. He hadn't noticed her, but if he lifted his head, he would easily spot her through the crowd. Heart pounding so loudly she was surprised people couldn't hear it, Marie darted back the way she had come.

Out of breath and face flushed with anxiety, she circled the complex and entered into a corridor through a side entrance. No one had followed her, so she must be safe for the time being. Sister Berenice was pacing up and down the length of the corridor, muttering violently to herself.

Upon laying eyes on Marie, the nun exploded. "Where have you been?" she roared.

Marie stopped short. She hadn't realized she would be missed. "There was a little girl here, Anne. She was burned in the bombing. I treated her and then found out that she was here alone, so I took her home." She fiddled nervously with the pockets on her smock. She had never seen Sister Berenice so agitated. It was an impressive sight.

The nun stopped and took several deep breaths. "We've been trying to make an account of everyone, and you were the only one missing. Next time, tell someone before you decide to run off."

Marie felt it was best not to argue and nodded meekly.

Sister Berenice pulled herself up to her full, not inconsiderable height. "Now, I must warn you that my nephew is here with the Governor while everyone tries to sort out how to deal with the situation." She threw a contemptuous look at the wall as if it were responsible for the present situation. "You need to be inconspicuous until he leaves, which, God willing, will be soon. I'm dealing with enough today. I'm not dealing with him too."

Marie didn't have a problem with that. She'd already dodged her former fiancé once and didn't want to have to do that again. Meeting up with Jacques wouldn't be much better than running into Claude.

"Do you know where I can find Sara?" Marie asked. "I need to talk to her."

The nun's eyes softened immediately. "Follow me," she said quietly.

She led Marie back out of the hospital into the courtyard. A bomb had landed there as well, but the damage was more superficial than in the building. Most of the garden had been blown away and the walls peppered with mud and missing a good number of stones, but the officials weren't coming here. Along the far wall, Marie could see three long bundles wrapped in white sheets. She stopped immediately. Sister Berenice looked back at her. She didn't say a word but just nodded.

Marie didn't move. She didn't want to go any closer. A lump was growing in her throat that she couldn't swallow. She didn't care which one was Sara. The thought of the feisty, young aspirant lying there, cold and lifeless, was almost more than she could bear.

"They're not going to stop." Sister Berenice's voice quivered as she stepped back toward Marie. "They'll even kill nuns. What is this?"

Marie put a reassuring hand on her arm. It was true. The hospital spire clearly marked where the hospital was. It wasn't an accident that they'd been bombed. The British didn't care who was killed; Louisbourg would be theirs.

Sister Berenice stood a moment longer in silence and then turned back to the building. "I am needed. Say your goodbyes. But remember that the living still need you." She walked away quickly, leaving Marie alone with the corpses.

***

Drucour and his minions left shortly after Marie was shown the remains of her friend. He had left frustrated that the hospital could not be housed at another location. That brought up an even more sobering issue. The decision to capitulate was one that Drucour alone could make. It was the 9th of July. So far, the siege had lasted only a month, and already he knew they could not drive off the British. Already they were running out of cannonballs and gunpowder. They had tried to plan for this, but the British were proving to be too much.

The situation in the hospital was not improving. Though it was spared any more damage, bombs were falling even more frequently all around the city. And since the hospital had been hit once, people no longer thought of it as a sanctuary but as a more dangerous target than people's homes. Everywhere she turned, Marie found panic along with illness and injury. No one felt safe within the walls. She tried her best to stay upbeat but felt her nerves rubbed raw. For every person she could help, there were two more who could not be helped.

The evening sun slanted through the windows, bathing everything in orange. Marie had been assisting two soldiers who had come in with bullet wounds, both to the stomach. One had expired almost as soon as he'd been laid down in front of her, but the other had bled to death as she'd tried vainly to staunch the flow of blood with her hands. After he was gone, Marie screamed at him to wake up, pounding on his chest. Father Laval had pulled her away, trying to stop the scene.

Close to tears, she went out into the courtyard and sat down on the outside stoop leading to the kitchen. She felt utterly hopeless. Her hands were still stained with the blood of the dead soldier, and bombs were falling without mercy. So many people had died in the last few hours that the courtyard was completely covered in rows of corpses bundled in white sheets. She laid her head on her knees, unsure whether she would ever have the strength to walk back into the hospital. How many more lives would end before Britain was finally victorious?

Just then, she felt a large, warm hand on her back as its owner settled his weight on the stoop beside her. It was Pierre. She leaned toward him and snuggled her head against his warm shoulder. The tears began and wouldn't stop. The dead soldiers, Sara, Nic, Anne—they all flashed before her eyes. Pierre lifted her onto his lap and stroked her back softly, murmuring reassurances into her ear as she shook in his arms.

For the first time that day, she allowed all her fear and despair to come to the surface. Pierre said nothing but gently rocked her until there were no tears left. Then she raised her head to look at him for the first time. He smiled sadly and pushed the damp hairs away from her face.

"I came as soon as I heard about the hospital, which was apparently hours after it happened." He held her tightly as if he could prevent another bomb from reaching her. "I've never been so scared as I was on the trip here."

Marie stroked his hair, covered in sweat and dirt from the battlefield. She could tell him what she felt. He wouldn't judge her. "I don't know if I can keep doing this."

The muscles around Pierre's eyes contracted with concern. "Are you hurt at all?"

She shook her head. "I feel like a coward for saying it, but I can't keep watching all these people die. There's nothing I can do, nowhere for any of them to go to be safe. And the British ... they knew they were bombing the hospital. They knew it!" She smashed her fist into her thigh in frustration.

Pierre nodded solemnly. "Yes, there's the spire—an easy target—but there are also the deserters. Soldiers going over to the British side, exchanging information for a chance at life."

Marie's anger, which was barely in check, boiled to the surface. Pierre was unjustly branded as a deserter, but here he sat after weeks of defending the fortress. "So much for loyalty," she spat on the ground. "Why don't we just give up now?"

"I know, beautiful," Pierre said, moving her gently out of his lap and onto the stoop beside him. "Everyone feels like it's hopeless. Not just you. And that is because it *is* hopeless."

Another explosion ripped through the air. "Sara died today," Marie said quietly.

Pierre wrapped his arm around her shoulders. "The young nun you were working with? I'm sorry."

They sat in silence, watching the clouds and smoke move over the city. The bombardment slowed down as night encroached, but it wouldn't stop completely.

"I saw Sophie today," Marie said miserably. "She now knows I'm here."

His body stiffened beside her. "Is she here?"

"No, her daughter was here alone when the mortars hit, and she was burned."

"Of course, she was," Pierre muttered furiously.

"I didn't realize that the girl was Sophie's daughter. I just saw a child hurt and alone and took her home. I didn't realize it was Sophie's house until it was too late." There was a note of pleading in her voice. She needed him to understand that it was an accident. She hadn't meant to compromise them like this.

He rubbed the back of his neck and thought for a moment. "Do you trust Sophie?"

"Of course not," Marie said indignantly. "She's the same as ever, harassing me for being selfish and not thinking of Annette."

Pierre snorted. "Well, you can't stay here anymore then—not if there's a chance that Claude or Jacques could show up looking for you. Everyone here has enough to do without keeping you hidden."

"And what am I supposed to tell them? I've changed my mind? They're depending on me now!"

Pierre gave her a crooked smile. "Tell them your husband thinks it's too dangerous, and you have to do what your husband says."

"Like hell I do!" She pulled away from him, nettled.

He laughed and grabbed her hand. "I know that. I wouldn't dream of trying to force you. But they don't know that."

"And where would I go? sit in a tavern until a bomb drops on me?"

A pained look crossed Pierre's handsome features. "No amount of effort is going to save us now. The walls are starting to fall apart. The British can't even shoot the cannons in some locations for fear that the wall will give way. Madame Drucour starts every morning by firing a cannon at the enemy, but now it's getting too dangerous for her to climb the walls because they're so fragile."

Marie raised her eyebrows. "Please tell me you're joking."

"I wish I was," he replied heavily. "Would you leave if I asked you to?"

She studied him carefully. "By myself?"

"No, I would come with you," he assured her. "I'm not going to abandon you or the baby."

"You would desert?" She never thought he'd actually do that.

"Not desert—change assignments," he said slowly.

Marie looked dubious. "What are you talking about?"

Pierre stretched his legs. "Is Father Weber still alive?"

"Barely. Both his legs were broken today. He's in terrible shape."

"Is he conscious?"

"Not last I heard."

Pierre stood up and pulled her up with him. "Well, I think it's time we had a visit with him while he's still in the land of the living."

***

Thoroughly confused, Marie followed Pierre back into the stifling hospital. After the quiet of the courtyard, the noises coming from the injured seemed deafening. Marie led the way to the private room where Father Weber was convalescing. Sister Miriam passed them in the hallway and gave them a questioning look, but Marie just shook her head and moved on.

Despite the warmth of the night, a fire was crackling in the hearth, bathing the small room in amber light. Father Weber was no longer unconscious, though he looked terrible, his legs elevated, propped up on several pillows. He glared at Pierre when he saw him.

"Can't a man die in peace?" he said in his thick accent, now glowering at the pair of them.

"You're not dying," Marie replied reasonably. "You might not walk again, but you'll live to see the British conquer us."

Father Weber scowled from his cocoon of blankets, his white hair sticking up from his head as usual but looking somewhat limp. A plain wooden cross was suspended above the bed.

Pierre bent and whispered in Marie's ear. "Can you give us a moment?"

She didn't really want to, but Father Weber motioned for her to get out of the room. She stepped out into the corridor but stayed right at the door, so she could go back inside if anyone found her and demanded that she continue treating the injured.

Pierre approached the cot where the little priest was lying and stared down at him. Beads of sweat were glistening on his pale brow as the man fidgeted with his blankets.

"So you finally decided to accept my offer to take those documents," he said weakly. "I was starting to worry you'd never come."

Pierre smiled thinly. "Marie is pregnant."

"So I've heard. Funny how that puts things into perspective."

"I don't want a lecture," Pierre sighed heavily.

Father Weber gasped as he shifted his weight. He looked at Pierre, his pale eyes glossy with pain. "I knew Claude, you know. Not well, but I knew him."

Pierre looked startled and glanced behind him at the door.

"Don't worry about running, young man." The old priest laughed and then moaned as the vibrations shook his body. "By the way, I never told Claude where to find Marie when she lived in his home. It was the scullery maid, listening at the locks for bits of information. She was ill two months ago when you removed Marie from the house and missed that vital conversation. I'm afraid Claude treated her to the same attention he paid his niece when he found out the maid couldn't tell him where Marie had gone."

Pierre sat down in the chair opposite the cot.

"I met Marie after you'd been sent to Montreal. She was assisting at this hospital. I was actually a patient here. I'd slipped on ice and fractured my knee cap. There isn't much to do when one's knee no longer works, other than sit and wait for it to heal. Much like now."

Pierre grimaced as he thought of the injury.

Father Weber smiled. "Yes, it was very unpleasant. However, your dear friend spent time every day talking to me. She would sit and draw for me, and I quite enjoyed watching her do that. She has a remarkable talent for it. I'm afraid I'm not a very interesting companion, but she made an effort to see me every day no matter how busy she was."

Pierre nodded. "She's like that. She's spent a lot of time feeling lonely, so I think she wants to make sure no one else feels that way."

The little priest nodded. "She definitely made the time pass more easily. She told me about Claude too. What he did to her. Once I recovered, I met with Nic, trying to figure out how to get her out of the situation, but Claude was always a step ahead." He sighed heavily under the weight of the burdens of the last few years. "I tried to befriend Claude, or at least communicate with him, to see if there was some way he could be persuaded to stop, but it didn't work. He's not right in the head. Something is missing there. I've never met someone with the devil inside him like that."

Pierre pursed his lips and looked away.

"Claude told me about you. Or some version of you. Of the ruckus you caused as a young man. Marie never mentioned you, as far as I know, to anyone. I did try to get a second opinion on the matter, but unfortunately, I chose my colleague Father Allard. He merely validated everything Claude said about you."

Pierre laughed darkly. "I'm afraid I was quite the little demon when I was in school. Father Allard compared me more than once to the spawn of Satan. I can't say I blame him after some of the things I did, although he deserved a great deal of it."

"Father Allard was always a little high strung," Father Weber commented, the corners of his mouth twitching. "I'm afraid that I thought that by denying your marriage to Mademoiselle Lévesque, I was protecting her from a lifetime of continued hardship. While I could not protect her from her uncle's wrath, I could protect her from you." For the first time, the priest looked remorseful.

Pierre wasn't sure what to say, although many things were popping into his head.

"Please forgive me," the small priest whispered.

Pierre bowed his head. "I can't. At least not tonight." He stared into the flickering flames.

Father Weber's eyes followed the hulking form as Pierre stood and paced around the room. "Will you give me what I came here for tonight?" Pierre asked bluntly.

The priest nodded. "Yes. You will need to leave immediately."

Pierre stopped, his back to the priest, staring out the window. "An acquaintance of Marie's saw her today, and she can't be counted on for discretion. Marie will have to leave the hospital tonight."

"I can make excuses for her. But this is a dangerous trip."

Pierre shrugged. "Is it any more dangerous than staying here with the bombs falling?"

"Possibly not, but the British will be patrolling the area."

Again, Pierre seemed unconcerned. "In '45, I left with three other men and made it to Quebec. At that point, the British were systematically trying to conquer the entire island. That's not happening this time. Most of the British are staying put around the fortress."

"Most of them but not all of them," said Father Weber, "and if you get captured ..."

"If I'm captured, I'll do everything I can to make sure that Marie gets to safety," he said with finality. "Believe it or not, I do love her ... very much."

The Prussian nodded. "Montcalm may give you an honourable discharge from the army in appreciation for carrying these documents to their destination."

Pierre looked more closely at Father Weber. He had been so focused on escape that he hadn't thought of the consequences for his military life—in this case, good ones.

"At the very least, you'll finally be promoted. Your days as a cadet will be over."

Pierre turned his face toward the door so as not to betray his feelings. The promise of freedom from the army without deserting was too tantalizing. He pushed the door open. Marie was standing so close that the door almost knocked her over.

"Were you eavesdropping?"

"Trying to, but the door was too thick," she said unapologetically as she scurried back into the room. "What's going on?"

Pierre glanced at the bed, but Father Weber was feigning sleep. He sighed. "The priest has information that needs to get to Montcalm in Quebec."

Marie's eyebrows shot up. She wasn't expecting this. "What?" she asked blankly.

"Letters have been gathered by people here in Louisbourg about the British invasion plans for the continent. Obviously, he can't go to Quebec with two broken legs." Pierre rubbed the back of his neck.

Marie had to agree with him there. Even before Father Weber had broken his legs, he would never have been called athletic, and he wasn't a young man either. From what Pierre said about the journey, it would be a difficult one.

"He wants me to go. Us, if you're willing. We can escape the bombardment, Claude, Jacques, all of this." He waved his arms around the room. "It would give us a reason to leave that wasn't desertion."

His eyes were intense. He was telling her, giving her the option. He wouldn't force her, but it was clear he had thought it through. While his voice was calm, he stood on edge, his shoulders tight with tension.

Marie motioned him over to the corner, as private a place as they could get. The priest was still pretending to sleep. "How dangerous is it?"

Pierre shrugged. "I don't know. It can't be worse than staying here." As if to reinforce that point, cannons rumbled in the distance. "The British aren't patrolling the entire island the way they were last time, and I escaped last time." He hated himself for putting Marie in this position. If anything happened to her or the child, he would never forgive himself. "In return, Father Weber will marry us."

Marie tried to keep the excitement out of her voice. "He would marry us tonight?"

"Yes."

"But how do we get out of the fortress? The entire area is surrounded, isn't it?"

"I think you'll find there's a way out if the proper resources are arranged," Father Weber called from the bed. He had obviously been listening to every word.

"People are starving because we're running out of food. There's no more medicine. Wouldn't it be better to use those resources to provide nutrition?" Marie tried to keep the tone of accusation out of her voice.

Father Weber seemed deeply amused by her question. For the first time since they'd entered the room, Pierre thought he looked genuinely entertained.

"Believe it or not, Marie," the priest said, "there are issues more important than food at the moment." Marie looked dubious. "It will be far easier for the two of you to sneak out in the dead of night than for a ship full of supplies to come in past the British defences."

Marie felt Pierre slip his hand around hers. She squeezed it in acknowledgement. "How did you get this kind of information?" The idea of the tiny priest as an agent seemed rather ridiculous.

Father Weber's white hair quivered as the priest replied with indignation, "I have my sources."

Marie gave Pierre a searching look.

"I wasn't crazy about the idea at first," Pierre said quietly in her ear. "But now that you're pregnant and Sophie knows you're here …"

Marie felt a slight panic rising in her chest. "But how do we get out? How do we get there? Quebec is over a thousand miles away."

Pierre wrapped his arms around Marie and pulled her close. "It's an awful risk, love, I know." He looked very serious.

Marie nodded. He wouldn't force her to go, but the possibility of a new life was worth the risk to him. Was it worth it to her? This was madness pure and simple, but it was so tempting to escape Louisbourg and everything that had happened here, to get away from Claude, to leave the army life behind legitimately, and to avoid deportation to France. "I'll go pack my things," Marie said quietly and walked out of the room.

Father Weber looked absolutely delighted, a feeling that Pierre found irritating at the present moment. The priest pointed to his cassock hanging from the back of the door. "In the left pocket, you'll find the documents."

Pierre did as instructed and fished around in the black depths of fabric until he found a grubby leather packet, tied neatly with string. Pierre lifted the bundle, turning it over and over in his hands. "You'll make our excuses for us?" he asked nervously. He couldn't bear to live through a second accusation of desertion.

The priest nodded. "Trust me, no one will call you a traitor when you deliver this."

Pierre laughed warily. "If there's one thing you can count on, it's that I don't trust you."

"What other choice do you have? I am a priest." He made this pronouncement as if it settled the matter.

Pierre stared back, his blue eyes accusing. "I've known many a crooked priest. I even knew one with a few children. You never betrayed Marie's whereabouts, but with all the power of the Catholic church and the French government," he said sarcastically, holding up the packet, "you never rescued her from the situation."

"I did the best I could with the knowledge I had," the priest said, showing no trace of embarrassment.

Pierre turned back to the fire and watched the flames, his thoughts far away.

"There is nothing for you here except death, destruction, and deportation."

The soldier nodded. He knew the battle was lost. It was only a matter of time before the fortress capitulated. Why Governor Drucour continued to hold out was beyond him.

"But am I really saving Marie from anything? I'm taking her away from the bombardment, Claude, and Jacques and throwing her into the wilderness with the Redcoats." Pierre leaned back, his jaw working furiously.

"She's already made up her mind. A woman like that can't be forced to stay home while you fight all the battles."

This wasn't the solution Pierre wanted, but the fantasy of a life free from the restrictions of Île-Royale was too tempting to resist. The priest knew it too.

Marie opened the door quietly, her small bag of belongings hanging limply at her side. She was determined. Pierre stepped over to her and kissed her gently. There was no going back now.

PART SIX: FLIGHT

Chapter 15

ON THE NIGHT OF JULY 9TH, MARIE AND PIERRE LEFT the hospital as man and wife, feeling more relieved than joyful. Marie felt like a traitor for leaving the hospital when so much help was needed, but no one seemed to blame her, or Pierre for that matter, when she told them what the two of them had decided.

The air outside was thick with gunpowder and the smoke from nearby fires, and cannons roared in the distance. The bombardment was never-ending. Stone buildings stood with huge open gashes. Roofs had been blown away and the remaining structures streaked black from the resulting flames.

Though it was well past dark, the streets were full of people. Soldiers were moving supplies slowly through the dark streets, their progress impeded by the rubble that choked the roads. People walked among the ruins of their homes and businesses, trying to salvage what they could from the wreckage. There was a feeling of detachment. No one spoke to anyone else. Everyone moved as if covered in their own cocoon of protection. Pierre held Marie tight, although no one stopped to notice them. The feeling of desperation was palpable as they dashed through the streets.

"Where are we going?"

"My father's house."

"Oh ... why ... ," Marie started to ask, but just then a mortar exploded one street over, causing them both to duck as stone and mortar billowed high into the air. There was no point in trying to carry on a conversation.

The Thibault residence slowly materialized out of the inky darkness. The door was unlocked, and Pierre walked in without a second thought. The place was as silent as a crypt. Marie dug her fingers into Pierre's arm harder than she meant to. The silence of the place frightened her, especially after so many weeks of noise and chaos at the hospital.

"Hello?" Pierre called. No answer. He groped along one of the hallways, searching blindly for some source of light. Before long, he ran into a table, knocking over the candlestick that was standing on it. Groping in the darkness he found the flint box and struck a spark. A small circle of amber light cast long shadows along the wall. "Hello?" Pierre called out again. There was still no answer. He turned to find Marie in the dim light.

"Have they all left?" Marie asked incredulously. It seemed remarkable that the house could be empty of all life. It was one of the few buildings in Louisbourg that had sustained no damage. It was obviously in an advantageous location.

Pierre nodded absently. "I thought they might. There's no one here to look after, no point keeping up appearances with the house. Might as well go where they want to."

Marie found the emptiness frightening. Silence fell between them.

"Pierre?" Marie said after a few moments, but he wasn't listening to her. Absorbed in his own thoughts, he stared blankly around the small circle the candle illuminated.

"Pierre ... are you all right?"

Pierre shook his head. "I'm not sure about all of this," he sighed.

"All of what?"

"Leaving," he said heavily.

"We don't have to go to Quebec," Marie said quietly. "Whatever deal you made with Father Weber, surely you can get out of it. We can stay here and wait for Drucour to capitulate."

"But Quebec was the price of our marriage, Marie. Besides, do you really want to stay here? Even if we survived and were deported to France, I'd still be a cadet. Cadet here, cadet there. It doesn't make any difference. And being married to a cadet is no life for you."

Marie didn't say anything. She did want to get off this miserable island and all that had happened here—though she knew she'd be leaving without saying goodbye to the people she loved.

Pierre turned to face his wife. "There was a time when I thought I knew the answers to everything, but not anymore. If we stay, there's death and the chance that Claude will find you; if we go, we could still be killed or worse."

Marie walked over to Pierre and gave him a tender embrace. They stood there for a few minutes, feeling the weight of their decision resting heavily on them. "We may never know what the right answer is," Pierre said, "but the choice has been made. It's too late to go back."

"When did Father Weber first ask you to do this?" Marie leaned her forehead against his chest. She could feel him stiffen under her touch.

"When I first asked him if he would marry us. Apparently, he had hoped to get the documents off the island before the British arrived. He wasn't successful and was getting anxious. He was hoping I would be desperate enough to make the trip."

Marie nodded but didn't say anything. It didn't make her feel much better that others had turned down this trip for being too dangerous.

"I'd be less concerned if there wasn't the child," Pierre said, drawing Marie in closer. "I have no doubt of your ability to run around the wilderness dodging Redcoats ... but with the child ..."

Marie sighed. She hadn't told him about the morning sickness yet. It was probably best to let him discover that on his own. "I'll be all right," she said finally.

"I won't be able to live with myself if anything happens to you or the baby."

Marie snorted. "You think you're the only one who'll be suffering if I run into problems?"

Pierre let Marie go and sighed, deflated. "No, of course not."

Marie changed the subject. "When do we leave?"

"Tomorrow at dusk."

"Why not tonight? I thought we needed to leave as soon as possible."

Looking embarrassed in the dim light, Pierre rubbed his nose. "I wanted one more night with you before ..." His voice trailed off.

Marie wrapped her arms around him. She could feel the bandages she'd placed on the wound in his right side. "It won't be the last time," she promised. He kissed the top of her head.

Pierre then stood back from Marie and said, "I need to find my father's compass and map before we do anything else."

"You think we'll be able to find anything in there?!"

"Well, I at least have to make an effort. I know the road to Port Dauphin, where we should be able to find a boat to take us off the island. But we have to stay off the main road. I can't promise I know my way through the woods." Pierre took the candle and pushed open the study door. It was just as bad as Marie remembered it—worse if possible.

Pierre cleared a spot on a small table and put the candle down on it. Then he walked over to his father's desk and slowly began to sift through the teetering piles of paper there.

Marie busied herself inspecting one of the bookcases. "How did your father ever get anything accomplished?" she asked.

Pierre shrugged, unconcerned. "The entire house would have looked like this if not for Madame Cloutier. He forbade her from ever entering this space. I think she spent at least an hour a day attacking his bedroom."

Most of the papers in the bookcase were bundled together with string, and Marie took each bundle out, one by one, to figure out whether it might contain a map. She was also keeping an eye out for a compass, which could have fallen in behind the papers. As she was starting in on the second shelf, something caught her eye.

"Pierre?" she called, lifting a particularly heavy bundle off the shelf.

"Hmm?" He was entirely immersed in ruffling through the papers on the desk.

"You should look at this. It's addressed to you."

Pierre looked up, puzzled, and took the bundle from her. Then he sat down behind the desk in his father's chair and started opening the package. As Marie gazed at him for a moment, she was struck by the remarkable resemblance between him and Augustus. She turned back to the bookshelf and resumed her search.

Suddenly, Pierre yelped in disbelief.

"What on earth is the matter?" she asked, rather annoyed. He'd scared her half to death.

Pierre didn't seem to hear her; his attention being completely focused on the stack of papers in front of him. Marie walked around the desk and peered over his shoulder.

Pierre looked up, startled, as if he'd forgotten she was there. "It's from my father."

Marie very much wanted to say something smart, but the look on his face made her think better of it. "What does it say?"

Pierre didn't say anything for a while. He looked as if he'd seen a ghost. He just continued to stare at the papers in his hands. Marie was beginning to worry he was having some sort of fit.

"Pierre," she tentatively put a hand on his shoulder.

"He sold all his ships," he said, handing her the first few pages. "The ones that went from France to the West Indies and from the colonies to France. Sold them to someone in France. He left me all the money." Pierre bit his lip, unsure of how to proceed.

It took a moment for his words to sink into Marie's consciousness. "The ships are gone? But how is he going to make a living?" Years ago, in France, Augustus had lived off his savings, but that wasn't something he could do for the rest of his life.

"He doesn't have to," Pierre said quietly. "He's dead." Pierre purposely avoided her eye and gazed over at the window, which, of course, revealed nothing but darkness.

"Why didn't you tell me?" Marie put the papers she was sorting on top of a pile she'd created, moving closer to him.

Pierre shrugged his broad shoulders. "I've been too angry with him to care." Suddenly, he was trembling, the papers clutched in his hand shaking as he fought to control his emotions. Marie wrapped her arms around him, not sure how she felt.

"I'm sorry, Pierre," she whispered. His knuckles were white, clenched into fists on top of the desk. She could feel his muscles contracting under her touch.

Pierre sniffed and took a deep, shuddering breath. "I never thought ... I ... ," he mumbled incoherently. Marie felt her heart break for him. Pierre had spent most of his life trying to gain his father's approval—working so hard to be ready to take over the shipping business, going all the way to Quebec and becoming successful there without ever gaining any affirmation from Augustus. Pierre had finally given up and distanced himself from the man, becoming more and more angry and bitter. Marie couldn't blame Pierre for his stunned reaction.

"He did care," Marie murmured softly into her husband's blond hair.

Neither of them said anything for a long time. Pierre kept staring at the window, consumed by his own thoughts. Marie was at a complete loss for what to say, so she simply held him until he was ready to talk.

"He had a strong sense that he wasn't going to survive the siege," Pierre whispered at last. "Most of the militia aren't going to live through this. I don't know if it's age or lack of expertise, but they are being mowed down like grain. Every time a cannon goes off, the militia goes too."

"I'm sorry," said Marie, realizing that any response in these circumstances would be inadequate.

"I saw him right before he died. They came and got me, took me to where the dying were kept." He rubbed the stubble on his chin. "A musket ball to the stomach. It took a long time, but I didn't get there until the end."

"Did he say anything?" she asked gently, continuing to stroke his hair.

"Sorry." His blue eyes were bright. "That was it. That one word." He paused as if wrestling with a great internal burden. "I didn't forgive him. Not then."

"You didn't do anything wrong," Marie said gently. "You can't always forgive immediately."

He leaned his muscular frame against her body. He looked up at her, smiling sadly as he stroked her face. "You're all I have left. You and our child." He touched her stomach underneath her many skirts. "All that will remain after I'm gone. I don't ... I can't lose you too."

Marie stood beside him and wrapped her arms around his neck. "I love you," she whispered into his ear.

"I know." He leaned his head against her stomach. "What about the baby?"

"We belong with you. I don't know which choice is better, but I'm not leaving you."

He wrapped his arms around her and pulled himself to his feet.

"Are we staying here tonight?" she asked.

He shook his head. "No, we'll get some things and then leave. I have far too much guilt to stay here."

***

The inn was small but clean, or at least cleaner than Marie was used to in such establishments. Pierre knew the couple that ran it. He'd served with their son on the mainland. The inn was quite full and the tavern more so, but when Pierre mentioned that it was his wedding night, the owners practically danced off to find them a space.

"We already had our wedding night," Marie said crossly. "They're probably going to give us their bed now."

Pierre grinned. "We have a long trip ahead of us. It'll be a long time before we get to sleep in a bed again."

Marie rolled her eyes. "Is sex all you think about?"

He winked.

It turned out that the owners didn't forfeit their bed, though they did apologize profusely for the state of the room given. Marie didn't see a problem with it. It was clean, and the mattress seemed free of fleas and other pests. The only possible issue was that there was a second door leading to the servant's rooms downstairs, but she insisted that it be kept locked.

The plan was to leave the following evening at dusk—under cover of darkness—and the reassembling British army would make it easier to slip through the enemy lines. Both Pierre and Father Weber felt that this was the best time for their departure. Knowing nothing of war tactics, Marie simply agreed to follow the instructions. The very few belongings that they had sat packed in a rucksack by the door. Their important papers, from Father Weber along with the money Augustus had left Pierre—in paper and gold—were wrapped and hidden in Pierre's coat.

Pierre stripped down to his shirt and crawled onto the bed, flopping onto his stomach.

He motioned for Marie to join him. Mindful of his injured side, she slipped in beside him, curling into his body's heat. He wrapped his long arms around her, drawing her closer.

"I've missed you," she murmured into his chest.

"That's why I wanted to leave tomorrow." He smoothed the hair away from her face and shoulders. "I feel like we'll never have enough time."

Marie traced the arch of his eyebrows with her fingertips.

"If we're separated," he began, but Marie cut him off.

"Please don't talk like that," she begged.

He rolled over and sat up. "But it's a possibility. If we're separated, I want you to take the money from my father and get to Quebec. It will be enough for you and the child. You'll be taken care of. Your Uncle Joseph, Renault, and my Uncle Tomas can all help you."

Marie pulled herself onto his lap and buried her face in the folds of his shirt. She suddenly felt very cold.

"I promise," Pierre continued, "that if I'm alive, I will find you."

Marie fidgeted with the end of the quilt. "Doesn't it feel as if God doesn't want us to be together?"

Pierre bent his head and kissed her long and slow. Finally releasing her, he held her at arm's length, watching her. "I don't really care, to be honest. But no, I think God keeps putting us back in each other's paths for a reason."

***

The sun was high in the sky when they awoke the next morning. As soon as Marie got out of bed, she spent over an hour retching. Pierre, who had never seen morning sickness before, was beside himself with worry.

"Are you sure this is normal?" he asked her over and over again, hovering close by. "Are you sure you don't need a physician? Maybe you should stay here if this is how your body is handling this."

"Let me stay here. That's a great idea. Why don't I stay at the hospital and wait for Claude to break down the door. I'd rather deal with the British than that sadist."

Pierre scowled but continued to hover annoyingly as Marie continued to be sick.

She found his concern somewhat endearing but mostly infuriating, and by the time she was feeling better, she wanted very badly to hit him.

"Pierre, I promise this is normal," she repeated for the hundredth time, rinsing her mouth with water.

"Are you sure? I've never seen this before."

"How many pregnant women have you been around?" she asked, exasperated.

He shrugged, proving her right, but that didn't stop him from grunting in disapproval. "I'm worried about you enough as it is. Childbirth isn't exactly safe."

Marie stretched out in bed, her stomach slowly settling. Pierre collapsed beside her, gently tracing circles on her belly. There would be nothing to see for weeks, but the baby was already wreaking havoc with Marie's constitution. Pierre's large hand on her stomach helped calm her.

"Are you terribly upset about the baby?" Marie asked after a time.

Pierre smiled. "No. I'm thrilled." He kissed her lightly. "I gave up a long time ago of any thought of being a father. When I joined the army, all thoughts of a regular life disappeared. I gave up." He stared at his wife with such tenderness that she felt her breath catch in her throat. "But I'm terrified of something happening to you or the child. There's nothing I can do to protect you or him, and it scares me."

Marie kissed him, a little breathless when he let her go. "What makes you think it's a boy?"

He chuckled. "You think I know anything about this?"

Marie pulled herself closer to him and laid her head on his chest. "I'll be all right." She could see his jaw flex and knew he didn't believe her.

He sighed. "I know you aren't happy about this but ..."

Marie interrupted him. "I'm feeling better about it now. The shock's over, even if I'm still petrified about the future."

"You're not the only one," Pierre conceded. "Sometimes I think getting off the island will be the easy part."

After a moment, Marie remembered the question she hadn't had the chance to ask the night before. "Do you know how Father Weber became a spy?"

Pierre laughed, brushing her hair away from his nose. "He's not a spy."

Marie looked confused.

"He gets other people to spy for him. Specifically, a man named John Clarke."

Marie rolled to face him. "Is he related to Sara?"

"Who's Sara?" he asked.

"She's the English girl I worked with at the hospital," she reminded him. "She was there the night you came in for stitches. She ..." Marie couldn't finish the sentence.

"She died, didn't she. I remember now." Pierre squeezed Marie's arm to comfort her and thought for a moment. "He must be a relative. There aren't many Clarkes in this part of the world. Is she from Boston?"

Marie nodded.

"He must be her father." Pierre paused for a moment and scratched his chest. "Anyway, this John Clarke was originally from Boston and should have gone back when Louisbourg was given back to us. But his wife wouldn't leave Louisbourg, so they stayed. John really missed Boston, so to help ease his homesickness, his brother would come to visit. The brother took notes about how the French had changed the fortress and what hadn't been repaired since '49, among other things."

"John Clarke didn't take him to see all this, did he?" Marie felt shocked and slightly betrayed. Sara had been so adamant about trying to disprove all of the preconceptions people had about her. Had Sara's family helped the British after all?

"I don't think Clarke thought anything of it. At least not right away. But eventually, his brother expected John to continue sending updates to Boston. About a year ago, John went and confessed what had happened to Father Weber. I think he felt that as a fellow foreigner, Father Weber might be more sympathetic to him. John was terrified of being banished from the fortress or worse."

Marie snorted in disbelief. The officials wouldn't have had enough time to try him, and if the public discovered he was a British agent, they would have killed him before any legal procedures could have started. "Being banished would have been the least of his problems."

"Exactly." Pierre laughed. "Well, Father Weber isn't one to miss an opportunity, so he basically blackmailed Clarke into becoming a spy for the French. Threatened to turn him over to the populace."

Marie looked shocked. "He didn't?"

Pierre laughed darkly. "He did. Apparently, Clarke jumped in with both feet. He wrote all sorts of letters to his brother, claiming to have knowledge of the inner workings of the garrison here. He even travelled to Boston and Halifax, meeting some of the handlers and agents for the British. He sold them outdated information, and eventually, after many nights over ale, the British started reciprocating. The British believe they have moles within the government and civil service of Quebec. Clarke passed that information on to Father Weber."

Marie nodded, impressed. "So there are names in here?" She reached for the little bundle and ran it through her fingers.

"Names and reasons why the person has been named. Among other things."

"Are they correct?"

Pierre shrugged. "That's the mystery. Montcalm needs to know there are possible moles within the government and civil service. Apparently, James Murray, the British General, has deep pockets and is paying people in Quebec. But there's a chance that the British never trusted Clarke and just fed him false information to distract us. But it's too much of a risk not to at least look into it."

Marie held the package up for Pierre to see. "Did you read what's in here?"

Pierre nodded and wrapped his large hands around the bundle. "Yes, but you're not going to. In case we're captured." He answered her quizzical look. "If the British think you're helpless and ignorant, there's a better chance that they'll let you go."

"I am not helpless or ignorant," Marie said crossly.

"I know." Pierre grinned and kissed the tip of her nose. "But they don't need to know that."

With that happy thought, Marie placed the bundle back on the table beside their bed, trying not to think about the possibility of capture. She came closer to Pierre's warm body. "Father Weber has classified information. Sara's father is a spy. Is there anything I should know about you?"

"I'm madly in love with a beautiful woman," he laughed.

"I meant something I didn't already know."

***

The sun was low in the sky in the late afternoon of July 10, 1758 as Marie and Pierre began to pack their few belongings for the coming journey. Other than the clothes on their backs and the papers, there wasn't much else. Having escaped from Quebec as a child with nothing, Marie had grown up feeling very little attachment to physical things. It didn't bother her that she would be starting over with nothing from her previous life.

The bombardment that day had been relatively light, but the British were certainly making up for it now. Bombs were falling like rain and the windows in the inn were shaking in their frames, but thankfully, no cannonballs fell on or near the structure.

Pierre filled a second rucksack with the little food that was available. It was decided that Pierre wouldn't carry any weapons on his person other than a pistol and dagger in his belt, in case they ran into British soldiers. Being escapees from Louisbourg would be a sticky enough situation, but if it became obvious that one of them was a French soldier who was away without leave, their case would be even more difficult. He had traded in his uniform for regular clothes the night before, but that wasn't a complete help, since every able man was fighting the British in uniform or not.

Marie was pinning her hair up as Pierre stepped out to the tavern below to see if there was more food and ale to be had. Finishing, she crossed the room and looked out the window. The fortress was bleak and crumbling in its present condition, far different from its prior majestic appearance, and yet it was still home. She felt a pang of sadness that she and the fortress would both be gone soon.

There was a light rap at the door and Marie shook her head as she crossed the room. After Pierre's concern for her, his greatest worry was going without food. And though food was, of course, in short supply throughout all of Île-Royale, Pierre was well aware of what a few *livres* could accomplish. Marie laughed, imagining how much must be crammed into his arms.

"You're a glutton, you know that," she yelled at him.

As soon as she unlatched the door, it slammed open, throwing her against the wall. She tried to scramble to her feet but felt herself pushed against the wall by the compact form of Claude-Jean des Babineaux. She tried to scream, but he pressed his muscular forearm into her windpipe, blocking her air supply. She wrapped her arms around her stomach, instinctively trying to protect the life inside.

"Where the hell have you been?" Claude spit into her eyes. She gasped for breath and tried to kick his shins.

"Think you can just run away, huh? You little bitch!" His fist smashed into the side of her head, causing stars to burst before her eyes. She was getting dizzy and desperately gulped for air. She tried to scream, but only a groan escaped her.

"Where have you been?" he screamed again. "Answer me!" He jammed her body against the wall causing a spasm of pain to shoot up her spine.

She gasped, clawing at his arm. "P-P-Pierre."

Claude laughed. "You always think you can run away …"

"Let her go!"

Claude's grip on Marie slackened a fraction of an inch. He glanced behind him. Pierre stood at the end of the short hallway, his pistol trained on Claude. Claude grinned, a horrible manic look, and his dark eyes shone with a kind of irrational pleasure. For the first time, Pierre fully understood how unstable the man really was.

Pierre took a slow step forward. "Let her go, Claude." He locked eyes with Marie, who continued to claw at the arm at her throat. They were so close to freedom, but Claude truly wasn't ever going to stop. "Claude!" Pierre shouted.

"Ah! The *habitant* returns." Claude's lips curled away from his teeth, making him look like a cornered dog. "You're supposed to be dead."

Pierre froze. Suddenly, he couldn't breathe. "What are you talking about?"

Claude seemed to forget all about Marie and let go of her. Marie crumpled to the floor, coughing and grasping for breath. Pierre wanted to run to her but stayed focused on the man in front of him.

"Deserters are shot," Claude said calmly, completely unconcerned about the pistol aimed at him. "General Picard promised me I'd never have to deal with you again."

Pierre's brain jammed. "It was you." He saw Marie struggling to her knees, still trying to regain her breath.

Claude moved forward. "For the amount of money I paid, you'd think they would have followed through."

"Leave her alone." Pierre could feel the butt of the pistol slick in his hand. He tried to stay calm, but panic that he wouldn't be able to get Marie to Quebec, away from the clutches of this madman, was beginning to overwhelm him.

Claude laughed. "And what are you going to do to stop me? You're a farmer, a coward, just like your father. He was never brave enough to face me …"

The crack of the pistol reverberated through the small space.

***

Claude's body pinned Marie against the door. Pierre crouched down beside her and pulled her to her feet.

"Are you all right?" He held her head between his hands, examining her, his fingers tracing the impact zone on the side of her head. Without waiting for an answer, he turned and looked at the body, blood blossoming from its chest.

Claude's dark eyes, glassy with the absence of life, glared up at him. Pierre stared down at the man. The last eight years, everything Marie had been forced to endure, the life that had been stolen from him, it was all the result of the body in front of him. He smashed his foot against the head, hearing bone crunch under his boot.

Shouts and footsteps started thundering down below. While the bombardment was loud, it couldn't cover the roar of gunfire in such a small space.

"Come on!" Pierre kicked the corpse into the hallway, grabbed Marie's hand, and pulled her back into the room. He threw the deadbolt across the door, grabbed the rucksack, and fled down the second staircase with Marie in tow.

Gasping and coughing, Marie did what she could to keep up with him. Her throat burned. She felt dizzy. She knew she was slowing him down.

They ran through the kitchen and out onto the street. Ferdinand was waiting outside the door. He took one look at both of them, then heard the shouts behind them. In an instant, he understood enough of the situation.

"Go! I'll send them another way," his deep voice urged.

There wasn't time to thank him. Pierre wrapped his arm across Marie's back and under her armpits, trying his best to move her along. Her skirts caught around her knees, slowing her progress more. Shouts came behind them as they ducked into an alley, coming out on the next street. Pierre led Marie through a maze of rubble-strewn alleys and passageways until, finally, he deemed it safe to stop.

Marie leaned her arms against the wall, still trying to catch her breath. Pierre stood in front of her absolutely beside himself with the events that had just transpired.

He was oblivious to her as he paced back and forth, trying to calm down. Finally catching her breath, Marie turned to face him. He couldn't meet her eyes. She could feel herself shaking. It felt as if ice had settled into her bones. She looked down at her bodice to see it covered in blood spatter. She tried to wipe it away with trembling fingers.

"Marie?" Pierre rushed toward her with concern. She was dimly aware of his grip on her shoulders before she fainted.

***

As the world came back into view, she realized she was lying on the cold, dirt surface of the alleyway, her head resting on Pierre's thigh. It took her a moment to remember why she was there. Then she shot up into a sitting position, staring wildly around the alley. "They're going to hang you," she gasped.

Pierre leaned over her and pulled her toward him. "Only if they find me. We'll be gone shortly."

The panic that was rising in her chest was threatening to choke her. She stared at him without comprehension. "They're going to kill you," she repeated.

Pierre tried his best to soothe her. "No, they won't. Not if we leave now."

Marie gazed at him, trying to understand. "You killed him."

He gripped her shoulders. "He did this!" Pierre was too worked up to be quiet. "The last eight years! Everything we've been through was because of him! He wasn't going to let you go. I never really believed that. But he wouldn't have. You would have spent the rest of your life looking over your shoulder!"

Marie's eyes filled with tears, and she buried her face in her hands. Pierre pulled her close as she broke down completely. Relief and fear waved over her in a confusing concoction. She gripped Pierre's jacket in an attempt to stay connected to the present. It was over. Claude was dead. But she was still afraid.

Pierre stroked her back gently. Slowly, her heart rate returned to normal and the tremors in her hands ceased. He couldn't believe that he'd actually killed Claude. He leaned against the wall, trying not to be sick. He'd wanted to kill the man ever since he first laid eyes on Marie, beaten and broken in the Babineaux manor. But he'd never believed for a second that he would actually do it.

"We need to go, beautiful," Pierre whispered in Marie's ear. "We need to leave before anyone finds us."

Marie looked at him fearfully. "They'll be looking for you."

"No, they won't," he replied. But he didn't look completely convinced. He helped her to her feet, dusting the dirt from his breeches.

A mortar exploded at the end of the alleyway, and Marie covered her mouth to silence a scream as Pierre pushed them both against the wall, shielding her with his body. As the dust cleared, he grabbed her arm and dragged her away from the scene. Already, she could hear the voices of people coming to investigate.

Pierre pushed his hat low in an effort to shade his face, his arm still protectively around Marie's shoulders. No one looked their way. Everyone was too consumed in their own loss to notice.

They came to the harbour, gloomy and destroyed, in the last light of the day. The charred, exposed ribs of broken hulls shone in the water like skeletons, scarlet in the dying rays of the sun. Fishing boats still floated in the harbour, deserted and forlorn. The massive forms of the few remaining French warships loomed above the dark water.

The British had stationed themselves at the lighthouse across from the harbour. Perfectly positioned, they were able to launch an offensive that slowly destroyed the remains of the French warships stationed at Louisbourg. For whatever reason, the British were happy to allow a land assault that night, so no conflict engaged the sailors there. The cannons and mortars screamed through the air but the glassy surface of the harbour was undisturbed.

"That's all that's left?" Marie asked quietly, staring at the forms of the massive ships.

Pierre nodded grimly. "The *Prudent* and the *Bienfaisant*. Two of the few ships we have left. Everything else has been destroyed or captured." Marie stared at the sparse collection of fishing boats bobbing uselessly at the docks. She could envision the four hundred British men-of-war ships waiting in the Atlantic just out of sight of the harbour walls. It suddenly struck her how doomed they all were. "I didn't realize that was all that was left."

Pierre shook his head. "We aren't long for this world. Once Louisbourg falls, the rest of New France is next."

Marie stared over the docks, trying to fix the image in her memory. She wouldn't be coming back, and even if she could have, the place would no longer be here. She felt a sudden stab of pain at the thought of leaving what was so familiar. She hadn't said goodbye to Elise or Annette. Whatever happened to them, she would probably never see them again. She glanced at Pierre and saw some of her grief reflected in his face. "Should we not stay in Quebec?"

"Let's worry about getting there first," he said gruffly. "But no. I think France is the safest option."

The darkness gathered around them. Lanterns and torches marked the way of French sailors and soldiers who were preparing for the next day. Pierre led her away from the sounds and lights of the resistance, down some rocks to a deserted part of the water's edge. Marie stumbled and fell several times in the growing darkness but eventually made it with only her hands skinned.

Pierre had his doubts about their mode of transportation. It was a birchbark canoe floating quietly on the water. It seemed tiny compared to the canoes the Algonquins and *voyageurs* travelled in. But close up, Pierre could see that it was large enough for the two of them and probably for a third as well.

"Where did this come from?" Marie asked.

"Father Weber has two broken legs. He's not dead." Pierre threw the rucksacks into the bottom of the boat.

"I thought the British had us surrounded." Marie could feel the adrenalin beginning to pump through her veins.

Pierre bent to whisper in her ear. "They are, but there's a belief that there's a break between camps farther up the cove. We're going to try to sneak up

446

through there. Besides, the mist is coming in an hour. No one will be able to see three feet in front of them."

Marie's face blanched. Pierre gave her a meaningful look. If she chose to turn back, he would understand. She shook her head a fraction and climbed into the bow of the canoe. As she'd never been in one of these vessels before, the process wasn't graceful. Water sloshed over the sides, soaking her skirts.

Marie turned to her husband. "You're sure about this?"

Pierre shrugged. "Straight to Baie des Espagnols. Apparently, the harbour there is still functioning."

"Someone will take us to Quebec?"

"Or at least off the island. We're on our own now." He gave her a swift, searching look, but she didn't argue.

Marie shivered and pulled her cloak around her, even though the night was warm. Pierre sighed, knowing all too well how she felt. He climbed into the stern of the canoe and pushed off into the mist. "Do you want to paddle?" Pierre whispered.

"What do you think?" Marie hissed back, her nerves stretched too far to be polite. She had always thought of herself as self-reliant, but she was realizing she didn't have the skills for this voyage.

Pierre said nothing but silently steered them through the water.

The mist, now more like a fog, was quickly rolling in, obscuring the world in a swirl of white. It would be impossible for any casual lookout to spot them. They moved silently, far enough away from shore not to be observed by anyone on the beach but close enough for the vague outline of red spruce trees to guide their way.

Marie gripped the gunwales of the canoe so hard her hands were soon numb. All along the bluffs, they could see the pinpricks of fires burning from the British camps. A few times, the sound of songs sung around the fires floated out over the sea. The invisible enemy.

Pierre had ridden in a canoe many times when he was in the army. But Marie had never set foot in one, even though she'd grown up doing many things that were considered unbecoming for a woman of good birth. So the instability of the craft frightened her, and her every movement sent the vessel rocking on the water. She gritted her teeth together, trying to stay as still as possible.

Pierre saw her pose and gripped her shoulder. "You're doing fine," he whispered reassuringly. She turned back, eyes round with fear. He nodded in what he hoped was a comforting way and continued paddling through the black water.

Marie had no idea where they were going. She certainly hoped Pierre did. Every bit of shoreline looked exactly the same to her, and except for the faint outline of trees and fields, everything was obscured by fog. She turned around to see the fortress one last time but it was too late. The crumbling city was in darkness. They passed the lighthouse and Island Battery, now in the hands of the British.

Pierre heard a sharp intake of breath from Marie before he spotted the problem. Ahead of them, barely visible in the night air, were four drunken soldiers, wading into the water.

"Don't move." The command was so quiet she almost missed it.

The canoe slowly glided in the opposite direction, away from the oblivious soldiers. Pierre guided the canoe as far as he could, hoping that the camouflage of fog was enough to hide them. Marie glanced back at him, face devoid of colour. He tried to look reassuring. If the fog shifted, if any of the soldiers looked over and decided to investigate, there was nothing he could do. They were completely exposed.

It took the better part of an hour before the soldiers staggered back up the shore. But Pierre waited still, heart in his throat, unsure of when to move. He couldn't clearly see to the shore. He cautiously began to move the canoe forward when Marie threw out a warning arm. There was still someone in the water. He waited, overwhelmed with a feeling of gratitude for her presence. A few minutes later, she waved him forward, the soldier now back on shore.

As they reached the shore and finally exited the canoe, Marie was so relieved that her knees gave out for a few moments. She knew the path ahead was even more treacherous, but she was grateful to be off the open, unsheltered water. Pierre knelt down beside her, and they paused for a moment in each other's embrace, simply listening to their heart rates return to normal.

When they were out on the water, Marie had been wondering how, in the darkness and fog, they were going to find the specific spot between the two British camps that they needed to scale. Her worries seemed ridiculous now as she saw a massive rock slide of boulders, trees, and earth spilling into the water. It was no wonder the British hadn't camped there. The earth seemed to have split, spilling its contents for all to see. It had jutted out of the fog like some massive scar in the blackness.

Grabbing their few belongings out of the canoe, Pierre began to fill the craft with rocks. Then he drew his dagger through the side of the craft and pushed it out into the water, watching as it slowly sank beneath the surface with its heavy load. He turned to Marie and smiled.

"First part done." The moonlight reflected off his grinning teeth.

Marie grasped his hand as they crept cautiously away from the water. "Where are we going?" she whispered.

"Tonight, we need to get past the British lines. Then it should be less than a day to Baie des Espagnols." It had taken him longer the first time he'd escaped from the island, though it would have taken much less time if the forests hadn't been crawling with the enemy.

Marie nodded and followed silently. She was exhausted, and her shoulders ached from gripping the sides of the canoe for so long. She could only imagine how Pierre must be feeling after paddling them both.

The path was steep, and massive rocks and broken tree limbs made the climb difficult. Marie hitched her skirts above her knees and slowly crept up the landslide. She was painfully slow, unaccustomed as she was to running around the countryside. Pierre waited patiently, never complaining about her pace. He seemed to have the capacity to see in the dark, Marie thought bitterly. The tree roots and broken branches that tripped her never seemed to come under his foot.

It was an uneventful trip. Twice they had to crouch down behind a cluster of birch trees as the sound of footsteps drew near. The first time, the sound came from a clearly intoxicated British soldier relieving himself, the second time, the cause of the noise was a porcupine. Marie didn't want another encounter with either, although Pierre had expressed a desire to eat the animal.

As dawn neared, Pierre felt it was safe enough to stop and rest. He passed a small loaf of bread to Marie and began to wander around the area in search of a place to hide. Marie bit into the crusty loaf, savouring the fluffy interior. She knew Pierre had eaten only a few berries since their departure, but he wouldn't dream of eating any of the bread. He'd brought that for Marie.

"I think I found a cave we can sleep in," Pierre said, reappearing. "It's not much, but it will keep us out of sight," he said apologetically.

Marie smiled. "I'm so tired, I think I could sleep right where I am."

When they arrived at Pierre's proposed sleeping spot, Marie could see that it wasn't really a cave as much as an outcrop in the hillside. It was true, though, that no one would find them unless they were looking, and that seemed unlikely as an armed conflict was raging mere miles away. Pierre said he was fairly confident that they were a few miles from any camp. Marie followed him and crawled in.

She spread one of the only two blankets they had on the hard ground, lay down, and wrapped herself in her cloak. Pierre wiggled in beside her, draping one of the grey blankets over the mouth of the outcrop for protection. Marie saw the dagger clutched in his hand and was grateful for his protection. She thought it important to tell him so, but before she could say anything, she drifted off to sleep.

***

He awoke sometime in the late afternoon. An awful, acidic stink filled his nostrils. He looked around for Marie and then pulled himself out from under the rocky outcrop. He spotted her under a nearby sugar maple nibbling on the last loaf of bread.

"Did I wake you?" she asked as he sat beside her. It was a clear day, and the noise of the bombardment was so far away that all they could hear was the wind and birdsong.

"Actually, it was the smell." He rubbed the stubble on his face, trying to wake up his senses.

Marie looked embarrassed. "I'm sorry. I woke up feeling awful. I tried to get as far away as possible before I was sick."

Pierre dismissed it with a shrug and wrapped an arm around her. "I can't exactly blame you, as it's my fault you feel this way. But how are you feeling now?"

"I thought pregnant women were sick only in the morning," she grumbled, breaking the loaf in two and passing one half to him. She insisted he eat something more filling than berries.

"Finish eating and then we have to go."

"How much farther?"

"We'll make it by dawn." Pierre stood and stretched. "Can you swim?"

Marie looked startled.

"We have to cross Sea Miray."

Marie shook her head. "Nice try. Just because I haven't travelled as much as you doesn't mean I'm not perfectly aware of the bridge there."

Pierre grinned, scanning the area.

"Well, I tried." He looked off into the distance. "The road shouldn't be too far from here."

Despite taking his father's map and compass, he hadn't used either of them once. When Marie asked him about directions, he pointed to the stars, and they hadn't led them wrong so far.

Marie stood up slowly so her head wouldn't spin.

"Do we need the road?" Marie asked.

"It'll be easier than the undergrowth. And Father Weber's sources said the troops are staying near the fortress, so it will be safe. Besides, it will be dark."

Marie leaned backwards, stretching. Her body had not enjoyed its night on the rocks. The sooner they got off the island, the better. She wouldn't admit it, but tramping through the forest was wearing her out.

By the time Pierre and Marie left the outcrop, night had fallen—another foggy one, though the fog, at least, hovered only a few feet off the ground. The half moon illuminated everything. His fear that they would be captured by British soldiers was lessening the farther inland they travelled. However, he would happily have taken some cloud cover to add to the protection of the darkness. At last, they reached the dirt road and hugged the edge, trying to stay in the safety of the shadows.

An hour into their journey, they spotted the first proof that the British invaders were not all clustered around the fortress. A small farm house lay in ruins, the remaining timber and fields scorched black from fire. Marie stood in silence for a moment, taking in the macabre sight. The few possessions that remained were scattered over the blackened ground, anything of value having been looted.

"What happened to them?" Marie asked quietly. She'd heard the stories but had never seen anything like this.

Pierre stopped reluctantly. He wanted to leave as quickly as possible. If they were near destroyed settlements, they were closer to the army than he had previously thought. "Hopefully, they made it to Louisbourg before the British came." Pierre looked skeptical.

Marie took a step toward the house. Pierre put a hand on her arm and drew her back. "Whatever happened, it's too late now."

They walked in silence for a time, passing a few more burned and demolished settlements, possessions deemed of no value scattered along the fields, the carcasses of livestock butchered and festering on the ground. The

British were looking for vengeance. Pierre had seen this before, the last time he'd fled from Île-Royale. The idea was to destroy the next year's crops to prevent the population from coming back. This type of behaviour was common in Europe. Marie was seeing this all for the first time, and Pierre could tell it was affecting her.

"Is it worth this?" she asked after a time as they passed an abandoned wagon, the contents long gone.

Pierre shrugged. "Is Louisbourg worth all this destruction?" He laughed bitterly. "Is anything worth all these lives?"

Moments like this reminded her just how much time they'd spent apart. She'd learned from Nic not to ask questions about battles. Whatever information was shared was all that would be given. But more than once, she'd seen the haunted look in Pierre's eyes and knew he had suffered in ways she would never understand.

Pierre sighed. "Since Europeans came here, there's been nothing but blood. Fighting with the Natives, fighting between France and Britain and Holland. For what? some furs, cod, and money?"

Marie said nothing. The anger in his voice was frightening; she'd never heard it there before.

"There was a soldier from France that I served with. He was older than most of the cadets, older than me. He'd joined the army to avoid arrest. I remember him saying that Louis cared about New France only as long as there were enough furs and cod to keep his mistresses at Versailles happy."

"You believe him, don't you?"

"Well, that man could sell water to cod, but I think I do." Pierre continued to watch the road for any signs of life, his hand resting on his pistol.

"That's why you want to go to France." Marie nodded to herself.

The massive shoulders shrugged. He knew Marie had hated the years she'd spent exiled in France, but it seemed like the safer option. "The British will be coming for Quebec next. That much is certain. Louis won't supply the colonies well enough to defend themselves because he has his own problems. The war in Europe isn't going well."

The two then walked in silence along the edge of the road, trying to stay in the shelter of the trees, both wrapped in the cocoons of their own thoughts. Suddenly, Pierre threw out a warning arm. Marie glanced around, terrified. She'd heard nothing.

Pierre scanned the road and surrounding forest, searching the black terrain for some lurking creature. He stood in front of Marie, sheltering her from the unseen threat. Her eyes combed the surroundings, but she could see nothing but trees.

She felt something press against her stomach, and looking down, she discovered the packets of documents from both Father Weber and Augustus. Her fingers fumbled as she tried to slip the leather bundle into her skirt pocket. Then she saw the moonlight reflect off the edge of the compass as Pierre slipped it into her hands.

Her hazel eyes found the piercing blue. She shook her head in panic, suddenly realizing what was happening. He nodded slowly and deliberately.

She clutched the compass to her chest, aware for the first time of the tears cascading down her cheeks. "No," she whispered.

Pierre looked away for a moment, keeping a wary eye on the edge of the trees. "You have to." He was speaking quickly. "There's three of them, over at the top of the hill." Marie followed his gaze. There were indeed three Redcoats walking directly toward them, weapons raised at the ready.

"They've seen us. You need to run as fast as you can. Go north for a while."

"What about ... ," she began. She couldn't leave him now.

"I love you." He gave her one swift, piercing look as he drew his pistol. "I'll keep them distracted."

"Pierre, I can't," she gasped, looking at the advancing soldiers. They were shouting, but Marie didn't understand.

Pierre gripped her hand but continued to watch the soldiers. "Yes, you can."

She shook her head and tried to hold him one last time. He gently pushed her away. "I love you." As he turned, he gave her one last swift smile before walking to meet the enemy. She ran, pushing her way through dense forest, away from the shouts and screams. She glanced back and saw the Redcoats push Pierre to the ground, muskets pointed at his head. The soldiers were pointing at the forest, clearly interrogating him as to her whereabouts. That was the last she saw before she fled. Branches ripped at her skirts and skin, and she tripped over roots and unseen obstacles. She could feel her heart beating against her rib cage. She stopped only when the stitch in her side forced her to.

Gasping and alone, she collapsed against the trunk of a maple, vomiting and sobbing until her legs could no longer support her. Gutted, she crawled over to a group of rocks, leaned against them, and waited. If he was alive, he would come after her. She didn't doubt that. And she encouraged herself by remembering how Pierre had fought off the three drunken privateers who had attacked her the night she broke her engagement with Jacques. Then a nasty little voice inside her head said those were drunk pirates, not trained warriors.

Her body was shaking, and she wrapped her cloak around herself. The blankets were back in the field with Pierre. She waited, the ice in her chest growing thicker with each passing hour. She stared down at the small collection she carried, stained with tears.

The moon was high in the sky before she thought of moving. She didn't want to leave. Leaving was admitting that he wasn't following. What would the British do to a captured French civilian? Surely, they wouldn't think he was a soldier. But what would they do if they found out he was one? Her stomach churned unpleasantly and she was sick again.

Clearly, there were more British soldiers in the area than just the three who'd apprehended Pierre. So Marie knew she was in more danger staying here than running, and if she was captured now, it would be a terrible way of repaying Pierre. However, her joints were stiff and unwilling to move. When she tried to stand, her knees gave out from under her. What if Pierre was already dead? She pressed her hands against her eyes, breathing deeply.

It took several attempts before she finally dragged herself off the forest floor. She had never been to this part of the island before. It was madness to keep on tramping through it now, alone in the dark, when every fibre of her being wanted to turn back.

In Marie's mind, every sound represented an enemy soldier. Every step was one farther away from wherever Pierre was and whatever had happened. She was consumed with guilt. Guilt that she had run when he'd told her to, guilt that she'd left him, guilt that the little life inside her was now alone with only her protection. However, there was little to do now but move forward. If Pierre was alive, he would find her. *If* he was alive.

Marie fought back tears most of the night. Twice she had to stop to catch her breath, to remind herself to keep going. More than once she called out for him, hoping somehow he would materialize. How many times had she said goodbye to him over the years, thinking it was the last time. She felt the grip of his hand still firm against her fingers. She stared down at the too-large silver ring, glinting in the soft moonlight. She told herself that the soldiers hadn't shot him. She had to hold on to that.

Sea Miray stretched before her, the moonlight shimmering off its rippled surface. A bridge extended across the body of water, silhouetted against the night sky. A brief wave of hysteria washed over Marie as she recalled Pierre's earlier teasing.

She stood on the edge of the shore, debating whether it was safe to cross. There was no cover on the bridge, so if she walked across it, she would be completely exposed. Carefully, she followed the water's edge until she reached the sturdy wooden boards jutting out of the inky blackness. She saw and heard no one but that meant nothing.

Heart pounding, she ran as fast as she could along the bridge to the other side, not stopping until she'd reached the safety of the forest there. Panting, she spotted a confused chipmunk eyeing her suspiciously. Marie laughed at the little creature and then carried on, following the edge of the road as best she could. She met no one, friend or foe. As the eastern sky slowly lightened, streaking the sky with pink and gold, she saw the cluster of houses that made up the village, settled against the clear, shimmering water of Baie des Espagnols. Fishing boats bobbed peacefully in the bay, untouched by the destruction happening just a few miles away.

Exhausted, Marie found a small tree near the edge of the water. She wrapped herself in her cloak and curled up under the tree's protective branches. It was too early to approach any of the cottages, though as a single woman, she posed little threat. Her last thoughts as she drifted off to sleep were of the heaviness in her womb and the father her child might never meet.

Chapter 16

SHE WAS DREAMING. SHE WAS SURE OF THAT. They were children of ten, walking home from school. Nic had started it or that's how Marie felt. He'd been bothering her all day, teasing and pulling on the ribbons of her braids. Being the mature child that she was, Marie had called him every name she could think of. Nic had retaliated by throwing a giant glob of mud all over her favourite green dress. She was livid, and instead of doing the sensible thing and rushing home to tattle, she'd launched herself on her brother, wrestling his face into the mud and sitting on him until he'd begged for mercy.

Her victory had been short lived. As they'd walked down the street, two of Nic's friends, one being Pierre, had caught sight of them and slung so much mud at Marie that by the time the two of them had arrived back home, they were almost unrecognizable. Annette strapped them both, then forced them to bathe and clean their clothes before forbidding them to go outside for three days except under her supervision. Nic's ears had burned as his aunt chaperoned him around, and he hadn't spoken to Marie for a week.

The sound of children playing jarred Marie back to reality. The morning sun was still low in the sky. She'd slept for only a few hours. She felt awful but pulled herself up and looked around. A small group of children had crowded near her, too afraid to approach closely. She smiled tentatively and waved at them. I must look like quite a sight, she thought, dishevelled and covered in dirt. The youngest pulled back in fear, but a girl of about eight walked up almost close enough to touch her.

"Who are you and what are you doing here?" the girl asked confidently, gazing up at Marie with her hands on her hips. Her upturned nose was sprinkled with freckles.

Marie smiled and tried her best to brush her hair from her face. "I'm looking for a boat."

The girl shook her head and frowned as if worried about Marie's sanity. "There are no boats here. Only our fishing boats, and they don't go out anymore or the British will catch them." The other children murmured and nodded their heads.

Marie nodded. "This is Baie des Espagnols, yes?"

Another of the boys from the group, heartened by his companions' interaction with the stranger, stepped forward. "Yes, Madame. Are you lost?"

Marie shook her head and turned toward the water, thinking. So she had to convince a fisherman to ferry her out of here. That wasn't going to be easy. The banging of a door brought her out of her thoughts.

A tall, plump woman came thundering out of a nearby cottage, shooing the children as she went. But she stopped when she saw Marie sitting in front of her. She looked for a moment as if she'd seen a ghost, and one of her hands flew to her throat. Marie realized that she must look worse than she thought. "Who are you, and what are you doing here?"

Marie stood up, trying her best to rid her clothes of the dirt and grime from the journey. She tried to smile, but the muscles wouldn't work.

Although surrounded by a dozen curious children, some of whom were undoubtedly her own, the woman was probably younger than Marie. She looked torn between concern and suspicion.

"I'm from Louisbourg," Marie finally blurted.

The woman's eyes grew round, and she took a few steps back. "Nobody comes from there," she whispered. "The siege." She crossed herself.

Marie looked around. Panic was bubbling in her chest. She hadn't counted on people not believing her. "I did," she said quietly.

The deep lines of worry on the woman's forehead grew deeper with concern. "What happened?" She sent some of the children back to her cottage. They reappeared a moment later, carrying a chipped mug full of sour ale.

"My name is Madeline," she said, passing Marie the drink. She said nothing more but waited. Marie took a deep gulp of the burning liquid and tried not to cough. All around her the dirty faces of the children were still peering at her.

"Are they all yours?"

Madeline shook her head and pointed to three who had frizzy, curly brown mops like hers. She may have shared drink with the stranger, but she clearly didn't trust her. Marie cleared her throat and tried her best to explain. The words were hard to get out and she choked when she spoke of Pierre, but when she was finished, Madeline looked convinced if not very sympathetic.

"We have only fishing boats here," she hedged, continuing to appraise Marie. "Maybe someone would take you to Miquelon." But the woman didn't seem truly convinced of this possibility.

"I can pay them," Marie said hastily, "whatever they want." She paused for a moment, considering how to proceed. "I'm pregnant," she swallowed.

"Anywhere off the island and I can make my way from there." She could hear the pleading in her own voice.

Madeline looked reluctant. "Most of the boats are out right now, getting what they can close to shore."

Marie nodded.

"But there are two who may be able to help," she said almost to herself. She looked very reluctant to share any more information. "Follow me."

Marie handed the ale cup to one of the children and followed Madeline, the gaggle of children clamouring in their wake. The village was made up of small cottages with thatched roofs and no chimneys. It felt far more remote here than in the bustling fortress.

Madeline walked purposefully toward one of the homes lining the wharf and knocked. Marie stood a way off, not sure what position she was supposed to play in the negotiations. The door was opened by a bad-tempered, middle-aged woman. The conversation between her and Madeline lasted less than a minute before the door was slammed shut with remarkable force.

It looked as if it took a great deal of self-mastery for Madeline to carry on. She moved away from the house with an ugly look and started walking away at a fast clip. "That woman is the most miserable human being," she spat as Marie rushed to keep up.

"I appreciate this," Marie said quietly.

Madeline waved a large hand and kept walking. Marie had a distinct suspicion that the woman wasn't helping her out of the goodness of her heart or out of Christian charity, but from a desire to no longer have this stranger in the community. If the British hadn't molested this village yet, she couldn't blame Madeline for not wanting an escapee from Louisbourg to attract the attention of the enemy army.

After a few minutes, they approached a rather shabby cottage. An ancient man answered the door. Marie thought he looked old enough to have personally welcomed Cartier when the explorer had first arrived in what was now New France. She couldn't hear what Madeline was saying, but the wizened old man nodded and stared openly at Marie.

Some agreement must have been reached because before she knew it, Madeline had said her farewells and wandered back to her home with the children following closely behind. Marie turned to face the old man. His wrinkled face broke into a toothless grin. "Well, come on, sweetie. Come on in." He motioned her into the poor quarters, hunched almost completely over with age. "I'm eighty and seven. I shan't hurt ya."

Marie was surprised by how quickly he moved about the small room, which was kitchen, bedroom, and living space, all in one.

"Now, ol' Mad Maddy says ye be needin' to get to Quebec."

Marie nodded. She was desperate to make travel arrangements, but she doubted this man could make such a trip. He looked as if a strong wind could blow him away.

He seemed to know what she was thinking. "I'm Bernard." He thrust a hand, twisted with arthritis, at her. His grip was surprisingly firm. "I may be an old seaman, but at least I know my way around the ocean," he wheezed merrily through his nose. He seemed completely unperturbed by her lack of enthusiasm.

"You can take me to Quebec?" Marie asked, still amazed that the little creature could walk, never mind sail.

Bernard ran his hands through what little white hair he had left. "Well, no," he conceded. "My son died last year and he was my right-hand man. I can't move as fast as I once did. Me grandson helps now, but he has a baby on the way next month. Can't be gone too long," he grinned, showing soft pink gums. "I can take ye to Miquelon."

Marie wanted to point out that the island of Miquelon was terribly close to Newfoundland, which had belonged to the French since 1713. She thought for a moment, still standing awkwardly near the door. She was tired and sick, and her head was beginning to ache from all the tension. She rubbed her eyes.

"In Miquelon, ye can find someone to take ye to Quebec. The bastard Englanders aren't there and lots'll still 'elp a woman in need."

"All right," Marie smiled. Despite her reservations, she found Bernard entertaining. Also, he seemed to be the only one willing to take the chance.

"Excellent!" He clapped his long fingers together. "When would ye want to leave?"

"As soon as possible."

"Wonderful!" Bernard exclaimed. "I haven't been out in weeks. Me grandson thinks I'm of a weak constitution." He shook his head as if that was the most foolish thought in the world. "I told 'im my father fished for his whole ninety-two years and died at sea, and I expect to do the same."

Marie bit her lip to keep from laughing. "That's quite impressive."

"Aye." Bernard rooted around the kitchen for his fishing gear, only half listening. He seemed elated about the prospect of this unexpected trip.

"Do you happen to know anyone in Miquelon who could take me to Quebec?"

Bernard straightened up, his arms full of equipment. "Aye, sweetie. I was born there. Me wee brother still lives there. Only seventy and six. He's got some connections."

Marie felt immediately relieved and grateful that Madeline had found this man. He hoisted a large rope over his shoulder.

"Should you really be carrying that?" Marie stepped forward to help.

"Nonsense," he snorted. "I'm still alive. Besides, this is terrible work for one who's pregnant."

Marie stopped short. "How do you know that?"

He grinned, gums gleaming. "When ye've been around as long as me, ye just know things. Besides, Mad Maddy told me."

Marie laughed.

***

It took a few hours, but eventually, Bernard announced that they were ready to leave. His grandson Saul had been reluctant to go, but he'd been persuaded to join them. He did not share his grandfather's optimism that he was strong enough for such a trip, but the old man had shouted him down. No doubt, Marie thought, Saul had been convinced to come largely because he was afraid of what would happen if his grandfather was allowed to navigate the waters alone. At last, the three of them were standing on the small deck of the *Françoise*, named after Bernard's late wife.

Saul was compact and muscular. He had five children at home, with another one on the way, and his wife wasn't happy that he was "abandoning" her as she put it. Saul also made it quite clear that he felt shepherding one lone woman to Miquelon was a waste of time.

"We're only going to the island," Bernard said soothingly when Saul complained for the tenth time. "As long as the weather stays pleasant, you'll be back home in a few days."

Marie moved away as the two of them squabbled with each other. She sat at the end of the boat, on a small wooden bench, cloak wrapped around her shoulders, slowly watching Île-Royale disappear. Deep in her bones, she knew she would never be returning, and her heart ached as she watched the misty forests grow smaller. Her life and everyone she knew and loved was on that island. Her thoughts then turned again to Pierre. She prayed that he would be preserved, that somehow he had lived through the encounter in the woods, but the longer she was without him, the more pessimistic she became.

The fortress would fall, and everyone in it would be at the mercy of the vengeful British. She thought of Anne, Sophie's small daughter, and the tiny and elderly Sister Agatha at the hands of the conquering enemy and wiped away a tear.

Marie still did not know what had become of Elise. There had been no word from her since Nic's death. Moving away from Île-Royale, Marie knew she may never know what had become of her sister-in-law. She prayed Elise was safe, perhaps finding refuge with her mother until the boats left for France, but Marie couldn't know for sure.

The boat finally turned out into the open ocean, its small sails snapping in the breeze. Then, as the boat began to roll with the waves, her stomach writhed in rebellion. She leaned back against the solid wood of one of the sides, trying to steady herself. The smell of sea salt filled her nostrils as she tried to focus on her breathing.

Bernard came and stood beside her, watching her discomfort with great amusement. "Have yer never been to sea before, sweetie?" His pale eyes were dancing with delight.

Marie glanced at him through half-closed eyelids. "I have. Many times. I was born in Quebec. But this trip isn't agreeing with me."

The old man laughed, the few wisps of hair still attached to his head dancing in the wind. "Yer just need yer sea legs."

"I doubt it." Her head was spinning. She lay her forehead on the damp edge of the bench, but that didn't help. If she had had anything much in her stomach, it would have been coming up.

Bernard continued to stand a safe distance away, looking pleased. "My wife had twelve kids, ten grown. I remember those days."

Marie slowly made her way back to the bench, her eyes shut firmly, trying to imagine ground. "Doesn't Saul need you?"

Bernard continued to chuckle. "I've been demoted. The first mate feels he can handle it now that we're in open water. Thinks he knows more than me." He shook his head good-naturedly.

Marie smiled despite herself. "I'm sure he's quite capable."

Bernard nodded. "He's a good lad. Don't judge 'im too harshly."

"Don't worry. I'm not. And I can't blame him for wanting to stay with his pregnant wife," she said wistfully.

Bernard nodded and leaned his twisted body against the withered wood of the boat frame. Suddenly, Saul rounded the corner, his dark hair standing up in the wind. He looked displeased, although for all Marie knew, that may have been the way he looked all the time.

"We're making good time," he growled, his muscular arms crossed over his chest as he glared at the pair of them.

Bernard nodded pleasantly. "That is good. The trip isn't agreeing with Madame."

Saul grunted. "That's a shame."

Bernard glared at his grandson. "Ye use yer manners, please. Ye're in the presence of a lady." He stood and shuffled off to check something, throwing daggers at his grandson as he went.

Saul looked chastened and slightly embarrassed to be alone with Marie. Marie tried to look reassuring, but she was more concerned with preventing a trip to the rail.

"I'm sorry," Saul mumbled.

Marie nodded, her eyes closed against the rolling water. "It's all right. I don't blame you for not wanting to leave your family. Especially with your wife the way she is."

"It's just with the British about ... she's very nervous."

"We all are." Marie risked a look at him. It was hard to sympathize with them when they had obviously been protected from the battles so far.

"You're from the fortress?" Saul asked as if that was impossible.

Marie nodded but looked out at sea, the grey-green water blending into the sky at the horizon. These people were only a few miles away from Louisbourg. How could they not be affected?

"How bad is it?"

"When you get home," Marie said, "you need to get your family out of here." She continued to look out over the water.

Saul scoffed, then realized she was serious.

"Louisbourg isn't going to last much longer. When it falls, so does the rest of the island. They won't be merciful."

The sailor looked at her for a long time, trying to determine whether she could be trusted. She stared back, too exhausted to care. Eventually, Saul shook his head and huffed back to the front of the boat.

***

Marie spent most of the journey with her head over the side of the boat. The rest of the time she spent dozing, curled up on the small bench. The illness was worse if she sat inside. The men largely ignored her, but Bernard would come to check on her every few hours.

They made good time. After three days, Miquelon came into view. The rocky shoreline, topped with green foliage, stood guard over the small port.

Marie was exhausted and her throat was raw. Saul happily accepted her payment while Bernard accompanied her onto shore. The smell of sea air and fresh fish mingled together, reminding her strongly of home.

Miquelon was tiny. It held no more than a few streets of jumbled fishermen's cottages, other homes, and taverns.

"This is where I was born," Bernard said proudly, leading Marie away from the bustle of the harbour. "France owned the island then as it still does, but ships came from all over: France, Spain, Holland, England. There was even one from Africa once." He grinned at the distant memory. "You could travel the world without leaving the town. But now ... ," he gestured to the predominantly French crowd, "it's just the same as anywhere else."

Marie was more concerned about finding a place to eat and sleep than about the island's history. They had managed to slip in without the officials noticing, and she wanted to stay invisible. As a woman on her own, she was at an extreme risk, even though she was French and a widow, not a woman of ill repute. "Can you recommend a good place to stay—safe for a woman travelling alone?"

The old man pointed to a nearby inn and winked. "My brother's daughter runs that place. You'll be safe there." He puffed out his thin chest proudly.

Marie nodded, even though she would have preferred a different place based on this one's outward hygiene. The grubby windows and piles of discarded trash around the entrance did nothing to add to its charm. But she wasn't about to insult Bernard after all he had done for her.

"Thank you," she said, turning to the elderly man.

He bowed his already bent frame and kissed her hand. "It was me pleasure, my dear. Not every day does an old man like me gets such an adventure. But I really must get Saul home to his family before he leaves without me."

Marie smiled. "Good luck."

Bernard nodded. "Yer need it more than me now. Things will work out." He turned and was swallowed up by the crowd.

Marie watched him leave and then entered the inn.

***

She ended up spending a week in Miquelon before she was able to board a Quebec-bound ship that was willing to take her.

Her first impression of the inn had been correct. Le Roi was cozy and served excellent food, but the accommodations left much to be desired. Upon first entering her room, she'd stripped the bed and slept wrapped in her cloak. Every day before she crawled in, she would do her best to rid the mattress of any unwelcome bedmates.

She slept for two days straight. Two glorious days when she hadn't been continually tormented by thoughts of Pierre and all those she had left behind. When she finally woke up, she ate a huge amount of food—an embarrassing amount of food. Surprisingly, it all stayed down.

"So you do actually want me to eat?" she asked her belly at the end of the third day. She was lying in bed, trying to keep from thinking about Pierre.

"Maybe we'll actually get through this." There was no response, not that she'd expected one. It was still too early to feel any movement from the child she was carrying.

The landlady may have been Bernard's niece, but she seemed incredibly suspicious of Marie. This, along with the fact that Marie didn't want to explain why she urgently needed to get to Quebec, meant that the stern woman was of no help in recommending anyone who could take her there. Frustrated, Marie left the inn during the day to search for a ship's captain who would take on a lone French woman.

It was a frightening search. Few boats were even willing to make the journey to the capital. The tiny island was relatively untouched by the war, and the seamen sailing from there didn't want to be involved with a woman who had just come from Louisbourg. It was too much of a risk, taking on a passenger tainted by the war. Who knew what her real mission was? Finally, when she had exhausted almost the entire harbour, she met a captain willing to allow her onto his boat. It had cost her a great deal and Marie knew that Pierre would never have agreed to the sum, but she was desperate to get to the capital.

The *Archille* was a large fishing boat, big enough to employ several men. It had come from Bordeaux and was resting in Miquelon before moving on to Quebec. Marie's stomach had been churning all day but had so far behaved. She'd been able to keep her breakfast down and was optimistic that the trend might continue until she set foot on the massive deck of the *Archille*. The smell of masses of unwashed bodies crammed into the vessel overwhelmed her as she stepped onto the gently bobbing boat. Marie put a hand on the railing to try to steady herself. Meanwhile, the sailors were eyeing her with curiosity—a woman travelling alone. And this time, there was no Bernard to explain the situation or protect her. She felt the hairs on the back of her neck stand up as the vessel pulled away from shore.

Captain Étienne Gauthier was a burly man, his face weathered from years of working out in the sun and wind. He smiled good-naturedly at Marie, flashing a mouth of missing teeth. He had a jovial personality and a booming laugh, and Marie liked him despite the amount she'd paid to board his ship.

Gauthier had been Captain of the *Archille* for ten years. Born in rural France, he'd stumbled onto a ship at the age of ten and never left the seafaring life. He'd seen many things, including the inside of a British prison. Not surprisingly, he hated the British, and that made him sympathize with Marie's plight. Feeling desperate for a means of travel, Marie had confided in him about the information she carried. It was a foolish decision, but it had brought her the results she wanted.

Captain Gauthier studied Marie shrewdly for a moment before approaching her. He offered his hand. "Welcome aboard, Madame. If you need anything during your voyage, please do not hesitate to ask."

Marie nodded, trying not to faint as the ship pulled up its anchor and moved out into open water. The familiar feeling that existed during the short boat ride here was growing in her abdomen. Not now, she pleaded inwardly.

Captain Gauthier was leading her to her accommodations, and he was saying something, but she didn't hear him as she rushed to the starboard side and threw up into the ocean.

✳✳✳

Pierre leaned against the rough wooden post that was holding the tent up. His ankle was chained to the post, but he wouldn't have tried to run even if he hadn't been in restraints. He was sitting in the centre of the British camps, facing the fortress. For some reason, his captors were keeping him alive, but he knew that if he was caught trying to escape, they wouldn't hesitate to put a bullet in his brain. The soldiers knew he'd been travelling with another person, and his refusal to tell them anything was how he'd ended up here.

The canvas sides of the tent snapped in the wind. It had been eight days since his capture on the dark road. He had refused to say anything—not his name, where he was from, or how he had come to be in the woods. One of the soldiers had eventually hit him with the butt of a musket in a fit of frustration. Pierre lost consciousness and woke up with a terrible headache, his cheek pressed flat into the mud with several irate British soldiers standing over him.

Once he'd been brought back to Louisbourg, he'd received several blows that reopened the gash in his side, but eventually they gave him up as a lost cause and left him alone.

He leaned against the tent pole and dozed while the world moved around him. He thought of Marie, relieved that she had escaped. He knew that much, but how far had she been able to travel? He felt a sickening swoop of pain at the thought of her alone and pregnant in the wilderness, fighting her way toward Quebec. His job was to protect her and he had failed. Keep her safe, he prayed. I don't care what happens to me, just keep her safe.

Eventually, a physician had come to see him. It was pronounced that he wasn't about to die, so the British could go on ignoring him. Near sunset, while the cannonballs and mortars still rained down on the fortress, a group of men passed by the entrance to the tent. It took him a moment to understand why the short boy in the middle looked familiar.

"Gérard!" he roared, fighting to get to his feet. "Gérard, you coward!"

The teen looked terrified when he realized who was shouting. Now that Pierre looked more closely, he recognized the people with the boy—other members of the Louisbourg garrison who had clearly deserted in exchange for their lives. Pierre staggered to his feet. The world spun, but he didn't care. He was so angry he could barely see straight. He pulled against the ropes holding him in place and continued to scream. Men were running toward him, trying to hold him back and calm him down, but he fought against them. Finally, he'd been tackled to the ground before losing consciousness.

Pierre had woken up chained to the tent and had spent the last week there with minimal food and no company. He swung between furious anger and despair, with nothing to distract him from his thoughts. He was completely powerless against the destruction raining down around him.

A British soldier who spoke fluent French had been brought, somewhat reluctantly, to try to pry information from Pierre about conditions inside the fortress. Pierre didn't understand why he was bothering with him. Clearly, there were deserters around who would be more than capable of explaining how bad things were.

He spent his time trying to figure out a way to get out of his situation. He assumed that he was being kept alive to be used as a bargaining chip when Drucour finally surrendered the fortress. His explosion at the deserters solidified the suspicion that he was an escaped citizen. However, the British would be in for a rude surprise when they found out their prisoner was also a murderer. Pierre was at a loss to see how this wouldn't end up with him at the end of a rope.

The flaps of the tent opened, and a new soldier entered. He was younger than Pierre, tall and lanky, with sandy hair that fell across his face. His eyes widened in horrified shock as he recognized the prisoner. For a moment,

Pierre was thrown back in time, thousands of miles away to when he had been a prisoner in Montreal. He forgot he was on the sunlit plains of Île-Royale, facing the fortress and surrounded by the ocean. He could feel the suffocating darkness as he and all the other forgotten men tried to find hope to live one more day.

He gazed back passively, though he too felt the jolt of recognition. He remembered John Anderson as a scared fifteen-year-old boy, thrown in prison for theft. Though his father was someone of importance in Virginia, he could do nothing to arrange the release of his son. The boy had been caught shortly after the war's conclusion when Canadians were feeling particularly hostile toward the British. The teen had arrived in Montreal on an Acadian's boat with others who still considered themselves French. He hadn't actually stolen the bread. That was someone else in his party. However, Anderson had been thrown in prison and left there for two years to learn a lesson. Upon his release, he'd been sent to the British army.

Pierre and Anderson had shared a cell with several undesirable prisoners. Fights sometimes broke out, and the guards did little to stop them. One night, a Frenchman took offence to something Anderson had said and attacked him with a sharpened bit of metal, stabbing the young man down the left side of his face. Pierre had pulled the enraged Frenchman off the boy, pinning the snarling offender to the floor until the guards decided to intervene.

The attacker was taken away, and they never saw him again. Anderson hadn't lost his eye, but it was a close call. Most of the left side of his face was twisted with scar tissue. From that time on, there had been a cautious camaraderie between the two.

"When did you get out?" Pierre asked with as much disdain as he could muster. Anderson might have been a friend once upon a time, but his presence in this situation was more unnerving than Pierre cared to admit.

The British man licked his lips nervously. "Just a few days after you. My father was eventually able to sway the government to negotiate me out of prison." He smiled nervously. "Did they let you out of the army?"

Pierre suddenly regretted having shared his life story with Anderson. It had seemed like a good idea at the time—during the freezing, dark nights in the dungeon at the bottom of the prison. "What do you want, Anderson?"

Anderson cleared his throat nervously. "I haven't told anyone who you are. As far as I know, the deserters haven't said anything either. You're still an enigma."

This was a pleasant surprise, but Pierre tried to hide his reaction.

"Also," Anderson continued, "there were scouts sent out to try to find the woman you were with when they captured you."

Pierre's head snapped up. No one had asked him about Marie since he'd arrived back at the fortress. He had hoped they'd forgotten about her.

"They haven't found her," Anderson said hastily, correctly interpreting the look on Pierre's face. "There's no body, no trace of her whereabouts. The only thing the scouts could find was that a boat left from Baie des Espagnols but that it was gone a few days. The fisherman who operates it says he was taking his elderly grandfather out for a ride on the ocean. The scouts believed him, but that's also roughly the amount of time it would take to get to Miquelon and back. She got off the island."

Pierre stared at the canvas wall without seeing it. If what Anderson said was true, and he had no reason to think it wasn't, Marie had made it off the island safely. He tried his best to hide the relief that was suddenly erupting in his chest.

Anderson studied Pierre carefully. "Is she that girl you wouldn't stop talking about?"

Pierre was surprised that Anderson would remember that piece of information. "Yes."

Anderson nodded. "I thought she might be. I figured you'd want to know. I would if it was me." He stood awkwardly for a moment before turning and exiting from the tent.

Chapter 17

THE ROCKING OF THE BOAT DIDN'T HELP the morning sickness. Instead of being nauseated in the morning, Marie now felt dizzy and ill for most the day. The ship's surgeon had been called, but having very little experience with expectant mothers, he gave up in frustration after she didn't get her sea legs after a few days. She'd been on the ship for over a month now and still didn't have them. By the Captain's orders, no one asked her any questions, but odd and appraising looks followed her wherever she went.

She spent most of her days locked up in her cabin with the windows thrown open, trying to avoid the smells of the rest of the ship. The problem with being in the cabin, however, was that there was nothing there to distract her from the constant thoughts that churned around in her head. The more she thought, the more likely it seemed that Pierre was dead. If the British hadn't killed him in the field, they would have taken him back to Louisbourg. He would be recognized and probably executed for Claude's murder.

She felt completely empty. She shouldn't have left him. If she'd stayed by his side, she could possibly have changed the outcome. How, she didn't know, but she would have tried something.

For the first week on the ship, she hadn't moved from her bed at all, other than for the occasional bite to eat. It hadn't seemed important. The leather bundle was hidden under her pillow, but she didn't even care about it any longer. Nothing seemed important: Louisbourg, the British invasion, life. She was so ill that her lack of activity hardly mattered. Her time on the *Françoise* had not been an anomaly. She couldn't keep any solid food down, and what broth and water she was able to consume didn't fare much better.

Before leaving Miquelon, she'd procured a small bag of dried mint leaves. She found that if she put some of those into copious amounts of boiled water with a large amount of sugar, her stomach would settle enough that she could keep things down. However, it wasn't enough to keep her nourished. She was losing weight at a remarkable speed and was becoming very weak. To improve her health to some extent, she tried, once a day, to lie in the warm sun on the deck. Usually, someone would help her get out of her cabin and walk along the rolling deck to a spot near the rail where she could curl up in a quilt.

As much as the trip made her head spin, she tried to find joy by watching the long, thin strips of farmland pass by. It was nearing the end of August, the 20th, to be exact. The harvest was beginning and the fields were filled with golden wheat. Despite the war, the river was filled with *voyageurs* in canoes, fishing boats, and massive merchant vessels travelling along the rushing currents. The Saint-Laurent was safe in this location.

A shadow fell across her face, blocking the welcome heat from the sun. She looked up to see Captain Gauthier smiling genially at her. "How are you feeling today?" he asked, completely unaffected by the movement of the waves. Not for the first time, Marie felt a pang of envy. She smiled as graciously as she could. "About as well as I have been." It was her standard answer. In truth, she felt terrible and was beginning to worry about the long-term effects of the morning sickness on both her and the child. Her dress was becoming roomy despite the hard lump that was growing in her middle. Once she arrived in Quebec, she still had to survive the winter, and Gauthier had promised her that Quebec and the rest of the colony were already suffering from food shortages.

Captain Gauthier laughed. "I am forever grateful I wasn't born a woman. My wife had seven children. I don't know how she did it."

"Did she have a choice in the matter?" Marie asked, still feeling grumpy.

Gauthier paused for a moment. Then his booming laugh filled the deck. He slapped the railing he was leaning against in amusement.

Marie closed her eyes and breathed deeply through her mouth. They were nearing the end of their journey, but she felt as if it would be a never-ending purgatory.

"Do you have any ideas about what you'll do once we reach shore?" Gauthier asked conversationally.

Marie opened her eyes a fraction of an inch and shook her head. He'd been enraged when he'd learned of Pierre's capture by the British but had refrained from speaking about it further. Sensing her fragile state, he usually kept their conversations to tales of his adventures on the high seas.

"I have family there. My husband's family is there as well," she sighed. "I'll be fine." She turned her face back to the passing shore and took a sip of tea to prevent further questions.

Gauthier turned and followed her gaze. "No matter how many times I travel this river, I'm always amazed by the beauty of it."

Marie nodded, only half listening.

"We should be at Quebec in a week."

Marie's eyes snapped open. "Only a week?"

Captain Gauthier smiled. "Just as well. I'm not sure you'd survive if it was much longer."

Five days earlier, the harbour of Louisbourg had less than a handful of warships standing between it and the might of the British navy. Then, on July 21st the British sent volleys from the lighthouse and had struck three ships that burned for most of the day. That evening, as the light of the sun sank below the Atlantic, *L'Enterprenant,* a seventy-four-gun ship, exploded. Pierre had heard the terrible sound of the wooden body breaking outward over the regular commotion of war.

Now only two ships were left.

No one had let him out of the tent, but he'd heard the reports, the bragging of the British officers as they laughed at the misfortune of those trapped inside the ship. How the people in the fortress were surviving was unknown. Pierre had seen the fortress a few weeks before as he and Marie were fleeing and couldn't imagine anything still standing.

Two days later, the King's Bastion, the largest building in the colony and the symbol of French power at the tip of the continent, was hit by a hot shot and caught fire. Men had rushed to put out the fire, but the British had simply gunned them down.

The walls were crumbling, and every cannon blast sent more of the ramparts cascading to the ground. It was the first siege all over again. There was so little ammunition left that as the King's Bastion burned, the French had scooped up the British cannonballs and shot them back from where they'd come.

Pierre burned with anger at the British for destroying his city and his people. He could hear some of the soldiers placing bets and laughing as the plumes of smoke rose above the walls. He was also furious at Governor Drucour, who kept the fortress fighting. Pierre had heard that the hospital had been hit several more times and was sick with relief that Marie wasn't there.

The Displaced: Fall of a Fortress

But why hadn't Drucour surrendered? Louisbourg wasn't just a military base. There were civilians in the fortress, including women and children, who shouldn't be exposed to any more bombardments. He had heard the British casualty numbers were fewer than 150 men, but more than three times that many civilians had died in Louisbourg.

He had woken up early that morning of July 26th, still in the tent. The last two warships in Louisbourg harbour had either been captured or burned the day before. He could see the mist swirling near the ground through the canvas flaps of the tent entrance. Something was different. Mornings were always filled with the thundering of rolling cannons and soldiers running to and fro. Three nights before, the British had dropped three hundred mortars on the town. The air was still choked with the thick smoke from the fires and explosions of that bombardment. But this morning, there was a current, like a spark, running through the crowd of soldiers he knew were only feet away outside the tent. Something had happened.

He waited, heart in his throat. Finally, he heard it: the scream of the crowd growing louder and closer. The shouts of victory. Louisbourg had fallen into British hands for a second time.

A Redcoat entered the tent. His face was unreadable. He stood over Pierre, a thin smile spreading across his face. "They finally surrendered." He spoke in perfect French.

Pierre closed his eyes and bowed his head in silent prayer. The people had nothing left. They'd lasted six weeks—much longer than Pierre thought they would and long enough to protect Quebec from an assault that year. But four thousand civilians as well as the garrison were now at the mercy of the victorious British army.

Keep her safe, Pierre prayed. And she was safe. At least from whatever was about to unfold within the walls of the city.

***

The last time he'd looked at Louisbourg, Pierre had believed he would never see it again. Yet here he sat, in a jail cell in the King's Bastion, shackled to the wall by his ankles. Captain Smith, a weasel-faced British officer who had taken an unfortunate interest in Pierre's fate, had happily informed him that he would stay here until the ships arrived for the deportation. Deportation to France was one of the better options available to the townspeople.

As long as Pierre stayed alone in the cell, he was relatively safe. No member of the French government had come to claim him. Maybe he would be forgotten. He stretched out on the stone floor with nothing but a little straw strewn over it for comfort. Montreal had been worse. At least here, no one was pestering him.

The city lay in ruins and the citizens were humiliated in defeat. The garrison was livid that Drucour had capitulated when they still had fight in them, while the civilians had begged him for weeks to spare them from the ongoing destruction. Having satisfied no one, Drucour now had the unenviable task of trying to broker a peaceful transition with the conquerors. It wasn't going well. In less than two days, there had been several riots as well as fights breaking out between the warring factions of French and British.

The upper storeys of the King's Bastion stood charred, the remains smouldering from a lone cannonball that had started a fire in the last days. They had never stood a chance. Being outnumbered and abandoned by France, it had only been a matter of time before the fortress would be captured.

The deportations would start soon. If Pierre was allowed to board one of the boats without the French discovering his identity, he had a chance of making it to Quebec. As a colonist by birth, he would be the perfect person to send there to fight. But all he cared about was to get there to Marie.

A guard came down the hall. It was the man Anderson. Pierre hadn't seen him since he'd come to deliver him the news about Marie. He looked very uncomfortable. Unfortunately, Anderson wasn't alone. Whoever accompanied the British soldier was important and French. He was dressed in the muted blue of the French uniform, but it wasn't dirty and covered in the grime of battle like the uniforms of the rest of the soldiers. The thin officer stared down his hooked nose at Pierre without saying anything. Pierre stared defiantly back.

"Who are you?" Pierre asked, as it seemed the visitor was in no hurry to speak.

"My name is Joseph Esprit des Groseilliers. I am the Intendant here."

Pierre kept his face impassive, but he realized he was in trouble. The Intendant answered only to the Governor, whom he assumed was busy dealing with the fallout of the defeat. Groseilliers was obviously here to find out who he was. Unfortunately, Groseilliers would have known Claude and the circumstances surrounding his death.

"May I ask who you are?" Groseilliers asked delicately. Something about his sneer made Pierre guess that he already knew the answer.

Pierre stared straight ahead of him, refusing to acknowledge the official.

Groseilliers waved Anderson away and moved closer to the bars. "I asked you who you are, soldier," he said in a dangerous voice. "And I suggest you tell me before I have you hanged."

So he knew he was a soldier, Pierre thought miserably, still not looking at him.

"You escaped," Groseilliers announced. "But you didn't desert to the British."

Pierre nodded. "I had information from Deiter Weber, a priest, to give to Montcalm. That's why I left."

He could see that this information surprised the official. However, he was able to cover the shock almost immediately.

"I see," he said uncertainly. "And may I ask where this information is presently?"

"My wife has it. She is on her way to Quebec as we speak." Hopefully.

Groseilliers's dark eyes narrowed. "I'm afraid ... forgive me, but I find that story to be a tad unbelievable."

"Go ask Father Weber. He can tell you."

A nasty smile played over the Intendant's thin lips. "Deiter Weber died three days ago. I'm afraid you'll find there's no one to back up this lovely little story of yours."

"I didn't desert," Pierre said flatly.

Groseilliers ignored him. "Your name. May I suggest that you cooperate with me before I make your life difficult."

Pierre gave a hollow laugh but didn't answer.

"There's a murderer wanted. He killed a man before the fortress fell." Pierre didn't move. "Matches your description: tall and yellow haired, a soldier. There was a woman with him. An accomplice, so to speak. She was the niece of the man who was killed." Pierre's throat was very dry. The muscles in his throat were constricting. "It would be a shame if word made it to Quebec that she was wanted in connection with murder."

"Leave her out of this," he growled, springing to his feet. He knew Groseilliers was trying to goad him into confessing, but his nerves were stretched thin as it was. He stared at Groseilliers's face through the bars, mere inches from his own, chest heaving with emotion.

Groseilliers grinned wickedly, showing crooked yellow teeth. "Your name then."

"Leave my wife out of it," Pierre hissed.

Groseilliers looked slightly amused. "You're in no position to be making demands, soldier."

"You're going to hang me either way."

Groseilliers considered Pierre for a moment. If Groseilliers had known Claude, he must think Pierre a monster.

"Please," Pierre begged. "Leave my wife out of this."

The muscles around the Intendant's dark eyes softened slightly. "Fine."

"Pierre Thibault."

Groseilliers showed no emotion but simply nodded. "Excellent." With that, he turned on his heel and walked out.

Pierre slumped against the wall. He had tried so hard to protect his identity from the British and had been successful for the most part, but now the truth would be known. Deserter, murderer, and whatever else Claude had told Groseilliers while he was still alive.

The hours ticked by. He watched the sun travel past the window opposite his cell. Night fell, but still no one came. Staring at the small patch of sky, he could see a few twinkling lights in the darkness. The murder of a dead French official wouldn't be of great importance to the British. They were too busy trying to quell the anarchy in the streets. However, he had no doubt they would happily comply with the hanging of a French soldier. After all, one more dead Frenchman was one less Frenchman the British needed to worry about.

He must have drifted off because when he opened his eyes, it was noon of the next day. Captain Smith arrived in front of his cell, a look of ecstasy on his face that couldn't mean anything good. Pierre had hoped for the familiar face of Anderson, but he wasn't there.

Smith thrust a document through the bars of the cell. "Can you read?" It was almost impossible to determine what he said through the merriment in his voice. "You hang tomorrow. Make an example of you, they will. People won't be so keen on rebellion when they know we'll hang 'em."

Pierre didn't pick up the document until he heard the door bang shut behind the Captain. He couldn't read English, but that didn't matter. No trial, just a decision by someone to exterminate him. Obviously, the new regime was more than happy to comply with the French in this regard. He thought of Marie. The beauty of her face swam before his eyes. He curled into a corner, rested his head against the wall, and finally broke down.

***

Pierre sat in a corner of his cell with his head leaning against the wall. It had been a long day. The waiting was the worst part. He wished they would just get it over with. So many times before, in battles scattered across the continent, he had thought he would die, and yet he had survived them all only to be hanged here in the fortress—the place he once called home and thought of as a refuge.

All the other cells along the hall were empty. It did surprise him that tonight of all nights there were no rebels locked away with him. He would like to have heard the stories they had to tell. But, no, he was alone on his last night. Alone with his thoughts. Always thinking of Marie, to keep her with him until the end.

He could hear Anderson shuffling around down the hall. The man was on guard for the night, the officials not realizing the two of them had a connection. Pierre wished the man would be quieter. It wasn't the noise of a bored man trying to occupy himself, but the anxious movement of someone grappling with an inner demon.

Finally, Pierre had had enough and he called out, "What's the matter, Anderson? Never guarded a dead man before?"

Silence followed and Pierre leaned back, satisfied.

Suddenly the pale, pointed face of Anderson appeared at the bars. Pierre was so startled he slumped right down to the floor.

"What the hell! Do you not make noise?" Pierre shouted.

Anderson looked at him with concern in his eyes. Pierre found it irritating and turned away. But Anderson continued to stare as if Pierre was some sort of spectacle at the market. Annoyed, Pierre rounded on him, feeling very much like a caged animal. "What do you want?"

Anderson sucked in a deep breath. "I-want-to-know-why-you-killed-that-man," he said so quickly Pierre didn't catch it.

"Excuse?"

"I want to know why you killed that man. The one they're hanging you for."

Pierre took a deep breath and let it out slowly. He cracked the knuckles in his left hand. "What do you care?"

Anderson looked terribly embarrassed, his entire face turning a deep crimson. "Well, it's just ..." He fumbled with the words, looking down at his scuffed boots. "You saved my life years ago, an enemy British prisoner. I don't understand why you would save my life but kill one of your countrymen in cold blood."

Pierre snorted. "You really think I'm that noble? Besides, I didn't save your life."

Anderson bobbed up and down on his toes waiting for an answer. He looked so ridiculous that Pierre laughed unkindly.

He just wanted to be left alone. Alone with his memories. Anderson was annoying him, but if the guard would leave him alone, there was no harm in telling the story now. It would all be over soon.

"It was my wife's uncle," he stated blandly, staring directly into Anderson's pale eyes. "The man I killed. He abused her and I caught him doing it again. I killed him for what he did to her and was going to continue doing as long as he was alive." He glanced away from Anderson, who looked enthralled by the few sentences.

Pierre shifted his weight, trying to get comfortable. "Her uncle put me in the army and in prison."

"Was she worth it?" Anderson wasn't being an idiot. He really meant it.

Pierre stared at the wall. He had mentioned Marie to no one since they were separated on their way to Baie des Espagnols, and he didn't want to mention her now.

"There's been no account of a woman being found in the woods by anyone," Anderson said quietly. Pierre began to chew the inside of his cheek. "There were still patrols after the scouts came back. A lone woman, that's something that would have got around." This conversation didn't mean anything, and Pierre knew it. He would never see her again—and would never see his child. For a moment, he couldn't breathe.

Anderson continued to stand at the bars, and Pierre continued to ignore him. Marie could be anywhere. He hoped and prayed with all his heart that she was on a ship to Quebec, but a small part of his brain always brought an image of her dead to his mind.

"She was pregnant." It was out of his mouth before he even thought about it. His eyes burned, and he turned away.

Anderson paced up and down the hallway. Pierre turned back to his corner and tried to bring Marie back to him. Keep her safe, he prayed again. He closed his eyes, remembering her chestnut hair and her wide hazel eyes that sparkled with laughter.

A few minutes later, Anderson was back, having abandoned his pacing. He nodded to himself as if something difficult had fallen into place. Pierre cracked one eye open but said nothing. He heard the rattle of keys and the whining of moving metal as Anderson unlocked the door to his cell and opened it.

Pierre didn't move from his spot. "What are you doing?"

Anderson fidgeted for a moment, unable to keep still. "You saved my life."

Pierre scoffed. "I did no such thing."

"Yes, you did."

"No, I didn't. I stopped someone from taking out your eye and even then, I didn't do a very good job. He wouldn't have killed you. I'm sure the guards would have intervened eventually."

Anderson laughed bitterly and shook his head. "Not for a filthy Englishman, they wouldn't," he sighed. "I owe you my life. I can't stand by and watch them hang you."

"If they find out you helped me escape, they'll hang *you*."

Anderson shrugged. "Only if they find that out." There was silence for a while.

"How are they not going to find out?" Pierre was torn. He didn't want to be held responsible for the death of Anderson, but if freedom was being offered to him, he was going to take it. He studied Anderson carefully. The Englishman seemed determined. "What are you suggesting?"

"I can only get you out of the fortress. After that, you're on your own."

Pierre thought for a moment. He had no food, no money, and only his shirt and breeches for clothes. He was battered and wounded from his captivity, but he had to try. He owed Marie that much. Besides, it would be better to die under the stars in the open than by a hangman's noose.

"I got off the island once before. That wasn't the problem."

Anderson unlocked the shackles and went back to his pacing. Pierre stood in the open doorway, scarcely hoping that they would be successful in this plot.

Anderson stopped at the other end of the corridor, his face illuminated by one of the torches on the wall. "All of the patrols are stationed on the northeast and south sides," he called down to Pierre. "If you go northwest, you should be fine."

"Are you sure?" Pierre had no desire for further run-ins with British patrols.

"The battle's won, mate," Anderson reminded him. "We're all under British law now. Just keep your head down."

Pierre didn't have to be told twice.

"Do you know how far the closest settlement is?" he asked. "One that the British didn't destroy?"

Anderson thought for a moment. "At least thirty miles northeast."

Pierre bit his lip. That was at least nine hours on foot. But he could do it as long as no one spotted him.

Anderson hesitated for a moment. "Follow me." He grabbed the torch and threw it into a puddle of water. Then he took hold of its brass holder and bashed it against the lock on the bars, over and over until the lock bent. "There now, that's damaged."

Impressed by his thinking, Pierre followed as closely behind as possible.

The fortress was empty in the darkness, a curfew had been implemented in an attempt to contain some of the tension that had arisen between victor and conquered. Anderson and Pierre went away from the centre of the city toward Queen's Gate. The gate stood open, with two guards standing lazily by.

"Say nothing."

Pierre nodded. It wasn't hard. His heart was pounding in his throat.

The soldiers perked up as Pierre and Anderson drew closer. "What's going on?" one of them asked. Both men smelled strongly of drink. At least the blame for his escape could easily be placed on more than one Redcoat.

"I'm taking this man to the cemetery," Anderson said with a great deal of authority for such a low-ranking soldier. Pierre wanted to point out that the cemetery was on Rochefort Point, through the Maurepas Gate, but none of the British seemed aware of this. "Why?" The guard on the left spat on the ground. "The dead are already gone. They should be buried within the hour."

Anderson sighed impatiently. "I know that. He was away when his son's body was taken. He never got to see it." This excuse had a ring of prophecy to it that made Pierre deeply uncomfortable. He tried his best to look like a grieving father, and that wasn't difficult, given his current state of mind.

The guards turned away impatiently. They didn't have time to deal with grieving Frenchmen. "Good of you to take him," the one muttered and then looked away, as if afraid he would be called upon to join in the grief.

As soon as they were out of sight of the guards, Anderson stopped. "This is where I leave you. Most of the troops have either left or are in the fortress, but be careful. There are still two camps out here." He pointed in their directions. "Also, there are still soldiers around. I can't promise the patrols are exactly where I said they were. If anyone asks, you're going home after foraging for food. I say less than an hour before your absence is noticed."

Pierre nodded and looked across the fields. There was very little cover until the safety of the forests, and the forests were a distance away. Sensing his hesitation, Anderson shrugged off his coat. "Wear this. They won't look twice at you from a distance."

Pierre held the thick, woollen fabric in his hands. "Why are you doing this?"

Anderson grinned. "You saved my life once. In a different time, we were friends. That counts for something."

Pierre nodded. "I can't thank you enough."

Anderson's smile widened. "I need you to do one thing for me."

At this point, Pierre was willing to give him anything.

"Knock me out."

Pierre scoffed.

"I'm serious. I'll tell them you escaped and made off with my coat when I tried to stop you. You're a big guy. Shouldn't be too hard."

Pierre laughed. "You save my neck and in return you want a broken face."

"It'll save my neck." Anderson glanced behind them. "We're running out of time."

"Thank you," Pierre said sincerely as he raised his fists.

"Go find your wife."

Pierre nodded and threw a right hook into Anderson's bad side. The soldier grunted and stumbled. Pierre waited for him to recover before knocking him out with a blow under the chin.

"I'm really sorry, Anderson," he said, standing over the unmoving form. Then, with one final look behind, he ran off into the darkness.

***

The capital's harbour lay before her, shimmering in the afternoon sunlight. After the demolished harbour of the fortress, this seemed picturesque enough to have been a painting. She hadn't been here since she was a child and was whisked away to the strange land of Île-Royale. She had thought she might remember something, some long-forgotten memories that would resurface now that she was actually in Quebec, but there were no memories—only the strange newness of a bustling city.

The air smelled clean, with only fresh air coming off the water. She didn't realize what a difference several hundred pounds of salted cod could make. Everything was so modern and well kept here—unlike the fortress, which was, first of all, a fortress and not a terribly prosperous one at that. Function came before form every time.

After almost six weeks at sea, Marie was exhausted and very weak, but she did somehow remember the route to her uncle's house. Annette used to talk a lot about the city and how she used to walk from place to place. After a longish walk and doubling back when she missed a turn, Marie finally arrived at Uncle Joseph's two-storey stone cottage. It looked the same as it always had, with its patchwork garden surrounded by the short wooden fence that couldn't even keep the rabbits out.

Marie knocked and entered the house. It was as still and silent as a crypt.

"Hello?" she called, moving toward the kitchen at the back. "Anyone home?"

A round, pink face peered around the corner. The full white cap on top of the woman's head gave her the appearance of a mushroom. "Who are you?" she demanded, wiping her hands on her apron. "You can't just walk in here!"

"Are you Madame Guitton?" Marie asked, concerned that her legs would give out soon.

Madame Guitton nodded but looked ready to tackle her.

"I'm Marie Lévesque ..." Before she could go any further, the housekeeper's mouth had dropped into a large "O."

"I'm so sorry," she gushed rushing forward. "Your brother wrote to tell me you'd be coming, but I completely forgot. Come here. You look dead on your feet." She led Marie over to a cushioned armchair by the empty fireplace. "I haven't seen you since you were a little girl. You look so much like your mother."

It wasn't true, but Marie appreciated the sentiment. She collapsed, feeling weaker than she had ever felt in her life. She was dirty, starving, and exhausted.

Madame Guitton hovered nearby. "My dear, you finally escaped."

Marie leaned her head back against the chair. Yes, she'd escaped, but the story she hadn't told Madame Guitton was far more complicated than that.

***

It was September 13th before Pierre arrived in Quebec. As he stepped off the boat, he knew for sure that he was no longer on Île-Royale, as the wind was completely devoid of the scent of cod. He smiled as the fresh air hit his face. Louisbourg was finally behind him. He tried his best not to think of what he would do if he discovered that Marie had not made it.

It had taken over a fortnight to find anyone on the island willing to speak to him. He had had to burn Anderson's coat to prove he really wasn't British military. Then, finally, he found a fisherman in a far-flung part of Île-Royale by the name of Charles Daniau. He'd agreed to take Pierre to Quebec only because he was fleeing from the invaders himself. Pierre had nothing to offer in exchange for the journey. The deportations had started, and Daniau had no intention of being a part of them.

Despite his pessimistic attitude and crusty exterior, Pierre quite liked the man. Daniau, in turn, had been enthralled by Pierre's stories from the army, his escape, and his return to Louisbourg. In Daniau's tiny boat, the journey had been treacherous and its captain swore they would never make it. But eventually, they arrived in the bustling harbour of the capital, soaking wet and starving.

Daniau left Pierre as soon as they passed the first tavern. They'd run out of spirits after a week and the lack of alcohol had almost done the old seaman in. Pierre stood on the road, unsure of where to go. If Marie had arrived, she would have known no one in the city. He assumed she would have gone to her uncle's house, but he had no idea where that was. He could search for Tomas, but he had no desire to deal with his family at the moment. He wanted his wife.

Dominique Renault was the only name that came to mind. If nothing else, Renault could tell him the address of Marie's Uncle Joseph. So he headed over to see his former employer. When he arrived at the office, it looked as unchanged as ever. The spacious apartment above the office that he knew so well still had the ugly blue curtains in the window. The bell tinkled as he pushed open the door. For a moment, he stood in the doorway, silently appreciating the stillness and faint scent of ink and paper. His heart ached as the memories came flooding back, the life he had had here that was stolen from him.

Renault was sitting behind his desk, in the same position he could always be found. He looked much older now, his hair and chin mostly white. His back had begun to bend with the arthritis and his hands looked almost useless, although there was a quill clutched in the right one. He sat open-mouthed, gazing at the visitor for some time until speech returned to him.

Then he stood up so quickly that he knocked his chair over. As speedily as he could, he crossed the room and threw his arms around Pierre in a bear hug. "You're alive!"

For one brief moment, Pierre thought that his fate had never been communicated to his mentor.

"Marie was sure you were dead." Renault released him, holding him at arm's length, his yellow eyes sparkling.

"She's here?" It felt too good to be true.

Renault nodded.

497

Pierre's strength finally gave out. Renault helped him onto a nearby chair. "It's all right son," he said quietly.

Pierre hung his head down as relief washed over him. Renault waited quietly, with one hand on his shoulder. "I can take you to her. She's staying at her uncle's place."

Pierre cleared his throat and looked around the room.

"How is she?"

Renault continued to keep his hand on Pierre's shoulder. "The journey didn't go well, and the pregnancy seems to be making life very difficult for her. She was very ill and lost a great deal of weight."

Pierre began to stand in alarm, but the old lawyer kept him seated. "She's been recovering very well since she arrived. There's nothing to fear."

"Can you take me to her?" Now that he knew she was alive, he had little interest in anything else.

Renault smiled kindly. He knew better than to suggest food or a change of clothes. "Of course, follow me."

***

Joseph Dumas lived on the other side of the Upper Town, so it was a bit of a walk, but that gave Pierre and Renault time to catch up. Pierre asked the Procurator General about the preparations and defences that Quebec had in place.

Renault sighed heavily. "What you see around you is what has been prepared."

The city looked the same as it ever did. Pierre gave Renault a questioning look.

"I have spoken to Marie at length about the siege at Louisbourg and what went on in the last days. The other leaders, Montcalm, Vaudreuil, and Bigot, will want to have an official statement from her, but I thought this best given her fragile state." He paused. "I am aware of the terrible situation Louisbourg was in before the siege ever started. Goodness knows France was no help to you. But there is a feeling among a great deal of the population here that a stronger people could have lasted longer and could possibly have been victorious."

Pierre felt as if he'd been punched in the stomach. Renault nodded sadly.

"But how could they?"

Renault continued walking at his slow, steady pace. "These people have not seen war in many decades, and there are few who remember the violence of the last attack. You experienced this last time you came here. The citizens of Quebec know nothing of the horrors of the island and choose not to believe much of what they do hear ..."

Pierre didn't say anything for a long time. Renault finally broke the silence.

"I know nothing of what you intend to do now that you are here. I know Marie has given information to Montcalm, but that was the extent of her plans." Uncle Joseph's house was now in view. Renault stopped, wanting to finish before Pierre left him.

"I never hired another assistant. You are welcome back at any time."

Pierre nodded. "There are some things you may want to know first, though."

The lawyer smiled. "Your wife told me all. I think you will find a very capable lawyer if you ever wish to fight those charges."

Pierre chuckled.

"Now go see your wife. You know where to find me."

Without thinking, Pierre threw open the door, calling Marie's name. The young maid standing on the other side of the room screamed in alarm. Apologizing profusely and explaining who he was didn't seem to help the situation. But Madame Guitton finally arrived on the scene and sorted the problem out.

"She told me you were dead." There was a hint of accusation in her voice that made Pierre want to point out that his current circumstances weren't a bad thing.

"Well, I survived, and I would like to see my wife," he said bluntly, matching her sour tone.

After looking around the house for Marie, the housekeeper and the maid concluded that she was out. Where, no one had any idea. She had a tendency to wander around the city at times. Pierre grumbled under his breath.

While he waited, he cleaned himself up somewhat and then accepted food from the still suspicious housekeeper. Unable to sit still, he left a note for Marie in case she returned while he was gone. Then he let himself out, full of frustration and nervous energy.

It felt incredibly immoral and naïve that life had continued along as normal here in Quebec. The people of Acadia had been deported and Louisbourg lay in ruins, her inhabitants' future uncertain at best. Quebec was next as the British prepared to focus on the capturing of the capital. Yet life still went on, the streets teeming with people going about their daily lives, unconcerned about or unaware that the British forces would be invading within a year.

Worse still, Pierre doubted that Montcalm and the others would take the situation seriously. If they couldn't see the loss of Louisbourg for what it really was, how could they possibly protect the rest of New France? Pierre kept on storming his way through the city, trying to calm down. He turned down streets blindly, paying no attention to where he was going.

Suddenly, he found her sitting by the well in the square of Place Royale, a basket of food lying at her feet. He felt his breath catch in his throat as he paused at the corner, staring at her as she sat, taking in the city around her. She looked healthy, but he could detect lines of strain around her mouth and eyes. There were also dark circles under her eyes that only appeared when she hadn't had enough sleep. Her hand dropped to the tiny swelling of her belly—his child. He watched in amazement as she crooned and stroked her stomach, utterly unaware of the world.

Pierre knew that she wouldn't survive the three-month trip to France until after the child was born, and that wouldn't be happening until early spring. Once the ice melted, though, it would be too late to leave. By then, the British navy would be descending on them. And there was no escape.

Marie spotted him then, a look of utter amazement on her face. He smiled shyly and waved. An empire hung in the balance, but they would be forgotten in history as the high-placed heroes and villains played their roles, fighting to control New France.

For one mad moment, he wanted to take her and run, away from all this, to the dangers of the wilderness, away from the politics, desires for personal glory, and war. But the conflict would find them. It would find every soul in the country.

Marie stood up with such haste that she knocked over the basket at her feet. She left it there, though, not caring about anything except Pierre. She pushed her way through the mass of people between them, crying out his name as she went. Then she flung herself into his arms. As he lifted her off the ground, he felt her tears mix with his own and their child pressed hard against his stomach. He lowered her slowly to the ground, unwilling to let go.

Their fate was sealed.

The End.

To The Reader

If you enjoyed reading this novel, please take the time to write a short review on Amazon.com at
www.goo.gl/c6XkKo

Get notified about the next book in The Displaced Series by subscribing at www.friedawatt.com/contact

Thank you,

Frieda Watt